Scarborough House

Scarborough House, overlooking the Hudson River, is a place people will scheme, seduce, steal and even kill for. It is a house many struggled to possess and some survived to make a home.

Marcella Paxton, a child of the slums of New York City, has learned to survive the rats, the filth, the despair of poverty. When she and her family escape to a more respectable part of the city, Marcella rebels. Refusing to be shackled by her mother's rigid propriety or her father's prosaic ambitions, she decides she *will* have the good things in life, and do whatever is necessary to get them.

Bradford Dalton – the means for Marcella's escape – is handsome, rich, and fleeing an unhappy marriage. He is the heir to Scarborough House.

Brad and Marcella begin a stormy and passionate affair, scandalizing New York society. They become partners in business and enjoy their social success, oblivious to danger, gossip, and impending ruin.

Inevitably, their ambitions and transgressions touch the lives of others: family, friends, and a growing collection of enemies. The illusion of respectability Marcella cherishes begins to crumble as, one by one, members of her family disown her, and rumours of Brad's infidelity replace the security of her love for him.

Brad is torn between the demands Marcella makes and his loyalty to his young son, Nicholas – and to Scarborough House. He is forced to lead a double life. Marcella, knowing Brad will never leave his wife or son, nonetheless refuses to give up her dream of possessing what is most important to him. Scarborough House becomes her obsession.

In fact Scarborough House becomes the focus of many lives – of tearing and mending of the fabric of families, careers, marriages, and homes. Three generations of Daltons and Paxtons are drawn to and repulsed by the great old house. For all of them – those who have it and those who want it – Scarborough House becomes the symbol of their destiny, of hopes realized and dreams destroyed.

Against the backdrop of nineteenth century New York, Sharon Salvato has created the saga of a passionate love affair, of illusions and ambitions, of war and peace in two families. From the opening of the Erie Canal in 1825 to the turmoil of the Hudson Valley in the 1840's, from the seamy depths of the slums to the gaudy frivolity of Flash Age saloons, she weaves the compelling story of Scarborough House.

Scarborough House

Sharon Salvato

COLLINS
St James's Place, London
1976

William Collins Sons & Co Ltd
London · Glasgow · Sydney · Auckland
Toronto · Johannesburg

First published in Great Britain 1976
© 1975 by Sharon Salvato
ISBN 0 00 222448-8

Made and Printed in Great Britain by
William Collins Sons & Co Ltd Glasgow

In memory of my mother, Alice Day Zettler

Acknowledgments

There is no tonic more fortifying than encouragement and belief. Many people have freely given this to me as I wrote this book: my husband Guy, with his patience at my long hours and his faith in me; my children, Chris, Greg, Steve, and Dan, for always thinking and letting me know that mothers who write are all-right people; my agent, David Hull, who ever assures me I can do things I am not so certain of; and my editor, Mary Solberg, to whom this book and I owe hours of work, unflagging enthusiasm, dauntless patience, and a valued friendship that was formed during the writing of *Scarborough House*.

Contents

BOOK ONE

Chapter One

The *Seneca Chief* left Lake Erie on October 26, 1825, drawn into the waters of the canal by four of the best, most perfectly matched gray thoroughbred horses to be had. The great lead barge, resplendent in red, white, and blue bunting, carried Governor De Witt Clinton and a party of dignitaries on its first trip to the East. When the flotilla reached the Atlantic, it would bring to the wilderness a link with civilization, and to civilization a rare view of the birds and animals of the wilderness, carried aboard one of the other barges, *Noah's Ark*.

No sooner was *Seneca Chief* in the canal than the first cannon at Buffalo was fired, carrying the message that the Erie Canal was open. The cannon fire, relayed from town to town along the four-hundred-and-fifty-mile route the barges would follow, thundered the news from Lake Erie to New York City that the *Seneca Chief* was on its way to the Atlantic.

Bankers, lawyers, tradesmen, housewives, schoolteachers—everyone knew it was coming; many began to prepare for the celebration at its arrival. Marcella Paxton had hardly been able to contain her excitement since the first time her father had told her about it. She loved his stories about her world and the importance of events like this nearly as much as she loved her mother's stories of pretty ladies and rich gentlemen.

"Charlotte!" Marcella whispered into the darkness. Her younger sister was curled into a compact ball, her face to the wall. Marcella could never tell if Charlotte was awake or asleep, but she couldn't imagine anyone would have her face so close to the dank wall of their bedroom if she were awake, so she gave her a poke in the ribs where she knew Charlotte to be most ticklish. Charlotte jumped, bumping her knee against the paper-thin wall.

"You girls go to sleep in there! It's late," Papa's voice called out. "Stop the nonsense right now!"

"Charlotte, I know you are awake now," Marcella whispered happily.

"Be quiet! You made me hurt my knee, and I'm going to tell on you."

"I am going to wear a beautiful pink dress with real lace to the celebration. And I shall look grown-up and beautiful, and my slippers will match perfectly, and...."

"You don't have a pink dress. Mama will make you wear your pinafore."

"I'm pretending! And anyway, I am going to have a pink dress someday."

"It'll look awful with your red hair. Mama said...."

"Mama said, Mama said! That's all you ever say. I *am* going to have a pink dress, and I'll look lovely. Maybe Mama can't wear pink with her red hair, but I'm different!"

"That's what you say. Everyone will laugh at you."

"No, they won't."

"Mama says you are not a lady, Marcella. Mama says you have ideas that . . . that. . . ."

"That what?"

"I forgot. Do you think Mama will really let us go to the celebration?"

"She has to! Papa promised."

"But maybe she won't."

"Then Papa will take us by himself."

Charlotte was quiet for a long time, and Marcella gave her another poke in the ribs. "Stop it! You're gonna get us both in trouble."

"I thought you went to sleep."

"Well, I didn't. I was thinking. Mama doesn't want to go. I know she doesn't. I bet she won't let us."

"I am going!"

"Ha!"

"Why are you angry?" Marcella whispered.

" 'Cause you say stupid things. You always think you can do whatever you like, Marcella Paxton. Mama is right—you do ask for trouble. Go to sleep, I don't want to talk to you anymore."

"I can't sleep."

"Well, I am going to tell Mama if you don't let me alone."

"Don't you want to go to Albany?"

Charlotte didn't answer, and Marcella didn't poke her in the ribs again. She would tell on her this time, Marcella knew. She also knew that Charlotte would never admit how much she wanted to go to the celebration until Mama had stated her preference. Until then she would leave it to Marcella to express all the excitement and reap all the trouble.

Charlotte was asleep. This time Marcella was sure. But the night was full of phantoms for Marcella—captains of giant barges toiling mile after mile through farmlands and cities as they made their way back to her world from the mysterious wilderness that lay beyond the mountains.

The next morning, John Paxton had not even had time to swallow his first spoonful of porridge before Marcella was upon him with her questions. "When do we go, Papa? How much longer is it before the *Seneca Chief* comes to the Hudson?"

He smiled at her. Was there anything at all that Marcella didn't consider the most important thing in her whole life? He doubted it.

He glanced at his wife, hoping to read in her face this once that she shared his joy about Marcella. But Hilary's eyes did not meet his. She was too occupied with braiding Charlotte's hair. Her concentration was absolute, and he knew she was deliberately ignoring him and Marcella.

"Hold still, Charlotte! I can't braid properly if you wiggle around every time you hear a voice. You can hear Papa perfectly well without seeing him." She gave Charlotte's braid a tug.

Charlotte squealed but turned anyway to see her father's face. "Today? Does it mean we go today?"

"No! I know that much, silly. The cannon means the *Seneca Chief* has begun the journey," Marcella said, placing her hands on her hips and scowling at her ignorant little sister. "How long does it take to travel out of the wilderness, Papa? Will they be attacked by wild Indians?"

"Might be." He grinned. "You can never tell what might happen on such a wild and woolly trip. And you never know what lurks in all those dark and haunted woods. Magical forests they are!"

"Such nonsense to fill their heads with!" Hilary said loudly. "Come to that, I think the whole trip is a very bad idea, John. I wish you would not persist in raising their hopes like this. You know full well the trip is too costly, and we haven't a penny to spare."

"It's a great event," he replied. "Everyone in the city who is able to be there will be. You don't want to miss all that, Hilary."

She looked at the two girls and then back at her husband. "Go to your room, Marcella. You, too, Charlotte. I have things to discuss with Papa. Not a word from you, Marcella. Go to your room!"

Hilary turned back to John as soon as the door had shut. "What I want and what I can have are not always the same thing, as you well know, John Paxton. And when it comes to the things that are dearest to my heart and my own desires, we both see the difference between what is possible and what isn't. No, Hilary, I say to myself, you cannot have a decent roof over your head, you cannot buy your children pretty clothes, or be known as a lady yourself. We haven't the money. Now you come smiling to me, wanting to spend a month's salary on an outing because some fool made a trip down a ditch dug by a bunch of beer-drinking Irishmen!"

"Now, Hilary, no need for that," John said soothingly.

"You gave me your word that the important things would come first! Every penny was to go for the new house, and now you have let Marcella encourage you to fritter it all away on nonsense. Sometimes, John, I find myself wondering who is the parent and who the child."

"I've never broken my word once it's been given, Hilary. I'll not start with you, nor will I disappoint Marcella. You are far too hard on her. We can't live our lives like moles, never taking part in the world around us. You'll get your house, but I'll not be buried under your discontent and misery until that day comes. We'll celebrate with the others on the day the *Seneca Chief* arrives. It's a great event, and that's all I wish to hear of the matter."

"It's an expensive outing we can do without," she said, this time more softly. He glared up at her. "I am not arguing with you, John. I was just going to make a suggestion. We could go to Greenwich or even to Sandy Hook and see more than enough. It would not be so expensive as a trip to Albany, and still the girls would see the most important part of the celebration."

John thought about it for a moment and then gave a curt nod. "Call the girls back into the room."

Marcella looked on as her father told them of the altered plans. Charlotte's eyes gleamed, happy that she now knew for certain that she should be in favor of going.

"Mama!" Marcella cried, knowing immediately who was responsible for the change in plans. "We'll miss all the celebrations! We can't. We just can't! It is the most important day of my whole life, and Papa promised!"

"We'll miss nothing, Marcella," Hilary snapped, "and please don't speak to me in that tone of voice, or I shall send you back to your room with a mouthful of soap! We'll go to the celebration at Sandy Hook. It is the most important."

"Papa?"

"You heard your mother."

"But you promised! You told me. . . ."

John Paxton shook his head in warning at the angry little redhead.

He glanced around the room. His bright little daughter had no business being in this dark room. Even when he lit every lamp in the house and Hilary scolded him for being wasteful, it was dark. The smell of decay and filth was everywhere, built into the cracked walls and ground into the plank floors. The stairwell, like a dark pit running from the top of the tenement to the bottom, funneled noxious air into each flat, together with the poisonous hates of the people trapped in buildings like this one and the despair that had already destroyed them.

It wasn't so bad for him. He had grown used to it—except at moments like these, when he was too aware of his daughters and his wife. Then he thought of what places like this had done to other families, and his own seemed so fragile, so easy to damage.

He put his hands out for Marcella to come to him. "You'll not miss your celebration. Perhaps I can arrange for us to be on a boat when the flotilla is met at Tenth Street." Marcella climbed up onto his lap and snuggled close to him.

"I wish I could see all of it, though, Papa. Do you know what? I wish I was the Hudson River, or at least a drop of water in it. Then I would see everything! Even the bottom of the barge." She giggled.

"Did you hear that, Hilary? The girl wishes she was a drop of water so she wouldn't miss anything. What an imagination, eh?"

"Nonsense! Encourage her to use her imagination with her studies. There is no reason why she can't do better than she does."

Marcella looked at her mother, remained silent for a while, and then began to play with the edge of her dress hem. "And do you know what else I wish, Papa? I wish I was one of the wealthy, important people who will ride on the steamships and go to the ball after the celebration. If I were a lady, and we didn't live here, I would be going. Mama said so."

"John bristled. "Now listen to her! That's the kind of nonsense *you* put into her head!"

"Don't argue in front of the children, John. I put nothing of the sort in her head."

"If I gave my word to you about the house, so did you give your word that this pretense of being something we're not would end," he grumbled. Hilary looked away. Automatically she reached out and took hold of Charlotte. She began to unbraid the already perfect braid.

"Mama, you've already done my hair." Charlotte winced as the single strands of hair caught and pulled. "It's Marcella who still needs doing!" Hilary didn't seem to hear. As she undid the braid and methodically began to brush Charlotte's hair again, she glanced at the small window at her side. It was the only window in the room, and she thought of it as hers alone.

"You make these girls look down on what they are. Always wishing for will-o'-the-wisps, thinking that all they need to be happy is a pretty gown and a damned parasol."

"Don't swear in front of the children, John," Hilary said, looking out the window.

"Swearing won't hurt them half as much as your filling their heads with nonsense."

"Why must you fight me so? If you'd put half the energy you spend in demeaning my efforts to make ladies out of your daughters into making a decent living, we would soon have the money to live in a decent neighborhood. And then my nonsense, as you put it, would be the one thing that might make these girls acceptable to respectable people. I'd not have to pretend if you would do your duty by us! I wouldn't have to pretend we were from out of town when we go to market, trying to hide our origins."

"I like Mama's market game, Papa," Marcella said, looking up at him. "Everyone says I am pretty when we play the game, and Charlotte and I get to dress in our best dresses, and sometimes we get a lemon ice—when it's warm—don't we, Charlotte?"

"It isn't real," John said sourly. "We are what we are, and I don't like it when I see you pretending to be what you aren't. Why, Hilary, if I were to meet you on the street in my work clothes, you'd cut me dead rather than have one of your respectable toadies see you talking to me. I'm an honest man, and I work hard for what we have. You have no right to make these girls look down on their father."

"And I don't want my girls known as Five Points girls!" Hilary shouted at him. "Be as proud as you want. I'll be ashamed as long as we live here. I want a good life for them. I don't want them scrubbing day and night in the darkness because there are no windows in the room. I don't want them knowing what it is to see bugs crawling on their babies as I saw on mine. I hate this place, John. I can't help it. I am ashamed. I am ashamed to death."

He muttered something so low in his throat that even Marcella couldn't hear it. He gave Marcella a push, sending her off the end of his knees, picked up his beaver hat from the stand, put on his coat, and went out, leaving Marcella bewildered.

"Go on outside and play for a bit," Hilary said in a monotone, patting Charlotte's head.

"Papa's very angry," Marcella said.

"No, not angry, just tired. Tired and unhappy. I suppose I should learn not to push so, but it is for you I do it—and Papa, too. Remember that, will you? My girls. You'll be something. Wait and see, you girls will be respectable, important. You'll have better than Five Points. You'll be something to be proud of . . . my girls." Her voice became more and more distracted, and by the time she had finished, she seemed not to be talking to them at all.

The girls stood waiting for their mother to go on, to sit in her chair by the window and tell them a story about the beautiful people in fancy dress who awaited them just outside Five Points.

The noise of a cart on the street below brought her attention back to the girls. She smiled wearily. "You do like my stories, don't you? But you must remember they are not really stories, they are true. That is the way people should live, the way you girls will live someday. Not just stories. . ." Her voice trailed off again. Then she pulled herself up and spoke firmly. "But not today. You go outside, but mind you stay away from the ragamuffins! And Marcella, if there is the slightest sign of disturbance, I want you to come in right away! No standing around to gawk. Do you hear?"

"Yes, Mama," Marcella said meekly. Any excitement would far outweigh the momentary pain of her mother's scolding. But nothing happened that day or the day after. Through no fault of her own Marcella was for the next week a model daughter.

The flotilla led by the dazzling *Seneca Chief* made its way to Albany on November 2. The city greeted it with daylong celebrations. Speeches continued for as long as the speakers and listeners could endure. Guns saluted the big barges with deafening enthusiasm, competing with bands and musicians, parades, and throngs of people. At night the city sparkled with bonfires atop every hill.

The following day, the gold-and-white steamer *Chancellor Livingston* arrived to escort the barges downstream. Twenty-four guns and a brass band saluted the flotilla as it passed West Point.

By November 4, the *Chancellor Livingston* and *Seneca Chief* had reached lower Manhattan just off Tenth Street, where the steamboat *Washington*, carrying a deputation from the city of New York, met the flotilla. The entourage doubled and then trebled as hundreds of smaller, privately owned boats joined the procession. Cheers went up on both sides of the flotilla. Those in the water were echoed by those on the land all along the route to Sandy Hook, where the flotilla was met by the schooner *Porpoise*.

"Papa, look! There it is. Look at it, Papa, look!" Marcella squealed, pointing to the barge called *Noah's Ark* with its cargo of two of each animal and bird native to the wilderness.

John smiled down at her. She was radiant, her hair flying in the wind, brighter and more beautiful than any flag that adorned the barges.

"But where's Noah?!" she laughed.

"Marcella! Lower your voice," Hilary snapped. "People can hear you. Do you want them to think you are ill-mannered?" She maintained her social smile as she spoke to her daughter, but touched her hand to her forehead as if it hurt her.

"Is that really Noah's Ark, Papa?" Charlotte asked.

"Not really. It is just like Noah's boat because it has the animals on it. Now look what's happening, Charlotte. Look on the *Seneca Chief.* Watch, Marcella."

"On the *Chief,* two bright green casks were placed at Governor Clinton's feet. He looked out over the crowd and lifted the first cask. "May the God of Heaven and earth smile propitiously on this work accomplished by the wisdom, public spirit, and energy of the people of the State of New York." He raised the cask high for everyone to see and then emptied its contents over the side of the barge. The waters brought from Lake Erie plunged down and mingled with the waters of the Atlantic Ocean.

The fleet returned to Manhattan, where everyone disembarked at the Battery.

"Will that be all?" Marcella asked wistfully and looked up at her father. He took her by the shoulders and turned her to face the street, where the parade had already begun.

Bands were playing, and the cannons thundered joy and approval of the great wedding of the waters. It seemed the whole city was celebrating. Speeches of great length were delivered to those who liked them and to those who simply needed the excuse of a long-winded orator to garner a few moments' sleep. Out of the tangle of people four trumpeters emerged, leading bands. A grand marshal appeared, followed by delegations of tradesmen; the parade that followed was nearly five miles long.

The Paxtons missed nothing. As John led them into the ranks of the parade, even Hilary seemed caught up in the furor and excitement. She seemed blissfully unconcerned as Marcella bobbed in and out of the paraders in most unladylike fashion, followed doggedly by Charlotte. Aside from her one chastisement of Marcella, Hilary was enjoying herself as much as her children and husband.

Finally, winded and tired, they let John steer them toward Fraunces Inn. When they entered the inn, John fully expected a lecture from his wife about the money they could not afford to spend on lunch at a restaurant. Instead, however, he noticed with dismay that she was glancing furtively about, comparing the clothing her daughters wore to that of other little girls. Whenever either of the girls spoke, she bit her lip, dreading that in some way their speech would give away their background. She made a point of informing the woman standing next to them, "We're from up north of here, but we do so love for the children to take part in any event of consequence that we felt obliged to come to the city today."

John took her by the arm and hurried her away. "I don't want you telling people those damned stupid lies of yours, Hilary!" he whispered loudly. "I'll never understand why you do it. That woman hadn't said a word to you. Do you think we wear Five Points like a brand?"

"I don't seem able to help it. I am always so afraid that they'll know," she murmured, looking down at her hands. The next moment she was fussing with Marcella's glove, trying to remove a smudge from the palm.

19

In spite of their unpleasant exchange, John enjoyed his meal, relishing the fact that the Paxtons were sitting together in a restaurant, well dressed and well fed, just as though they could afford it. Marcella and Charlotte peered out the windows, afraid to miss the slightest bit of excitement outside. From time to time they pointed at something on the street, whispered secrets to each other, and giggled incessantly.

For Charlotte, it was as if one of her mother's stories, told by the special window, had opened up and allowed her to walk into it. Everything was as Hilary had said it would be. The ladies carried tiny parasols and nodded agreeably. Their dresses were adorned with lace, and they smelled sweet. They talked in low, soft tones. It was like a foreign language compared to the way Five Points women talked. Even the men were different, polite and attentive to the ladies. Not one of them smelled like the men who lived in Charlotte's building.

She looked across the table at her mother. "Those weren't really stories at all, were they, Mama?"

"What weren't, dear?"

"Those stories you tell Marcella and me. They are real, aren't they?"

"You can see for yourself, Charlotte. They are real—at least for some people."

"They are going to be real for me."

After dessert, John sat back and hooked his thumbs in his waistcoat pockets. "I suppose you girls are too tired to go out and join in?"

"We're not tired. Not a bit, are we, Charlotte?"

"What do you say, Hilary?"

She nodded and drew on her gloves, a sure sign she not only agreed but was nearly as eager as they. So in the late afternoon sun of that November day, the Paxtons joined the clusters of singing people outside, and like everyone else, they ended their day in front of City Hall. The building was dazzling, bedecked with hundreds of lights. Fireworks lit up the autumn sky, leaving everyone with visions of song and color and history.

For some there would be a grand ball to end the day. But the Paxtons, more tired than they could ever remember having been, spared hardly a passing thought for the ladies and gentlemen who would dance away the hours until dawn.

Even at that hour Five Points throbbed with the sounds of the dirt street and the shops that lined it, the gambling houses, the tenements, the grogshop, the houses in whose doorways women stood beckoning. The celebration day had been a day away from all this. For once, Hilary thought, she had heard music, real music, and laughter that meant only merriment and not the coming of another street battle. She had stood before City Hall and seen a building alight, and walked streets brightened by whale-oil lanterns. For once, as they turned onto Orange Street, they could look up at the tenement, black against the night sky, with anticipation of sleep and dreams of a good day.

* * *

The day of the canal celebration marked a change for each of the Paxtons. As so often happens when people see life outside of their daily limitations, each of the Paxtons had grown. They had seen something better, something they wanted more than what they had. Nothing visible marked this change, and none of them spoke of it, but it was as real as if they had been physically transformed.

Hilary had always hated Five Points, but now she hated it with an intensity that threatened to swallow her up. Someone had once told her that the street was paved in stone. She had never seen a stone on Orange Street, except as part of a barricade for one of the street fights. All she had ever seen as she walked that street was muck and filth, layer upon layer, cleaned only by the pigs that ran loose until someone caught them for supper.

She hated Five Points and what it was doing to her and her children. Too often she had wakened in the night to hear the sound of rain spattering onto the floor in her room. Too often she had had nightmares of sinking slowly into the mire of the streets.

There was never any respite. Five Points was as alive as she was, breathing its own malignant air. She had lived too long with the constant expectation of disaster it represented, a growing dread she had never been able to communicate successfully to her husband. The argument they had the day after the celebration was a wearying repetition of countless others.

"My God, Hilary, what do you think I do when I leave the Points in the morning? All I do is work until my back is breaking. Is that what you envy?"

"How can you be so blind, John? At least give me the satisfaction of knowing you're glad to leave here, if I cannot leave myself."

"You dramatize. You would have done well as an actress, Hilary."

She glared at him, close to tears. "Is it dramatizing when I see the woman downstairs?"

"There are a lot of women downstairs."

"Aren't there! And all crammed into one flat, jostling one another and fighting for the one bedroom. It really doesn't matter which one I meant, John. Take any one of them and look, if you've eyes to see. Have you any idea how old Mrs. Kelly is?"

"I don't even know *who* Mrs. Kelly is."

"She is just past thirty, and she has had a child every year of her life since she was sixteen years old. Three are alive, and look at them, their tiny, pinched faces, sour and sick. John, they will be that way all their lives, if they live at all. Why can't you understand? I don't want to stand by day after day until I see Charlotte and Marcella look like one of the Kellys—or worse yet, come to an age where they might . . . where they might fall prey to one like Amos Kelly." She shuddered, thinking of all the times she'd seen groups of boys marching down the streets to fight rival gangs, watched the barricades go up as the street came alive with the shouts of impending violence.

"We won't be here when the girls are old enough to start worrying about men," he said softly.

Hilary shook her head. Even if she had to sacrifice her own pride to go to work as a maid in a rich man's house, she thought, she would get the money to take her two daughters out of Five Points before it was too late. "You won't understand what I'm telling you, no matter what I say, will you?"

She watched him turn from her and take his coat from the nail. "I'll be back late this evening. Not before seven, or possibly eight."

As he left the house, he tried to shut out the filth and joylessness. It wasn't easy; yesterday he had realized he didn't like what his wife had become.

He remembered the day she had told him she would marry him. That day he had felt blessed beyond worth. She had been a wisp of a girl, her gentle charm as elusive as the breeze. She had drunk in life in great gulps and given it back twofold when she smiled. Where had all those days gone, he wondered.

She had known they would have to live in the Points for a time—at least until John, as he put it, could get on his feet financially. She had accepted that as she had everything in those days—full of optimism, seeing it as an adventure, a challenge, knowing both of them could and would meet it. What had happened to her to kill that faith?

He hitched up his pants as he walked along. He loved her, she knew that. Not once had he been faithless, and that was saying something, especially in the Points. Hilary knew that, too. She knew as well as he that she was the only woman he had ever wanted.

Was it, as she had said, living in Five Points? Of course he was aware of the gangs—the Dead Rabbits, the Plug Uglies, the Bowery Boys, and God knew how many others—but they didn't affect his family. They were a part of the street. Hilary would raise his girls to be good, God-fearing women. The street couldn't affect them. He could see that, if Hilary could not.

He looked up and saw the last few leaves, frostbitten and bright, clinging tenaciously to the trees. He was out of Five Points. He sighed.

Maybe the Points was more than he gave it credit for; maybe Hilary was right. Whatever the cause, he did know that Hilary had become a woman frightened, critical, and always on guard against traces of what she called "commonness" in her family. He did breathe deeply and began to look at the beauty around him the moment he knew the Points was behind.

As he walked toward the river that day, John Paxton decided that he would move his family from Five Points. For now, he would tell his wife nothing about his plans. From the beginning Hilary had said she would have a house on Eighth Avenue someday. He had laughed at her then, for it was a very fashionable street, and she might as well have asked him for a palace. By now, the fashionable people had found new streets and moved to them, leaving Eighth Avenue merely respectable. But Hilary's dream had not changed. And John Paxton would see to it that it came true.

John had always been a handy man, a jack of all trades and master of many. Whatever complaints he had about his city, lack of work was never among them. Summer or winter, he put his cart to use as a tea-water cart, sawyer's cart, ice cart, or porter's cart. People were always in need of services. There was seldom a day when he had nothing to put into the box in which Hilary hoarded the money to buy her dream house. He had often smiled to himself on his way home, thinking of the hoard he had accumulated, which his wife knew nothing about. He had his own account in a bank, and he walked along Bank Street with the best of them to deposit his money.

On Orange Street and even in his own home John Paxton might be called of no account and poor, but on Bank Street at least twice weekly he was known and greeted as a man of substance. What joy it would bring him to take his wife by the hand and lead her to the house he had bought for her without having touched her precious money box.

Chapter Two

As often as he could that winter, John Paxton made his way up the Hudson River along with dozens of other men. The entire river valley hummed with industries—tanneries, cement plants, stripping yards—growing and shaping the future of New York City. Some of these were too far upstream for John to make the trip daily, so he became involved in the business of cutting and storing giant blocks of ice from the Hudson, to be used all summer by the people of the city. The job had to be done in the coldest months, when the river was frozen to a depth of at least ten inches.

"I must be daft to like this." He grinned at the shivering man next to him.

"You come all the way from the city?"

"Every year!"

"You're daft!" the man muttered as he went off to find a saner companion.

John smiled after him and went back to carving out the giant ice blocks. After he cut them, they were carried by the conveyers up to the large storage houses that lined the banks of the Hudson. There the ice would be kept until the city began to melt in the summer's heat. Working on the river in the dead of winter, his fingers stiff and his nose bright red in the cold, it was hard for John to imagine how much in demand the ice would be in the months to come. But the money he deposited at the end of each day had a way of reminding him that his work was going to be worth at least as much to him, come spring, as it was to his boss right now.

Fom Hilary's point of view, that winter was an intolerable drain on her strength. John had absolutely forbidden her to go to work as a maid; even Hilary had not dared press the matter. There was little to keep her busy in the flat where they lived. She had too much time on her hands, most of which she spent worrying about her daughters.

Marcella, who had her twelfth birthday that winter, seemed as always to cause her more concern than Charlotte did. It occurred to Hilary that in some very real way Marcella was changing. Perhaps, she thought, it *had* been the celebration that had affected her daughter. To Hilary's alternating delight and consternation, Marcella was becoming less like a child and more like a woman.

She plunged into housekeeping, an eager pupil of all Hilary could teach her. Her mother watched with some chagrin, and a growing sense of her own uselessness, as Marcella cleaned, cooked, and did more and more of the family's marketing.

Her daughter's physical development was no less worrisome to Hilary. The little girl was fast giving way to the beautiful young woman. It was all too clear to Hilary, especially when she considered for whose eyes Marcella's beauty would be displayed. With each passing day, Hilary's fear for her grew.

One evening, as she sat by the window, waiting for John to return from the river, the fire bells began to clang. Hilary listened for the number of bells; the call was for Five Points.

Hilary bolted out of her chair, sniffing the air. Nothing—that was a relief. At least the fire wasn't in their building. Still, one could never feel safe. In Five Points fires spread quickly and in all directions.

After a quick glance at both her daughters, she began to gather her hoard of house money from the dozen places in which she had hidden it away, carefully deposited in jars and boxes. Always afraid someone would find it and rob her of the only hope she had, she had never kept it in one place. She hurried from one hiding hole to the next, counting it as she gathered up each small cache. Every once in a while she would stop, raise her head, and sniff the air like an animal.

Marcella watched her mother for some minutes and then took her opportunity to escape. Down the steep, darkened steps and out into the slushy streets she ran.

She raced for Cross Street, pushed and jostled by heavyset women, urchins, and men forcing their way to the front of the throng, only to be forced back again by someone faster or stronger. The street was alive with fearsome excitement, a mixture of people's peculiar desire to see the worst happen and their fear that it would.

Those who ran alongside Marcella knew that at least it was not their particular tenement that was going up in flames, and no one but the unfortunate victims had much concern for the burning building. Their attention was riveted on the battle for the pump. Which of the volunteer fire-fighting forces would arrive first and claim the water pump as their prize?

"Grab de barrel! get it there!" A heavyset man screamed the battle cry. As Marcella ran furiously to keep up with him, his beaver hat flew off his head in a gust of icy wind. Marcella stopped just long enough to retrieve the hat from a half-frozen puddle. No Dead Rabbit would be seen without his badge of honor. Clutching it tightly in one hand, she tore off down the street again.

At the burning tenement, she saw the young man who had lost his hat perched atop the barrel that covered the pump, fighting off the front-runner from the fire brigade from the Bowery. He and his boys had just arrived, lugging a barrel of their own. On their heels came the racing, pounding feet of the men and boys from her district—the Dead Rabbits and the Plug Uglies. Marcella held her breath as they all converged on the man whose hat she held. All she could see was a melee, arms and legs flailing.

The fire raged, spitting out chunks of fiery tar and cinders onto the crowd below. Hunks of the roof, flaming bits of tinder, cloth, and wood covered the streets, melting the ice where they fell. At the edge of the crowd Marcella waited until the fight began to break up. The Plug Uglies, allies of the Dead Rabbits, secured the pump, and the first shower of water finally reached the building.

Within minutes the fire was under control, but there was not much of the building left to save. Now the fire fighters concentrated on keeping the blaze from spreading to the rotted buildings on either side. As soon as it was apparent that they would succeed, the crowd dispersed, hurrying through the cold streets to their homes, the night's excitement over.

Marcella stayed, still clutching the hat. Once the serious business of fire fighting was over, the men became merrier, paying less and less attention to the smoldering ruin behind them. Marcella brushed away a smudge on the crown of the hat and walked toward its owner.

Several blocks away, Charlotte stopped to brush a bit of mud from her stocking. Like other children, she loved the excitement of a fire, but unlike the rest of them, she had walked to see it. Hilary had told her that ladies did not run down the street, and to be sure, having seen all the well-dressed ladies at the canal celebration, Charlotte imagined it would be most difficult to run with parasols, lace, and ruffles.

As usual, Charlotte missed most of what there was to see. She arrived just in time to hear a mighty cheer go up on the street in front of the still-smoldering building. Then she caught sight of the person responsible for the cheer.

Marcella was far above the crowd, perched on the shoulder of the man whose hat she had returned, her arms outstretched, laughing just as loudly as Rosie, who lived down the street and wasn't nice. Charlotte clapped her hand over her mouth, looking in all directions to see who else had noticed Marcella's disgrace. Clusters of people had stopped at the sound of new commotion, and they, too, were laughing. Charlotte ran all the way home.

"Mama! Mama!" she screamed as she entered the front of the building. "Mama! Come quick!"

Hilary clasped her hands to her eternally queasy stomach, trying to quell its pitching. She hurried to the head of the steps, peered down into the darkness to wait. She had no doubt that whatever Charlotte wanted to tell her had something to do with Marcella. Her eyes didn't adjust to the darkness.

"Mama!" Charlotte panted as she suddenly appeared in front of Hilary. "She's doing it again. Marcella—Marcella—she's—making a . . . a . . . spect-tickle of herself. She's. . . ."

"Is she all right?" Hilary screamed, shaking Charlotte by the shoulders.

Voices from doors along the long stairwell cried out for quiet.

"Mama! Stop it, Mama. You're hurting me!"

Hilary stopped. She looked at Charlotte for a moment in silence. "Where is she?" she asked finally, fighting back nausea. She leaned heavily against the rotting stair railing and listened to what Charlotte had to say. Slowly she sank down to the top step and put her head in her hands.

Oblivious to the look on her mother's face, Charlotte chattered on. "She's on Cross Street, and they're all dancing around her and shouting. Mama, she is sitting on some man's shoulder! And he said she's a new member. Is she, Mama? Is Marcella going to be a Dead Rabbit? Can ladies be Dead Rabbits? Hellcat Maggie isn't a lady."

"Charlotte, be quiet! Don't even mention people like that." She pulled Charlotte's pigtail sharply. "I don't know where you hear these things." She got up and took her apron off as she walked back into the flat. She smoothed down her hair, put on her best street coat, and followed Charlotte to the rescue of her elder daughter.

Marcella was being carried in triumph back toward Orange Street. She looked up and caught sight of her mother and sister long before Hilary reached her, but she knew it was already too late to scramble down from Lou's shoulder. Lou would not put her down, anyway. He was deliriously happy, and slightly drunk.

"That's my mother," she whispered frantically, wiggling and nearly toppling Lou's hat. "Put me down. Hurry!"

"It's her old woman!" Lou shouted to the rowdy group behind him. The crowd moved toward Hilary, cheering her now as Marcella's mother.

"This your girl?" Lou shouted cheerfully. "She saved me damned hat!"

Hilary turned her head to one side slightly as the odor of whiskey reached her. Taking a step back as Lou moved nearer, she replied, "That was thoughtful of her, I am sure. Now if you will be so kind as to put her down, I shall take her home and put dry and clean clothes on her."

"I'll take the little girl home for ya, ma'am. No trouble at all."

"Is she a member now?" Charlotte asked shyly.

"She sure is! Dead Rabbits and Plug Uglies, too. Do you want to be a Dead Rabbit?" He gave Charlotte's cheek a pinch. The tears welled up in Charlotte's eyes.

"Aw, did I hurt you? I didn't mean to. It's these big hams of mine. Not fit for pretty little cheeks."

"No," she sniffed. "You didn't hurt me, but I don't think I can join. Thank you, anyway."

"Hey, you there! Will, come on over here and give the little Fire Top a ride." Another beaver-hatted man hurried forward, smelling of smoke and sweat, and lifted Charlotte to his shoulder before Hilary could say a word.

"Let's go, Mom." Lou gave Hilary a smart slap across her shoulders. "Lead on!"

"Put them down. Put them both down now."

"Now, don't be like that," Lou said smiling. Behind him the men began to grumble. "Let us take the little girls home. They're having the time of their lives. Ain't that right, girls?"

Hilary held her ground, staring icily at Lou. Steadily rising voices and noisy catcalls suggested everyone's patience was wearing thin. Shrugging his shoulders, Lou told Will to put Charlotte down next to her mother. He lifted Marcella from his own shoulders and put her down next to her sister.

"Never come near them again," Hilary said through clenched teeth. "They're not like you."

Lou looked from her to the little girls, smiled at Marcella, waved, and then turned back to the gang. "Let's go now, boyos!" he shouted, and before Marcella could wave back, they were gone.

Hilary didn't speak a word all the way back to Orange Street. Marcella was shut in the windowless little room she shared with Charlotte, under threat of later punishment.

Nearly an hour later Hilary came into the bedroom. She looked into the gloomy dusk and saw her daughter huddled against the wall on her bed.

"You have shamed us all," she said finally.

Marcella looked up at her, her dark eyes shining. "I didn't do anything wrong. I gave the man his hat, and he put me on his shoulder just like Will did to Charlotte. She isn't being punished. I didn't do anything!"

"You encouraged that man. You were laughing, enjoying it. I saw you myself, young lady, so don't bother to tell me your stories! You've disgraced yourself and humiliated me and shamed your name."

"I did not!" Marcella shouted. Before she realized what she was doing, Hilary had slapped Marcella's face. Immediately she backed away, her hands trembling. She had never hit a child like that before, and she wanted to slap Marcella's defiant face again.

"Don't leave this room, do you hear me? No supper. You stay in this room until you can manage some decency and respect!" Hilary rushed from the room, slamming the door behind her.

Hilary released the doorknob and walked slowly to her chair by the storytelling window. Once she would have been watching the street below to see John's broad-shouldered shape making his way home, counting the minutes until she saw him again. No more. No more after today. This last nightmare had been real—the fire, Five Points, the filth. It was all too much.

And then in that lightning-swift moment when she had seen her daughter on Lou's shoulder, beautiful in her happiness, alive and vibrant, Marcella had suddenly become a stranger to her. Marcella had gone beyond her and driven her to use physical violence against her own child. And she knew that day that John could no longer help. After that afternoon, there was nothing and no one on this earth that could help her.

The sooty snow seemed to smear, not clean, the tiny window. Time has

27

won, she thought. After all the times she had waited in dread when she wasn't sure what it was she was waiting for, today she knew. She had no more time. Marcella was gone from her.

Marcella was no longer just a pretty little girl. She had seen that today. The man had known it, too. How was she to tell this to Marcella? It was bad enough that Marcella had been a child in this horrible place, but to become a young woman here, that was intolerable.

Marcella had already developed qualities Hilary considered unseemly and vulgar. She talked too freely, she laughed too loudly, walked too fast, was careless in her mannerisms, and much too inclined to touch when no touch was necessary. Her nature made her headstrong to start, and Five Points was making her cheap.

Hilary, lost in her thoughts, did not notice that John had entered the flat.

"Hello! Hello there! Has everyone lost their tongues?" He took off his coat and hung it on the nail by the door. Charlotte waved timidly, but still no one spoke. He looked around the nearly empty room and then back to his wife.

"All right, what is it this time, Hilary?" he asked, giving up the attempt to be cheerful. Hilary did not answer.

"It's Marcella, Papa," Charlotte said in a near whisper. "She's been bad again."

"Where is our bad girl, and why isn't supper ready?" he asked, glancing at the empty table. "Say something, will you? What has she done? What's happened? Where is she?"

"I'll fix supper," Hilary said, pushing herself out of her chair. John crossed the room and took her by the shoulders. She struggled weakly, then gave up.

"It can't be all that bad," he said gently. "Where is Marcella? I'll get her to tell me all about it."

Marcella was sitting on the edge of her bed when he came in and closed the door behind him. She leaped up and raced across the room and into his arms. Before they had sat down on the bed again, she had begun chattering about the day. She recounted everything, including how angry Hilary had been when she had come after her.

John listened solemnly while Marcella spoke. He couldn't approve of what she had done, and her open admiration of Lou disturbed him somewhat, but he sensed it was that more than anything else that had upset Hilary. As Marcella continued to talk, he tried to see her as the sinner her mother saw. She was not as quiet as Charlotte, it was true, nor was she as ladylike as Hilary. But he wondered if Marcella's real crime was not that she enjoyed herself too much. When she had finished, he gave her a mild scolding, softened by a wink and a hug. Then, cautioning her to look properly remorseful, he led her into the main room of the flat.

Hilary looked up as soon as they had entered. "She's being punished. Go back to your room, Marcella."

"She is sorry for what she did, Hilary, and she hasn't eaten yet. She can go back after supper. Tell your mother you're sorry, Marcella."

"I am sorry, Mama. I didn't mean to upset you."

"She is being punished."

"Hilary, it's not as bad as all that. Let the girl have her supper first. She has apologized for what she did."

"I am not going to argue with you, John. If you insist on my obedience to your wishes, I have no other recourse than to obey. I shan't prevent her from eating."

"Don't make this out to be more than it is," he said, annoyance creeping into his voice. She stared at him for a minute as if she might say something, but then turned and slowly stirred the mixture in her bowl. "Take a dish to your room, Marcella," John ordered.

"We eat at a table! We haven't become animals yet," Hilary snapped.

"Then, damn it, sit her down and feed her like any natural mother would and stop your infernal bleating!"

The supper meal was passed in silence, as was the usually sociable hour that followed before Marcella and Charlotte were sent to bed. Tonight Hilary's deadened hopes and John's anger sat like two cold, heavy stones in the middle of the table.

For once Marcella was grateful to be able to slink off unnoticed into the dreary but less tense atmosphere of her room. Hilary left the table as soon as the meal was finished, returning to her chair by the dirty window. Charlotte cleared the table and washed the dishes as quickly as she could. From time to time she looked over at her father, his face lined with silent resentment, and then at her mother, who stared out blankly at the freezing rain.

"I'll be going further up the river tomorrow," John said finally. His voice sounded terribly loud in the quiet room. Hilary said nothing. "It is a hard trip in weather like this. I won't be home for a few days."

At last Hilary stirred and turned her chair to face her husband. "You'll be home by the week's end, won't you?"

"Most likely."

She sighed. "I am sorry you are angry, John, but there is nothing I can do about it."

"Can or will?"

"Both, I suppose. I know you think I am wrong, but I am not. One day you'll see, and then it will be too late. So I am sorry. I really am. That is all I can say. Good night, John. I wish you a good trip."

Charlotte hastily placed the last dish on the sideboard and hurried past both of her parents to the comfort of her room.

"Good night, Mama. Good night, Papa." She kissed each one lightly and dashed for the bedroom.

"Marcella!" she whispered, once inside. "Why do you have to go and make everything awful around here all the time? Mama is mad at Papa, and Papa is going away. All because of you!"

"Where is Papa going?"

"He is staying up on the Hudson. He won't come home."

Marcella flopped back down on the bed, putting her arms behind her head. "That's just because it is cold and nasty out."

"That's what you say! He's very angry at Mama, and all because of you. I don't think you are very nice."

"Mama doesn't either. She is always mad at me, but I really didn't do anything bad. I just wanted to see the fire. I didn't know that man would put me on his shoulder when I gave him his hat back. You were on someone's shoulder, too. Why didn't Mama get mad at you?"

"It was your fault that he picked me up, not mine. Mama knows who started all that trouble."

"Charlotte, you're just like Mama. I wasn't bad. You just think you know everything."

"Is that so!"

"Yes, that's so!" Marcella replied, and for once it was she who turned over and curled herself into a small ball, feigning sleep. Charlotte gave her one good poke in the back.

"I don't like you, Marcella Paxton. I wish you weren't my sister!"

Chapter Three

A month before, Hilary might have told John all the shadowy things that haunted her. But this time, she decided, it wouldn't change anything, so she didn't bother. If John had wanted to, he could have read the signs as well as she. He had lived in Five Points just as long. Either he didn't care enough, or he didn't want to know. He left the next morning before Hilary was awake.

Hilary awakened from a nightmare, as she often did. In those last minutes of morning sleep when dreams can be so vivid, she saw again the men of the street and the fight.

The race for the water pump the day before, she knew, would trigger a street fight between the rival gangs. It always did; nearly anything could be used for an excuse, and the fire was a better excuse than most. Not a week went by that there wasn't some confrontation between the Bowery Boys and the Five Points gangs. It was a near certainty when the pride of the volunteer fire brigade was at stake.

The pitched street warfare fascinated Marcella. Hilary had never permitted the girl to watch or be on the street during one of the fights, but then Marcella never obeyed. At the slightest opportunity, Marcella would be down on the street before Hilary even knew she was gone. Now there was the added danger of Marcella's being singled out and favored because of Lou.

Hilary knew she had only to wait one day, two days, perhaps longer, but it would come, and on that day she would again have to go down onto the street to disentangle her daughter from the riffraff, praying nothing too horrible had happened. Each time it would be a little worse, until finally it would be too late altogether. She got up from her bed, shivering.

Five Points had always been a blight, but it got worse with each passing year. Set low in a hollow of land that should have been left a marsh, the area had become a refuge for outcasts from many countries as well as for people who had lost out on the good life in the New World.

It was a natural breeding ground for crime, like a rabbit warren with its interconnecting passages beneath the tenements and low-roofed sheds that could and did hide many a crime and a criminal. Crime and violence were not mere occurrences in Five Points, they were a way of life, as the names of the streets attested—Battle Alley, Bandit's Roost.

When Hilary heard policemen casually remark that Five Points managed to average at least one murder a day, she couldn't help wondering which of the people she passed on the street would be gone tomorrow or by whose hand they would leave this world. For days after hearing that comment, she found herself tiptoeing through her own building, wondering if any of the people who lived there with them were murderers.

When she mentioned her fears to John, he laughed at her. "There are murderers all over the world. What makes you think some of the finely dressed men and women you are so fond of rubbing elbows with are not just as guilty?"

She remembered his words so clearly; now, they seemed to reflect his attitude toward everything. Again he had left her, belittling her fears, and it was she who stared out of the window and saw and heard the signs of the coming fight.

The street was slowly coming alive. Carts normally used for business in the more respectable parts of the city were now loaded with great stones dug from the streets and bits of rock and wood taken from houses and fences. Three times in the last two days she had seen people running with rifles and muskets in their hands.

Five Points women, whom Hilary hated with every breath she drew, were talking in their wild and jeering way about their men, promoting the feeling that the battle would be one of honor. Their talk made her think of the poor fools who called themselves the American Guard. They were to be found on every street corner, denouncing England as if America were still at war with the mother country.

In spite of her hatred of Five Points and her dread of what it could do to her family, Hilary thought its inhabitants pathetic. To have in life only the primitive battles waged for reasonless causes was pathetic beyond all bounds, as far as Hilary was concerned. She would rather die than call that life. It was like a bog, an oozing marsh, sucking, gurgling, trying to drag her and her own down into it.

For several days she had tried to keep both girls by her side. Charlotte, very nearly as frightened as her mother, had presented no problem whatever. John's not coming home had upset her very much, and she was still angry with Marcella.

"Won't he ever come back, Mama?"

"I think he'll be back this weekend, dear."

"It's too cold for him to come all the way home each night. You are so silly, Charlotte," Marcella said peevishly. "Mama, when can I go outside? Why can't I play for a little while?"

"Marcella, stop nagging. I said you couldn't go out, and that is final."

"I have to go outside. Just for a minute."

"You'll do no such thing!"

"But, Mama, I must. I have to use the privy!"

Hilary stopped what she was doing and looked suspiciously at her daughter. Then she shook her head and smiled. "Put your coat on and your scarf. It is terribly raw outside today."

She had become ridiculous in her suspicions and worry. The poor child felt compelled to ask permission to relieve herself. Hilary turned her attention back to the matter at hand and began pouring lye into the boiling kettle in which she was making soap.

When Marcella returned to the flat nearly half an hour later, Hilary was furious. "You lied to me! What am I going to do with you, Marcella? I have had Charlotte out looking for you for the last ten minutes. The poor child is frightened out of her wits and frozen to the bone!"

Marcella stood rigid and defiant just inside the doorway. She hadn't taken her coat off.

"Where were you? Where did you go?"

"I just took a walk."

"Where? Who were you with?"

"No one. I just took a walk all by myself."

"Did you see him?"

"Who?"

"That man, that awful man!"

"Do you mean Lou? He isn't awful."

"Did you see him!?"

"Yes, he was on Ragpickers Lane with the rest of them."

"I knew it. Oh, my Lord, I knew it!" Hilary gasped. "Did he—were you with him? Is that who you took a walk with?"

"I told you, Mama, I took a walk all by myself. Lou waved at me. Why are you so angry with me? Why won't you let me go outside? I didn't do anything wrong!"

Only a small, choked sound came from Hilary's throat. "Go put dry stockings on. Your feet are all wet. I'll fix our supper. Charlotte, you change yours, too." She turned away quickly so the girls wouldn't see the tears in her eyes.

There was very little for her to fix dinner with, and there wouldn't be more until John came home again and gave her some money. She would not touch the money she had hoarded. As she cut the few vegetables they had and made them into a puree for soup, she thought of the expression on Marcella's face as she had stood in the doorway protesting she had done nothing wrong.

Lou had broken through the veneer of reserve Marcella had had regarding the gangs. She liked Lou, and Hilary had to admit there was no reason why she should not. The man, in spite of what she knew him to be, had been kind to Marcella, had been an exciting, romantic figure, fighting the blazing building and then singling her out for attention. Marcella was at the age for heroes and crushes, which made Hilary's task all the more difficult. Short of locking the girl in her room day and night, she could do nothing to keep Marcella out of the midst of things.

Hilary sighed loudly. She hadn't felt well lately and had blamed it entirely on her worry over Marcella and the crawling despair of ever leaving Five Points. Only in the last few days had she considered another possible reason for her occasional nausea—but it brought her no comfort or cheer.

She was near the end of her childbearing age, and the thought of another baby to be born and waste away on Orange Street was more than she could bear. Slowly her mind and her face began to grow blank, and once again she took up her post by the storytelling window, staring vacantly at the streaks of soot.

The Dead Rabbits emerged from Paradise Square and came down to the barricaded end of the street near the intersection of Cross Street on a clear, frosty morning. The air crackled with the icy cold—and something else. Marcella, who seemed to have acquired a sixth sense about the tempo of the street, was out of the building that morning before Charlotte was awake or Hilary had thought to look in on her.

Marcella knew, as she dressed in the cramped space of her bedroom, that what she was doing was wrong and that she would be punished for it. But she also knew she would be caught and punished if she did nothing worse than walk down the street or say hello to one of the women who stood in the doorways of the tenements with their best dresses on.

Today her mother could catch her doing all of these things. The thought made Marcella shiver in the cold room, but it wasn't fear that made her teeth chatter—it was excitement.

As she raced down the street on her way to the barricades, Marcella waved to anyone and everyone. With her coat flying open and her thick red hair unfurling behind her, she looked as wild and ill-kempt as any other street child.

She spotted Lou almost before he was within calling distance. "Lou! Lou! I want to help, too!" Lou turned at the sound of her voice and stretched out his arms for her to run to him.

"Come on, Fire Top!" he laughed, lifting her high above his head. He walked over to the side of the road and put her down among a group of women there. All of them were smiling or laughing, enjoying the scene between Lou and Marcella. They welcomed Marcella to their ranks.

Favored by Lou, this daughter of the most uppity woman in Five Points was a real novelty. Those who didn't take to Marcella because of her personality and spirit encouraged her to stay because her mother had refused to see them, to acknowledge their existence. So, in spite of some less-than-kind comments about her ladylike ways, Marcella was sheltered with the other women along the sides of the buildings.

Lou himself showed her which tunnels and passages to take if things should go wrong for the Dead Rabbits.

"It don't happen often, you see, but you gotta know these things if you want to be a part of us." Marcella looked up at him in awe. "You run as fast as you can. Just follow the way I showed you, and you'll come out all right, Fire Top."

Marcella clung to Lou's hand as if she were never going to let go. He gave it a small shake and smiled down at her. "I can't do much good out there if you don't give me my hand back."

She let go immediately and blushed to the roots of her hair. He led her back to the bedraggled group of battle-ready women. Bags of ammunition hung from their arms or shoulders; piles of rocks, cudgels, brickbats, and other weapons lay at their feet within easy reach.

With few exceptions, these battles were well planned. Both sides were prepared for them to go on for days—until army troops were brought out to stop them. They knew they had nothing to fear from the police, and even less to fear from an enraged populace. No one really cared as long as the violence was confined to Five Points.

If and when things got too far out of hand, the Twenty-seventh Regiment would be called out to put an end to the fighting, but that wouldn't happen until the police force had proved itself ineffectual again. It might be as much as two or three days before anything was done.

Marcella was all eyes and ears, listening to the women's tales of blood and mayhem from other days and other wars. As she looked from one woman to another, she wondered how she could have supposed they were just like her own mother. After all, she had seen them with their children, hanging out wash, or carrying market baskets. They had seemed so ordinary.

One woman in particular impressed the little girl. Marcella could not have said what it was about her that made her different. Not a large woman, but rather small and thin, she looked wiry. Her hair looked like a mass of curly brass shavings. Marcella stared at the woman's back and shuddered involuntarily.

"You lookin' at our Maggie?" one of the women asked.

At that moment a Five Points legend turned to give Marcella her first full view of her. Hellcat Maggie drew back her lips in a snarl, displaying front teeth that had been filed to points. Maggie had ripped the flesh from many a man and woman with those teeth.

Marcella could not take her eyes from those horrible yellow and blackened teeth, and would not have, had not Maggie, enjoying her new audience, thrust up her hands so the cold winter sun glinted on her fingers. Specially made, fitted brass claws sparkled in the frozen sunlight. Like Hellcat Maggie who wore them, the fingertips were a legend, said to have ended the sight and good looks of many a man in the Bowery.

The woman standing next to Marcella looked down at the little girl. "Don't worry. You're on the right side," she laughed.

Marcella fought down the urge to run home to her mother. Hellcat Maggie's eyes were wild, filled with hate and blood lust.

"She looks very . . . mean," Marcella whispered.

"She is! " one of the women shouted. "She eats little girls for breakfast. Ain't that right, Mag?"

Maggie looked up and found Marcella's eyes immediately. She began to move down the line of women toward Marcella. Marcella backed up flat against the wall of the building. Maggie flashed the deadly pointed brass fingernails before Marcella's eyes.

"Save it for when it counts, Mag," said a deep voice. Marcella nearly sank to the ground in relief as she saw Lou walking toward them.

"Who're you talkin' to? No one tells me what to do!" Maggie screamed and turned to face Lou. Laughing, Lou took Maggie, nails and all, by the shoulders, crushed her against his chest, and kissed her.

Marcella looked away in embarrassment and disgust that Lou would ever kiss that hideous creature. When she looked back, Maggie was grinning, her fanged teeth protruding under her lip as she slapped Lou on the shoulder.

"Watch the fingers, Maggie!" he yelped and jumped away from her.

"I'll murder 'em for you, Lou. I'll murder 'em!" The women at the sidelines, seeing the Bowery Boys advancing down the street toward them, echoed her cry. "Let's go get 'em!"

The fight began slowly, each side trying to see the weakness in the other before committing themselves to an all-out charge. When it did begin, Marcella could not distinguish one side from the other. She held her ears and her breath as guns went off all around her. She had never been so afraid or so excited in her life.

In spite of the bitter cold, she was warm and increasingly bold. Lou had told her just to watch this first time, not to go out into the fighting mob, but she wanted to run to the men, the brave men. Whatever they were fighting for, she was certain it was something just as glorious and grand as Lou was himself.

She didn't move from her place of safety under the overhang of one of the low sheds until the fight had gone to hand-to-hand combat. She could hear men calling for knives and cudgels. As soon as she could see where Lou was, she began to battle her way through the writhing bodies. Bumped, hit, and finally knocked down, she lay for a stunned moment in the slushy mud. Then she felt the sharp, hard pain of someone stepping on her leg or hitting it with a cudgel. For the first time she realized that this was no game and she would die if she didn't get up and move. Leaping up, Marcella hit, kicked, bit, and clawed her way toward Lou, dumped her little bag of weapons into his hands, and began to make her way back.

"Get under the shelter!" Lou screamed after her, but Marcella was too caught up in the blood and violence around her to pay any heed. Several times she saw Hellcat Maggie pummeling her victims, leaving them bloody and broken.

Frantically dodging fists and passing weapons, Marcella lost all track of time. Neither tired nor hungry, she had no idea that most of the day had passed or that five men were now dead and three others would die. Finally, the policemen who had been watching from the outskirts of the battle had gone to get help.

The fight was still in full force when John Paxton walked into the Five Points area on his way home. After a week on the Hudson he was eager to get back to Hilary and the girls, to take back the angry words he had left them with. This last part of the trip—the part that he had to walk because no coach would take him to Five Points without charging double—was the worst, and he was bone-tired and thoroughly chilled. Hearing the noise from the fight, he noted the direction from which the sounds came so he could avoid the brawl. It annoyed him mildly that it was so near his own tenement. He knew it would upset Hilary, and it also meant that at any time an odd bunch of fighters might make their way to his flat for a moment's rest, a hot meal, or more likely, a bandaging up.

As he turned the corner to walk the last block home, he looked over at the enraged crowd and, dumbfounded, saw the top of a head with flying strands of deep red hair bobbing in and out. He froze where he stood, belief not coming readily.

The police, armed with copper shields and nearly useless nightsticks, were moving cautiously along the outer edge of the fracas but doing nothing to stop it. Occasionally they extricated a single battler from the melee, only to beat him senseless and leave him lying in the mud. They, like everyone else, were waiting for the Twenty-seventh to arrive.

Seeing immediately that Marcella would be an easy target for the police, John began to run toward the mob.

"Marcella! Marcella!" His shouts were drowned by the noise all around him. He raced to the plank walkway, edging along the side of the building he had seen her run for. As he grabbed her by the collar of her coat, she whirled on him, fighting for her life. Her teeth bared, she bit and clawed like a cornered animal. Her fists flew, her nails tore the flesh on the backs of his hands and along the side of his neck, until he found himself close to striking her in pain.

"Marcella!" he screamed again as he managed to crush her twisting, turning little body against himself. "Marcella! It's me!"

"Papa?" She suddenly went limp.

John did not answer but began to pull her back toward the crowd so he could cross the street and get her home. If he were stopped by the police, he would just pray that she hadn't been noticed. Marcella pulled on his hand.

"Not now!" John snapped. "Come along. We have to get away from here!"

"Papa! Wait, Papa. I know how to get out. Lou showed me."

John stopped and looked down at her. "Go ahead. Lead, and I'll follow you."

She darted back to the side of the building and under the overhang of the shed. Soon they were in a labyrinth of connecting passages. John lost his sense of direction in the circuitous route, but minutes later Marcella brought him back out on the street not ten feet from the door of their tenement.

"My God!" he breathed, stopping only long enough to wipe the blood from her face and his own. There was nothing he could do about her torn coat or the deep scratches that covered him, or the cut that still bled just below Marcella's hairline.

"Go upstairs," he said in a strangely quiet voice. He followed her up the long, dark staircase five flights until they came to their door, then pushed Marcella into the flat and sank down into his chair without a glance at Hilary or Charlotte.

"Oh, my God!" he moaned, both hands cradling his head. He looked up at Hilary. Charlotte was cowering in the far corner of the room, sobbing to herself.

"She could have been killed! How did you let it come to this?" he shouted. "Sitting there by that damned window, day in and day out! She might have been killed! You knew what was happening. Damn it, the whole street is alive with it. You knew! You knew!" His voice cracked, and he fell back against the chair.

Hilary's shoulders began to shake, racked with silent sobs. John's feelings were confused—tenderness for his wife, mixed with his own feeling of despairing helplessness. He looked away from her.

Marcella stood, dirty, blood-streaked, and tattered, near the door to the hallway.

"Go to your room, you little bitch!" he screamed. Marcella's eyes widened in horror and filled with fear as she scrambled for her room.

"Don't—don't talk like that. Charlotte—" Hilary choked out.

"By God!" he screamed. "You'll let one run the streets and do nothing, but let me say 'bitch' and you have plenty to say. You damned, unnatural woman!"

"I tried! I couldn't stop Marcella. I couldn't."

"How did you let it get so bad with Marcella? Why didn't you come to me while there was time?"

"I did! Oh, John, I did. I told you and told you. I begged you to get us out of here, and you mocked me and made fun of me." She dissolved in a flood of tears. "You left these godforsaken streets and went into clean air, leaving us behind. Don't tell me I should have stopped it. I couldn't. I tried and I couldn't. I tried and tried." Hilary paced the room, her eyes wild.

He was frightened by the woman in front of him. She in no way resembled the gentle woman he had married. She stood across the room from him, raging and screaming incomprehensible words to him. In a daze, John tried to make sense of what Hilary was ranting.

"I'll kill it! I'll kill it! Do you hear me, John? I'll not bring life into this place. As God is my judge, I swear I'll not let it be born."

He ran to her and took hold of both her thrashing fists, pinning them to her sides to keep her from pounding at her abdomen. She was strong beyond what he thought possible. He struggled with her, trying to get her to their bedroom, out of Charlotte's sight. Kicking the door of the room shut behind them, he felt her stiffen in his arms. Awkwardly he stood holding her, not knowing what to do next. She was no one he knew—a stranger. This wasn't Hilary, any more than it had been Marcella whom he had seen earlier out on the streets. What was happening to all of them?

"Hilary," he pleaded. "Hilary, please. Oh, God, please. Sit on the bed. Come along. Hilary—" He forced her down on the edge of the bed. She stared fixedly at the floor, her hands now clasped tightly on her lap. Over and over she repeated, "I'll not have it. I'll not bear the child."

"We are leaving here, Hilary," he said, kneeling by her side. "I'm giving my word. Hilary, do you hear me? I'm taking you out of here. We're leaving Five Points." She made no response.

"I'll not bear the child. I'll not. . . ."

"Hilary, listen to me. Please hear what I am saying. The child—the child won't be born here. It's all right. The child will never see Five Points. I promise you. We won't be here when the child is born. Can you understand? Do you even hear me? Say something . . . say something to me, please. . . ."

Well over an hour later, he was able to get her to lie down and fall into an exhausted sleep. John sat by her side, afraid she would awaken and harm herself or the child she carried.

When she awakened before the sun had fully risen, Hilary remembered very little of what had happened the night before. She glanced over and saw John slumped in the chair he had dragged from the main room. As soon as he heard her stir, he opened red-rimmed eyes and staggered to her side, telling her in what had now become a litany that she could have what she had always wanted—a house of her own, a yard, and a neighborhood that was respectable.

Chapter Four

In the morning light the import of John's words came to Hilary. "Do you mean what you are saying for now, John? I know you mean to take us from here. You always have. But do you mean we can leave now?" she asked softly.

John struggled to keep his eyes open and focused on hers. "We can look for your house this very day. I mean it for now, Hilary."

"How can we? I mean the money—I haven't near to enough."

He made an effort to pat her hand, missing and touching only the edge of her dress instead. "We can leave now."

She bit her lip to keep from asking how. At Charlotte's entrance into the room, she raised a finger to her lips. Charlotte tiptoed over to her mother.

"John? Are you asleep yet?" she whispered. He murmured. Hilary shook her head at her daughter and watched her move cautiously out of the room again. When she had gone, Hilary covered him and then followed Charlotte out the door.

"Where is Marcella?"

"She is in the bedroom."

"Tell her I wish to speak to her."

Charlotte hesitated. "She won't come out. I asked her before."

"Do as I ask, Charlotte. Marcella will come out."

Charlotte reluctantly did as she was asked. A moment later she returned to the main room without Marcella. "She says she doesn't feel well, Mama. Mama . . . Marcella is crying."

"And well she should." Hilary stood and smoothed down the front of her dress. She walked purposefully over to the door of the room Marcella shared with Charlotte. There she stopped and looked around the flat of three rooms. "We were lucky, you know. In spite of everything we have been lucky."

"Yes, Mama."

"Perhaps I have done you a disservice, Charlotte. What I have told you about Five Points is true, but it has never been your father's fault. Know that. There are five families in all of the Points that have three rooms for themselves as we have. Your papa did that." She opened the door to the girls' bedroom and walked in.

Marcella lay on the edge of the bed, her face puffy, her body still attempting to cry long after her tears had dried. Looking at her, Hilary felt angry rather than sympathetic.

"I asked that you come to the front room to talk to me."

"I don't feel good."

"I doubt that any of us do after the events of yesterday. I have managed to stir myself, and so shall you. Come with me immediately."

Marcella moved to the edge of her bed. "Lou's dead, Mama."

"Wash yourself before you come to me."

"Don't you care?"

"I do. Wash yourself and then come to me and we will talk."

Marcella came out into the main room and began to wash in the brackish water Charlotte had carried up from the street pump earlier that morning. It was cold, and it never smelled good, but this morning it seemed worse than usual. She moved slowly, aware that Hilary was watching her the whole time. Hilary suddenly got up from the chair on which she sat and came over to Marcella. She pushed back the hair from her daughter's forehead, exposing the gash Marcella had gotten the previous afternoon.

"You will carry a scar for your activities."

"I am clean now."

"On the outside, Marcella. You have much to do before you are clean on the inside, and that is where it means the most."

Marcella sobbed, but there were no tears. She looked up at Hilary. "I didn't mean to be bad. I didn't know what would happen."

"What you meant or what you expected is not the point, Marcella. What is important is that you didn't know who you were or what you stood for. You did things that people like us should never do. Your papa told me earlier that we are going to leave Five Points. We will be living in a new, respectable neighborhood. Do you know what that means, Marcella?"

She nodded her head. "We will be like those people you tell us about, like the ones at the celebration."

"Your father and Charlotte and I will be, Marcella, but what of you? It is not merely the clothes those people wear that make them different from Five Points, it is the way they live, and more imporant, the way they think and behave. About you, Marcella, I am not sure."

"Am I like the Five Points people?"

"I don't know. Are you?"

Marcella said nothing. "This"—Hilary's arm swept around the whole room—" is not Five Points. Your father has always kept us safe from the worst of it, and Lord knows this is bad enough, but it isn't the true Five Points. You have always liked this, haven't you, Marcella? I think I always knew that was at the heart of it."

"I do like it, Mama. You and Papa are here."

"Well, we are leaving, and before we do, I am going to do something I should have done long ago. You and I, Marcella, are going to see Five Points as it truly is. There will be no memory ever to draw you back to this place when I am finished. Now get dressed suitably. We are going out." Hilary finished and went to the nail and took down her coat. "Charlotte, if your papa wakens before I have returned, tell him I have gone to do some shopping. Be sure to tell him Marcella is with me."

Marcella followed her mother out of the building. The street was very quiet that morning. People were crowded about the streets as usual, but their talk was subdued. Several times Marcella heard Lou's name mentioned. She could hardly believe it when Hilary stopped to speak to one of the women. Marcella had never seen her mother speak to any of them before; she had gone out of her way to avoid them.

"When is this man Lou to be buried?" Hilary asked the woman standing near the entrance to one of the grogshops.

"God rest his soul!" the woman replied in a thick Irish brogue. "The poor thing, poor dear soul."

"When is he to be buried?"

"Day after tomorrow."

"Where?"

40

"Where?" the woman laughed bitterly. "Potter's Field, and lucky at that."

"Thank you," Hilary said and turned to Marcella as they began to walk again. "Did you hear what she said?"

"Yes."

"Potter's Field, and lucky. Do you think he is lucky, Marcella?"

"No."

"But he is, my dear. Five Points people don't always get such a burial." They came to the entrance to the back passageways that Lou had shown Marcella just the day before. Without hesitation Hilary turned into the labyrinth.

"Mama! How did you know about this?"

"There is little of Five Points I don't know about. Hurry along. Don't drag so."

"Where are we going?"

"To the Old Brewery."

"But, Mama! You said we were never allowed near there."

"That is Five Points, and now, Marcella, you will see it, and along with it, a grave that is more typical of what one can expect down here."

"I don't want to go!"

"Oh, but you have earned it, and now you shall see what you chose to become a part of. Hurry, Marcella, don't make me drag you every step of the way." Hilary jerked her hand, and they turned into the three-foot-wide walk that encircled the Brewery. The alleyway called Murderers Row reeked of refuse and human filth. It led to a fifteen-foot-square cellar room into which as many as sixty people were crowded.

Hilary threw open the door, and like animals the people inside shrank from the invasion of light into their den. There was a great muttering and stirring as bodies both black and white clambered over one another, retreating from the invasion.

Hilary paid no attention to any of them. She walked through those who parted to let her pass, and over those who did not. Marcella stumbled along behind her, gagging at the smell of the damp, decaying room. Tears of fright spilled out of her eyes. Hilary stopped before what seemed to be just a spot in the floor. "A little girl was buried there," she said to Marcella. "That is a Five Points grave. Look at it and don't forget it."

Marcella looked down and saw nothing but the hard-packed earth of the cellar. Hilary swayed a little. Automatically her hand went to her abdomen. "Let's get out of here. I don't feel well." She wiped perspiration from her lip and brow. "The little girl is not there now."

"How do you know she isn't?" Marcella asked. "What happened to her?"

"Mrs. Sweeney and I went to the Seventh Regiment and told them to clear out the pack of murderers who were staying there at the time. She is now decently buried."

Hilary took her through Cat Hollow and down Donovan's Lane, past the house where the Shirt Tails, another Five Points gang, hung out, and finally into the path called Cow Bay. Cow Bay was a cul-de-sac surrounded by tenements that seemed to lean against each other for last-ditch support. Hilary pointed at one of the buildings, which had a rickety staircase on its side.

"We have never lived like that. Your papa saw to it. If you want to be Five Points, Marcella, and be proud of what you see in Lou and the others, at least now you will know what it is you are proud of. Do you know why they have that staircase on the outside? There are no stairs in the building. There are no apartments. If Papa had let us live in a place like that, we would have been thrown in with as many people as could fit in the room."

"Can we go home now?" Marcella clutched her mother's hand more tightly than before.

"Not quite yet. There is one more place I want you to see." Hilary led Marcella out of Cow Bay and back into the confusing lanes. She stopped before a horrible wooden tenement of about four usable stories. The bottom floor was so deeply sunk into the uncertain ground that no grown man could ever have stood straight up at its one end.

"This is where Lou and his mother and brothers lived."

"Mama . . ."

"The Gates of Hell. That is its name, and it isn't far from wrong, Marcella. Now we will go home."

Marcella followed her, silent, as they made their way home.

When they returned, Hilary set about preparing the kind of dinner none of them had had for some time. Suddenly she seemed possessed of new and purposeful energy. "Marcella, go down and fetch some water for your father. He'll be awake any moment and will want a good wash. See if you can find the tea-water man. I'll want a pail." She took several pennies from her coat pocket and handed them to Marcella.

Marcella did as she was asked, while Charlotte, pouting at being left out of the "shopping trip," helped Hilary prepare the supper.

"Such a puss you are," Hilary chided her. "You have missed nothing."

"Why couldn't I go?"

"There was no need, but you can go shopping with me tomorrow—all by yourself."

Hilary's good humor and sense of purpose stayed with her all that night and through the next day. After her shopping trip with Charlotte, she announced to Marcella that they would be going to Lou's funeral.

The following morning they went to Potter's Field together and saw from a distance the small group of people around Lou's coffin. There were no pallbearers, only those who had cared enough to rise early in the morning and carry the pine box to the burying ground.

Hilary walked briskly toward the cluster of his family and a few of the Dead Rabbits. The coffin was placed by the side of the freshly dug grave, and the lid opened. His mother leaned over to kiss her son farewell. Marcella found herself standing beside the coffin. She had only to look and she would see Lou. She kept her head down, staring at the ground. Hilary pushed her forward.

"He was a good man, Marcella. Or he might have been. But I want you to see what Five Points does to its good." She turned her child's head so Marcella had no choice but to look down into the misshapen face. He had been washed and prepared as much as his mother had been able to do, but the marks of violence were deeply impressed in the dead flesh. Marcella trembled violently, struggling against her mother's iron grip. She began to wail, her own small voice joining that of Lou's mother.

"Let her go!" Hilary looked up to see Will, the man who had been with Lou the day of the fire, and who had carried Charlotte on his shoulder. "Don't do that to Fire Top. Let her be."

Marcella, released from Hilary's grip, continued to whine frantically, her lips drawn back into a grimace. Will looked at Hilary, waiting for her to do something, then went to Marcella himself and comforted her.

By the time Hilary brought her home, Marcella was quiet and subdued. "We'll neither of us ever mention this again. I have shown you the worst of Five Points and what it does to those few who are good. Go to your room, rest, and begin to look forward to the new house."

Marcella nodded dumbly. She wanted only to hide, to be alone, to forget what Lou had looked like in his coffin.

Hilary bustled about the three rooms of their flat with more energy than she had shown in weeks. When John returned with his cart from a day of selling sand to the women of better neighborhoods for their kitchen floors, his dinner was ready and waiting for him.

"What do you say we look for that house tomorrow?" he said. "You did yourself proud with this dinner."

Hilary placed another generous slice on his plate. "If we are to live on Eighth Avenue, you'll have to get used to eating good food. We can afford it, can't we? I mean, there is no point in leaving here if we must continue to behave as if we hadn't."

"Don't take the slum with us, you mean?"

"Something like that."

"We can afford it. If you're careful, that is—and I know you are. But I wish you could get your mind off Eighth Avenue. We may not be able to find a house there."

"We'll find a house. And it will be on Eighth Avenue, mark my words. I've waited and prayed for too long. I know it is there."

As it turned out, Hilary and John spent many days hunting for the house. Most of the places that were for sale were not to Hilary's taste. She was tireless in her search, resting only at John's angry insistence.

"You've got to think of that child!" She knew he meant it. She also knew that it was the unborn child that would take them out of Five Points. She did as he asked, handing over to her daughters her household responsibilities. Both Charlotte and—to Hilary's surprise—Marcella were not only willing but eager to help.

Marcella had barely stirred from the tenement since the day of Lou's funeral, going out only when she was asked to fetch water. She no longer talked to the people in the building or on the street. Her father, who had never seen Marcella so inactive or unsmiling, asked Hilary about it several times.

"She is just growing up, John. You didn't expect her to be a baby forever, did you?"

"You're sure she isn't taking sick? She seems cold all the time, and I haven't seen her smile for days. That isn't like her."

"She's fine. There isn't a thing wrong with her that our new home won't cure."

Beyond this often-repeated conversation, Hilary would say nothing. When John talked to Marcella, he got nothing but evasion. After a time he gave up trying to find out what was bothering Marcella and instead redoubled his efforts to find the right house for all of them.

The house he finally found on Eighth Avenue was the most welcome sight Hilary had ever seen. Three narrow stories high, built of brick, this house would never sink into unstable ground. The brick had been painted red—freshly painted—and the mortar shone white and brilliant under its coating of paint. Although it was not grand, or elegant, it was clean, fresh, and decidedly respectable—a fit place from which to launch her daughters and the new baby.

John told her they could move as soon as they wished, for the house was vacant. Much to his surprise, she refused.

"Why not? You've done nothing but talk about getting out of here—"

She laughed and patted his hand. "It is just that the landlords will set their new rents on February first. . . ."

"We're not renting the house. I told you, I bought it."

"Let me finish, John. They set the rents on February first. There are always adjustments, and there are always people who cannot or will not meet those adjustments. So we, too, shall wait until May first, the accepted moving day and no one will even notice us."

"But there is no reason to wait. We have no rent to pay, we don't need the three-month grace period to find a house. It makes no sense!"

"John, please listen to me. Everyone moves on May first. The streets are always crowded with movers. If we move on that day, no one will pay us the slightest attention. They won't even realize we are coming from here.

"When we leave Five Points, I want to leave completely. I don't want anyone to know where we came from—ever! Please, John, we're so close to moving. After May first we will never again have to breathe the words Five Points."

"Whatever you wish, Hilary."

In a sense it was a relief to him. For four months more, he could remain just what he was, a man with a cart and a knack for knowing who would need his services and pay the most. After they moved, John knew his cart would also be a thing of the past.

Chapter Five

Hilary, too, wanted time. She needed to recoup some of the strength that this winter had drained from her. She was tired, too tired even to rejoice properly in her long-awaited freedom from Orange Street.

With great self-discipline and determination, she forced herself to take proper care in packing the few possessions she would consider taking with her to the new home. Early on, she saw that they would never have what might appear to be a suitable quantity of belongings. They would look poor. She sent John out in search of boxes, which she filled painstakingly with paper folded to look as if it protected pieces of china and crystal.

"Be certain they are packed tightly and neatly, Charlotte. Everything one does is a sign of what one is. Shall we be thought of as shoddy before we have even gotten into our new home, simply because we have neglected to do an adequate packing job? I should think not!"

"But, Mama, how is anyone going to know unless they look in our boxes?"

"No one is going to look through the boxes, Charlotte, but we must do as good a job as we can, so if they were to look, we would be proud. See? This box looks exactly as if it were carrying china." She stood back to admire her work. "Imagine that these will be inspected, and that will help you to do good work. Always remember, a job worth doing at all is worth doing well."

"That's what the monitor at school tells us," Marcella said, looking down into Hilary's packing box. "Where will we go to school when we live in the new house, Mama?"

"I don't suppose you girls will be going to schools much after we leave here. You're growing up." Hilary looked at Marcella and forced a smile. She had not yet found a way to reestablish her affection for Marcella. She had tried, and Marcella had tried, being as obedient and helpful as it was in her nature to be, but this child had slipped away from her. Somehow she bore the marks of all Hilary was determined to forget, to erase from her life.

While Hilary and the girls prepared to move, John Paxton was tending to the financing of their home. While with the depletion of his bank account he would once again have to watch every penny, he was entering a new era in his life. He was a landowner—or in real estate, as he preferred to think. It was no mean achievement. After all, how many men in his position would have held on so long and saved enough to buy a house?

There was a pleasant, solid feeling about owning property, he thought. Perhaps this was the direction his checkered career should take. Though he had very little money with which to begin, he could make plans. He would save his money, placing it in his account twice weekly as he had in the past, until he could purchase another modest piece of property, then another.

The city of New York was changing rapidly, more rapidly, he believed, than anyone realized. More and more people were crowding into less and less space. John Paxton intended to buy property north of the city. Although many spoke of the farmlands of Brooklyn, and others believed the city would grow toward Greenwich, he held firmly to his belief that Fifth Avenue, which now ended in an unpaved, muddy path above Tenth Street, would eventually go north to the very end of the island. In any case, that was one area where land was cheap enough for him to be able to buy.

In the meantime, the present concerned him deeply. He had hoped that Hilary would be her old self again, once she knew for a certainty that they were leaving Five Points, but he could no longer fool himself. His Hilary was gone forever.

Marcella, too, weighed heavily on his conscience. Hilary had finally convinced him not only that he shared in the guilt for what had happened to his daughter, but that he was in great part responsible for it because of his lack of attention and concern. He saw in Marcella a child cut off, drawing on her own meager inner resources for guidance and reason.

John had never been told about the trip around Five Points or the visit to Lou's grave, or he might have understood Marcella better. As it was, he saw a child adept as always at seeing what she chose to see, at pretending to be whatever she wished to be. Apparently she wished to be like her mother. John watched her become a grotesque little replica of a woman, too quiet, too meticulous without her singular joy and zest for life. It worried him, but nothing he tried seemed to help. Apparently Hilary no longer cared.

One night, when John came home bearing a gift, Hilary greeted him at the door and kissed him coolly on the cheek. Polite practice, he supposed, for the time when they were respectable residents of the Avenue. He smiled and handed her the parcel he carried.

"Take care and hold it upright."

"What is it?"

"Unwrap it. It's not all that much, just something I thought you might welcome."

Hilary quickly unwrapped the package. It was a nicely designed oil lamp and a goodly supply of whale oil. She smiled and hugged it to herself.

"Careful! I think there is oil in the lamp. You'll spill it. Shall we light it?" he asked, removing the candle from the table.

"Oh, no! We'll save it—for our new home."

"Don't be silly. We won't wear it out by using it, and I can get you more oil. Let's enjoy it. May is a long way off."

"Only a little better than two weeks, John. Not so long."

"Let's enjoy it, Hilary."

Reluctantly, she put the lamp on the table and stood back as John lit it. It brightened the room so much better than the wavery candle flame, but it also made more evident than ever the condition of the place in which they lived. He turned the lamp down.

In spite of John's suggestion that she get someone to help her with the last-minute preparation of the new house and the moving, Hilary had insisted on doing everything herself—packing their belongings, buying the basic furniture they would need in the larger house, scrubbing and painting the new house from top to bottom. In the end, the task fell primarily to John and Marcella. Hilary, for all her protests, simply could not manage alone. She went to the house with them and supervised, examining the colors used and the neatness of the job.

Both Marcella and John grew tired and short-tempered under her constant criticism and direction, but when they had finished, the house did look fresh and new. Again John tried to persuade Hilary to get help.

"You'll be wanting help when we move, in any case. What does a few extra days matter, Hilary? Hire someone to come in and give you a hand."

"No," she said flatly. "Not yet. Do you really think that I have come this far only to bring someone in here now, to see how we live? I'll not have anyone. No one. Not until we are settled."

"Get someone from around here to help you at this end."

"Let a Five Points harlot in here? You have taken leave of your senses, John Paxton. I'll thank you not to bring up the subject again."

"Do as you wish, then. If it pleases you to wait until we have moved, then we shall wait, but I still think it is no more than foolish pride. This is far too much for you to do in your condition."

When May 1 arrived, Hilary was tired beyond measure. Fortunately it was a bright, mild day. As Hilary had predicted, the streets were filled with people bustling to and fro, changing neighborhoods, houses, and apartments.

The Paxtons joined the others on New York's traditional moving day. Hilary felt no embarrassment when they loaded up John's cart; if John had not been busy moving his own family, his cart would have been put to the task of moving some other family.

The move was accomplished with amazing ease, and they received little or no attention from anyone.

"I'll hand it to you, Hilary. You were right. All your fussing and packing has done this just right."

"I've told you so often, John, I'd think you'd grow weary of hearing me. It is the small things, the ones you think go unnoticed, things like wearing clean white gloves, or properly packing a box, that distinguish one class from another."

"Which class do our paper-filled boxes put us in?" he asked mischievously, putting his arm around her waist.

She sat down heavily on one of the packing cases and looked around her. "It really is a lovely house, isn't it? It has a feel about it—a feeling of home, just as I knew it would. I think I'll make a sampler for the dining room. Would you like that? It's our first home, John. Our very first. We begin life right here and now. Nothing will ever go wrong again."

Even before they moved in, they had made plans for the eight-room house. Off the central hall to the immediate right was the parlor, which Hilary had decided to use only for the most formal occasions. Behind that room, joined by sliding double doors, was the main parlor, which the family would use daily. It, too, could be entered from the hallway. On the left side of the hall was the dining room, and behind it the kitchen.

Upstairs, the master suite consisted of John's and Hilary's bedroom and a sitting room for Hilary. Of the two other bedrooms, one would be used for John's study, and the other for Charlotte. Marcella and the new baby, if it was a girl, would be housed on the third floor. If it happened to be a boy, either John's study or Charlotte's bedroom would be given over, and Charlotte would join her sister in one of the spacious rooms on the third floor.

"I am going to put the bedroom in order," John said, clearing his throat. "You need a good rest."

"I'm fine. It has been a long day. I should be tired."

"I agree that you should be and that you are. So I am going to set up the bedroom. Then Marcella and Charlotte and I will see to putting the downstairs in order. We can manage perfectly well by ourselves."

"Maybe a little rest . . . A nap would be so nice."

He bounded upstairs to the bedroom. Sometime during the past week she had hung curtains at the window, sheer curtains that would let in light and air from the two long, wide windows.

John laughed to himself as he opened both of them and breathed deeply of the mild night air. Hilary hadn't cared for the room's panels of leather and had painted the walls around them a soft blue. It would be some time, he guessed, before Hilary surrounded herself with darkness of any kind. As long as she didn't have the leather itself painted, he didn't mind. He left the room and went down to get his wife.

Josephine Loretta Paxton was born in the heat of summer's end in 1826. Like her sisters before her, she was crowned with the deep red hair of the Paxtons. Josephine was a tiny baby, a smaller, daintier version of Marcella.

Marcella and John were both amused and delighted by the resemblance. For the first time since they had moved from Five Points, John saw some spark of the old Marcella return to her.

"May I hold her, Papa?" she asked when Josephine was no more than a few hours old. The midwife placed the baby in Marcella's arms, showing her how to hold her, with a strict warning of what might happen if she did not do exactly as instructed. Marcella sat, afraid to move, for several minutes before her fascination overcame her restraint, and she relaxed. John, completely enchanted by his new daughter, tried to get the infant to take hold of his finger. When the midwife came to take the baby to Hilary, John and Marcella both gave her up with reluctance.

As the weeks passed, it became clear that Hilary would be slow in recovering from having this child. After the long winter pregnancy and the move, she needed most of her strength simply to hold her own and had little to spare for Josephine.

The birth of her sister and her mother's inability to care for either the baby or the household represented a new kind of challenge for thirteen-year-old Marcella. She had no choice but to become the woman of the house. To her own satisfaction—and to her father's enormous relief—she rose to the occasion.

John had counted on Hilary's strong, active hand in running the house frugally until he had his financial feet firm again. He was especially worried that he would have to dip into his remaining capital to keep the house operating properly. Perhaps they had moved too soon. Every penny had to be watched if they were to succeed. He had gotten them out of Five Points, but even he was not so much an optimist as to believe that there was any hope for them if they should fail here.

A great load of worry was shed from John's shoulders when Marcella proved to be as able a housekeeper as her mother. She was eager to learn and thought of the task as a game or adventure. With the diffident aid of her father and the matter-of-fact advice of the neighborhood women, Marcella hired a wet nurse for her baby sister. She made John's shaving soap, the household soap, and the candles with such exuberance that John could do little but laugh in happy pride.

He loved being able to join in, to contribute to her task. Hilary had never let him near her when she was cooking or doing anything she considered women's work, but Marcella was different, and he took profound pleasure in encouraging his daughter.

As soon as April arrived, John could be seen leaving his house in the hours before dawn, hurrying to the foot of Seventy-fourth Street. There he joined a friend in a small boat for one of his favorite occupations—shad fishing. In the quiet dawn they drove the slim oak poles into the bottom of the Hudson. The sound of the sledges echoed across the river. Then they stretched ropes from pole to pole, ready to entangle the shad.

Their method marked them as city fishermen confined to the shallows, but John didn't care. The first time he went out for the shad that year, his catch was meager, not enough to sell. He took them home to Marcella, eager to teach his daughter how they should be prepared.

"Papa! They are beautiful!" She touched the lavender-and-silver-scaled body of the fish. "Oh, they are so beautiful. Look at the color and the shape. This one has red mixed in with the silver."

John laughed and picked up the fish. He turned it over in his hand. "This is the one you'd pick as best, is it?"

"It is the prettiest."

"It's a buck. Not so good as the roe." He put the shad down and picked up another. He ran his hand over the fish, over the bulge below the belly behind the dorsal fin. "This is a roe. You can tell by the bulge and the coloration. If you ever have occasion to buy shad, remember that and take the roe."

Marcella nodded solemnly and looked up at him. "But why should I buy them when you are such a good fisherman? You bring home all we can use and then some."

John nearly blushed with pleasure at Marcella's enthusiasm. He wondered how long Hilary's ideas of propriety would permit him to be seen with the rough men who fished the Hudson. He had already given up the all-night fishing he enjoyed so much, the dark nights when the fishing was best and the running shad looked like blue-white lights racing through the water. He shrugged. "Maybe you'll marry a man who won't like the water or fishing, and then you'll buy fish, my girl. You never know."

"Oh, I'd never marry anyone who didn't like the river. Never, never! What kind of man could that be?"

Again John laughed. "Watch, Marcella." Quickly he cut the back of the first shad's neck and let it bleed. "Wipe it off with a clean cloth, Marcella," he said as he picked up the next fish.

They worked in silence until the job was done, and then he called her to come and watch what he did. He opened one fish and emptied the belly. He then filled it with vinegar and sewed the fish back up, placing it in a baking pan.

"Now you do the others."

"Can't I fry them? I much prefer the olive oil to the vinegar, Papa."

"This is better for your mama." Marcella immediatley agreed and went to work on the remaining fish, humming little snatches of tunes, while John watched. How much she has changed, he thought, in such a short time. What had they called her in Five Points?

"Fire Top," he said out loud. Instantly he was sorry.

"Please don't call me that, Papa."

"I won't—ever again. I don't know why I did. Sometimes your Papa doesn't use his head."

"It's all right," she said with forced cheerfulness. "Now tell me why I must use the vinegar. Can't I just bake them?"

"It melts the bones as the fish cooks," he said, almost apologetically. Suddenly he felt uncomfortable in the kitchen. The closeness was gone, at least for the moment. "You'll be all right now. You don't need a heavy-handed man in your kitchen." He wiped his hands on a towel and left.

Marcella flourished in her new position as woman of the house. Without realizing it, she began to replace her mother, both in her own eyes and in the eyes of the rest of the family. The wonderful fantasy of "playing house" became real. Above all, Marcella needed to be valued and given proof of that value. Her father generously provided that proof in his obvious pride and pleasure in what she was doing.

Actually, Marcella had taken what place was left in the family framework and made of it something to satisfy her own need. Charlotte cared for her recuperating mother simply because Charlotte was the only one Hilary permitted to be around her. If Marcella brought her supper tray, Hilary turned her face to the wall. She claimed Marcella was clumsy and inclined to spill things, which was true more often than not, since Hilary berated and criticized Marcella constantly. Whatever belated attempt Hilary had made to teach her daughter caution and control in a place like Five Points had been a total waste, she was convinced. Hilary's nightmares were no longer of Five Points, but of Marcella, whom she now saw as thoroughly tainted by association with that place.

For Marcella, her mother's room was the repository of a vague, chilling sense of reasonless guilt. Outside that room, she was becoming the picture of refined young ladyhood. No one but Hilary would ever have suspected her daughter of the wild, headstrong abandon of which she had once been capable.

Outwardly Marcella displayed no difficulty in adjusting from the riotous atmosphere of her old home to the quiet, socially conscious neighborhood in which she now lived. She made friends with the neighbors on either side, eliciting daily offers of help. A willing pupil, Marcella basked in the approval of these women, and they, for their part, liked nothing better than to share their favorite methods and recipes for keeping a proper household.

In spite of the ladies' and all Marcella's efforts, nothing seemed to make the slightest favorable impression on Hilary in the months following Josephine's birth. Fortunately, her mother's lack of approval was something to which Marcella was long accustomed, and it did not hamper her actions in the least. Her first decision, for example—to hire the maid her mother had never gotten around to hiring—was not nearly so difficult as presenting to Hilary the facts of the accomplishment. Calling upon Charlotte for support, Marcella was able to assure Hilary that utmost caution had been used, and that the girl had not come from Five Points nor did she suspect that the Paxtons had. Once Hilary's chief bogey had been driven away, she took the new maid in her stride, accepting her services as if she had been born and bred to it. When Marcella hired a cook, there was not a word of caution or criticism from her mother. Nevertheless, the gap between Marcella and her mother grew, bridged only by the remnants of parental possessiveness and a sort of interfering curiosity on Hilary's part.

Little about Marcella suggested she was still a child. By the end of the first year in their new home, Marcella had a poise most women hadn't acquired by the second year of marriage. Paying no attention to the girls of her own age, she mingled and spoke with all the women she knew on an equal footing. Marcella seemed to have parted with her childhood the same day the Paxtons had parted with Five Points.

Her bedroom mirror, too, reflected her feelings of adult self-importance. Almost overnight, Marcella, in her own eyes, had become beautiful. No one else had ever denied her attractiveness, but now she saw it, too. She reveled in it, exploited it, amazed and delighted by the effect her beauty had on those around her, especially on men.

While women might dream, Marcella believed, only men could make a dream a reality. After all, hadn't it been her father who had loved her? Hadn't it been Lou who had made people take notice of her? Hadn't her father bought this house—not her mother, who had spent all of her life longing for it and dreaming about it?

Charlotte made no bones about telling her older sister exactly what she thought of her excessive vanity.

"Are you in front of that mirror again?" Charlotte asked one night as she breezed into Marcella's bedroom. "If Mama knew what you do up here all the time, she'd have you down on the second floor with the rest of us so fast you wouldn't know you were gone."

"She never comes up here." Marcella turned to study the other side of her profile.

"I could tell her."

"Why should you? You're as welcome to use my mirror as you care to be. I don't see anything wrong in what I am doing."

"That's probably what Narcissus said, and tell me what good he ever did himself. You'll do worse than him. It would be just like you to fall right into the pool of your self-image and drown."

Marcella giggled. "Not I! I am not in love with my image. I am concerned only with what others will see when *they* fall in love with it."

"If they can manage to climb over your mountain of conceit!"

"What conceit?"

Charlotte stared at her, openmouthed. "What conceit?"

"I'm not conceited, Charlotte. I don't care at all for people who are, you know that very well. But why should I pretend that I am not pretty? I am."

"You're awful and a liar as well."

"It's better than being jealous like you!"

Charlotte huffed out of the room, forgetting whatever it was she had come for.

When Marcella went out later in the day, taking with her some of the money she had masterminded out of the weekly allowance she was given to run the house, she bought Charlotte a soft, many-colored shawl as a peace offering. But as often happened, Charlotte was given only the privilege of admiring it on her sister's shoulders.

Chapter Six

John Paxton's worries about his own and his family's financial fortunes at the time of their move to Eighth Avenue proved to be groundless. Almost as soon as they had moved into their new house, his prospects began to brighten, and within a few years he had secured a responsible position in an iron factory, supervising the production of the iron stoops and facades that were so popular on the downtown buildings.

There was little John hadn't tried at one point or another in his working life up to that point—cutting ice and hawking fresh tea water from door to door, selling sand, being a porter, for a time even lighting the whale-oil streetlamps.

All of that was past now. From time to time he caught himself wondering why he had allowed so many years to pass, why he had spent so much of his young manhood in back-breaking laborers' jobs when, he told himself, he could have been on a road to success like the one he was on now.

His work brought him to the edge of the expanding construction business, encouraging some of the plans and even more of the dreams he entertained of becoming a land developer. He began to invest, first with several friends, and later, as he was able to save more of his growing salary, without them, in small tracts of open land.

As the city grew, his careful investments began to pay off. Over a period of four or five years, John Paxton looked increasingly as if he would become a prosperous man. His slow but steady climb up the ladder of financial success was reflected more and more in his family's style of living.

For her part, Hilary took to the new prosperity with the driven, curiously joyless single-mindedness of one whose dreams have been deferred too long. During her long convalescence following Josephine's birth, her physical frailty had confined her to bed much of the time, and in her mind at any rate, justified laying on Marcella the burdens of running the household and caring for the baby.

Having recovered, however, Hilary seemed to have made a virtue of her frailty. Headaches, overexertion, and occasional dizzy spells mingled with what she saw increasingly as the trials of being a mother at home. As often as she could, she fled this host of troubles, commencing a full-fledged campaign to become socially accepted and respectable.

She invited the neighborhood ladies in for afternoon tea, knowing that propriety would dictate a return invitation. She joined almost every social and charitable women's group that would accept her, and began an everlasting round of socializing. Always, it was Charlotte she had in tow, while Marcella remained at home with Jo.

As those first few years passed, it was hardly surprising that Marcella became the baby's surrogate mother, encouraging her first few steps, nursing her through colds, telling her stories, answering her incessant questions. Nor was it surprising that the family became more and more divided, had less and less in common.

For the most part, Hilary was perfectly content to leave Marcella to her own devices. She had never understood her daughter, she convinced herself, and there was no reason to believe she would begin to understand her now. That Marcella seemed capable of running the household efficiently and keeping Jo occupied surprised Hilary only as often as she thought about it, which was not often.

Occasionally, in a fit of guilt, Hilary would confront Marcella about her way of dressing Jo, or the frequency of Marcella's outings on the Hudson, or the tenderness of the cut of meat Marcella had brought home from the butcher. Marcella soon learned that it was pointless to argue with her mother, much less to reason with her, at these times. She would listen sympathetically until her mother had finished, promise to see what could be done to rectify the situation, and go on as she had before. For Hilary, venting her angry guilt seemed to suffice.

During these years, there were only two issues on which Hilary gave Marcella no peace: Jo's schooling and Marcella's social life—or lack of it. When Jo was five years old, Marcella decided to enroll her in a Free School. The minimal formal schooling she and Charlotte had had, they had received at such a school. After visiting one nearby and speaking with the headmaster and several teachers, Marcella announced to the family at dinner one night that she had made arrangements for Jo to attend the following fall.

Hilary would not hear of it. "I won't have my daughter attending a common school. She'll have a tutor, and when she is old enough, she will attend a finishing school. That is all I want to hear on the subject."

All her husband's attempts to change her mind had no effect, and so, in short order, Hilary hired a tutor for her youngest daughter. Miss Potts, the woman selected after numerous interviews, was proper almost to the point of extinction. As far as Marcella was concerned, she practiced and preached the most blatant form of bigotry she had ever seen, but long experience with her mother's views of morality and propriety had taught her to keep her opinions on the subject to herself, and she did.

Within a year Marcella's dim view of Miss Potts's opinions and teaching methods was vindicated—by Hilary, to Marcella's great surprise. Her mother complained more and more often of the frequency with which Jo quoted Miss Potts on every conceivable subject, until she could tolerate it no longer. Miss Potts was let go, politely but firmly, with the admonition that she not turn her next charge against the child's parents.

Though Marcella was not the least bit sorry to see Miss Potts go, she also recognized that now she would have to contend again with the effects of Hilary's direct involvement in Jo's education. The silent tug-of-war between Hilary and Marcella, with Jo in the middle, resumed.

On the other target of Hilary's criticism, Marcella's social life, Marcella could scarcely avoid being involved. Hilary had begun some years before to express to her husband her concern about the proper launching of her daughters and their eventual marriageability. Her inroads into the social life of the community had given her a welcome opportunity to look over the crop of her friends' eligible sons, whom she measured against her daughters as prospective husbands.

Her efforts on Charlotte's behalf had paid off. Charlotte had met and become very much interested in a young man by the name of Martin Henderson, a state of affairs about which Hilary never ceased reminding Marcella.

"Martin Henderson and his mother will be spending the weekend with us," she announced to Marcella one summer evening. "I do believe that young man is very seriously interested in Charlotte."

Marcella chuckled. "Martin seems very serious about everything."

"I wouldn't get saucy if I were you, Marcella, especially not at your age. At least Charlotte has a young man to consider. It is more than can be said of her older sister."

It was a conversation that, in one form or another, they had had more times than Marcella cared to think about. Charlotte, she thought with a little condescension, had neither the ambition nor the desire to look further than someone like Martin Henderson. She would be satisfied with him, his meager income, and his equally meager prospects of becoming anything of note in New York City. As for herself, she would not settle for anything less than exactly what she wanted.

She expressed only the last thought out loud.

Hilary was incensed. "You needn't carry it that far, Marcella! Perfect men are hard to come by."

"I didn't say perfect, Mama. I just said the kind I want. He must have a certain spark, a vitality. I shall know it when I see it. After all, I was only twelve when I recognized it in Lou."

"Marcella, please don't deliberately try to pick an argument with me. I have told you before that Lou, considering what he was, was a nice enough young man. As to the other, you are like all young women your age. You're a dreamer where men are concerned. The first thing I know, you'll be dragging some thin-shanked lad in here and telling me he is your Adonis!"

Marcella snorted. "Has Martin finally gotten around to asking Charlotte to marry him?"

"That tactic will do you no good whatever," snapped Hilary. "It is only a matter of time with Charlotte and Martin. He is a cautious and responsible man." She smoothed the front of her skirt hastily and then looked up at her daughter. "What about that man—Jack McClellan—you've been seeing lately? What's wrong with him? He is a nice man."

"Mama! I don't love him!" Marcella turned away abruptly, and with some effort, lowered her voice. "Why should Charlotte be cautious and careful about what she does, while I should grab the first male creature who offers himself?"

"You are so caustic, Marcella, and so defensive. I can't say a thing without your twisting it and making it into something we both regret." Hilary sighed loudly. "Charlotte and I have such nice little chats. I try so hard with you, but you just wear me out."

"Well, Mama, why don't you lie down and rest, then? Surely you can get over this talk with an hour's sleep."

Hilary hardly noticed the edge in Marcella's voice. "I think I shall. Be a dear and tell Betsy to bring me my violet water for my forehead. It throbs so."

"Of course, Mama. Is there anything else I can do for you?"

"That's thoughtful of you, Marcella, but no. I think you are right. What I need is a good nap, and I shall feel fine again. Do remember the wise advice I have given you, dear. It is always given with your interests at heart. You know that, don't you, dear?"

Marcella watched her mother walk from the room, thinking, as she always did, that her mother was a silly, shallow fool. It was always easier to entertain the thought than to allow for the suspicion that in spite of her mother's callous way of expressing it, she was right. Perhaps she would be a spinster, living alone for the rest of her life.

There was nothing wrong with Jack or any of the other young men she had met, Marcella admitted to herself, except that by marrying any one of them she would, she was sure, become just another version of Hilary Paxton or any of the other women who lived near her. There was so little difference between them, one's conversation the duplicate of another's, one's dress differing only in color from that of her neighbor.

There were agonizing times when it seemed that the wild, free feeling of being able to meet life on any terms, of being marked for something special, had been crushed out of her. She would have to keep her mind's eye on the dream, she knew, or it would never happen.

She turned abruptly from her reverie, suddenly remembering her promise to have Hilary's violet water sent up to her.

Chapter Seven

One horribly cold winter's night in 1835, fire swept New York City, leaving disaster and ruin in its wake. What added to the horror was that the water pumps that served the growing city, inadequate for even normal use, were totally useless in combating a fire of such magnitude.

Volunteers raced for the holocaust, many of them still dressed in the top hats and ruffled shirts they had worn to the theater earlier in the evening. They hooked up the fire carts to the pumps, began to spray the flames, and then watched in horror as the water shot up into the air and froze as it came from the hoses.

New York was going to burn, and they could do little but watch it go. Outlying communities that, under normal circumstances, could be relied upon to help, were unable to get into New York because there was no transportation sufficient to get them over the unpaved and rutted roads just outside the city. Even Broadway wasn't paved past Tenth Street. New Yorkers were left alone and isolated with their blazing town. Only by blowing up the burning buildings were they able to stop the fire from spreading.

As it was, the Wall Street area suffered tremendous damage. Most of lower Manhattan was a charred mass of ruined buildings.

As a result of the fire, three things happened in the city, all of which had an important impact on John Paxton's life and business. Perhaps most important to the future of the city was the building of the Croton Reservoir. For the first time New York would have running water. This ended the tea-water-cart business. Despite some heartfelt nostalgia about his days as a peddler of tea water, John was not terribly regretful about the demise of that institution.

He was now captivated by all the talk and furor about the so-called bathing room. It seemed to him that it might be a small measure of the delights of heaven to have a room in which one could take one's ablutions. Of course, his stumbling block was Hilary. She, along with most New Yorkers, considered this an unhealthful and immoral thing, to be used only on a doctor's orders. But John wanted a bathing room, and he was determined to get one.

The second turn of events affected John's business ventures more immediately. With the exception of a few old iron-stooped buildings such as the City National Bank at 52 Wall Street, that section of town had burned to the ground and needed rebuilding. Old mansions of earlier years were converted into offices, banks, and places of trade. Flagging replaced the old planked sidewalks in front of the new buildings. Iron facades, which everyone hoped were fireproof, were installed. Within two years after the fire of 1835, what had once been a heavily residential section of the city had become almost entirely a business district.

The fire's devastation, combined with the phenomenal growth of the population of the city, created an enormous demand for new housing. The property that John had been buying ever since they had left Five Points—his worthless marsh-, scrub-, and farmland—rocketed in value as the city began to sprawl into new areas.

As John had expected, it began to move northward past Tenth Street, section by section. As Fifth Avenue changed from a street of residences to one of shopkeepers, the usual dismay was expressed as those who had lived on that street saw it being taken from them by commerce of all manner. Houses were torn down, to be replaced by modern facades of granite.

To John, the sound of the workmen's hammers was echoed by the sound of coins dropping into his pockets. Wherever business went, residents went farther out, always keeping a respectable distance from the stores that made their money. And the Paxton family fortunes took yet another turn for the better.

When the Croton Aqueduct was completed, Marcella was twenty-three years old and Charlotte was nearly twenty-one. Neither had married. It didn't concern John, who was much too busy marveling over his shrewdness and good fortune, but it did bother Hilary immensely.

Charlotte had been seeing Martin for three years, and while Hilary admitted it to no one, she had begun to look upon him with a wary eye. It was one thing to be a responsible, stable young man, but quite another to take up the best years of a young woman's life and then do the unspeakable by doing nothing whatever. To add to the dreadful things she periodically imagined about Marcella, she now added the unhappy vision of Charlotte as a pining old maid with no Martin and no prospects. Publicly, however, she told anyone who cared to listen that Martin was a fine man, and that he and Charlotte were as good as settled.

At home, she gave Marcella no peace. "Surely one of these men must appeal to you, Marcella. You can't possibly find something wrong with every decent man who comes to the house. Charlotte has had no difficulty in choosing a fine, upstanding man. Why can't you be more like she is? Why must it always be you who are so hard to please? One of these days you'll please yourself right out of the running!"

"I see no reason to marry someone I don't care for."

"You have always been stubborn, Marcella—terribly headstrong, and wrongheaded in the bargain. Sometimes I believe you do it simply to spite me—after all I have suffered for you. I shall never understand you. Your entire ungrateful manner is unbecoming and strange."

"I should think you would be pleased, Mama. You have always worried about my interest in men. You used to say I'd run off and be married to someone unsuitable if not disreputable. Do you remember? Well, I remember, and here I am, as respectable as blueberry pie, unmarried and still at home like a good daughter."

"At the age of twenty-three! I can hear the spite in your voice. You have done it deliberately. I stopped your wicked tendencies when we left Five Points, but that didn't stop you, did it, miss? You simply went to the other extreme. One way or the other you get yourself talked about, Marcella Paxton! At least I prefer people to think you are a bit strange rather than wonder whose man you'll be after next."

Marcella forced a laugh. "Really, Mama, you can't seriously be implying I would have been a lady of the evening?"

"I am simply saying you are extreme in whatever you do. You didn't become a child bride, so now you have elected to become a spinster."

"I've not elected to become anything. I simply have not met the man I'd want to live my life with. Is that really so strange?"

"What's wrong with Tim White?"

"Nothing. But what is right about him, Mama? He is unattractive, unrich, and unlovable."

"Such a crude mouth you have! He's a dear boy."

"I don't like dear boys."

"You'll outsmart yourself one of these days, young lady! Mark my words. If you think you can marry whomever you please just because you have a pretty face, you have another think coming."

A few days later, John expressed a desire to go to the opening of the Croton Aqueduct. Some of the finest architects in the country would be present at the celebration, and John, who was making plans to enter land development properly, wanted his knowledge to come from the best. There were to be parades, speeches, a banquet, and though it wasn't planned, there were sure to be horse races.

Hilary was singularly unenthusiastic. "I am too tired. After I've told you how utterly fatigued I have been of late, you surely can't expect me to go tramping out into the country to see an overgrown cistern! I would be dead on my feet and bored as well."

John had no better luck with Charlotte.

"Oh, Papa! I am sorry, but Martin is taking me to Vauxhall Gardens. I really can't tell him I won't go now. He has been planning this."

John grinned. "Think this will be the big day, do you?"

Charlotte blushed. "I don't know, Papa, but he did make it seem an important day. I mean, he has talked as if it might be special."

"Then you had better go, and wear your prettiest dress."

When Marcella, Josephine, John, and Tom Bascomb, one of John's colleagues from work, left the house shortly before noon, John was as anxious and eager as a little boy. The moment the carriage wheels stopped rolling at the aqueduct, he was out and off in hot pursuit of his new career, leaving Marcella and Josephine to their own devices.

Tom Bascomb, who had been brought along to take John's place as escort for the afternoon, considered the entire enterprise something of an imposition, but he dutifully followed the two girls wherever they led him.

John's day was more tedious than he had expected. Normally beer and whiskey would have been present to shorten speeches, or at least to provide some small escape from the courtesy of paying attention. Today's celebration had fallen into the hands of the temperance people, however, and it was appropriately pious, dry, and wordy. Only the good, pure water of the Croton Aqueduct was used to toast another New York triumph. John found it next to impossible to begin a conversation with any of the men he sought out.

He had made arrangements to meet Marcella and Jo at Croton Cottage after the ceremony, but since he was quite late, Marcella and Jo sat for some time sipping tea as slowly as they could. When other people began to come in for dinner, taking one empty table after another, Jo began to fidget.

"When do you think Papa will get here, Marcy?"

"Don't gawk around like that, Jo—people will think you are staring at them. Mama would have a fit."

"Well, people are looking at us, and I am hungry. Besides, I don't think they like us sitting here when so many are waiting to sit down. That man with the apron on keeps looking at us."

"Don't worry, Jo. Papa will be here soon. You know how he is. He has most likely gotten to talking with someone and forgotten the time."

"But, Marcy, I am hungry, and he might not remember the time for a very long time. Papa does like to talk."

Marcella smiled. "Mr. Bascomb, I think Jo is right. We may be in for quite a wait. I think it is best if we go ahead without him. Papa won't mind, so will you please order for us?"

Tom Bascomb's long face showed his dismay. "Perhaps we should wait awhile longer. Fifteen minutes. I am certain Mr. Paxton would prefer that."

"I think not," Marcella persisted. "Jo is right, people are looking strangely at us, and they are standing waiting to be seated. Order dinner for us now." She, too, began to look around the room.

Marcella was in high color this afternoon, dressed in a close-fitting suit of deep burgundy. She attracted attention wherever she went, but today she was particularly lovely, and few men resisted the impulse to allow their eyes to rest on her. Several times she glanced up and looked down again quickly, lest she be thought bold.

Then she happened to meet the smiling gray eyes of a man sitting with an attractive, aristocratic woman at one of the small corner tables. He was a big man, and bold as brass, staring at her openly and with obvious pleasure. His hair was black and wavy, his face rugged. She didn't lower her eyes but stared as hard as he, feeling a stirring of excitement inside. The woman seated with the man said something, to which he nodded. The woman glanced in Marcella's direction but gave no sign that she had seen her.

"Marcy, what are you looking at? You told me it wasn't nice to gawk. Aren't you gawking?"

Marcella's laugh was high-pitched and a bit too loud. "I guess I was, at that." She gave the man one more meaningful glance and turned back to her own table.

By the time her father arrived, the food on her plate was still untouched.

"Such a waste," John complained as he sat down. "Glad to see you went ahead and ordered. If I had known what I was getting into, I could have taken a walk with you and had a much better time." He tucked in his napkin. "It's certainly agreed with you, Marcella. Even if you are my daughter, I still say you're the best-lookin' woman around."

Marcella blushed deeply. "We had a lovely time, Papa. The esplanade is lovely."

"Lovely?"

"Well, yes, it really is. I am sure it will be a more popular promenade as soon as people learn of its charm."

"It is too far out to be very popular right now, but I suppose for those hardy creatures who don't mind jolting over the country roads it may well earn some degree of favor. And who knows, Marcella, you may be right. Forty-sixth Street may yet become a main part of the city. The way it is growing, anything is possible."

"I'd like to come here again—often, in fact," Marcella said.

"And what about you, Jo? Do you feel the same way?"

Jo made a face, crinkling up her small nose. John looked back to Marcella. He couldn't remember the last time he had seen her look that way, so beautiful, so vibrant. Automatically he glanced about the room at the various men present, but he saw none sitting alone, so he decided it must have been someone she had met while walking.

On their return to the city, Hilary was given a full report of the trip to the aqueduct by everyone but Marcella, who kept her pleasure private. All she said was, "It was a nice outing, Mama. Jo and I both enjoyed it, but you were wise in not going. There was a great deal of walking and not much to see. I am sure you would have been fatigued long before it was time to come home."

"Your father seemed to think you had had an especially good time. In fact, he is convinced you met someone there, someone who caught your interest. Who is he, Marcella? Do tell me!"

"I did not meet any interesting men, Mama. I didn't meet any men at all, only a few ladies walking as we were."

She hadn't met him, she thought later. She didn't even know his name, nor did she need to, for it hadn't been the man himself who had fascinated Marcella. It was the vitality that she had sensed in him, seen in his eyes, the way he moved and carried himself. Whatever it was that she felt in herself, had sensed in Lou—she had seen it in that man as well. It hadn't been a fantasy. She could recognize it. The man at Croton Cottage had had that same quality about him.

In the weeks and months that followed, Marcella spent more and more time alone. Partly it was a defense against Hilary's nagging, but mostly it was to dream—of what she might do, whom she might marry, and how wonderful it would be to be famous, adored, and important. She thought of a stage career—not for the first time—and she might have talked it over with one or both of her paents, had she not known what Hilary's reaction would be.

Often she escaped to the river to spend time riding the steamers. Why she felt nearer to her dream when she was on the river, she did not know, but it was true. The only person she didn't mind having with her was Jo.

Hilary grew increasingly resentful of Marcella's fascination with the Hudson and her strong tie to Josephine, but she had virtually given up her attempts to keep Marcella from going.

"Why must you ride up and down that river? It is aimless, and—I don't understand you, Marcella!"

"I know, Mama. I don't mean to upset you. I just feel drawn to the river. What more can I say? I like it, and I like the land and the houses above the city."

Years later, Marcella would say that it was the dark star that guided her whole life that had led her to the river. And she may have been right. For from that time on, the Hudson would and did play a determining role in her life.

Chapter Eight

On a Sunday afternoon the following spring, Marcella's dark star led her back to the Hudson. The entire family was to go for an outing. When her father had suggested the trip, Marcella had anticipated protests from her mother, but none had come. Hilary seemed perfectly content and even a bit pleased about the Sunday afternoon on the river.

They boarded the *Chancellor Livingston*, joining the other respectable families on the deck. John led his family to the railing to look down into the swirling water. The great wheel began to turn, churning the water into foam. Marcella smiled to see her mother looking around the giant ship with eyes as wide as those of any other first-time traveler.

"I had no idea the boats were like this, John."

"What were you expecting?"

"Well, I don't know, but certainly not elegance such as this. We must be on a very special boat indeed."

"Steamship, dear. Steamship or steamer, but not boat. The captains of these ships are very proud men."

"Oh! I see. Steamship, and this one is called the *Chancellor Livingston*?" Hilary looked from the gilded eagle atop the flagpole to the elaborately carved and painted figurehead that hung proudly far out over the river. "Mrs. Wenger will be most amazed when I tell her how really elegant the *Livingston* is."

"Mama, wait till you go downstairs." Jo tugged at her mother's hand. "There are beautiful chandeliers, and the staterooms are decorated very nicely."

"Are they really, John?"

"They are. You'll see them all when we go below later for dinner."

"Well, Marcella, I must confess I have misjudged you entirely. Had I known you were spending your time on a boat . . . ship such as this, I might have joined you rather than criticize you. Marcella—"

Marcella did not hear her mother. Her heart was pounding. The man and the woman standing right next to her father were the same two she had seen in Croton Cottage. She knew he had seen her, too, and he had remembered her; there was no doubt.

"Marcella! Whatever is wrong with you? I was speaking to you," Hilary said, annoyed that her apology had not been acknowledged.

"Yes, Mama, I heard what you said," she replied distractedly.

"You should have described the steamship to me. You should have known I would approve of this kind of place."

John laughed and turned to the couple next to him. "It's her first time aboard," he told them. "I am John Paxton. And may I present my wife and my three daughters, Charlotte, Marcella, and Josephine?" He extended his hand to the other man, who introduced himself as Bradford Dalton. The woman with him was his wife, Annette.

Soon John and Bradford Dalton were caught up in conversation. The ladies, a bit more concerned about formalities, stood apart, each taking the other's measure. After several moments, Mrs. Dalton cleared her throat quite noisily. Her husband turned to her and smiled. "I am sorry, Annette, we didn't mean to exclude you ladies." Suddenly he pointed to the fire that sprang from the smokestack of the steamer. "Hold on tight, ladies. I think we are about to pick up speed."

"Oh, John! Are we afire?" Hilary cried out.

"Nothing like that. Another steamer is coming alongside, and we will give him a run for his money, that's all."

"But the flames! It will catch us afire, I know it will. John, what shall we do?"

Bradford Dalton chuckled. "They have put more fuel into the firebox, Mrs. Paxton, that is all. It is really nothing to be concerned about. The fireman adds pine logs and ties down the safety valves to get more power. We'll be quite all right."

"Mama, just watch the other ship," Marcella added. "You won't even think about the firebox if you keep your mind on the race. It is so exciting."

"It looks terribly dangerous," Hilary insisted. "Supposing we bump into something?"

John sighed noisily. "Would you rather I took you below? We could go to the salon if you'd rather. I am sure the Daltons wouldn't mind staying with the girls for us."

Hilary looked from her daughters to Bradford Dalton and then to the smokestack shooting out flame and cinders. "No. I'll stay here. It is far too dangerous to leave the children. I don't see why we couldn't have had a nice Sunday afternoon ride on the river as we had planned. Why must they race?"

Marcella remained near the highly burnished railing, trying very hard to concentrate on the water and the other ship. She was unable to resist stealing a look at Bradford Dalton as he lounged against the rail not two feet away from her. Several times her guarded glances met his, studying her with an intensity that made her cheeks flame.

"Wouldn't you know!" Charlotte said suddenly. Marcella whirled around, startled, to see Charlotte standing with her palms turned up, looking at the sky.

"Now what?"

Charlotte gave her a blank look. "What's the matter with you, Marcella? It's raining! Can't you feel it?"

Marcella began to laugh, letting her pent-up feelings rush out with the laughter. She put her own hands out, catching tiny droplets, then rubbed them against her cheeks. "Oh, it is! It is raining! Look, Mr. Dalton, it is raining."

"Marcella!" Charlotte whispered. "You're acting like a goose. Stop it. What will the Daltons think of you?"

"What *will* the Daltons think of me?" Marcella repeated boldly.

"Hurry, girls!" Hilary called as she hustled Jo toward the lower level. Fortunately, she did not notice Marcella at all. Annette Dalton stood for a moment staring at the beautiful young girl who stood near her husband. Then she turned to him, her face expressionless.

"Are you coming, Brad?"

When he didn't answer her, she turned away from him and followed Hilary and John below.

Marcella couldn't keep the smile from her face. "Your wife is angry, Mr. Dalton."

He returned the smile and took her hand. "You enjoy the rain, Miss Paxton. So do I. Anger has no meaning in the rain, don't you agree?"

Marcella and Brad walked the decks, laughing and talking about the sky and the river. Each burst of windblown spray that flew into their faces whipped through Marcella's brilliant red hair.

By the time they joined the others, they were wet to the skin. Marcella's dress left a trail of water wherever she walked

"Marcella! What in the world . . ." Hilary sputtered. "Where have you been? Surely not standing on the deck all this time. Mr. Dalton, I hold you responsible for this! You should have better sense than to allow a young lady to stand in the rain on a deserted ship's deck. Mrs. Dalton, surely you understand. . . ." Hilary looked angrily from one Dalton to the other.

"I accept the responsibility, Mrs. Paxton," Brad said smoothly, "but I shall not offer an apology for one of the nicest afternoons I have spent in many a day. Your daughter is a most unusual woman, most refreshing and excellent company. Annette, can you imagine finding someone with a passion for stormy weather to match my own?"

"She'll dry out," John said heartily. He smiled at Brad. "You worry far too much, Hilary."

Hilary glanced at John and wondered if this, too, was some strange custom known only on steamships. One could expect nearly anything on a floating hotel where no one needed a proper introduction to become dinner mates or friends for the afternoon. Her face softened its lines when she looked at Annette Dalton, composed and serene as always.

Annette turned her cool gaze on the wet face of her husband. "I am pleased for you, Brad, but you really must learn to be more considerate. Miss Paxton's passions may match yours," she purred, "but her constitution may not be up to the same challenge. She is a young, unmarried woman, as well. She has a reputation to think of. You were most inconsiderate all the way around."

"How right you are, Annette, as always," Brad agreed with a slight bow. "Mrs. Paxton, Miss Paxton, you have my apology after all. As Annette has pointed out, I gave not the slightest thought to Miss Paxton's health or her reputation. I beg your pardon."

"It isn't necessary, Mr. Dalton," Marcella said before her mother could open her mouth. "My health is excellent, and my reputation is my own. On no account need you apologize or have misgivings. My constitution, Mr. Dalton, is up to nearly any challenge offered to it." Marcella, looking magnificent in spite of her dripping clothes and wet hair, smiled sweetly at her mother, who was shocked, and at Mrs. Dalton, who was not.

Marcella hadn't the slightest doubt that Bradford Dalton had understood perfectly well what she was willing to agree to. Time proved her correct, although it took more time than she would have preferred.

However certain Brad might have been about his feelings for Marcella, it was no easy matter to see a young, unmarried woman when one was not an eligible suitor. He had to make opportunities. John Paxton was a little surprised, but thoroughly delighted, that a man of Bradford Dalton's position and wealth sought him out so often. Always Brad was correct and courteous when he called at the Paxton home. He never singled Marcella out for concern or interest, and yet it was there. John knew it—and ignored it. Hilary, on the other hand, was all a-dither.

"What does he want with us, John?" she implored one evening after Brad had left.

"I don't believe he *wants* anything, dear. He is just a friendly man. I have no doubt seen him for years, but not knowing him, did not single him out for attention. Now he has been called to my attention, and obviously we frequent the same places. That is all, I am certain."

"And I am equally certain it is not! No, it is more," she insisted. "No matter what you say. I can feel it, and I am never wrong about these feelings, John. I can feel it when he comes into a room, and I can feel it in Marcella. I don't like him. I don't want him near Marcella. Do something about it, John. I don't want him near her!"

John patted her hand benevolently. "He hasn't been near her, has he? I am the one who sees him."

"Well, why would he want to see you if not to get close to her? And do you know he has sent flowers to the house? Ostensibly to me, but you know as well as I that they were never intended for my pleasure."

"Hilary, calm yourself. You react too strongly. The man has sent flowers to you. He has seen me in places of business. What can I accuse him of? What has he done?"

"I don't know, but I know I am right! I can't put my feelings into words very well, but I know what I know. Marcella is headed for no good."

"Marcella? She doesn't even know I have seen Dalton unless you have told her. She probably doesn't even know how upset you are. I'll wager she'd have a good laugh if she did. The poor man hasn't done a single untoward thing, and you have him hung for a goat."

"It isn't what he has done, John. It is what he is thinking. No! That's not right either. Oh, I don't know! Now see what a fool you have made me sound!"

John had laughed at her, but he knew Hilary was right. But he was just as certain that there was nothing he or anyone else could do to stop it. He would always be able to protect Josephine, and he knew Charlotte would be all right on her own, but Marcella—he could only hope Marcella would be better off with Brad Dalton than some of the other fates that might have befallen her.

"Come along now, Hilary. Smile for me and have a little faith." She looked up at him questioningly. "Faith in your daughters. Faith that each of them will choose what is good and natural for themselves. You can do that, can't you?"

She shook her head.

"No? And why not? We've done well by them . . . taught them, given them the best we could."

"It is enough for the younger ones, but Marcella was too long in Five Points, and to be honest, John, I have never been able to be as good a mother to Marcella as I wanted. Somehow I just could never care for Marcella properly."

Uncomfortable with the tenor of their conversation, John stood abruptly.

"Shall we go up to bed?" he asked wearily. "I'm sure things will straighten themselves out if we just have patience."

However worried Hilary was about her daughter and Brad Dalton, Marcella had come to believe that she might never see him again. She had only memories and one of the roses from her mother's excursion bouquet pressed into her diary to remind her that Brad had really existed. When Martin and Charlotte finally set a date for their wedding—after some healthy prodding from Hilary—Marcella was for the first time in her life jealous of her sister. Why, she wondered, couldn't life be as simple and secure for her as it was for Charlotte?

It was on the occasion of Charlotte's wedding in the spring of 1838 that she saw Brad for the third time in her life. As the wedding party came out of the church after the service, Brad was standing there on the sidewalk, looking at Marcella. But he made no move toward her, and if any of the rest of her family noticed him, they chose not to comment.

It was a disappointing and frustrating day for Marcella. She could not go to him, nor even speak without calling attention to herself, and again she had to be satisfied with less than what she wanted.

Her problem was very simply that she had no idea of how to arrange their meeting. It had always sounded so simple when she had heard her mother's friends gossiping about a questionable woman who was known to have met her lover in the early afternoons. But Marcella, it seemed, was never free to see him, and if she were free, she hadn't any idea as to where to find him.

Shortly after their marriage, Charlotte and Martin moved into a tiny house not far from the Paxtons'. In some ways it was a boon to Marcella. Hilary never questioned her when she said she wanted to visit Charlotte every day, so she was free to leave whenever she chose. Sometimes she did spend the afternoon at Charlotte's, but more often she went only for a short visit and then spent the rest of her time by herself mooning and moping over the problem of how to see Brad Dalton.

When she finally did see him again, she was thoroughly unprepared. She and Jo had gone to Washington Square one Thursday afternoon, as they regularly did, and Marcella was in the midst of dickering over the price of a goose when she heard Brad's voice behind her.

"She'll take that one at the price stated," he said, pointing to the finer of the two geese.

"The bird is more than a pound heavier!" the meat man protested.

"Your price is too high to start."

The man glared at Brad and shrugged. "Excuse me, miss," he said, placing the bird carefully into her basket.

Trembling with excitement, Marcella paid the man and then reached down to pick up the basket.

"Let me carry that for you. How have you been, Jo?" Brad looked down at the wide-eyed little girl standing next to Marcella.

"What are you doing here, Mr. Dalton? Do you do the shopping in your family?"

"Sometimes. In fact, I'll let you in on a secret if you won't tell anyone."

"What is it?"

"Well, you mustn't tell because my wife would get very upset if she knew I had told anyone, but I am a much better shopper than she is."

Jo nodded solemnly. "That is too bad, Mr. Dalton. I think a woman should do the shopping. Marcella is a very good shopper. Papa says she is a wizard. She will never have her husband doing her marketing for her, she is much too bright. Isn't your wife bright?"

Brad laughed heartily. "About some things she is very bright, but then about others. . . ." His voice trailed off. "But you won't tell her I told you!"

"Oh, no! I never tell secrets."

"Good. Now! Have you ladies had lunch yet? No? Then we shall have to remedy that."

"I still have some marketing to do, Mr. Dalton." Marcella was astonished at the calmness in her own voice. "Could we just finish that first? Or would that detain you too long?"

"Detain me? I came here to see you, didn't you realize?" Brad looked Marcella full in the face.

Marcella blushed deeply and looked down at the sidewalk, unable to trust her voice.

"Oh, that was very nice of you," Jo bubbled. "Lots of people come to see Mama and Papa, but seldom does anyone come to see us, do they, Marcella?"

"Oh, I imagine a good many come to see Marcella. Young men, at any rate."

"They used to," Jo said earnestly. "But Marcella told them not to come back, and now they don't. Mama said she was a silly fool for doing that."

Brad turned to Marcella and gently took her arm as they began to walk. "I wonder why you told them to leave, Marcella?"

"I believe you already know, Mr. Dalton," Marcella said quietly.

"If I am not mistaken in what I know, Miss Paxton, then we should not be calling one another Mr. Dalton and Miss Paxton."

"No, we shouldn't . . . Brad."

At first she met him at the market every week when she went, or occasionally at a restaurant when she was supposed to be at Charlotte's house. Josephine, who nearly always accompanied her, became a favorite of Brad's. He always contrived to involve her in a secret of some sort, so that the meetings with Mr. Dalton were never spoken of in Hilary's presence. There was no doubt that she enjoyed both the attention paid to her by this handsome man and the exciting, secret outings she and Marcella shared with him.

One day he took them up the river to show them the huge Greek Revival mansion that was his.

"That's Scarborough House," he said, pointing up to where it showed through the waving trees.

"Oh! It is beautiful," Jo breathed. "Can we come and visit you one day?"

Marcella glanced at Brad. "I don't think so, Jo. We don't really know Mrs. Dalton that well. She might not care for unexpected guests just dropping in unannounced."

"Why can't Mr. Dalton tell her when he goes home that we are coming to visit the next time we are out?"

Brad cleared his throat. "Normally I could, Jo, but not right now. Mrs. Dalton is expecting a baby, and we must be very careful of her for the time being." He looked up at Marcella, who was staring at him in disbelief. Abruptly, she turned away from him and walked across the deck to the other side of the steamer.

Brad hurried after her. "Why did you walk away like that?"

"You didn't tell me Annette was going to have your child."

"It is the normal course of things for married people."

"Perhaps, but are you the norm for married men? How can I mean anything to you if she is going to have your child?"

"Marcella, there is something we are going to have to understand from the outset. I am married. That house, Scarborough House, is a part of my life that demands as much from me as any love ever can. An heir to that estate is important, Marcella. I can't and won't deny it, nor will I let you pretend that life with Annette doesn't exist."

"You realize what you offer me?"

Brad looked away and nodded his head slowly. "It is all I have to give you."

They parted that afternoon with mixed feelings. Brad gave Marcella an address to which she could dispatch a message if she wanted to see him again.

Marcella wasn't sure she did. Brad was right—she had been pretending. She wanted marriage, and in her own way, she wanted respectability as much as Hilary did. Her dismay at being reminded about Annette and Brad's country home was matched only by the chagrin she felt at not having recognized her illusions for what they were.

She had assumed Brad lived in the city. She had never considered estates and obligations and lives that had nothing to do with her or him when they were together. She was not at all sure she wanted to settle for the small part of himself he offered, nor was she sure she could share him with Scarborough House, Annette, and the unborn heir.

On the day of the final outing, Brad had neglected to involve Jo in any secret. She told Hilary all about the beautiful house that sat atop a hill overlooking the Hudson River.

Hilary was frantic, reducing Jo to tears. "You saw that Mr. Dalton? Where? Where was he?" Immediately she sought out Marcella.

"Marcella! Josephine tells me you saw Mr. Dalton. When was this and where? What were you doing with that man?"

For a moment Marcella said nothing, not sure which outing Jo had told

Hilary about. Taking a chance that it had been the last, she spoke as calmly as she could. "We took a ride on the steamer, Mama. He happened to be aboard the same one. He lives on the Hudson."

"And I suppose you spent the whole afternoon with him?"

"We could hardly get off, Mama."

"Don't be saucy with me! I won't have it, nor will I have my daughters exposed to the influence of a man like that! Marcella, I shall tell you but once, so listen and heed. Never go on those ships again without your father or me to accompany you."

Silent, Marcella looked at the floor. Hilary's voice softened. "I am not blaming you, Marcella. I am trying to protect you from an unscrupulous man. I know that man has intentions toward you that he has no right to have. Just the other day I heard his wife is expecting their first child. What kind of a person can he be?"

Marcella shrugged despondently. "I think I'll take Jo out for a walk, Mama. Perhaps I'll go see Charlotte for a while."

"I'll come with you!"

"I won't go near the river, Mama."

"Nevertheless, I'll come with you. I'd not put anything past that man."

"Mama," Marcella pleaded, "you can't follow me everywhere I go, and I can't stay inside the house for the rest of my life."

Hilary slumped down into a chair, rubbing her hand over her forehead. "Of course not. I am being silly, aren't I? Please be careful, Marcella."

Marcella remained under close watch for the next several weeks. That she had no chance to reach Brad only intensified her desire to have of him what she could, on whatever basis she could manage. If that meant she could only fit into his life as a mistress, she decided, at least that was more than she would have without him.

Carefully she made plans. She reestablished the pattern of going to Charlotte's house daily. When she thought it had been accepted as a part of her daily routine, she sent a message to Brad, saying she wanted to see him.

The next afternoon she walked with Jo to Charlotte's house and dropped her off. Charlotte, who was pregnant, welcomed the company and help of her little sister. Marcella told Charlotte she would come for Jo at the end of the day. For her part, Charlotte assumed that Marcella had returned home to her own chores. Instead, she met Brad.

"I didn't think you would send the message," he said. "Did it take you so long to know what you felt?"

Marcella told him what had happened during the intervening weeks. "So you see," she concluded, "it has been very difficult to get out of my mother's house gracefully."

"But you are sure now?" he wanted to know. "You know the way things are, and still you want to see me?"

Marcella smiled ruefully. "I won't pretend that I like it, Brad, because I

69

don't. I'll never stop hoping that one day it will be different. For the time being, though, I do understand, and I accept it."

The clandestine meetings continued for some weeks. While Marcella looked forward to them, she was also acutely aware that they satisfied neither Brad nor her. She was also sure that time would run out for them. She would not always be able to leave the house so freely. Sooner or later Jo or Charlotte would say something, or Hilary would come to Charlotte's house when Marcella was supposed to be there and wasn't.

Marcella wanted more, and she sensed the same restlessness in Brad. But no matter how often they discussed it, the answers were always the same. He was married. He would soon be a father. The more she listened to him talk about the child, the more certain she was that Scarborough House and the baby would be her true rivals.

"He'll be the third generation of Daltons here, Marcella. I am going to name him after his grandfather. My father was here when this country began, and now my son will see it pass the centennial."

Marcella laughed. "Aren't you a little premature? It may be a little girl."

"That child is my son."

When Nicholas Dalton was born, it became clear to Marcella that in some unalterable way she would have less of Brad. But she wasn't willing to give up her dream easily. She threw caution to the wind, seeing Brad as frequently as she could, and for as long as she could.

It was not long before Charlotte pieced the truth together. Between the few things Jo had let slip as she helped Charlotte with the new baby, and Marcella's long absences and her high spirits, Charlotte was sure that something highly improper was going on in Marcella's life. She sent a message by Jo for Marcella to come to see her.

Almost the moment Marcella entered the house Charlotte was upon her. "Marcella, you can no longer use Jo as you have been doing. I won't let you do it."

"That's a fine way to say hello! Aren't you even going to show off young Martin to his aunt?"

"The baby is asleep. I want to talk to you. I know all about it, Marcella, so there is no need to lie to me."

"Dear heavens, Charlotte, you sound so dire. What do you know all about?"

"You and Mr. Dalton."

"Oh!"

"Is that all you have to say? 'Oh'?"

"What should I say? If you know, you know. It won't change anything. I am going to continue to see him."

"Not by using Jo as an excuse! I am warning you, Marcella. It is bad enough what you are doing, but to involve an innocent like Jo—"

"Oh, for the love of heaven, don't be so dramatic! What have I done to Jo?

He has taken her to lunch with us on occasion, and we have gone for carriage rides and on the steamer. How is that going to taint her?"

"Marcella, he is a married man. Whatever Jo doesn't realize now, she is growing up, and soon she will understand exactly what you are."

"And what is that, Charlotte?" Marcella demanded.

Charlotte looked away. "I didn't mean that exactly. I know you aren't that kind, but what will people think? And his wife . . . what of her? It is wrong, all wrong. There is simply no justification for what you are doing."

Marcella was unmoved. "I have never been so happy in my whole life. I love him, surely you can understand that."

"What you feel isn't love."

"What is it, then?"

"That is beside the point. I can't stop you from doing what you will, but I want your promise you won't include Jo in these . . . meetings of yours ever again."

"You are making too much of everything, Charlotte. Jo has no idea what is going on."

"Jo is fourteen years old, Marcella! She knows a great deal more than you give her credit for."

Marcella looked hard at Charlotte. Then she sighed and let her hands drop to her sides. "Very well, Charlotte, I won't take Jo anymore. She expects to go with me tomorrow. She is coming here, and I am going with Brad. I won't change those plans, but I won't take her anymore after that."

"Will you promise?"

"Yes. Yes, I give you my word, Charlotte."

"Good! Let's just hope it isn't too late. She has had quite a lot to say about it of late. You know Jo and her rights and wrongs. She is very unhappy about the whole thing, Marcella, because she loves you very much."

As Marcella walked home that evening, she thought about what had been said. If Charlotte knew and Jo was on her way to knowing, it wouldn't be long before Hilary did, too. She believed her father already knew or suspected, but that didn't matter half so much as Hilary's knowing. Even if John disapproved, she could count on him to understand.

The following afternoon Jo was in an exceptionally good humor. She was in the midst of her first crush, a young man she had met the previous afternoon while out with her mother. She chattered on and on about how handsome he was, and how polite. She was quite sure she would never get over him as long as she lived.

Marcella had never heard Jo talk this way before. She had to give Charlotte credit for having seen her younger sister changing first.

They stood at the street corner where they were to meet Brad. Suddenly Marcella's head went up, and she smiled broadly.

"Isn't he beautiful!" she exclaimed.

"Terrance?"

"No, silly! Brad." Marcella pointed at a carriage far down the street.

Jo squinted. "How can you even tell it is him? I can't see a thing."

"I can tell, and so could you if you weren't as blind as a bat."

"But he's inside the carriage. You cannot see!"

"Yes, I can!"

"Marcella . . ." Jo said quietly.

"Yes, Jo, what is it?" Marcella asked absently, still watching the approaching carriage.

"Tell him you won't see him anymore."

Marcella looked down at Jo's serious face. The wheels of the carriage made sharp sounds against the cobblestones as it pulled up next to them.

"I'll be back by five, Jo. I'll meet you right here, and we can talk as we walk home."

"Please don't go, Marcy," Jo pleaded, taking her sister's hand.

Marcella pulled her hand free. "I'll be here at five, Jo." She turned toward the carriage door.

"I won't be here. I just can't!" Jo cried and ran away down the street toward Charlotte's house. For a fleeting moment Marcella wanted to run after her, but the driver was opening the carriage door. All she saw was Brad.

"I thought you would never get here!"

Dramatically he pulled out his pocket watch. "As a matter of fact, I am here early."

"When I wait for you, Mr. Dalton, even early is late." She kissed his cheek and settled close beside him on the seat.

They had no plans for that day, so they decided simply to take a drive around the city. Perhaps later they would have a good run down Third Avenue. There was always someone to give him a good race, and Marcella loved it.

For now they both leaned back, letting the sun make them sleepy and enjoying being together.

Suddenly Marcella sat up straight. "Shall I show you where I once lived?"

"If you want," Brad replied easily.

Marcella gave the driver directions and ignored the look he gave her. Brad, who had paid no attention to what she had said to the driver, sat back to enjoy the ride.

Before long, however, the noise and the smells from outside attracted his attention.

"Where the devil are you taking us, Marcella? Did you give the driver the right instructions?"

"I did. We are going to my old home."

"Your home? You didn't live down here! Where are we?"

She pointed to a sagging tenement on their left. "That's the building I was born in. Isn't it attractive?"

Brad, horrified, put his arms around her, as if to shield her from the people milling about the streets. "It wasn't as bad as all that, Brad. Five Points is just a place, and these are people just like any others."

Brad grimaced. "They are not like any others. How could they be?"

72

The driver had had to slow the carriage's pace to avoid running over a small group of ragged children playing in the muddy street. One or two of them now approached the carriage door, hands outstretched, begging. Another urchin grabbed hold of the back of the carriage, anticipating an exciting ride down the filthy street.

Brad shuddered involuntarily. "It's criminal," he growled. He shouted to the driver to drive out of the area immediately.

"What is criminal, Brad?" Marcella asked quietly.

Brad sat back and straightened his waistcoat with a tug. "Allowing this place to exist."

"What would you do? Burn it down? This area was built originally as a recreation area after they filled in the Old Collect Pond. When it was discovered that the ground wasn't solid, it was abandoned by the developers. If there weren't a Five Points, some of these people would have no place to go at all."

"That doesn't make it right. Something should be done about this place."

"You sound like an idealist, Brad Dalton." She looked at him for a moment and then spoke again. "I don't believe this is the first time you have come in contact with a place like Five Points."

She paused to look out at the neighborhood into which they had driven. The streets were as dirty as any streets in New York, but the buildings were a little more solid than those of the Points. "If you really felt strongly about it, you would do something besides talk."

"What makes you so sure I wouldn't like to?"

As they drove on, Brad began to explain to Marcella the plans he had for becoming involved in the politics of the city, the discussions he had initiated with several civic groups regarding the need to do something about areas like Five Points.

Suddenly Marcella laughed. "You are a reformer, Brad! A hell-raising, pulpit-thumping, notice-craving reformer!"

"I guess I am at that," Brad chuckled. "Leave it to you to make me see it." He glanced up, noting the sameness of the brownstones they passed.

They fell silent. The carriage proceeded down a quiet street. Suddenly Marcella sat bolt upright.

"Oh, Brad, look! Look at that house. Isn't it the loveliest house you have ever seen?"

"They all look alike to me," he said.

"Please tell the driver to stop. I want you to see it, too."

"Which one is it?"

"Back there. Three—no, four houses back."

Brad instructed the driver to turn the carriage around. "I don't see how you can pick any one out from the others," he said to Marcella.

The carriage moved slowly back down the street until Marcella cried out for the driver to stop. "Do you see it, Brad?"

"See what?"

"Oh, Brad. I'm disappointed. I was so sure you'd notice right away."

He shook his head. Marcella got out of the carriage and hurried to the gate in front of the brownstone. When Brad caught up with her, she took his hand. "Over the door!" She pointed. "Don't you see the letters up there?"

"I'll be damned," he said and laughed. The letters, carved in the stone over the front door, were his own initials.

"Now do you agree it is the most beautiful house in the world?"

"I agree with anything you say. As long as you are with me I haven't a disagreeable bone in my body."

"And when I am not with you?"

"Then I am nothing."

"Perhaps I had best always be with you in that case."

"Perhaps."

Chapter Nine

Three months later, almost to the day, Brad took Marcella back to the brownstone. This time the driver stopped and came around to the side to help her from the carriage. The house was hers. Brad had bought it for her, and the deed was in her own name.

"Do you like it?" he asked as he opened the door. "Is it what you thought it would be?"

"Oh, Brad, it is beautiful," she said, looking at the blank wall of the entry hall.

Suddenly Brad began to laugh. "Which of us is crazier? I am asking you about a house you have never seen the inside of, and you are telling me an empty wall is beautiful. God, I love you." He swung her into his arms and carried her inside to the front parlor.

Like most brownstones, the house was narrow, with high ceilings. They walked through the parlor to the dining room. On the other side of the hall, Marcella was delighted to find another parlor.

"This will be my sitting room. From this window I can see the whole street, and I will know just when you are coming. Maybe I should call it the waiting room instead."

"You'll never be kept waiting. I'll be with you whenever you are here."

Marcella looked away from him. She walked to the window, where she stood for a moment, silent. "There is something I should tell you, Brad. I have been meaning to for some time, but I just kept putting it off. I was hoping things would change, but they aren't going to."

He glanced around for a place to sit. "I should have had them leave some of the furniture. The only piece they left is an old bed upstairs," he said. "They wanted to sell the house furnished, but I thought we would like to do that ourselves. Shall we sit on the steps?"

He led her toward the back of the house, where the staircase was tucked away in the hall leading from the kitchen.

"Now tell me what it is that you have been putting off for so long."

"Maybe there is nothing to tell, but somehow now that you have actually bought this house. . . ." Her voice trailed off, and then resumed, "Do you know, Brad, that I have a star—a dark star that no one else can see, and it guides my life?"

He shook his head in mock dismay. "Is that what you wanted to tell me? Let's go look at the upstairs." He started to get up.

"Brad," Marcella said, putting a hand on his arm, "Charlotte knows I have been meeting you. Jo knows, too—I mean, in a different way than she knew before. And I am sure my father does. I may. . . . Could I just live here in this house, I mean?"

"When did you find out about Charlotte?"

"The day before we saw this house. You see what I mean? We were meant to find this house. I really do have a star."

Brad was very quiet for a long time. The sun went behind a cloud, and the hallway suddenly became dark. Marcella shivered and hugged herself.

"I should never have let this happen," he said finally. "I knew better."

"Brad, I'm not regretting anything. I wouldn't exchange knowing you, loving you, for anything the world had to offer, not even my own family. I am not at all sorry. I don't want you to be sorry either."

"But what have I done to you?" he asked, putting his arm around her shoulders.

"You have made me happy."

"Marcella, are you sure? Can you really love someone as you say you love me?"

Marcella nodded, unable to speak.

"I've wanted to be with you for so long," he said softly. "Come upstairs with me now."

He carried her in his arms up the stairs and down the hall past the bedroom that would be hers. He gently put her down on the bed in the guest bedroom and lay down beside her. Marcella got up from the bed and crossed the room to the windows, where she pulled the heavy draperies across the filmy curtains. The room was bathed in a dusky rose as the sun came out from behind the clouds and touched the draperies with light.

Slowly she turned and waited for him to join her. Then she began to unbutton his jacket and then his waistcoat. Her face was radiant as she turned to allow Brad to unhook her gown and then her bodice. He ran his fingertips gently across her naked shoulders, his head swimming with the intoxicating scent of roses that filled the room. Finally they stood, as if in a dream, unaware that there was a world other than their own, naked and seeing each other for the first time.

Brad never took Marcella Paxton. Beginning with this first day in the house, Marcella and Brad entered into a mutual bond of acceptance, something

Marcella knew she would guard jealously all their life together. The romantic discovery of one another and the mystery of the promise they shared was something Marcella treasured. Their lovemaking belonged to a private world, protected and tender.

As they lay together that afternoon, Marcella knew she would move into the brownstone with Brad. She would become the mistress of Bradford Dalton in a way all the world could see and judge. She had no illusions that they would judge her gently. She was going to make herself an outcast from everything her mother had ever valued. On this hazy, quiet afternoon, it all seemed worth the price.

She came home with Brad that afternoon much later than usual. Hilary had already started supper without her. She was greeted by an icy silence from Hilary when she entered the dining room.

"Where have you been, Marcella?" John asked, hoping her answer would prevent the storm that was bound to come from Hilary.

"I took a carriage ride, Papa. I had some things on my mind, and I wanted to be alone for a while."

"Weren't you to bring Josephine home at five o'clock?" Hilary asked. "Or do you now think it is acceptable to allow your youngest sister to walk the streets alone?"

"Jo said she didn't want me to meet her this evening," Marcella said simply. She looked over at Jo, whose eyes were red-rimmed from crying.

Hilary poured herself a glass of water and set the pitcher down on the table. "I believe you have a great deal of explaining to do, Marcella, but it will not be over dinner. I would like to see you in your father's study after we have finished eating."

Marcella spoke a bit too quickly. "I would like to see Charlotte before I talk to you. May I visit with her for a short while after dinner, before I see you?"

"I think there is no need to drag Charlotte into this. She has a family of her own, and I am quite sure Martin would want no part of your particular problem," Hilary said. "Eat your dinner, Marcella. It is getting cold."

Marcella looked down at the plate. Generous slices of pork, yams, and greens were all covered over with gravy that was beginning to congeal. "I am sorry, I just don't seem to be hungry, Mama."

"It doesn't surprise me in the least, but it is a sin to be so wasteful of good food. You forget too easily, Marcella, what gifts of life you have been given."

"Hilary, you are ruining my dinner as well," John said from the head of the table. "I thought you said we wouldn't discuss this until after dinner." He looked sadly at Marcella and went back to cutting his pork methodically.

Dinner seemed never-ending. Marcella's head filled with partial sentences, fragments of explanations. Nothing coherent came to her.

Hilary would think the worst no matter what the truth, but Marcella dreaded what the wrong words might do to her father. She wished she had had the good sense to talk this over fully with Charlotte when she had had the opportunity. Now there was no way to go back a day or even an hour.

Then it came time to go with her mother and father to his study. Marcella took a seat in the dark, paneled room. All three Paxtons sat in silence, each waiting for someone else to begin. Surprisingly, John took the initiative.

"Charlotte came over here this afternoon, Marcella. She brought Jo home. She was crying and very upset, and Charlotte didn't think she should come home alone. Naturally we were concerned. We expected you to be with Jo. Marcella—" His eyes beseeched her.

"I was with Brad Dalton, Papa," she said softly. "I think you already know that. I am sure, under the circumstances, Jo has already told you."

Hilary did nothing to disguise the bitterness in her voice. "It is disgusting. How could you let an innocent child like Josephine become involved in your sordid relationship with a man like Mr. Dalton?" She glared at her daughter, then looked away. "Of course, you understand that neither your father nor I will put up with this. Your father has worked long and hard to bring us to where we are. In one disgusting sweep you are making a mockery of all we stand for, all we have worked for. I won't stand for it, Marcella. I forbid you even to see this man again."

"There isn't going to be an easy way to tell you this," Marcella began quietly. "I tried to think of a way to make it easy, but there is none."

"Surely you aren't going to tell us you are having a child by this creature!" Hilary gasped.

"Hilary, please. Marcella isn't that kind of woman. Don't talk like that," John said, looking pained.

Hilary whirled on him. "Are you telling *me* how to behave?"

"In this instance I am," he snapped. "Let the girl speak."

Marcella took a deep breath, no longer able or even wanting to put it off. "I love Brad Dalton. I know you are aware of it, Papa. I am sorry it couldn't have been a nice, respectable relationship that would have ended in a nice, proper marriage like Charlotte's, but it isn't, and I can't help that. I love him, and I intend to live with him."

"Over my dead body!" Hilary shouted. "I'll have you put in a convent first. Go to your room this minute and never speak that man's name in this house again."

Trembling, Marcella forced herself to speak calmly. "We have bought a house, Mama. Brad bought it and gave it to me this afternoon. That is where I have been all day today. I will live in that house as soon as we can get it properly redecorated and furnished. I am sorry you had to find out this way."

Hilary sat in stony silence, her back ramrod-straight. In her mother's eyes Marcella saw all the resentment and hate that had built up over the years. When Hilary spoke again, her voice was cold and deliberate. "You'll leave this house first thing in the morning. You will not speak to Josephine again, and you will never return to this house. From this day on, I have no daughter named Marcella."

She got up from her chair, straightened the front of her gown, touched her hand to her hair, and left the room.

Afraid to look at her father, Marcella looked down at her hands. His heavy breathing punctuated the otherwise silent room.

"Papa, I wouldn't willingly hurt you for all the world," Marcella told him. He said nothing. She heard him blow his nose. "I can't ask you to bless what I am doing, but Papa, please tell me you don't hate me!"

"I don't hate you, Marcella." His voice was so low she could barely hear him. She ran to him and threw her arms around his neck. "Papa, I do love him. I tried not to, but I have loved him for so long."

Her father held her close and wept. "At such a cost, Marcy, at such a cost. Is he worth it? Isn't there any other way? Could I send you away for a time, just long enough for you to be sure? Europe? We have the money now. Would you go? Marcy, I can send you anywhere in the world. Won't you go, child, won't you just try to forget him?"

"Time wouldn't matter, Papa. I think you know that, too. Maybe Mama has been right all along. Maybe I was born to go wrong. Papa, I love you. Love me, too! Please tell me you do love me."

"I will always love you. No matter what, Marcella. You're my little Fire Top, you know. Try to be happy . . . and Marcella, remember if . . . if ever you need anything, I am still your papa. Nothing will change that." He held her tightly for a moment and then released her. "Let me be alone for a time. Come in before you go to bed for the night, but let me be alone for a time."

She kissed him, wiped the tears from her eyes, and stood up. "I love you very much, Papa." Then she went to her room to gather up and pack her belongings.

She went briefly to her mother's room to ask if she might borrow a family trunk or two to transport them. "I will return them to you, Mama. I'll bring them back tomorrow afternoon."

"I am not your mother," Hilary snarled. "Please refrain from insinuating a relationship between yourself and me. You will take nothing from this house that is not yours. *Nothing!*"

"Mama!" Marcella cried at Hilary's back. She turned and ran upstairs to her own room, sobbing.

Taking the sheets from her bed, she began to fill them with her clothes and the few books she would take with her. There wasn't much else Marcella could claim as her own—a couple of figurines she had purchased for her mantel, a print of a painting, a pastoral scene. The picture would have to remain; it was too unwieldy.

She tied the two sheets into bundles and dragged them to the side of the room. She would have to pay the cabdriver to come up and take them to the carriage for her. She went to her washstand, looked for a moment into the mirror, and then tossed cold water on her face. Her eyes were puffy and red-rimmed.

The hallway was empty and silent when she looked out. Hilary was nowhere in sight. Quietly Marcella went down the steps to the second floor and made her way to Jo's room. Marcella opened the door and went in without a sound.

"Are you asleep, Jo?" she whispered.

There was no answer. Marcella leaned over and kissed the child gently on the forehead and began to tiptoe from the room. She had nearly reached the door when Jo turned over.

"I'm not asleep, Marcella."

"I just came to say good-bye to you, Jo. I'll be going away tomorrow."

"Where are you going? Will you come back?"

"Oh, I will visit from time to time, and you can always visit me. I will have a home now, too, just like Charlotte has. Maybe you would like to come and spend afternoons with me sometimes. We will have a garden in the back and fill it with the most beautiful flowers in the world. Would you like that?"

"Will you be married now?" Jo asked.

"In a way, yes, I'll be married."

Jo looked away from her and put her head back down on the pillow. "You won't be married. Mama explained all that to me. Mr. Dalton already has a wife, and no one is allowed to have more than one wife."

"I can't explain all of this to you now, Jo. You are still too young. It is just like when you were very small and wanted to read books before you were able to understand what they meant. Do you remember that? You were always asking me to explain words you didn't know, remember? That is the way this is, but you will understand, Jo. When you are older. I would never do anything to hurt you, and I would never hide anything from you."

"Mama says you have been very deceitful, and she says what you are doing is wrong . . . a sin, a very bad sin."

"I love you, Jo. Do you think that is a sin?"

"No."

"Well, I also love Mr. Dalton. I love him very much."

They talked until Jo was so sleepy she couldn't keep her eyes open any longer. Again Marcella leaned down and kissed her goodnight, and good-bye.

The house was unnaturally quiet the following morning. John had left the house for his office as usual, but Jo was not there, and neither was Hilary. When Marcella went downstairs, she found the dining room unprepared for breakfast.

She sent an errand boy after a carriage. Every minute she waited seemed an hour. She walked through the familiar rooms and thought of the empty rooms of the brownstone house. How would she manage until she and Brad could furnish them?

When the cabbie did arrive, she found that she wasn't at all prepared to leave. She fought back tears as she pointed at her bundles.

The driver scowled at her. "I ain't no laundryman!"

"Just put them in the carriage, if you please."

When they arrived at the brownstone, she paid him well and listened to the odd sound the front door made as it closed behind him on his way out. Her new home sounded like an empty house. Would it ever really be a home to her? Today it was not home at all.

Marcella didn't touch the bundles, but left them on the floor where the driver had dropped them. She ran from the house, pulling on her gloves as she went, hailed a cab, and directed the driver to Charlotte's house.

"I just had to talk to you!" she gasped as she ran up the front steps to the door where Charlotte stood waiting. "You are the only one who can help."

"What happened last night? Mama was here with Jo at seven o'clock this morning. *Seven* in the morning! And she wouldn't say a word about last night. What happened?"

"Everything! Everything that could happen did, and it is awful, Charlotte. You have to help me."

"First tell me what went on. After I took Jo home yesterday, I knew the whole story was going to be told, so I went back to the corner where Jo meets you to wait for you. Where were you? I waited for nearly an hour."

"Let me have a cup of coffee first. I haven't had a bite this morning. Mama wouldn't even let me have breakfast in the house."

Marcella followed Charlotte to her kitchen and sat at the table while her sister scurried around the room, pouring coffee and toasting two slices of bread. "Do you care for anything else? Eggs?"

"No, no, just the coffee and the toast. I don't know where to begin. I wish I had met you last night. It would have been easier if I had known what was coming."

"Well, where were you?"

"Brad bought a house for me, and—"

"He did *what*? A house? What does he think you are? I hope you told him everything he deserves to hear about himself!"

"It is a good thing he did. I would be out on the street this morning if it weren't for that house. Mama has no daughter named Marcella as of last night. I am never to show my face in the house again, and I am never to talk to Jo. And that was none of Brad's doing, Charlotte. That is pure Mama." Marcella paused for a moment and then went on more quietly, "Charlotte, I am beginning to think this was bound to happen. If it hadn't been Brad, it would have been something or someone else."

Charlotte didn't speak for a long time. "Mama put you out of the house? She wouldn't mention your name this morning. I thought—knew—you had probably had an argument, but I thought she was just trying to make me realize how angry she was. You know Mama and her dramatics. But this! What are you going to do?"

"This morning I moved into the house Brad bought for me. What else could I do? That's what I want, anyway. I told them about Brad and the house last night. That's what caused the whole mess with Mama. I don't know what to do now, though. I want to see Papa. Even if he doesn't like it, he understands. Then there is Jo. You know I would rather die than go through life never seeing Jo again."

"Marcella, how *do* you get into these things? Why is it always you?"

"I don't know, but I do. Will you help me? Please say you will help me."

"What can I do?"

"Talk to Mama. Make her see things aren't as bad as they seem. I can't hurt Jo by seeing her, and I am not going to cause any trouble if I visit Papa sometimes."

"You must be insane. The saints themselves couldn't talk to Mama if all you tell me is true."

"Won't you even try?" Marcella asked, putting her coffee cup down on the table and looking directly at Charlotte.

Charlotte looked away. "You have some nerve, Marcella. You come here and want me to make Mama accept something that . . . that is so immoral and outrageous that it is improper for us even to mention it, and you want me to convince her it is all right, when I don't think it is myself."

"Charlotte, please, you are the only one I can turn to."

"I'll help you by telling you to tell that horrible man to go away and never see you again. Then beg Mama for forgiveness and go away—out of town, perhaps—for a while until tempers cool. Then maybe you can come back. But no one is ever going to convince any decent person that living as that man's mistress right out in public is all right."

"Then you won't help?" Marcella said softly. "I understand, I really do. But I love Brad. If I could marry him, I would. Do you think I like this?"

"Whether you like it or not has nothing to do with it. The man is married, Marcella. Think what you are doing to that family!"

Marcella looked away quickly. "Well, I guess I had better be going."

"You haven't listened to a word I've said," Charlotte sighed, sitting down across from her sister. "You never listen. It is always your way, no matter what, always you!"

Marcella brightened. "Then you will help me!"

"I'll try to talk to Mama, but not right away. But I will say something if I get a chance. I am not promising, mind! Only if there is a chance."

"Oh, I know you. You will find a chance." Marcella leaned across the table and took Charlotte's hand. "You will make one. Oh, Charlotte, what would I do without you! Thank you! Thank you! You and Martin will be the first guests Brad and I have for dinner in the new house."

"Oh, no! I said I would talk to Mama. I didn't say I liked what you are doing, Marcella. Don't ask me to come, because I will never set foot in that house of yours. Never!"

Marcella stopped smiling and looked at her sister. "May I come here to see you?" The unanimous disapproval of her family suddenly weighed very heavily on her. Would it always be like this? Would she be able to talk only to Brad for the rest of her life, because no decent man or woman would come near her?

Charlotte didn't answer for a moment. "You know I should say no. Martin would be very angry if he knew I'd seen you, especially after he hears about all this."

"Don't tell him," Marcella suggested.

"Ho! Even if I didn't, do you really think he wouldn't hear on his own? Nothing like this is ever a secret, Marcella. Come to see me, though . . . but not too often, and—"

"And when Martin is not at home," Marcella finished for her. Charlotte nodded and then looked away.

"I am sorry, Marcella, but that is the way it has to be. I still think you should reconsider. Can't you see what a miserable life you are making for yourself?"

"But I am happy with Brad, Charlotte. No matter what you say, I do love him very much."

Charlotte shook her head slowly. "I hope you know what you are doing. You are giving up everything in your life as it is now, Marcella. Are you sure Mr. Dalton is willing to do the same?"

Marcella wasn't sure. Brad didn't even know yet that she had left her family. What would she do if he were not willing to live with her?

Chapter Ten

Marcella left the brownstone at three-thirty that afternoon and went to the corner where she ordinarily met Brad. She still had not sent him a message, so he would be there as he always was, expecting to see her standing on the corner watching for his carriage.

When the carriage arrived, she didn't wait for him to help her in; she opened the door herself and hopped into the back, flinging herself into his arms.

"Hello!" He laughed and then stopped immediately. "What is wrong? Are you frightened?"

"Do you love me?" she cried. "Brad, do you really love me?"

"You know I do. What has happened? What is wrong with you?" He pried her loose from him so he could see her face; it was very pale and strained. "Marcella," he said softly. "Tell me what is wrong."

She moved away from him slightly. Her mind was in a turmoil, assailed by every doubt her family had aroused in her. She didn't know how to begin. What if he refused to stay with her in the brownstone?

He waited patiently, observing the changing expressions of her face and eyes. Then he took her hand and kissed it softly. "Don't try to tell me now. We'll be at the house in a moment, then we'll straighten out whatever it is. It can't be half as bad as you seem to think."

Marcella pulled away. "I don't want to tell you at the house, Brad. Take me someplace where we can talk for just a little while. I don't want to tell you this at our house!"

He frowned. "What is all this, Marcella? All right! We'll go someplace—the park. Will that be all right?"

She nodded. All the way to the park she sat, tense and anxious, on her side of the carriage, looking out at the passing houses. By the time the carriage had stopped, Brad was clearly very worried. As he led her to an unoccupied bench, there was a trace of annoyance in his movements to which Marcella was immediately sensitive.

"You are already angry, and I haven't even told you yet."

"I am not angry!" he said gruffly. "Now what is all this, and why do we have to sit out here with the pigeons? Why wouldn't you go to the house?"

"Oh, Brad, it isn't that. I do want to go to the house. It is you who may not wish to go to the house after I have told you what has happened."

His eyes narrowed. "Well, what *has* happened?" He crossed his legs and folded his arms.

Her head bowed, her hands limp on her lap, Marcella told him what had happened at her home the night before and what she and Charlotte had talked about earlier in the day. Brad said nothing as he listened, nor did he relax. He stared straight ahead, arms still crossed over his chest.

"Say something, Brad. I didn't mean for it to happen."

"The woman is a harridan," he said finally, his voice choked with anger. "You are sure she means all that she says?"

"She means it. I am hoping Charlotte will be able to soften her position a little." Marcella sighed deeply. "What shall I do if I can no longer see Jo? Brad, she means so much to me. I am sure I can see Papa. I can always meet him if Mama won't allow me to come to the house. But what of Jo?"

"Perhaps I should speak with your mother," he said more softly. "What kind of woman would put her own daughter out on the streets?"

"No. No, you mustn't even see her. It would make everything much worse. Let Charlotte talk to her. Charlotte is very good at that sort of thing, and I know she will do all she can. Please don't try to see Mama, Brad."

He looked at Marcella. "She blames me, then."

"No, not exactly. Mama ... well, Mama thinks I am bad. Maybe she is right. I've always been in the thick of any trouble we have ever had."

"If there is a fault, it is your mother's. You have no other relatives in the city? I mean, is there someone you can stay with?"

Marcella looked at the ground. "You don't want me to live in the brownstone?"

"Alone? How could you manage? It isn't even furnished."

Marcella stood up, fighting back tears. "Thank you for listening, Brad." She turned away. "As a matter of fact, I do have a cousin with whom I might stay. Leona Dowell might let me stay at her house if she could get her parents to agree. I think I had better see about it now, while I still have the light of day."

Brad reached out and grabbed her hand, pulling her roughly back onto the bench with him. "Now don't be all frosty and insulted. I didn't mean you shouldn't stay at the house. But it isn't furnished. There is nothing there for you right now. You've thought about this all day long and last night as well. Give me a few minutes."

She stayed where she was but said nothing.

"You do want to go back with your family, don't you?" he asked.

"I want to be able to see Jo and Papa."

"I can't let you live in that house alone, unattended, Marcella. You are such a headstrong, impulsive creature. You haven't given a single thought to how cruel people will be to you in that position. I can't let you do it."

She turned to him, her eyes blazing. "You can't permit me to live there or face scandal? What have I been facing for these past months? It is not I who am afraid, it is you! In the end, Brad, it comes down to whether you love me or not, and how much that love means to you. You don't want me in that house, and you don't want to be there with me! So just say it, and let's be done with it."

He stood up and again pulled her roughly with him to the carriage. On their way, the driver stopped twice. Marcella and Brad stayed in the carriage each time as the driver hopped down and did whatever Brad asked of him. Neither Marcella nor Brad spoke to one another until the carriage had stopped in front of the brownstone house.

"What are we doing here?" Marcella asked when Brad got out and began to help her down.

"We live here," he replied curtly.

The driver, carrying several packages, followed Brad and Marcella up the front stoop. "Take them back to the kitchen," Brad ordered and led Marcella into what would become their parlor.

"Damn it, why did I ever tell that woman I didn't want this place furnished!" he muttered and yanked the one remaining straight-backed chair toward him. "Sit down." He hurried out of the room, returning a moment later with another chair. "Can you cook?"

"I certainly can! I am an excellent cook."

He started to reply and then heard the driver of the carriage going down the hall toward the door. He jumped up from the chair, called for the man to wait a moment, and then turned back to Marcella.

"I need pen and paper. Do you have it?"

She hurried over to her bundles and came back with writing paper, slightly crinkled, and her pen. At the windowsill Brad wrote his message and instructed the driver to give it to his wife at Scarborough House. Then he turned back to Marcella.

"Tomorrow we will shop and get this place furnished. I will not live like this." He stretched out his arms for her to come to him. When she was close against him, crying softly into the front of his shirt, he said, as sternly as he could manage, "Don't ever doubt me like that again."

That afternoon Marcella promised faithfully, her face shining in happiness. As the weeks passed, however, she began to find that the consequences of her act of faith were not so simple at all. Their lives were not to be serene, and some of the complications began to be felt almost immediately.

Brad's reasons for buying the house were not so straightforward as they had first appeared. While it was true that he would never have bought it or thought of living in it if it had not been for her, he also wanted her name on the deed for a variety of reasons. Her pleasure was only one, and not the foremost reason, for Brad had decided to take Marcella's advice and learn to make use of the power his money, social position, and personality afforded him.

Since he had decided he wanted to enter politics, he now developed a protective instinct where his own name was concerned. The two women in his life had vastly different values, he realized, and he began to make plans about how and for what purpose he could use them. Marcella would be kept privately at the brownstone, while Annette would reside regally, as she liked, at Scarborough House, protecting it for his son.

Marcella was, by this time, fully aware of Brad's feelings about Scarborough House. In some way, the estate was sacrosanct. She resented his feelings for Scarborough far more than she did the woman he called his wife, for while she felt she had already won her victory over Annette Dalton, she hadn't made so much as an imprint where the house was concerned. There was no question in her mind that this alone was the most important thing in the world to him.

He talked of the estate so often that she came to feel she could find her way about it without ever having seen it, could walk through each room, down every pathway that wound around its grounds, and know exactly where she was going. Scarborough House—a place to which Brad Dalton would never take her—was something that could never be criticized nor openly resented. However he might love her, she would never set foot on that land by his invitation. Scarborough became as much a symbol and a threat to Marcella as Five Points had been for Hilary. It was something she had to overcome, for it had the power to take Brad from her.

The very first night they spent in the brownstone, his first thought had been of Scarborough House. Marcella wasn't so unreasonable that she didn't realize it was a natural reaction, but after all, hadn't she just given up her own family?

The following day Marcella was upset and moody all day long, and they argued about his family and hers. She wanted to see her father and her sister Jo. He had known from the outset that Annette, even if she did not know everything about him and Marcella, knew enough to use her most effective weapon against him—silence.

For two days he stayed with Marcella in the brownstone, helping her gather some furnishings and linens, stock up on the necessities, leaving all else to be taken care of at some other time. Then he left for Scarborough House to see his wife and family.

The ride to Scarborough House had never seemed longer to him than it did that day. He and Marcella had been seeing each other for some time, but this last step, it seemed, had sealed a troublesome bargain between them. He wondered how much his family already knew. Brad knew he could count on his father to react very much as Marcella's father had. Brad was his son, and nothing in the world would change that, but neither would anything prevent the disappointment or disapproval Brad's double life would cause.

When he arrived, his father was standing on the front lawn, checking the azalea bushes he had put in earlier in the year. At the sound of the carriage, Nicholas Dalton looked up and began to walk to the driveway toward his son's carriage. Brad's driver stopped as soon as he saw the older man. Brad jumped down from the carriage.

"Go on ahead, Max. I'll walk with Dad."

"I am glad you have come home," Nicholas said, clapping his large hand on his son's shoulder. "It isn't too late to set things straight."

Brad looked at him in surprise. His father's hard look told him there was no point in talking around the truth. He told his father why he had not come home two nights earlier, leaving nothing out. "So you see, Father, I love Marcella. She is a fine and decent woman, and she loves me, too."

Nicholas laughed grimly.

"I don't see that as funny," Brad snapped.

His father looked at him sharply. "It isn't," he said quietly. "Bradford, do you think you are the only man ever to find himself in this position?"

For a long moment Brad was silent. How curious, he thought. Here I stand, a grown man, feeling so much like a little boy who has been caught with his hand in the cookie jar. "No, I suppose I'm not, Dad. It's just that—"

"It's just that what?" his father interrupted. "My dear son, I am neither blind nor a fool. Did you really think your frequent meetings with this Paxton woman would escape everyone's notice? Did you really believe we would be spared the news by any and every gossip between here and the city?"

Brad groaned. At what point, he wondered, did I stop caring, stop thinking about these consequences? For a fraction of a second, he resented Marcella Paxton with all his heart.

"Bradford," his father went on, "you are a bit late. You already have a wife and a son, and you seem unwilling to compromise at any point. Seeing that woman is one thing, but if you do choose to live with her openly, you will be thrusting your sin into the faces of everyone around you."

There was a bitter taste in Brad's mouth, but no words to answer his father. The older man stood silently for a moment. Then he took Brad by the shoulder and gestured up at the house. Standing at the top of a slow rise, its bulk crowning the gentle hill on which it sat, Scarborough House looked golden and majestic as it faced the Hudson River. The Doric columns that ran across the front of the house stood out gleaming white from the yellowed brick.

"Annette isn't your only responsibility here, Brad."

"I know, Dad, and Scarborough means more to me that I know how to put into words, but—"

"It isn't just the house. It is Scarborough House, and the land, and the spirit of the land and its people."

"I know, Dad. You think I have let you down and turned my back on my home and the things you value. I haven't. Believe me, I haven't. Let's go up to

86

the house now. I should talk to Annette. I'd like to get it over with as soon as I can."

Old Nicholas shook his head slowly. "Always in a hurry. Get this over with, hurry to that, rush into something else. You are always in too much of a hurry, son. You pass the most important things in life and never even know they are there. Scarborough is the Daltons—not a house, Bradford, but a heritage, not brick but blocks of character, of what the Daltons stand for, of what we believe in."

Suddenly Brad smiled and put his arm through Nicholas's. "You never change, do you?" he chuckled. "A house built of fairy wings and leprechaun charms, or honor and chivalry and dreams cemented to dreams."

"I recall nothing about fairy wings in what I said to you. But then, you didn't listen to what I said. You never have, Bradford. You have always been too hard and too hurried to see what is right before your eyes. I happen to have wanted to talk of something quite serious."

"I'm sorry, Dad. What is it? I'm listening."

"Never mind that now. Your ears may be listening, but your mind isn't."

"It's just—Annette. What am I going to say to her?" He sat down heavily on the front steps.

The older man sighed and sat down beside him. "I am sure I wouldn't know. But I do hope that before you say anything you will regret, you make very certain that what you are doing is right. I won't have my grandson jeopardized by your carryings-on."

Brad was relieved to be able to change the subject. "How is Nick? You know, I've missed seeing that little fellow."

"He is a fine, healthy boy." Nicholas frowned. "And he hasn't changed that much in two days."

Brad's face fell. "It seems longer since I last saw him."

"It was your choice to leave him. You shouldn't. The boy will need you. He needs you now, and so does this valley. We are heading for trouble around here, Bradford. Ever since Stephen Van Rensselaer died, the tenant farmer situation has gotten progressively worse. It won't stop, Brad. This time they are going to fight the feudal system. I can feel it in the air."

Brad shook his head. "Nothing will come of it, Dad. It never has. The farmers have protested the system ever since the War for Independence. They may grumble, but there is no way for them to fight that system. The Van Rensselaers and the Livingstons have far too much power. A bunch of farmers aren't going to break it."

"But the system is unjust. We are a free country now. Those people have no right to hold that land as they do. The farmers have cleared it, made it workable, and paid for generations for the right to buy their land. It is their land, Bradford, morally if not legally."

"Dad, nothing is going to come of it." He stood up and brushed off his pants. "I have got to go to Annette now. We can talk about this some other time."

"You're turning your back on this, too."

"I'm not turning my back on anything. This is still my home, and I am concerned with the farmers, but not now, Dad. Not right now."

"You'll regret this, Bradford."

"Dad, listen to me. I'm not leaving. This is still home. It will always be home for me. I won't be here as often as I was before, but I'll be here."

"The rest of the time you'll be with that woman, I suppose."

Brad took a deep breath and let it out slowly. "It is only partly due to Marcella. I have been planning for some time to go into politics. There is so much to do, and I want to be a part of it. I always have, you know. That would keep me in the city more than I have been, in any case."

"That the story you are going to tell your wife?"

Brad looked up sharply. "It is no story. You know damned well it is true. I should think it would please you. All my life you have hammered into my head the glory of building a nation. This . . ." he said, sweeping his arm across the panorama, "all this was part of the beginning of the nation.

"Maybe I am not as romantic as you, nor do I have the gift of making things seem heroic, but I feel the same things. I also feel what happens to the people in the city. I want to have a part in changing some of the evils there. The job isn't done yet, in spite of what you may think." Brad stopped abruptly to kick at a stone in the driveway.

"That was a very pretty speech, Bradford, and if I believed it, I would be proud of you."

"What's that supposed to mean?"

"It means quite simply that I have been telling you about a critical situation in this valley, a situation just like the one you described. The farmers here are trying to change things, and they'll need help. From men like you. But where are the men like you, Bradford? The city, you say? Your world is here, son, and fight it though you may, that will never change."

"And what in hell am I to do about it?" his son asked angrily.

Nicholas shrugged. "Forgive me, son." His voice betrayed only a trace of sarcasm. "I know you have more important things on your mind. I shall see you later. I am about to take my grandson out for a ride in his pony cart."

As Brad watched him walk toward the stables, he had an overwhelming urge to follow and put Annette off for as long as possible. He turned reluctantly and went up the steps to the front door.

Carlisle hurried forward at the sound of Brad's entrance. "I am sorry, sir, I didn't hear you come to the door." He took Brad's coat. "Madame is upstairs in her sitting room. It is good to have you home, sir." Brad knew it was as much a warning as it was a greeting.

Annette sat in her sitting room with her back to the door. Her hair was pulled back from her face in a severe knot at the back of her neck. As always, her posture was rigid and straight.

He stood for a moment gazing at her. She looked almost Spanish, he thought. Her skin, like everything else about her, was smooth and blemish-free. She talked properly and even laughed with restraint. He could not criticize her, but neither had he ever been able to relax around her. With Annette he was too large, his hands too heavy to touch that aristocratic, fragile body.

As he walked across the room to her, his feet on the carpeting seemed heavier with each step. He leaned over and kissed her lightly on her cheek. While she did not draw away from him, she made him feel she had.

"Have you seen Nicholas?" she asked.

"Not yet. Father was going to take him for a ride in the pony trap. Annette—"

"I wish you would speak to your father about those rides. The child is far too young for that sort of thing. It is dangerous, and your father is much too willing to take chances with little Nicholas."

"I'll talk to him. Annette—"

"Please do. Just yesterday I happened to look into the stable yard and he was actually holding that baby on the back of a pony. He said he was going to teach him how to ride!"

"Annette! I need to talk to you."

Annette stared at the opposite wall. "I think your actions have said all that needs to be said. Your message only confirmed the worst of what we have already been privileged to hear from every local gossip. If you want someone to talk to, I suggest a confessor. I won't be dragged down by your sordid affairs, Brad. Don't try to include me in any of it."

"That is all you have to say?"

"That is sufficient. I assume you have told the young woman that this is an impossible situation, or you would not be here now. I shall accept that, but please don't mention it again." She glanced over at him. "We are due for dinner in less than an hour. You had better bathe, and you could stand a shave as well." She got up and walked gracefully to her own bedroom.

Brad watched her go, and then turned and went across the room to the other door that led to his bedroom. He had never liked the idea of separate bedrooms, but at the time it had happened there was little he could do. Annette had had difficulty carrying Nicholas the last two months, and the doctor had suggested it would be wise for her to remain in bed, and alone, during that time. So Brad had moved into the bedroom that adjoined her sitting room on the other side.

After the baby was born, the arrangement continued. At first he had suggested that he move back into the room, and then, as he began to see more of Marcella, it didn't seem so important anymore.

As he went into his own room, he wondered if he had ever really shared Annette's bed, if she had ever actually welcomed his presence there.

He was very tired. He lay down on the bed, his boots still on, without turning down the tapestry coverlet Annette had made. He closed his eyes and drifted off into the gray, troubled world between waking and sleep. He came to himself minutes later, awakening with the vision of Marcella in his mind.

He missed her already—her warmth and her desire. If he were in the brownstone house, he thought, he wouldn't be wondering how to approach the woman in the next room; he wouldn't have to pry and dig to find what her feelings were. Marcella would have told him through kisses and tears and words and longings. She would have delighted him and exhausted him. If it were Marcella who was his wife, he would have known by the end of this night that he would never return to the city.

After he had bathed and shaved, he returned to the sitting room. It was as though he had never left. Except for her change of clothing and the ruby earrings she now wore, Annette was exactly as she was when he had first come in.

She put down the tapestry she had been working on. "Oh, there you are! I wondered what was keeping you." She smiled at him—the same smile she bestowed on the servants after she had instructed them as to the particular way she wanted the silver polished or the floors buffed.

"Why didn't you come to see what had detained me? My door was open."

"I didn't expect you would need assistance."

Brad strode across the room to the window. "Are you going to keep up this cold, disinterested attitude of yours? There is no point to my being here if you are."

"What do you want of me, Brad?" she asked his back. "Did you honestly expect I would welcome you with open arms when you came straight from her? For months, Brad, you have humiliated me, made me an object of the crudest sort of gossip. Did you really think I was fooled for a moment by your lame excuses about staying in town for business? Really, Brad, I do have some remnants of pride left. I can't smile sweetly and say hypocritically that I am pleased to see you home. In many ways, Brad, it would have been simpler if you had never come back."

Brad turned to face her. "I haven't intended to hurt you. You know that, don't you?"

"It doesn't change anything."

"I am sorry that I have."

She laughed bitterly. Turning the tapestry over, she examined the back of it closely. With delicate, precise fingers she picked at a loose thread and tucked it under the drawn stitches. Then she put the tapestry down on her lap and looked up at some point on the wall.

"That is an entirely worthless sentiment, Brad. It changes nothing. Let me ask you something, and please answer me honestly. Do you love that woman?"

For a moment he was silent as he tried to gauge what effect his possible answers would have on her. "Yes, I do love her," he said softly.

"I am glad you said that. I wouldn't have believed anything else. Now one more question. Do you love me?"

He looked up sharply and met her eyes. They told him nothing. "Can you honestly say you've ever loved me?" he asked her.

"You haven't answered me."

"And I am not going to until I get a bit of the truth from you that you are demanding from me. Answer me, Annette."

90

She shrugged her elegant, slender shoulders. "You are my husband," she replied coldly.

"Am I?"

"Yes, you are, and as such I am obligated to you in loyalty and body, and—"

"I never wanted obligation from you."

"No!" she snapped. "You wanted the same kind of crudity you are wallowing in now. You wanted commonness and cheap emotion. I won't give that to you, Brad. I never would, and you have known that from the start. Why did you marry me if what you wanted all the time was a—what is her name?—a Marcella Paxton? I am sure you could have found any number of women like her on any street corner."

"I would have been more likely to find dozens like you," he snarled, "in any number of middle-class houses, gossiping and whiling away hours doing nothing."

The anger left her face as she consciously relaxed her body. Once more she looked as calm and imperturbable as an ivory mask. "I think we have said enough. We shall be late to dinner if we don't go down now. I promised Nicholas I would stop in the nursery to say goodnight to him. Will you join me?"

When they went to the nursery, Annette kissed the child on his cheek, holding fast to both his baby hands so he could not reach up to muss her jet-black hair. Then she left the room, leaving instructions with his nanny to make certain he was brought to her in the morning and not turned over to his reckless grandfather to be perched on the back of a pony again.

The baby, who was just learning to walk, toddled and fell and got up again, calling in an unintelligible language to his mother. He paid no attention to Brad until after his mother had left the room. Suddenly Brad realized that he had actually paid less attention and given less affection to his son than Annette had. He reached down, picked the little boy up, and started toward the door.

"Oh, sir!" cried the boy's nanny. "You can't take him out of the nursery. He is to go to bed. Madame will be very distressed. He mustn't go out of the nursery."

For a split second Brad thought to tell her he would take the responsibility for countermanding his wife's authority. Then he thought better of it. Annette would blame the woman in any case. He said nothing to the nanny but took the child outside to walk in the dusk.

He let the child wander where he chose, let his inept little hands attempt to pick the flowers in Annette's private garden. Nicholas had never been up so late, and his head was drooping sleepily on Brad's shoulder when he returned him to his nanny, wet and dirty.

When Brad left Scarborough House early the next morning, he didn't say good-bye to Annette, nor to his father. In many ways Brad left feeling like a stranger to his own home. He could not remember ever having acted the coward before, but he had this weekend, and he knew it. He had solved nothing. He had not even made a legitimate attempt. It left him with a gnawing sense of guilt.

Chapter Eleven

To Marcella it seemed that she and Brad had been cast adrift, as though all their bridges had been burned by some unseen hand before they were ever aware there were bridges to be crossed. Now they stood, alone and together, looking back at their families, cut off and alien from what they had once been. Neither of them had intended for things to happen so fast or so irrevocably, so while their situation formed a tighter bond between them, it also stirred up a desire, tantamount to a cause, to make everything right.

Brad wanted to maintain whatever civil balance he could between those at Scarborough and his life with Marcella. For her part, Marcella wanted her family to see and accept that she would have preferred to be married, but could not, that she loved Brad and had taken what she could get of him.

Charlotte had had little success with Hilary. Marcella saw her father at least once a week but had agreed that they would not meet under the roof of the Paxton house. Once John had come to see where Marcella lived, but he had been so ill at ease there that she had urged him not to come again.

Instead, they met in the park; sometimes he would take her to dinner at one of the smaller restaurants where they would not be noticed. If Hilary were ever to hear of their regular meetings, she would once more try to stop all contact between John and Marcella. Neither John nor Marcella was willing to risk that.

She had not been able to see Jo at all since she had moved out, and now Jo was sixteen years old. She was growing up, and Marcella missed her little sister more than she would have thought possible. She found herself picking arguments with Brad about Jo.

"If she wanted to see you, Marcella, she would," he told her.

"It's Mama who stops her, you know that. Jo would never deliberately stay away from me. She loves me, and you have no right to talk of her like that."

"Don't I? Where is your family when you need them? Who is it that stays here with you, provides you with a home? Your family? That precious mother of yours? Not even your father."

"Brad, stop it! I won't have you talk about them like that. Your family is no better. I don't see them running from Scarborough to be at your side. At least my father visited once. Where is your father?"

He slammed out of the room and the house. Marcella threw herself on her bed, beating her fists against the pillow in frustration and fear that Brad might be right. Jo might not want to see her.

Many times in their first year together Brad had left the house annoyed that he was not able to convince Marcella that none of her family was worth the mental agony she put herself through. Always she became defensive and protective; always he ended up being angry with her, and hurt. Always he was conscious of his own doubts and the cold wall of disapproval that separated him from his family at Scarborough House.

Even with the difficulties she had, Marcella was able to keep in touch with her family. She continued to meet her father and to visit with Charlotte. To Brad's amusement, Marcella took a gift to Charlotte on each visit.

"What have you got to bribe her with this time?" he asked as he watched her prepare to go to Charlotte's house.

"It isn't a bribe. Go back to reading your letter and stop teasing me."

"What have you gotten for her? Let me see."

She handed him the small box. "It isn't for Charlotte. It is for little Martin. She loves to have pretty little things for him, and you know she can't afford them on what Martin makes."

He held up the sweater, turning it around as though he were actually interested. "It will do nicely, Miss Marcella," he teased.

"As long as you approve, Mr. Bradford," she snickered, taking the sweater from him. She folded it and replaced it in its box. Brad chuckled and picked up the letter again. He had only read a few lines when she came to sit by his side.

"What does he say?" She riffled the edges of the letter. "He does write such long letters."

"Hmmm."

"Well, aren't you going to tell me what it's about?"

"Nothing that would interest you."

"Tell me, and we'll see!" she insisted.

"All right." He picked up the letter. "The farmers on the manor lands have to pay four fat fowls, fourteen bushels of winter wheat, one day's labor, and all the taxes due on the land they farm to the manor lords each year." He looked up at her. "Shall I go on?"

She nodded vigorously.

"This is the cause Dad wants to get me involved in. Every letter he sends is full of this stuff."

"But why? Is it really all that important?"

Brad leaned back, resting his head on the cushion of the sofa. "I honestly don't know. This has gone on for years—ever since the Revolution. There is no question that it is an unjust situation, and the farmers have cause to be unhappy, but whether anything can really be done, I don't know. Dad swears up and down that the whole thing is finally coming to a head after seventy or so years of grumbling, but—"

"What he really wants is to bring you back to Scarborough House."

"No doubt of that."

Marcella sat thoughtfully for a moment and then spoke. "You're not really interested in this—farm thing, are you?"

"Of course I'm interested." Brad got up and began pacing the room. "How could I not be? It is one of those odd things that happen from time to time. After all the planning that went into the formulation of our government, here is one little area of the country that still has a system right out of the Middle Ages, and there is no law to cover it."

"Why didn't they do something about it right away?"

"For the most part, the farmers have had an easy time of it," he explained. "If they had a bad crop year, no one pressed them for payment. If they had a good year, it caused no hardship to pay the manor lord. But just recently the Van Rensselaers have begun to collect payment and demand past payment. So the whole question is now very much in the mind of every farmer. He can't afford a bad crop now, and if he can't pay, he is liable to be put in prison for his debts and put off his land."

"But that's not fair!"

Brad laughed. "That's what my father keeps telling me."

"Why don't you do something about it?"

"What?"

"I don't know. Why doesn't someone change the law? What about the legislature?"

"It's been tried. There is a lot of power behind the manor lords, and it won't be broken easily."

"But—"

"That isn't fair," he finished for her. Just then the mantel clock chimed the hour. "You had better go to Charlotte's or you won't have any time to visit, and then your bribe will go for naught."

"I'll pretend you didn't say that, you scoundrel, and I will go and leave you all alone. But you see, you were wrong. I was interested in your father's letter."

"I should never have told you about it."

"Why not?"

"I will probably have to listen to both of you now. Dad is bad enough with his epistles, but if you start, too, before I know it, I'll be riding up into the mountains to help the farmers."

Marcella left shortly for Charlotte's house. Some days, like this one, she was able to go cheerfully and with hope, because she and Brad had shared something important. Marcella was doubly glad that it had had something to do with Scarborough House, and that she had been able to contribute something that might draw Brad closer to her, even when he was not in the city with her.

She thought about Brad's father, Nicholas Dalton. The long letters he wrote to Brad between Brad's monthly visits to Scarborough never ceased to upset her. Each time one arrived, it reminded Brad of things Marcella would like to have him forget altogether.

Then, too, Marcella worried about what happened when Brad left her for Scarborough. All his vows of fidelity to Marcella notwithstanding, she could not be sure ... Annette was his wife, after all. She was an attractive woman. Brad did care, more and more, it seemed, about his good name. The fantasies Marcella conjured up in Brad's absence left her sleepless more than occasionally.

Her relationship with her own family made life no easier for her. Often, she found her visits with Charlotte were no more than exercises in self-punishment. It had been nearly five years since she had moved into the brownstone house with Brad, and for five years Marcella had remained the beggar at the Paxtons' door. Not once in all that time had Hilary shown any sign of forgiving, much less forgetting, Marcella's sinful life.

When Charlotte told Marcella on one recent visit that Jo was going to be married, her impatience and determination grew to talk to her mother and somehow make things right between them. She pestered Charlotte to talk with Hilary more persuasively, and she nagged at her father until that long-suffering man broke their weekly luncheon date.

One day in late summer she went to Charlotte's house at a time she wasn't expected, hoping to catch Jo there. As she came up the street she could see Charlotte standing at her front door, talking excitedly to her neighbor. Charlotte had been crying.

Marcella waited at the side of the walkway for the neighbor and young Martin to hurry past.

"Hi, Aunt Marcella!" he called as the neighbor woman tried to hurry him back to her own house.

"Martin, go with Mrs. Johnson as I asked you, and do be a good boy. Come in, Marcella."

Marcella followed her sister into the dark hallway. "What is going on? Everyone seems to be in a state. Why have you been crying?"

"Oh, Marcella—Mama is terribly ill. She is ... We don't even know if she will recover. Papa is beside himself." She picked up a dress from a nearby chair. "Help me get dressed. I can never manage these hooks alone. Martin doesn't even know about it. He will come home from work and find me and little Martin gone and not know a thing!"

"Can't you send a message to him?"

"It would be much too costly. Mrs. Johnson will have to tell him later."

"I can send it for you. We can use my driver and coach."

Charlotte looked up at Marcella and then looked away. "I don't think so."

"Oh, for the love of heaven, Charlotte, the Lord will not condemn you for sending a message in my tainted vehicle."

"I didn't mean that. But Mama would hate it. She is so ill ... I just don't want to do it today."

"Never mind, I'll send a message to Martin myself." She jotted a note at Charlotte's small desk. "I am coming to the house to help. Will you at least accept a ride to Mama's house with me?"

"You can't go there!"

"Well, I am. If Mama doesn't need me, Papa does. I am going to help. After all, Charlotte, she is still my mother, even if she doesn't accept me as her daughter." Marcella sealed the envelope, went to the door, and instructed the driver to deliver the message and to hurry back for them. Then she returned to Charlotte's bedroom. "You haven't told me what is wrong with Mama."

"She has had a stroke. She doesn't know anyone. She didn't even recognize Papa. She looks awful, Marcella." Charlotte blew her nose loudly into a lace-edged handkerchief. "How will we manage? She has always been the center of everything—for all of us. Jo can't manage by herself, and ... oh, what will happen to Jo's beautiful wedding? Whatever will we do, Marcella?"

By a great effort of will, Marcella spoke calmly. "When did all of this happen?"

"Last night she didn't feel too well after dinner, and then sometime later— I am not too sure when—Papa found her lying on the floor in the hallway. She must have been trying to get to the bathing room. Now she is unconscious, and the doctor isn't certain she will ever wake up again. Marcella," she sobbed, "she can't die! She just can't."

"I am sure she won't," Marcella replied, taking Charlotte's hands in her own. "But sitting here crying about it won't help. Let's go now, Charlotte, I heard the carriage drive up a moment ago. We can do much more at Mama's house than we can here."

Charlotte hesitated for a moment, summoning up courage to repeat that she didn't think Marcella should go to the house. "It would kill Mama outright if she ever knew you had been there. And there is Jo—Marcella, I have always hidden this from you, but Jo wouldn't want you there either. It isn't Mama alone who keeps you from the house. It is Jo."

Marcella felt the blood rush from her face, and she felt suddenly dizzy. She clutched the back of Charlotte's chair. "Jo? Jo doesn't want to see me?"

Charlotte nodded but said nothing.

"I don't believe you," Marcella stammered. "Not Jo! She is like my own child. Jo always turned to me. You're lying. I am going to Mama's house now. If you want to come with me, do so, and if not, I'll see you over there."

She left the room at a near-run, grabbed her cape, and hurried to the carriage. Climbing onto the seat, she waited two long minutes for Charlotte to follow. When she did not, Marcella instructed the driver to take her to the house on Eighth Avenue. Charlotte walked.

In five years' time there was little difference to be seen from the outside of the house. The trees were larger, and the bushes that lined the front of the small yard were thicker and afforded the privacy that Hilary had always admired. Otherwise it looked just as it had the first day they had all seen it.

The brick was stained the same brilliant red, and the mortar joints were sparkling with fresh whitening. Marcella felt very young and strangely excited about coming back home. How far back would she be going when she entered this house again?

She stepped inside and found immediately that she wasn't coming back home at all. Hilary's ideas of elegance had taken full control. What had once seemed to Marcella to be a comfortable, well-arranged parlor was now a conglomeration of gilt chairs, two Belter sofas facing one another—when one would have been far too much—and innumerable small prints cut from calendars or bought from the mail-order houses, cluttering the walls. There was fringe everywhere—on every table, on the afghan that covered one end of the sofa. Between the doilies and the fringed table coverings sat Hilary's cut-glass bowls and the Lalique figurines of which she was so proud.

Everything was covered with a thin coat of dust. Marcella touched the edge of the sofa. Hilary must have been unwell for some time for her to have allowed so much dust to collect. She looked up to see her father enter the parlor.

"Marcella?" he said softly, not daring to believe his eyes. He came over to her, letting her put her arms around him. "It's a good thing to have you here. Mama is—"

"I know, Papa. Charlotte has told me all about it. I am only here to help. Mama won't know a thing about it. I'll stay out of the way."

"Maybe she'll feel different now. Maybe she can forgive a bit."

"Let's not worry about that now. We have plenty of time for making up and forgiving. Sit down and talk to me while I straighten this room a bit. You look tired, Papa. You are not taking care of yourself. Have you eaten anything at all today?"

He shook his head slowly. "I haven't been hungry. They don't want me in her room. I can't see her."

Marcella spent most of that afternoon in her father's house. By the time she left, the first floor was spotless and in order. She had not gone upstairs, and Josephine had not come down.

"Didn't you tell her I was here, Charlotte?" Marcella asked just before she left.

"I told her, but you know how it is, Marcella. Jo has her hands full. She has been tending to Mama all day."

"And she didn't have a single moment to say hello to me? Charlotte, I haven't talked to Jo in five years. Surely she can't hate me that much."

"I tried to warn you. Jo has always been like that, Marcella."

Hilary clung to life with a tenacity and determination that forced admiration. Within several months, the doctors were sure she would be back on her feet and active again. Though Marcella told herself she was glad for her mother, she knew that with her recovery Hilary would once again stand between Marcella and any hope she might have had of seeing Jo. Marcella's visits to Eighth Avenue ended.

Jo was married to Terrance O'Connor the following month, and Hilary was there with tears in her eyes as she watched Jo become the wife of the slender, dark-haired man with the turquoise eyes. Terrance was a happy, laughing man, an unlikely choice for Jo, for he hardly shared her rigid sense of propriety. He seldom had a spare penny, for one had only to ask and he would give it. As a result he had a good many friends, and almost as many enemies. But Jo loved him as she had never loved anyone or anything before in her life.

Marcella hadn't been invited to the wedding, but then, no one had thought to tell her she wouldn't be welcome either. That was enough. She watched Jo marry, and wept—a little in joy and a little in self-pity.

After the ceremony she went up to the couple along with the others. If Jo's smile faded the slightest bit when she saw Marcella, it was excusable. It had been a long time since the sisters had seen one another. Jo introduced her to Terrance. His smile was brilliant.

"Where have you been hiding this sister?" he grinned, taking her hand.

"Marcella hasn't lived at home for some time, Terrance. She—she has her own home," Jo said quietly.

"Oh, I know you, my girl. You were afraid to let me see her." He gave Jo an ungentlemanly poke.

To Marcella's amazement Jo smiled. "I was, indeed. Marcella is far too pretty, and intentions in a man like you are far too transitory to trust."

"You see what I have married, Marcella? A shrew, a jailer to my good spirits, and here I stand condemned to a life of this!"

Marcella laughed. "You look a very happy prisoner, Terrance. Will you and Jo stay here at Mama's and Papa's house?"

"No!" Jo replied, too quickly. "I mean, we will stay for a time, but then we are leaving. Terrance and I will live in Ohio."

"Ohio! Jo, that is—it is little more than a wilderness."

"You listen to too many tales," Terrance chuckled. "It is no longer. And my girl has a fancy for far-off places. It is not New York for her."

Soon thereafter, Marcella left. Whatever yearning Jo had for the far-off places Terrance had spoken of, Marcella knew that what Jo was really doing was leaving her home and Marcella's scandal. It wasn't so much what she wanted to see as what she no longer wanted to tolerate.

The next day she spoke with Charlotte about Jo's plans. "Can you tell me that Jo isn't leaving because of me?"

"I can't say that isn't a part of it, Marcella. Over the last five years the whole family has come in for some nasty gossip because of the way you lead your life. None of us likes it, but we put up with it. We haven't left."

"Jo is."

"Marcella! For once in your life wake up and realize that Jo's life is not tied up in yours as yours is in hers! She is going to Ohio because that is where she and Terrance want to live. It has nothing to do with you!"

Marcella looked at her doubtfully. Nothing Charlotte said made any difference to her. Whatever reasons Jo might give others, Marcella continued to believe that it was her scandal that was causing Jo to leave. Jo did not love Marcella any longer. She didn't even want to be associated with her. The wedding was no new beginning for Marcella. It ended a part of her life that she had treasured, and ever after, there would be a void where Jo's love had been.

She returned to Brad for comfort, determined to fill that void, and allowed him to catch her up in his burgeoning social life. Brad was becoming well-known in the city. The intensity with which he drove at his goals sometimes frightened Marcella, and always awed her.

While he came of a landed family, Brad needed to gain the financing necessary to become a force in a city that respected and bowed only to the successful.

In his climb to financial power, Brad had made but one mistake, and that had been forgiven him by those who had been wiser. He had begun speculating in stocks at a time when the New York Exchange was having problems, and he had gone to a rival organization called the Bourse. It took him little time to realize that the Bourse—or little board—catered only to those who hadn't the ability or intelligence to compete in the greater speculations. To deal on a small scale was the same to Brad as not dealing at all.

So when the old board moved its headquarters to the new Merchant Exchange Building at Wall and Williams streets in 1842, Brad made the move with it, leaving the Bourse behind him as though it had never existed. From that time on, his mornings were spent at the Exchange Building with all the other men in their swallowtail coats and tall hats. It was a gentleman's business, and Brad not only enjoyed it, he excelled at it.

While a growing number of prominent businessmen accepted Marcella as his hostess when he was in town, he still claimed Scarborough House as his residence. Annette's name was always on the tip of his tongue, particularly when anyone of importance was present. To the outside world he was a devoted husband, and Marcella was no more than a necessary convenience for the social obligations that were more easily met in the city. This fooled no one, but then no one was ungentlemanly enough to make comment, for they enjoyed being asked to Brad's house in the city. Whatever was said about Marcella publicly, privately they loved being near her, and there wasn't one who did not envy Brad his arrangement.

Nothing, it seemed, stood in the way of his ambitions or the realization of his dreams. Having the advantage of an old and established family name and the burning desire to succeed, Brad touched a common thread in everyone he met.

Among men who knew what they had come from and where they were going, Marcella was at her best. She knew them. She was just like they were. She understood and sympathized with their peculiar brand of ambition and could draw information from them like water from a tap. As a result, Brad often had the jump on the newest speculations before others knew what was happening.

During these periods of activity, neither Brad nor Marcella had the time or the inclination to struggle with the feelings of their respective families as they did at other times. Their lives were full and satisfying.

So one day when Brad received a letter in his father's handwriting, neither of them thought too much of it. Brad took the letter with him into the sitting room, where Marcella was curled up in a chair, reading.

She glanced up from the magazine. "What have the farmers been up to this time?"

"I haven't even opened it yet." He removed the single sheet from the envelope, turned it over, and then looked back into the envelope. "Apparently this is not one of his usual letters." He unfolded it and frowned.

"Well, what is it?"

"He wants me to come to Scarborough immediately," Brad said absently as he read the short message.

"Does he say why?"

"He says practically nothing. But I think he would have said if it were illness, don't you?"

"I do, but if it isn't that, what is it?"

"It is just possible the old fox is trying a new tack with me. He probably wants me there for his farm cause."

"Oh, he wouldn't! He wouldn't worry you like this."

"He would if he thought it would work. You don't know my father. If he is nothing else, he is persistent. It's damned inconvenient, but I suppose I'd better go."

"Can't you just send him a letter and tell him you're not interested in the farmers? We have a dinner party this coming Wednesday evening."

"We'll have to cancel it. Explain that I was called out of town. Besides, no one of any importance is coming."

"What about Eugene Timmins?"

"I can't do anything about him," Brad replied, immediately irritated. "What does he expect me to do? I can't cure him of stupidity, and I sure as hell have no intention of making up his losses to him."

"I think a small hint of what might be a good investment would make him a much happier man, Brad. He did lose his money following you in the first place."

"I didn't know what he was doing! If he had said something . . . but he didn't. He was a sneak, and he lost. We never had an agreement. What happened was his own fault, Marcella. Damn it, I didn't even know he had bought the stock. Everything that happened was his fault."

"You don't need to convince me. I believe you."

"I don't like that man," Brad muttered, a little surprised at his own vehemence.

"All right. Let's not talk about it anymore. I'll tell him you were called away on a family emergency, and that will be that. He won't believe me, of course. He will say you won't face him."

"I don't care what he says. I don't know why I let you talk me into inviting him here anyway. I think you like him fawning over you. I can't stand the man."

"I just don't like to see you have enemies," Marcella soothed, "not even one like Mr. Timmins. I want everyone to love you as I do. Now stop being nasty." She smiled and leaned over to kiss him.

"I have to leave right away," Brad said, heading for the stairs to the bedroom, "or there won't be time to see Dad this afternoon. Come on up and help me pack."

"How long will you be gone?" Marcella asked, scurrying up the steps behind him.

Brad walked into the bedroom and pulled a bag out of the wardrobe. "I really don't know," he said, throwing a few things into the bag. "It depends mostly on Dad and what he wants. If it is about the farmers, I should be back tomorrow evening."

"And if it isn't?"

"I don't know. I'll let you know as soon as I do."

"Oh, Brad, why must you go at all? Sometimes I get so angry at your father. You know there is nothing really wrong. Don't go. I want you here with me."

Brad stopped packing and looked up at her. "Don't do that. I have to go. I haven't been home for a long time, and I can't just ignore this. Whatever it is, it has Dad in a huff. I want to see him."

Marcella pouted. "And Scarborough and Nicholas and Annette and everything else." .

"That, too."

"And what about me?"

Brad sighed, closed the case, and sat down beside her on the edge of the bed. "You're a jealous woman, Marcella."

"I have reason to be!"

"Not a one. I don't visit you, Marcella—I live with you and I love you. I give you everything there is of me. All I can give to them is a visit."

"You make it sound so pathetic."

"Well, it is, in a way."

"Brad?" she said, taking his hand, "I have been thinking. . . ."

"Oh-oh."

"No, I'm serious. Lately, I have heard quite a lot about these farmers. Not from you, but from the people who come here. Maybe—" She looked up at him, debating whether to go on. "Maybe it is something you should be interested in. It might be what we have been waiting for, Brad—something to put you in the public eye."

Brad laughed, but his laughter served only to make her more excited and determined. "Oh, Brad, use it! Solve their problem, and then nothing will stop you. Just think of it!"

He held up a hand to stop her. "The farmers don't really want to go that far. They are grumbling and making threatening noises, but nothing will come of it. It never has in the past, and it isn't likely to now."

He finished dressing and went down to get his carriage. "Take care of yourself while I'm gone. I'll send you a message as soon as I know what is going on."

On the ride to Scarborough House, Brad found himself thinking about what Marcella had said. The Down-with-Rent War might just be enough of an issue to start his political career, at that.

Chapter Twelve

The question the antirenters posed had gone on for years. From time to time there had been real trouble. After one attempt by the Van Rensselaers to collect taxes and income on land they owned above Albany, there had been open clashes between the sheriff who had been sent to collect, and the farmers, who called themselves the Calico Indians.

The governor of New York had intervened, promising the farmers that the situation would be brought to the attention of the state legislature. Nothing of consequence had been done, however, and the battle had resumed. This time, however, it had not died off as it had in the past.

For those in the city, the Down-with-Rent War was a topic of conversation—one of those issues that caused people to say fervently that something ought to be done about it. But as with so many things, there was no one who actually wanted to be the one to fight the existing powers.

Marcella's urging reminded Brad that he had heard talk that there was a man on the side of the farmers who might consider running for governor. But he could not be taken completely seriously. The man had virtually no chance of being elected. Still, Brad couldn't get it out of his mind.

It was nearly dinnertime when he arrived at Scarborough House. Old Nicholas stood on the porch of the house, looking out across the fields. Brad called a greeting to him and vaulted up the stairs of the house to his side.

"I came as soon as I got your message."

"I'm glad you're here."

"Aren't you going to tell me what it's all about?"

The older man lowered his head. "I want you to do something about the situation here. Now, don't say anything. I'm not going to apologize for tricking you into coming. This is your home and your problem, and we need you."

Brad smiled. "I thought that it might be that, and I thought a great deal about it on my way up. I agree with you, it is a serious problem. But, Dad, is it any of our business? Do the farmers even want outsiders involved?"

Old Nicholas shook his head vigorously. "By the gods of hell, Bradford. I've heard it all now. We are not outsiders! This is our valley, and those are our farmers who are being done out of their due."

"Dad, we don't have tenant farmers on Scarborough property. We haven't since you were a boy yourself. Maybe we have already done all we can or should, by example. What do you think I can do? Mount my horse and ride off to the mountains bearing arms? More than likely one of them would shoot me on sight and find out at my funeral I had come to help."

"It is not a joking matter, Bradford."

"I am sorry, but I don't see what I can do."

"Your son will, by God! That young Nicholas has the heart of a lion. He will do what his father refuses to."

"I am not refusing, Dad. I just don't know what to do about it. I can put in a word with the governor if you think it would help."

Brad looked across the meadow to the south of the house and saw his son racing along, riding bareback, his body scantily clothed. "He looks like a little Indian out there."

Old Nicholas laughed. "He is an Indian. The farmers have formed their own militia, call themselves the Calico Indians. Nick plays at being one of them."

"Dad, I just got here. Let me think about it some more. We can go in and have dinner and talk later." He turned and started toward the door.

"I don't even want to talk to you about it, Bradford," his father muttered. "I can see we have nothing to say to one another."

"Then why am I here?"

"I wonder myself." The old man moved to get a clearer view of his grandson. "Nick and I will see it through alone."

Brad stopped. "Dad, he is only a small boy. You don't talk to him seriously about all of this, do you?"

"I do, indeed," the older man retorted. "That boy will be master of this house one day. I raised my son to shirk his responsibilities to the land and family. I'll not make the same mistake with my grandson."

At that point young Nicholas turned his horse and cantered back across the field at what Brad considered an inordinate speed for one so young.

"Is that Night Wind he's riding?" Brad asked.

"Indeed it is. I've given him to the boy for his own."

"You're not serious! That is far too much horse for a boy his age."

"Nonsense. He is becoming a man!"

"What has Annette to say to this?"

"Bah! Given her way she'd make a simpleton out of him. Velvet suits and lace collars! Nicholas is a good boy. He is fast approaching manhood."

"Maybe too fast. I will be taking him into town with me from time to time," Brad announced.

"You are too late, Bradford. The boy is Scarborough all the way through. Not even your precious city will knock that out of him. If you wanted him for your son, you should have been around here all these years. Now he belongs to me. To Scarborough."

There was more truth in that than Brad liked to admit. Nicholas did turn to his grandfather for guidance—and protection from the awful things Annette subjected him to, like dancing lessons and weekly socials with the ladies of the neighborhood. He was always happy to see Brad, but more as an audience for his accomplishments than as a father. Brad was someone to whom Nicholas owed allegiance, not someone he could trust.

Brad went into the house and straight up to Annette's sitting room. She turned at the sound of his footsteps. "Hello, Brad. When did you get back? Have you seen Father Dalton yet? No one is ill, if you have not yet discovered that. I told your father he had no business sending you a message like that. You were sure to think the worst."

"I guessed what it was about. I just talked to him."

"Sit down, Brad," she said graciously. "I was just about to have tea. Would you care for some?"

"Thank you." He sat down, feeling strangely formal and out of place. "How have you been, Annette?"

She smiled a bit, almost as if to acknowledge his discomfort. "We have all been quite well and content, considering. Father Dalton and Nicholas should be coming in after a bit. I imagine they are cleaning up." She poured Brad a cup of tea. "Have you seen the condition Nicholas runs around this farm in? The boy spends his days very nearly naked. I haven't been able to change that, but I have at least insisted that both your father and your son be properly attired and clean when they come into the house."

"Dad must have had a mouthful to say about that request."

"It was not a request, and he understood that. He has completely dominated the boy. In this, at least, I shall have my way. If you were here, things would be quite different, but as it is, I take a firm hand when and where I am able. In spite of my efforts, the boy is fast becoming a ruffian. At this moment his interests and sympathy are entirely consumed by these rabble-rousing farmers."

"So Dad told me. This is one bug he has gotten that nothing seems about to dislodge. I suppose Dad will never be happy unless he has a cause."

"It might behoove you to listen to him this time, Brad," she said earnestly. "It is no longer a matter of a few mountain farmers causing difficulties for the sheriff. It has spread throughout the valley, and it is only a matter of time before another outbreak."

Brad leaned forward in his chair. "It is really that bad? I hear talk in the city, but so far no one has taken it too seriously."

"They will take notice in time, I think. Several of the farmers have slaughtered their own herds rather than give them up in payment to the manor lords. They shoot horses from beneath riders, and more than once we have had a sheriff return tarred and feathered." She paused to put her cup down. "Brad, I do not approve of your father's involving Nicholas in it. Father Dalton keeps telling him he is a man, and the child believes him. He runs around here with that ridiculous dinner horn tied to his neck. I can hardly get him to remove it when he goes to bed at night."

Brad smiled. "He is going to warn the farmers of the sheriff's approach with his dinner horn, is he? He is a spirited little lad. My father is right, Annette. We have raised another defender of womanhood, truth, and a seeker of the Grail.

"But then," he said, getting up from his chair, "you seem to be right as well. Things have gotten out of hand—in many ways. I'll see to them." He walked over to Annette and for the first time in many weeks bent down and kissed her on the check. She put her hand up to the side of his face, and he kissed her firmly on the mouth.

He smiled in pleasure and surprise. "I haven't had time to unpack yet. How long have I until supper?"

She looked down at her hands and then glanced up at her husband. "The bedroom ... your bedroom is being redone," she said softly. When he said nothing, she went on. "I didn't expect you, or I wouldn't have had it done at this time."

"It's all right. Tell me where you want me to sleep. Any room will do."

"Perhaps your old room?"

"Perhaps that is best." He smiled and felt a surge of excitement. Annette had actually asked him to sleep with her! "I'll tell Carlisle."

"I am not asking you to leave Marcella, Brad. You needn't worry about that anymore."

"I'll wash up for dinner. It's good to be home, Annette." As he went into their room for the first time in a long time, he really did feel at home.

Old Nicholas had gone after his grandson. He was angry with himself for not having told Brad the whole situation in the valley, and with Brad for having seemed so uninterested. Momentarily, he regretted having sent the message to Brad. Let Brad lead his own life, he thought; he doesn't belong to Scarborough any longer.

Old Nicholas raised his arm and waved to his grandson. The child rode up and dismounted.

"Tie up the horse and come with me to the willow pond, Nick."

"Sure, Grandpa." He did as he was told and then came over to his grandfather. Hand in hand, they walked down toward the pond.

Nicholas Dalton had had that part of Scarborough landscaped and planted for his wife. A long curving allee of trees sloped gradually downhill, until it took a final turn and entered a small, secluded area. In the center were a pond and a summerhouse.

Nicholas and his wife Martha had gone to this place in the evening, and it had always remained theirs exclusively. No guest was invited. Even Brad had been there only a few times.

Nicholas took his grandson there often. Here the boy felt free to confide.

"Will Papa stay at home this time, Grandpa?" he asked as they approached the glen.

"I don't think so."

"Why not? Doesn't he like us?"

"He likes us. He loves us."

"Then why doesn't he stay? Doesn't Mama want him here?"

"Grown-up people are difficult to understand at your age, I'll wager. You'll find out later on, when you are a bit older, that papas are very busy men."

"Why doesn't Mama go with him?"

"I am not so sure I can tell you that. Who knows why a woman does or doesn't do a thing? Maybe it is too much of a task for her. Bradford does a good deal of entertaining and traveling in the city, I believe."

"Mama likes parties."

"Tea parties, perhaps." Old Nicholas put his arm around the little boy and held him near. "I wish your grandmother were alive to see you. How proud she would be of you, little Indian. You're a fine lad."

He looked at the pond with its mirror surface. The frogs sitting on lily pads were motionless, and the small blue-and-purple flowers turned motionless faces to the last rays of light.

"Grandpa?"

"Yes, Nick?"

"Will Papa help the Indians?"

Nicholas was silent for a while. "Maybe. Maybe so, if we ask him right."

"Please?"

"No, not 'please.' We will just have to let him know we want him. Sometimes, Nick, that is all a fellow needs. Just show him you want him here."

They sat quietly for a few more minutes, listening to the breeze rustle the branches above them. Old Nicholas stood up. "We'd better get back to the house, Nick. You still have to put that horse of yours in the stable."

They had just finished rubbing down the horse when they heard Gert calling them to supper. Old Nicholas made a face at his grandson and then hurried to obey. "Hope your papa's got your mama in a good mood, or you and I are both in for it."

By the time they arrived in the dining room, Brad and Annette were already seated.

"So there you are!" Brad said as soon as the two walked in.

Old Nicholas Dalton rubbed his hands together and returned Brad's smile. "Annette, did you see to the wine for this evening?"

"I asked that no wine be served."

"Nick, run out to the kitchen and tell Gert to bring up—what do you think, Bradford? Something light?"

Annette cleared her throat. "Father Dalton, you could have told Gert when she came into the room to serve us. I do wish you would not send the boy racing around with your messages."

"Nick's legs are younger and stronger than Gert's. She has enough to do," the old man said, rearranging his silverware and napkin. "Well, Bradford, it is good to have you home for a change. How long can you stay?"

"I haven't made any plans, Dad."

"Then perhaps we can persuade you to stay for a few days at least. Perhaps even a bit longer."

The dinner was a pleasant one. Annette did most of the talking. By the end of the hour Brad knew a great deal more about her and with whom she spent her time. Nicholas did not once mention the problem of the farmers. That, Brad guessed, would be the subject of their after-dinner conversation in the library.

Chapter Thirteen

When Brad and his father excused themselves and headed for the library, Brad noticed that Nick was following them.

"This isn't talk for you, son. Go with your mother."

The boy looked to his grandfather for support.

"Nonsense! Let the boy come along. He knows more about the situation than you by a long chalk."

Nicholas, smiling triumphantly, seated himself in one of the large over-stuffed leather chairs near the fireplace. Old Nicholas handed his son a cigar and reached into the second humidor and pulled out a striped candy stick, which he handed to Nicholas.

The older man came directly to the point. "I suppose you realize by now that I am determined to have your help, Bradford. I wouldn't have called you here if I didn't think it important."

"I knew it as soon as I read the message. I have been thinking about our earlier conversation, and then Annette has told me a little of what has been happening. I am beginning to understand your concern."

"This is the situation as it now stands: A fellow by the name of Smith Broughton is the leader. The Livingstons have gotten into the thick of things. I tell you, Bradford, this thing is completely out of hand now. Something must be done about it."

"Slow down, Dad, you're way ahead of me. What is all this about the Livingstons? What brought them into it?"

"The antirenters began publishing a newspaper out of Albany, a weekly sheet to report the goings-on and also to raise money for their movement.

"They began to demand that the patroons' titles to the land be tested in the courts. That put the fat in the fire. The Livingstons have a great deal to lose, as you well know. So it was decided that it would be better to break the movement here and now before the thing got greater impetus and force.

"They sent a spy to one of the secret meetings of the Calico Indians. He discovered that their leader, called Big Thunder, was in fact Smith Broughton. They arrested him, concocted some story of thievery, and threw him in jail without bail."

"Did anyone try to get Broughton out?"

"Of course they did. But with Big Thunder in jail, Livingston figured the whole movement would collapse. So they have been raising a hue and cry ever since, saying we need the state troops, that there is a rebellion afoot."

Brad puffed thoughtfully on his cigar. "Well, they aren't going to get far with that kind of tactic."

"I don't know, Brad. Governor Wright bows in the face of power such as the Livingstons'. They carry a lot of weight around here. Sometime this week the foot soldiers and cavalry regiments are due here. In our valley, damn it!"

"Calm down, Dad. Give me a minute to think."

His father leaned forward in his chair. "Does that mean you'll help?"

"I'll do what I can. But I have to think. I have a headful right now. I am going back to New York tomorrow. I'll hand over my business affairs to my assistant and Marcella. They can manage for a time without me, and then we'll see what can be done. I have a few other ideas, and I'll see to them while I am in the city tomorrow."

"Such as?"

"Such as a governor who will actually do something. Right now we don't have a law that protects people like tenant farmers. We need one, and if the situation is as serious as you indicate, my bet is that there is something already in the political works. I'll find out about it when I am in the city and throw our support to it."

"Are you going to join the Indians, Papa?" Nick asked. Brad had forgotten the boy was in the room.

"I suppose in a way I am, Nick. Would that please you?"

"You should talk to Asa Bishop," the boy said solemnly.

Brad looked up at his father. "Who is this Asa Bishop? You didn't mention him, Dad."

"Ask your son."

"Who is he, Nick?"

"He's the Black Hawk of the Indians," Nick said excitedly. "He led them, all the men from Woodstock and Boarsville and Shandunken, against the Livingston agents, Papa. He is one of the best, isn't he, Grandpa?"

The old man smiled. "He is, Nick. He's a good man."

"Well, Dad," Brad said, getting up, "I'll be leaving then, around noon tomorrow. I'll do my best to be back here the day after. If I can reach all the people I need to talk to right away, there should be no problem. Otherwise, expect me in a couple of days. I'll make it as short a trip as I can."

"I'll count on you. We both will," old Nicholas said, putting his arm around his grandson. "Nothing can beat a Dalton as long as he has another Dalton to count on."

Brad rumpled Nicholas's dark curling hair and left to find Annette. When he informed her of what he would be doing during the next few days, she was obviously delighted.

"I am so glad. We have needed you here. We shall have you for at least several days, won't we?"

"It would seem so. I don't think this is something that will be cleared up by a word here and there."

"I shall get busy and arrange some dinner parties. So many people hereabouts hardly believe you exist any longer, you are here so briefly when you do come."

"Annette, I don't know about dinner parties. I will be very busy, and I don't really know how involved in this I will be. You had better wait and see what to expect."

"We must entertain!" Annette said, a trace of irritability in her voice. "Brad, people seriously don't believe we are married any longer. I must be able to show them."

"Do whatever you wish, then, but I can't promise I will be available."

"You must be, Brad. You owe that to me. If you can take time out of your life for these farmers, you can certainly take some time for your wife."

"I said you should do as you see fit. I'll do my best to comply."

He left for the city the following afternoon. Stopping at several homes along the way to gather the latest news and promises of support, he was late in arriving at the brownstone. Marcella knew as soon as she saw him that something was afoot.

"Was it the Down-with-Rent War?" she asked, taking his coat.

"It was, and wait until you hear all that it entails. I have thought about what you said before I left, and I think it is feasible. I can make a name for myself with this—at least a start."

Marcella listened eagerly to everything he told her until he mentioned the redecorating of his own bedroom.

"What do you mean? Where did you sleep?"

Brad looked directly at her. "She is still my wife."

"You hardly need tell me! Brad, is that why you are going back? Is it Annette?"

"I have told you, Marcella, it is the antirent war and what it will do for you and for me and for *our* future. As for Annette, I can't help that, and quite frankly, I don't want to. Annette can entertain some men whom you cannot entertain. She can talk to wives. She has her place as well as you have, and if I can be on agreeable terms with her, I welcome it."

Marcella leaned back on the sofa. She spoke very quietly. "If that is what you want, I can't do anything to deter you, can I?"

"No."

Her finger traced the side of his leg. He uncrossed his legs and sat up straight on his side of the sofa. "You'll have to learn to accept the fact that I have a family, Marcella, and trust me."

"I trust you, Brad." She turned and lay down, putting her head in his lap. "Painting your room! I would have been far more subtle than that."

He began to play with the curls at the side of her face. "You are a subtle creature, aren't you?"

She turned her head to look up at him. "Terribly. Will you let it all go for naught?"

"None of it," he whispered and leaned across her to extinguish the lamp. The room was plunged into a soft, cool darkness. The light of the moon traced a path across the carpet.

"Shall I take you upstairs?" he murmured as he took her hair down and searched for the top hook of her gown.

"It is much too long a trip. Take me to the moonbeam, Brad. We have never made love in a moonbeam. Perhaps our memories will be caught in the silver light. Is that possible?"

"Stop talking."

"I love to talk to you. I love to talk to you now." She sighed as she felt his hands move over her body until she could no longer think of any words to say. She moved with Brad and against him, waiting and longing and anticipating the final moment of their lovemaking.

Afterward, as they lay on the carpet, she laughed.

He pulled her back against his chest. "How can you laugh?"

"Because I love you so, because you make me feel so alive! I can't hold it in, I have to laugh and talk and love you and touch you and—"

"What could I have done all those years I didn't know you? How did I exist then?"

She smiled up at him. "Why, Brad, as you told me earlier, you have a wife."

He said nothing. The moonlight outlined the side of her cheek. He ran his fingertips across her lips.

"She doesn't like to play, does she? She is serious and proper and a good wife, the kind of woman Mama told me to be."

"She is a good wife, the kind your Mama told you to be," he repeated.

The following day, Brad arranged appointments and meetings. Sympathy was running with the antirenters as he had guessed, but he saw immediately that something more was needed to push the situation through the final barrier of reluctance before the public would support the farmers in the coming elections.

They needed a candidate for governor, sympathetic and willing to change the law in their favor. If the support could be mustered, the man would be John Young.

He put off leaving for Scarborough that afternoon, deciding instead to take Marcella to dinner at Delmonico's and later to the theater.

"We'll go to bed early tonight, and I promise I won't keep you awake or talk all night or anything," Marcella said. "Tonight I'll be a good wife, too, but only tonight. Then you can leave early in the morning, and your father will be pleased."

"I think late afternoon is quite early enough, and anyway I don't think I can sleep anymore without someone talking nonsense in my ear."

He arrived at Scarborough before dinner the following day. When old Nicholas saw him driving up, he hurried out to meet him.

"Where have you been, Brad? You said you'd be back yesterday!"

"I said I would if I could. I had people to see. And I have some good news. Come on, let's go to the house. I'd like a good cool drink."

"The devils are prowling at night, dragging people out of their beds! The dirty cowards. Afraid to show their faces in the light of day. I knew it would come to this!"

"The farmers are attacking at night?"

"No! The soldiers and agents of the manor lords. They are throwing everyone in jail. We aren't safe here either. It is well known that we are sympathizers. No one is safe."

"Calm down, Dad, it can't be that bad."

Nicholas stalked off toward the stables. "Come with me," he shouted over his shoulder, "and I'll show you how bad it is." He told one of the stable men to saddle his horse and one for Brad, and they rode out across the green lawn and onto the golden meadow.

"Where are we going, Dad?" Brad called to old Nicholas's back.

"Breed's place." The old man urged his horse to greater speed.

Ebenezer Breed and old Nicholas had been friends for as long as Brad could remember. The land Breed now owned had once been a part of Scarborough; unlike some of the other landowners, Nicholas had sold his land to the men who had farmed it.

Moments later they came to a board house barely adequate for the family of five that lived there.

"It doesn't look as if anyone is here," Brad said, looking around.

"Mabel will be, and that girl."

"Louisa?"

"Yes, that's the name. They'll be here. More than likely they are hiding."

Nicholas cupped his hands around his mouth. "Mabel! Mabel Breed! Do you hear, woman? It's Nicholas Dalton. Come out!" He looked toward a patch of scrubby undergrowth in a grove of trees in front of the house.

Slowly the figure of a frail little woman emerged into the open. "Hello, Mr. Dalton, Bradford. The men aren't around." She turned and looked back into the thicket. "It's all right, Louisa. It's your pa's friend."

"Sure it ain't those men come back again? They's gonna get me, Ma, you know how they was lookin'."

"Hush and get out here. What can I do for you, Mr. Dalton? Eb is back. Want to see him?"

"I thought they threw him in jail. Where is he? Let me talk to him."

"He ain't up to much talkin'. Come on." She hurried back into the thicket, followed by Brad and Nicholas, and led them deep into the trees and down a steep incline. Both Brad and Nicholas were out of breath and panting when she stopped in front of a little shack sitting unevenly on the ground.

"He's in there," she said, "but he ain't in good shape. Don't worry him none."

Ebenezer Breed lay on a makeshift bed in the shack, his skin nearly black from the sun and covered with bright-red welts. He looked up through bloodshot eyes at his old friend.

"Nick," he murmured, raising his hand and letting it drop to his side again.

"My God, man, what happened to you? You break jail?"

Eb tried to shake his head and winced at the effort. "Never got to jail. Mabel will tell you. I just can't seem to talk too good."

Nicholas took a rag from a pail of water by his side and gently sponged his face. "Get Mabel in here, Bradford."

When she entered, he asked, "What happened to him, Mabel? He isn't fit to tell me anything. What went on here last night? Where are the boys?"

"Clem and Del went to join the others. They's not putting up with this no more. All them soldier fellows is goin' to find in these parts from now on is women and children. No more men!

"They come last night after the boys'd left. Eb and me was readying for the night, and in they storm, pretty as you please. Hauled Louisa out'n her bed and looked her over like she was some kind of slut, and then they took Eb. Put my man in chains and drug him right out'n the house.

"They had a wagon, dumped him in it, and off they went. I thought they was takin' him to jail, but now the man tells me they drug him around in the hot sun all day long. Like to kill him. Not sure they didn't. Look at him! Them and their bayonets pokin' at everything in sight!"

Brad sucked his breath in. "They used bayonets?"

"They used them. Lookin' for the boys. I told them no one was here, but they were mean, just lookin' for a reason to hurt. They took Eb."

"They ruined my milk cellar, too," Eb moaned. "A man works all his life . . . I ain't even a tenant farmer, Nick. What have I got to do with all this?"

Nicholas squatted beside the bed. "I think it was more against us than you, Eb. I am sorry it had to happen. Don't worry about your property, we'll take care of that. I just wish there was some way I could make this other right for you."

He stood up and turned to Mrs. Breed. "Mabel, I'll be sending a cart down here soon as I get home. We'll take Eb to the house where a doctor can see him. You and Louisa come along, too, for the time being."

"But, Mr. Dalton—" Mabel protested.

"Don't say a word, I won't hear of it. You're coming, and that is all there is to say."

"Thank you, Mr. Dalton. I appreciate it for the sake of my husband," she said, looking down at the dirt floor.

As Nicholas and Brad rode back to Scarborough House, Brad thought aloud, "I think the first thing I'll do is find out how widespread these attacks are. If this isn't an isolated incident, we should start publicizing the kind of activity that is going on up here under the silent approval of the governor. If this gets around, there is at least a reasonable chance to get a sympathetic man like John Young elected this time around. If we—"

Suddenly Brad's horse reared and screamed in fear. Stones of all sizes and shapes came hurtling out of the surrounding cover. Nicholas roared out an earsplitting cry as he, too, fought his horse.

"Sorry! Didn't see who it was, Mr. Dalton!" a voice called out. A man emerged from the woods, dressed in calico coveralls, his face painted like an Indian's, his eyes covered by a mask. "We heard about poor Eb and thought that young fellow with you was one of them come back to finish the old man off."

"You're likely to kill your own kind, you fool!" Nicholas shouted, not in the least mollified. "That's my son! Mind who you attack the next time!"

He kicked his horse's sides and tore off down the wooded path. Brad prodded his skittish horse to follow. They raced along for a quarter of a mile before Nicholas slowed his sweating, foam-flecked horse.

"Damned fools!" he muttered when Brad came up beside him.

"They didn't know who we were."

"And whose fault is that? If you'd been here all along, they'd have known you."

Brad remained silent. The ride back to the house seemed especially long, and Brad was happy to leave the horse at the stable yard for the groom to take care of. Old Nicholas, meanwhile, went to make arrangements for Ebenezer Breed and his family to be picked up and brought back to Scarborough House.

During the next days and weeks, old Nicholas rode like a cavalry courier across the fields, gathering information and carrying bits of news to anyone he met, completely ignoring the danger his activities invited. Often he was accompanied by young Nicholas. This annoyed Brad and frightened Annette, but neither of them could contain either the old man or the child. Neither of them saw any romance or excitement in fighting a war by Brad's method.

Brad sat at his desk, writing unending notes to the men he knew in New York City and in Albany. He kept a steady flow of information to the city and the newspapers about what was happening in the valley. Day and night, messengers arrived at Scarborough House, bringing responses and taking more of Brad's missives away with them.

During this time, Brad had little time to see Marcella. Although he was able to get into the city a few times, most of their communication was confined to writing. It became clear Brad was going to be gone for some time.

He urged Marcella to be patient, not to worry about him, and always to remember it was with her he wanted to be. He asked her to keep a scrapbook of all the newspaper clippings and articles concerning the progress of the war. Not only did he want them for his own satisfaction, but he imagined the nights he would spend with Marcella afterward, when they would look through the scrapbook as he told her in detail the part he had played.

He dreamed of sharing with Marcella all his new discoveries about his family and his home, and of somehow making her part of them. Once again, he felt completely a part of Scarborough House and a man of the Hudson Valley. His father did his best to reinforce that feeling.

One Sunday after a week in which there had been little war activity, Brad planned to go into New York. His father, as though he anticipated Brad's plans, took Brad aside and asked him to join him that Sunday afternoon.

"I had planned to go into the city, Dad. Do you mind?" he asked. He confessed to himself, however, that he was too tired to look forward to the ride.

"Of course not. How could I mind? If you have something more important to do, why, by all means—"

Brad laughed and shook his head. "If you must know, Dad, I'd really rather stay, anyway."

Sitting down to their Sunday meal at midday, Brad looked around at his family and felt a deep sense of pride and loyalty. His father was seated at the head of the table, obviously pleased that he had prevailed upon Brad to stay.

Young Nicholas, uncomfortable in his velvet suit, kept tugging at his oversized collar until he had covered it with fingermarks. The boy was quiet as usual, but his saucer eyes, gray and unfathomable, missed nothing. Shortly before the adults had finished their coffee, Nicholas slid down from his seat and disappeared from the dining room.

"Now where has he gone?" Annette asked. "That child has no manners at all, and I hold you responsible, Father Dalton."

The old man wiped his chin with his napkin. "You fret him too much. Let the boy alone, he's a fine lad. He needs the open air and freedom. How's a man to learn the treasure of the earth if he isn't allowed to roam it, to smell it, to love it."

"He'll be all right, Annette," Brad added. He smiled as his father began winding up to give Annette one of his lectures on the freedom of the spirit and the love of the land, the essence of patriotism and manhood, and anything else that came to him.

It didn't last as long or wax nearly so poetic as Brad had expected. Old Nicholas seemed anxious to be away. He didn't finish his cigar, another concession he had gained from Annette, who hated smoking in her home.

She sighed. "As usual, you defeat me by sheer length of breath." She nodded to both of them and excused herself from the room.

"Shall we be off?" Nicholas said to Brad, his eyes twinkling.

They went together to the stables where a cart was waiting for them.

"Why don't we take the carriage? It's more comfortable than this."

Nicholas frowned. "You're too soft all around. If you're coming, get in, and if you want cushions, go visiting with your wife."

Brad got into the cart, a small two-seater easily drawn by one horse. Nicholas barely touched the reins, for the horse seemed to know where they were headed.

In the back of the cart young Nicholas hid in the storage compartment under the seat. He shared it with several bags—feed bags—but he knew full well that feed was not what the bags contained. He lay silent, both frightened that he would be discovered and trembling with excitement. He could hear his father and grandfather laughing and talking as they rode, and he could tell by the jolting of the cart that they had turned off the main road.

Old Nicholas hopped down from the wagon, introducing Brad to the man whose legs Nick could see from his hiding place.

"What have you got?" the man asked.

"I've got one little beauty I'd like to try with the gloves. That suit you?"

"What are you betting?"

"What did you have in mind?"

"Ten?"

"Ten! A bit small. What do you say to fifty?"

They agreed on a bet of twenty dollars, and old Nicholas opened the top of the compartment. Nicholas cringed, pressing himself as far back as he could. Old Nicholas pulled out one of the sacks and walked off with the farmer. Sure that they were out of sight, Nick scrambled from his hiding place and hurried toward the barn he had seen the men enter. He slipped inside and hid behind some equipment stacked atop a wheelbarrow.

Both his grandfather and the farmer, who brought out a cock of about equal size, carefully drew padded gloves over their birds' natural spurs. Neither man wanted to use the gaffs, sharply pointed steel attachments fastened to the cock's legs. The gaffs usually caused a clean wound or a quick death and were preferred to the cock's natural spurs, which caused a dirty, tearing wound. In this case there was to be no battle to the death, only to defeat, so the gloves were used.

Old Nicholas and the farmer breasted the two cocks and then released them. They came together, beating one another with their wings and leaping into the air to attack with the glove-covered spur. The farmer's bird hammered into Nicholas's bird, knocking him to the ground. Fortunately, the cock was not hurt, merely off-balance, and recovered, battering away at the head of the other bird until it was stunned and staggering about.

Old Nicholas chuckled. "Will you call it my fight?"

"With gaffs, your bird would have been finished at that first fall," the man replied in ill humor.

"Will you call it? It was a gloved fight, not a gaffed one."

The man picked up his befuddled bird and put it back into the chicken run. While his grandfather removed the gloves from his own cock, Nicholas took the opportunity to run back to the cart and struggle back into his hiding place. He heard the men approach minutes later.

"I thank you for a pleasant afternoon," old Nicholas said happily. "I'll be seeing you next week, then."

"With gaffs, and for fifty," the man replied. "That cock of yours would have been gone if it weren't for the gloves."

"Well, sir, I'll tell you, without gloves this would not have been cockfighting. All a part of the game. It takes a good man to know which bird to fight the right fight. I'll look forward to our next meeting." Nicholas bit off the end of his cigar and spat it into the dust. "Good day," he added, and climbed into the cart.

They went to three other farms that afternoon. Twice the cocks fought with gloves and once with the gaffs. All three times old Nicholas was the victor. His grandson knew he would be in good humor for several days as a result.

Nicholas regretted having to keep his afternoon a secret, but keeping it a secret was better than risking a good, hard beating with Grandfather's greenwood switch. He lay in the back feeling each jog and rut in the road. In spite of the discomfort and the dust, he was getting sleepy, and had just let his eyelids droop shut when the cart stopped again.

"What are we stopping for? There is nothing here," he heard Brad say.

"You can come out now," old Nicholas said gruffly.

Brad looked to either side of the road. There was open field on both sides and no one in sight. "Who in hell are you talking to?"

"Your son. Come on out of there, Nick."

The boy lifted the leather top of the compartment and poked his head out. "How did you know I was there?"

"I saw you at the first stop. I damned near took your foot out instead of the bag with my bird in it."

"I didn't know you saw me. I am sorry."

"You should be. Haven't I told you no gentleman ever sneaks?"

"Yes, sir. You did tell me, but I didn't think about sneaking."

"No? What did you think about?"

Nicholas put his head down. His grandfather waited. "I am sorry, Grandfather."

"Lying is no better than sneaking."

"I wanted to know where you went, and I liked the fights. I like the gloved fights best."

"Well, now, that is better. Of course, you understand that there can be no more of this hiding and skulking about. One other thing you had better understand immediately, as long as you are striving to be a man—secrets must be kept from certain parties. Just a wise precaution."

"Mama is not to know?"

Old Nicholas chuckled. "What did I tell you, Bradford? He's a fine boy."

Old Nicholas scooted over to make space for his grandson. "Come up here in front with us. There is room between us."

The three returned home content with a day well spent, and there was not even a protest to be heard from Nick when his mother hurried him off to bed.

Brad kissed him good night and then went out to stand on the front porch of the house. The Down-with-Rent War was winding to a close. He could sense it. In any case, he had done his best. After the elections, win or lose, the war would end, and he would be leaving Scarborough House once more. Tonight he was very much aware that there was no way he could ever again mesh the two great loves of his life. Always he would be divided between Scarborough House and Marcella Paxton.

Brad began to look upon each succeeding day he stayed at Scarborough as something to be treasured. Reports still came in of herds being slaughtered, militiamen being attacked, and an occasional clash between a group of farmers and manor men, and he used these events to explain to Marcella why he needed to remain at Scarborough until the election took place.

John Young, a relative unknown, did win the election. It had seemed an impossibility. Many had placed their hopes on him, but few had really believed he had a chance of winning. On the day after the election, Scarborough House was swarming with men coming to thank Brad and his father for what they had done to secure Governor Young's victory.

"Well, it's all come straight at last, Bradford," old Nicholas said when the last man had finally left. "Ebenezer told me Governor Wright freed Dr. Broughton and the other Calico Indians right before he lost."

"He had nothing to lose. Governor Young would have done it, anyway. Now all we need to do is make sure the laws are changed."

"There is no question that they will be, is there?"

"I don't think so. It may take a little time. I imagine the state constitution will have to be changed, but there is no doubt it will be."

"Then we should toast that!" He lifted his glass toward Brad. "That, and to my son."

Brad spent a full day summoning the courage to tell his father he was returning to the city. After he had told him, he hurried up the stairs and packed his bags. He said terse good-byes to all the members of the household. Most of them begged him to come home again soon. Annette looked up at him for no more than a second.

"I didn't think you would be here much longer. I have been expecting this."

He said nothing to her. There was nothing to say. Regarding Annette, he no longer fooled himself. She had probably never cared for him. She had wanted to be married. She had wanted a son. She had never wanted him. If anything, their relationship had embarrassed her. Oddly enough, it had been this realization that had sent him back to her bed. It was one thing for him to have fallen in love with another woman, but quite another for his wife to prefer having no one to having him.

At first he had berated her, accusing her of having a lover. Anyone listening would have concluded that Brad, not Annette, was the wronged party. She had laughed at him in her cool, infuriating way and continued to work on her tapestry. One night he took her, violently, and then he knew he never wanted to touch her again, and he hadn't.

In Brad's mind, Annette had nothing whatever to do with Scarborough or with him. She was the one person he would be glad to leave. It was his father, and particularly his son, who had held him there. He put off saying good-bye to Nicholas until last.

Now that he was ready to leave, the child was nowhere to be found. He looked through the house and in all the gardens near to the house. He went to the stables last, for if Nicholas was riding his horse, Brad would never find him and would not be able to say good-bye. Night Wind was still in his stall, but none of the men working in the stable had seen Nicholas.

"Bring the carriage around to the front," Brad said sadly.

He walked slowly across the stable yard toward the front of the house, still hoping to find his son. Suddenly he felt Nicholas's small hand in his own. The boy tugged, and Brad followed him to the giant weeping beech at the side of the house.

Nick had made a fort inside, out of the twenty-foot circle formed by the drooping branches. This was Nick's favorite tree. "The leaves are so big, no one in the whole world can ever tell I am here if I don't want them to know. You won't tell anyone, will you, Papa?"

"You mean your mother?"

"Well, yes. She doesn't ever think to look here."

"I won't tell anyone, not even Grandpa."

"Oh, he knows. Grandpa knows everything. Sometimes he hides in here with me."

Brad had settled down cross-legged on the ground facing Nicholas. "You have fun with Grandpa."

"We do lots of things. I am not old enough to do some things, but he says I am growing very fast."

"Would you like it if you and I did some of those things together?"

"Oh, yes! Are you going to stay here?"

"No, but I'll come more often, and I would like to take you to the city with me sometimes. There are all kinds of things to do there."

Nick lost his look of interest. "I don't think Mama would let me go to the city. She doesn't let me go anyplace unless she takes me."

"I think we could talk your mother into it." Brad got up and brushed off his pants. "I have to be leaving now, Nick. Be a good boy while I'm gone, won't you? Think up some things you would like for us to do together."

"Why are you going? I don't want you to go."

Brad put his arms around him. "I won't be gone for long," he whispered. "Would you like to race to my carriage?"

Nicholas nodded and raced out from under the tree. Brad trotted along behind him. Again he wished he weren't leaving.

Chapter Fourteen

Marcella was quick to sense the difference in Brad when he returned. There was a wistfulness, a discontent about him that he tried to hide but could not.

The city now seemed cluttered and frantic. He had enjoyed the simpler, more active life in the country. No matter what attractions the world of business had for him, there was a part of him that responded to Scarborough as to nothing else.

Marcella remained silent as long as she could.

"Are you unhappy here, Brad?" she finally asked him one evening as he sat staring into the fire.

He looked up abruptly and grinned. "I am very happy. What made you ask?"

"You are not here, Brad. Your mind is far away. Sometimes I think you didn't really want to come back here at all."

"I was thinking about Nicholas. I wish you knew him."

"So do I, but wishing it won't help. You're not going back again? Not this soon."

"He wants me to take him ice-skating this winter when the pond freezes over. Actually he was all for skating across the Hudson, but he finally agreed on the pond."

"You aren't listening to me! You don't even know I am here. Don't you care?"

Brad saw the tears in her eyes. "I do care. I would not have come back if it were not for you, Marcella. I love you with all my heart."

"So you say! But really I don't mean any more to you than that monstrous old house!"

"I was not talking about the house. I was talking about my son," he said reasonably.

"Not really. You wouldn't pay any attention to him if he lived in the city. It is that awful place. It casts a spell on you!"

"And so do you. Weave your spells, Marcella, for Scarborough is far away. I am here, where I want to be."

For a time Marcella stopped talking about Scarborough House altogether. Brad's last stay there had stirred something in him that Marcella feared and could not seem to stop. He thought constantly of Nicholas. He talked about his father, about events that happened when he lived there. And he began to insist that Marcella get to know Nicholas. If he could bring Nicholas and Marcella together, he might somehow be able to put the two halves of his life back together.

Marcella not only did not believe it was possible, she didn't want it. While Brad fought to bring them together, Marcella tried her best to put it off. She didn't want Brad to bring Scarborough into their life at the brownstone. She also worried about the tales Nicholas, now eight years old, was likely to take back to his mother. Marcella was certain she could get along well with Nicholas, she simply did not want to. Brad was certain everything would be much better if she did. Neither considered Nicholas.

"I want you to know him, Marcy."

"And I think you are wrong, Brad. He isn't going to understand, whether he likes me or not." She began to pace around the room. "You know I want nothing in the world more than to share in every part of your life, Brad. But this time I am sure it won't work. He is both too old and too young to be brought into our lives. We have simply waited too long—or not long enough. Maybe when he is older he will understand."

"My dear one, you have all the facts right, but the wrong conclusion. He *is* too young to understand. He will learn to love you now, and then when he goes through that abominable critical stage all children seem to come into, his relationship with you will be established."

Marcella stopped her pacing and looked at him. "Brad, might there not be a time when—when we are truly together? When Nicholas might have more than simply liking me as a reason for being close to me?"

Both of them knew Marcella referred to marriage. She had done it often before. He didn't answer her for a long time.

"Why do you press this? It is kind to neither of us, and you know what I must say will hurt you, and it hurts me to say it."

She looked away. "I don't know why. I shouldn't have brought it up." She sighed deeply, then brightened. "Let's make plans for Nicholas's visit. We must make it a grand day for him. I shall have Myrtle bake the most delectable cakes, and then we shall play games. What might he like?"

"I am not sure, but if the pond in the park were to freeze, Nicholas loves to skate."

"I'll have skates here for him. Anytime he wants to visit, he can use them! Only for here. He'll like that, won't he, Brad?"

By the end of that week, it was cold and snowing. Marcella was up far too early on Sunday, waiting for Brad to return with his son from his overnight trip to Scarborough House. When the two of them appeared, covered with snow, on her front stoop, she opened the door before they had had a chance to ring. Her eyes rested first on Brad, then on the small boy holding tightly to Brad's hand.

Nicholas's face still bore a trace of his summer tan. His long black eyelashes shadowed eyes like Brad's, but darker. His hair, too, made her think of Brad's, Brad's when he was first awakening—dark and curling far too much to be well-groomed. He looked like a miniature David, brave and willing to slay the Goliath before him.

Brad gave the boy's captive hand a rough shake. "Nick, mind your manners. Greet Miss Paxton."

Nick put his head down, muttering into the collar of his coat.

"Won't you come in, Nicholas?" Marcella said cheerfully. "I am so pleased to meet you. Your father has told me what a fine boy you are. Come along."

Myrtle hurried from the back of the house, scolding Marcella as she came. "You won't never learn that I'm supposed to answer the door!" She took Brad's coat and Nicholas's from them. "Welcome home, sir."

Marcella frowned at her for using the word "home" and glanced apprehensively at Nicholas. The boy was staring at Myrtle but said nothing.

Marcella extended her hand to Nicholas. Very slowly he looked from Myrtle to Marcella, and then he reached up and removed his cap from his head, engaging his free hand. Brad gave his other hand a tug, propelling him into the parlor.

"I don't much like to hold hands with people I don't know well, either," Marcella said, pulling one of the more comfortable chairs closer to the sofa.

Brad, as he always did, settled comfortably on the sofa. Marcella, thinking Nicholas would want to sit beside his father, sat in the chair she had moved close to the sofa. She watched as the boy chose to sit, conspicuous and uncomfortable, on the only straight-backed chair in the room, some distance from Marcella and Brad.

"Wouldn't you care to sit over here next to your father, Nicholas? It is closer to us and much more comfortable."

"No, thank you."

Marcella shot a look at Brad. "Well, then, Nicholas, your father tells me you are quite a horseman. Tell me about your pony."

Nicholas made a face. "I don't ride a pony. I ride a horse."

"Oh, I see! And here I thought you far too young. Of course, I realize my mistake now. You are very nearly a man, aren't you?"

"In some respects. My grandfather tells me I have a ways to go in others," he said and immediately looked away.

"How would you like something to eat, Nicholas? Are you hungry after your trip? I am hungry and haven't even had a trip from the country."

"Well, I would certainly like something," Brad said, leaning forward and smiling at Nicholas, "especially after smelling the delightful odors that are coming from Myrtle's kitchen."

"I don't care for anything, thank you."

Marcella worked to make her voice light. "Don't be too hasty, Nicholas. I'll wager Myrtle has made something very special for us. She usually does, you know. When she knows that I am expecting visitors, she is always full of surprise goodies from her oven."

The disapproving little face stared at her mercilessly. "I am not hungry."

Marcella gave the cord a severe pull, and moments later Myrtle appeared, tray in hand. Nicholas paid no attention to the beautifully decorated petit fours. His eyes remained on Marcella.

Brad cleared his throat. "It is not polite to stare, Nick, even if the lady happens to be a very pretty one."

"My mother is prettier."

"Nicholas!"

"It is all right, Brad. He meant nothing by it. He should be loyal to his mother. Isn't that right, Nicholas? And anyway, I agree with you, your mother is a very beautiful lady, and the most beautiful in the world for you."

"Yes. And Father thinks so, too, don't you, Papa?"

Brad looked embarrassed. "There are many beautiful women in the world, Nick," he said finally, "as you will discover when you grow older. I would be hard pressed to say which of all of them was absolutely the most beautiful."

"I don't think it is hard to decide at all," Nicholas said in a steady voice.

Brad shoved one of the petit fours into Nicholas's hand. "Here, have a cake and stop talking about things you know nothing about."

Nicholas looked at him defiantly and replaced the cake on the tray. "No, thank you. I don't care for one. My mother says it is bad for my health to eat sweets between meals."

"Now that's something coming from you!" Brad burst out. "Is that Nicholas Dalton I hear talking? The boy who hides away in the compartment of the cart and rides with the Calico Indians? Since when have you been one to follow any rule, let alone that one?"

"Since today," Nicholas replied, unruffled. He got up from his chair and began to walk around the room, looking at the paintings and touching the small figurines and ornaments. He stopped in front of a small ship model. He held it up to the light and then turned to his father. "Is this the model of the *Clermont* that belongs in your study at home?"

"Yes."

"Why is it here?"

"Miss Paxton rode on that steamer and mentioned it. I thought she might enjoy the model."

"Grandfather and I thought it had been lost. We were looking for it. I shall return it to the study when I go home. It belongs at Scarborough House with the other ones." He began to put the small ship into his pocket.

"Put the ship back on the table, Nicholas. It belongs to me, and I shall do with it as I please."

"But it will be mine! You said—"

"Nicholas. Do as I say, and not another word from you!"

"Brad, please. Let him take it if he wants. I have enjoyed it long enough. Let's all play a game and forget about the ship. What sort of games do you like, Nicholas? Help me think of one that would be fun for all of us."

"I want to go home now."

"But you have just come. Please be a good boy. Come play a game. I only want to be your friend. We can have fun together if you will try a little. We were going to keep it for a surprise for you, but perhaps now is the time for it. Wait just a moment." Marcella disappeared, returning shortly with a gaily wrapped package. "This is something special for you, Nicholas," she said, handing it to the boy. "You may open it now."

Nicholas was about to refuse the package when Brad said, "Open it."

Nicholas took one look at his father's face, swallowed, and said in a near-whisper, "Thank you, Miss Paxton." He tore off the wrapping and opened the box.

"Do you like them?" Marcella beamed at him. The man assured me that these were the finest skates any boy could have."

"They are very nice," Nicholas answered, head down.

"Well, then, I shall tell you the rest of the surprise. We are all going to the park this evening to skate. There will be torches and many children. We will have a grand time. We'll go right after we have had supper. How does that sound to you, Nicholas?"

"I don't want to go to the park," he said in a low voice. "I would like to go home."

Marcella sighed. "Perhaps some other time, Nicholas. If you don't want to do that, why don't you come along with me to see about dinner. We will eat, and then you can leave."

Brad stood up. "Never mind, Marcella. I don't want you begging the boy. He shall get what he asks for. I will take him home, and once we get there, he shall be taught some manners. What you need, Nick, is a good firm hand —across the bottom."

"Brad, please don't, for my sake. Don't make things worse by punishing him."

"Do you hear that, Nicholas? She doesn't want you punished for your atrocious behavior. Isn't it too bad that you could not have been as nice to her as she wishes to be to you?"

Nicholas's huge eyes welled up with tears as he looked from one of them to the other. "I want to go home," he repeated in a small, choked voice. "I want to see my mother."

"Put the skates down and go see to the coats. Miss Paxton may give them to a poor child or one who deserves such a gift."

After Nicholas had got the coats, Brad sent him out to wait in the carriage. He stood in the hall with Marcella, watching Nicholas climb into the carriage.

He kissed Marcella on the forehead. "I'm sorry," he said. "She spoils him."

"I would, too, if he were mine. He is a beautiful boy, and I am afraid we were wrong about him. He may be too young to understand completely, but somehow or other the child knows about us and is defending his mother in the only way he knows, and that is by refusing my friendship. Don't punish him, Brad. Somehow what he has done is noble, I think. He makes me feel ashamed."

"You don't really mean that, do you?" he said, touching her face gently. "You're not ashamed of what we have?"

"Yes, for the time being, I am ashamed. But don't worry, Brad, it won't last. I am not noble. I wouldn't have been able to refuse the cakes and the skates. I am not like Nicholas, I am not good enough for my shame to last. As soon as you have gone, and I no longer see Nicholas's accusing eyes before me, I will be my usual self, wanting you, and needing you, and taking what I can have of you."

BOOK TWO

Chapter Fifteen

Marcella's brownstone became better-known generally—and notorious in some quarters—as the years passed. The face of the city changed, and Brad and Marcella held to each other, their relationship sometimes stormy, sometimes serene.

Brad's father had died in 1850, and Marcella's mother was now a complete invalid. Young Nicholas had never forgiven Brad for not being at Scarborough House when old Nicholas died, nor had Hilary yet forgiven her daughter sins now decades old.

It was both a sad time and a time of growing together for Brad and Marcella. What they could find in no others, they found in one another. As Brad become more successful, and Marcella came to accept the wealth and power that emanated from her life with him, they became as much business partners as they were lovers. He had put many assets in her name, and while she never thought of them as hers, she enjoyed the status and income such ownership provided.

Brad's fascination with political power, which had begun with his involvement in the Down-with-Rent War of the 1840s, had grown over the years. For a short time after the war ended, he had been the toast not only of the Hudson Valley but also of the city. All too soon, however, other events had captured the attention of New York political circles, and Brad, to his deep chagrin, had found himself on the periphery again.

Unwilling to give up his political ambitions altogether, he concentrated his efforts while in residence with Marcella on establishing ties with the major financial wizards of the city, men who he knew were the real powers behind the politicians. Those in the valley around Scarborough House, meanwhile, had not forgotten so easily what Brad had contributed to their cause, and it was here that he saw new opportunities for building a political base.

More and more often—and for longer periods of time—Brad traveled north out of the city, meeting with potential allies, entertaining visiting upstate politicians, offering to do what he could for this individual or that one in Albany. All debts, he knew, could and would someday be collected.

For all the plans and stories Brad shared with Marcella, she felt increasingly dispensable in Brad's life. Whenever his travels took him out of the city, she could not shake loose the suspicion—and the accompanying feeling of helplessness—that slowly but surely she was losing him. And what she was losing, Annette and all that she represented to Brad must be gaining.

Then, during the summer of 1860, Annette fell ill, and Brad was called back to Scarborough House. Marcella waited impatiently for his return. A month passed with no word from him. She thought of a dozen reasons to remain silent, not to write, but always it came back to the same thought—out of sight, out of mind. She had lived too many years with Brad to let that happen.

The loyalty she did not possess because of a legal document, she felt she had a right to expect because of time. In many ways, she thought, she had always been more his wife than Annette. Now all she faced was loneliness, while Annette had his attentions and his name, his son and his family home.

I am middle-aged, thought Marcella. I deserve something for what I have given. I am the only one who has ever really needed him. Annette is secure, and Nicholas is nearly grown now.

She wrote Brad a letter and sent it by personal messenger, giving the man strict instructions to deliver it into the hands of Mr. Dalton and none other. "Make it clear that this is a business matter that requires his personal and immediate attention."

The note was typical of Marcella. It said simply: "Brad, where are you? I love you. I need you." She didn't sign it, nor did she tell him that her mother had finally died of her last stroke two days after Brad had left for his most recent visit to Scarborough House.

The two days she waited for a response from Brad were brightened only by a visit with Charlotte, who was Marcella's sole link with her sister Jo in Ohio.

That afternoon, as they sat over coffee and crullers, Charlotte fussed about whatever problems were currently besetting her. Marcella, a little weary of hearing her sister's usual litany, asked whether Charlotte had heard anything from Ohio.

"Well," Charlotte began, "Jo did write, as you'd expect, when Mother died—"

"How is Jo?" Marcella interrupted. "Is she happy?"

"As happy as anyone can be who breeds like a rabbit. I mean, I am not prejudiced, but my God, those Catholics take everything so seriously! Jo has six children—and no end to them in sight!"

"I think of her mostly as a little girl with red ringlets around her face. And now—such a large family."

"Mind you, I don't hear from her often. But Leona Dowell—you remember Leona?"

"I remember her—a little stick of a thing with a prune face."

"She wouldn't thank you for that, but yes. Anyway, Cousin Leona also lives in Columbus. She claims Terrance is a very well respected man there. Very well thought of, I gather, but said to be a bit free with his money."

"How so?"

"It seems he has a great deal of sympathy for his countrymen wiped out by the Potato Famine, and as fast as he can, he raises money and brings them to this country, sets them up, goes so far as to provide farmland for them. All very admirable, but I do hope he has had the good sense to provide for his own family in case something should happen."

"I am sure he has. Jo would see to it, I should think."

"I don't know. Leona claims Jo has changed completely. You know what a proper little thing she was when she was small. Leona says she is quite gay, quick with a joke and laughing. Not like our Jo at all."

She put down her cup and looked quickly at Marcella. "But then, how far can you trust Leona's opinion? She doesn't approve of the O'Connors. I take it they are too boisterous for her taste." Charlotte pursed her lips, trying to look as severe as Leona Dowell. She and Marcella laughed until tears ran down their cheeks thinking of Cousin Leona.

Marcella returned to the brownstone in much better spirits than she had left it. Unfortunately, her good humor was short-lived.

The next day the messenger returned from Scarborough, bearing her own note to Brad.

"I gave it to Mr. Dalton, just like you said, but he said he was the wrong Mr. Dalton. He wouldn't take it from me, ma'am. I tried to tell him what you said."

"What was his name? Was it Nicholas?"

"Yes, ma'am, that's the name. A young fellow—big, strapping lad."

"What did he say? He must have said something else other than his name. Did he give any reason for not giving this message to his father?"

"He said the other one went on a trip with some friends to the Catskills. Said he'd most likely be back first of this coming week."

"Why didn't you tell me this in the first place?"

"That young feller told me not to tell you unless you asked."

"The next time I pay you, I expect you to tell me everything whether I ask or not," she said angrily.

When Brad appeared at her door nearly ten days later, there was nothing to indicate that his feelings for her had changed for the worse. In fact, he was most attentive and excited. Marcella feared she saw in his loving manner what she wanted to see, and not the truth.

"Why didn't you tell me you were going to the Catskills?" she asked before he had had time to sit down in the parlor.

"So you heard! I might have known I couldn't keep it a secret," he said happily. "Come and sit beside me and let me tell you how much I have missed being here with you. And then, if you do not already have all the details, I shall tell you all about my trip."

"I want to know about those friends of yours. Who were they? Or more to the point, who was she?"

"*She?*" he roared, slapping his knee. "She! Marcella, you are priceless. After all these years you can still ask a question like that. My love, you are actually having a fit of adolescent jealousy! 'She' was about half a dozen men and their wives."

"No one else? Not another woman who just happened to be along with the others, with no husband to accompany her?"

For a moment he didn't reply. Intently he began to brush some mud that had caked on the hem of his trouser leg. "This is beneath you, Marcella."

"There was, wasn't there? There was a woman. I knew it as soon as I got back my note unread and unanswered."

"Oh, for the love of God, stop dramatizing everything! There was no woman, not in the sense you mean."

"How am I to believe that? After all the time you have been gone, and not a word from you, how am I to believe you?"

"By trusting me when I tell you there was no one. By looking around you and seeing that I keep this house filled with the things that mean the most to me, things I love and you love—" He stopped short and dropped his hands to his sides. "How else can I tell you if you don't choose to believe?"

"What if I asked you to do something that might not be easy for you to do? Something that meant a great deal to you, and to me. Would you do as I asked, Brad, no matter what it was?"

He laughed uncertainly. "Don't I always?"

"Not always. We aren't married and never shall be. You wouldn't do that for me."

"You know that is not entirely by choice. I would if I thought I could."

"But you haven't. I am and always have been your mistress, and I will never be anything else to you."

"What are you getting at, Marcella?"

"What I want is a marriage of sorts. I can't have a real one, so I want second-best, a marriage of intent."

"What in the hell is a marriage of intent? What is it you want me to give you?"

"Something important to you."

"Such as?"

"Such as Nicholas," Marcella said, looking him straight in the eye. "Would you allow me to be responsible for him?"

"Nicholas?" Brad said, amazed. "What would you do with Nicholas?"

"Nothing. I don't want him. I just wanted to know if you thought I was good enough to raise him."

Brad's relief showed. "He's yours, my love, all six feet of him. Take him if you can catch him."

Marcella laughed. "He runs far too fast for me now, and he is a bit old to mother, so I will abandon that idea." Suddenly she was serious again. "Let's talk about the other great treasure of your life."

"Will you come to the point! What *are* you talking about?" He glared at her impatiently. "I don't know what has gotten into you."

"I want Scarborough House, Brad. Put it in my name. Let me be its guardian until it is time for Nicholas to take ownership. Do that, and we will be married for all intent. I know what that house means to you and your son."

"That house belongs to Nicholas. What would I tell him? Scarborough means more to him than anything else, more than it does to me. Why do you want it? What good is it to you?"

"It isn't really the house I want, Brad," Marcella said evenly. "It is the security it represents. I don't want to live in it. I don't even want to see it."

She paused and then hurried on. "Don't you see, Brad, it would be the same as a troth between us, a substitute for the bond of marriage we'll never have. Try to see what I mean. In trusting me with Scarborough, you give me a duty to protect it for your son. I want that, Brad. It gives me a part of your life I can never really have."

She looked down at her hands. "Sometimes when I . . . I look in the mirror and see the image there, and see what you see when you look at me, I wonder who that woman is. The Marcella I see isn't the girl I was when you met me, or the one I feel living inside of me. The one reflected in the mirror is getting old. I see lines on her face, wrinkles around her eyes. I don't want to be left alone and old, Brad. All my life is tied to you, and we both know that your life is no longer tied up in mine, not the way it used to be. Please try to understand."

Brad stopped his nervous pacing. "But why Scarborough? What has it to do with anything? You've never mentioned it before."

"I don't talk about your warehouses, or farms, or the miles of railroad track or any of the other things you have in my name either, and yet you trust me with those. What is the difference? Why will you trust me with those and not with Scarborough?"

"It isn't a matter of trust. I don't understand you . . . Why are you doing this?"

"You put those things in my name because it was to your advantage. You had nothing to lose. It wasn't a matter of trust, Brad, it was convenience. Now I want something to my advantage. Put my name on one more piece of property—one that does require your faith in me. Is that any more to ask than what you have asked of me over the years?"

"God, Marcella. Don't talk like that!" Brad slumped into a chair. "I don't know what to say to you. I don't understand any of this. Why?"

"I don't know, Brad. I guess you had never left me alone for this long before. Or maybe it is just that this time I realized what a fragile hold I have on you. At any time you could walk out the door of my house and never return. I have nothing you value except myself, and now I am not quite the self I once was. I have heard all manner of rumors—"

"Marcella," Brad interrupted, "there are always vicious people. That has nothing to do with you and me."

"But it does. Why did you just go off? Why didn't you let me know? Always we talked about things like that. How old was the woman last week, Brad?"

"How should I know? I wasn't with any woman, as you mean it."

"How old?" Marcella persisted.

"Twenty or so. She was—"

"That must mean eighteen or nineteen. She was young and pretty, no doubt, and madly in love with you. And you did enjoy yourself, didn't you?"

"You seem to be telling this story. You tell me, did I enjoy myself?"

Marcella ignored the sarcasm. "That is why I want Scarborough House. Annette has her security in the wedding band she wears. You will not leave your wife, I accept that now. But I also accept that I have nothing to keep you loyal to me. Scarborough will give me that security."

Brad shook his head slowly. "You have made both of us seem cheap."

"I am sorry for that, but remember what I come from. I am Five Points. You knew that before we began to live together. I made sure you did. I can't help it that it is cheap to tell you the truth as I see it, or to be frightened of being alone, or of losing you, or to be jealous of women who have your company when I don't. I have asked you for little in the past, Brad, but this is something I want. I need it."

"And if I refuse?"

"Then I shall sell all that is in my name and move away. Perhaps I'll go to Ohio and find Jo. Maybe after all this time she can forgive me. I gave her up for you, you know. She has never spoken to me, and I bore that because I loved you more."

He looked at her with disgust. "You can't sell those properties. You don't own them. This whole thing is no better than blackmail. It makes me feel dirty. Tonight *you* make me feel dirty."

Marcella fought the urge to cry. "That's too bad. But whatever you say, I do own those properties legally, and I can sell them. I have checked."

"You could go a long way toward ruining me if you did that."

"And you will destroy me—us—if you don't give me something to cling to, Brad, something I can believe in."

"That's pure nonsense."

"It isn't nonsense!" Marcella shouted. "Don't you see? I am losing you already. You didn't laugh me out of this, you didn't do anything, and above all you didn't give it to me. Brad, you would never have let something like this evening happen before!"

"Damn it! You say you want it, and now you are crying because I let you ask me for it. What the hell do you expect of me?"

"I'm not crying! And I do want the house. I need it!"

He didn't say anything.

"Will you put it in my name, Brad?" she whispered to his back.

His voice was low and very deliberate. "I'll consider it. But before I do anything, I want something from you as well. You say you need it. I won't pretend to understand. But if Scarborough should ever be put in your name, it would be done with the full understanding that the house belongs to Nicholas and to his sons after him. I want that in writing, Marcella, and I also want it in writing that you will not sell those other properties without my consultation and agreement."

"All right, Brad. If that is the way you want it, then I will give you that. Just as soon as I have it in writing that Scarborough is mine."

"I want your word now! Before I do anything about Scarborough."

"There certainly isn't much trust left between us, is there, Brad? Maybe there never was any to start with. Perhaps we have always been fooling ourselves."

"There was," he said. "There was for me—until today."

"Really? Then why did I know everything was over for us as soon as I heard you were in the Catskills? How could you have gone off with someone else and still claim to have the same feeling for me you have always had?"

"Perhaps if you had listened to me when I first came into the house, you would have understood. But you had already judged me guilty of everything your imagination dreamt up for you."

Marcella looked at the floor.

"I was in the Catskills," Brad continued, "with several men and their wives for a meeting. They had heard, among other things, about my part in the organization of the campaign to aid the antirenters years ago, and they thought I might make a good political possibility. The goal you and I had worked for so long was finally going to happen.

"I couldn't get back here right away, and I didn't want to tell you news like that in a curt, formal letter. I wanted to tell you myself, to let you share in it completely. I could only do that by waiting until I could get back here."

He walked over and stood before Marcella. "The young lady you mentioned was the daughter of my host. She is twenty, by the way, not eighteen or nineteen. And I did wine her and dine her. I spent as much time as I could with her and all of her family. She will no doubt marry the young man she chattered about incessantly before the year is out."

Marcella began to weep silently, shaking her head back and forth.

"And before your jealousy conjures up any more ghosts, I'll tell you I was charmed by her freshness, her innocence, her trust in me—and by the sweet way she expected me and all men to be honorable with her. I thought of her romantically, too. Many times. I thought of her with my son. I thought of how he would feel for her, or someone like her, what I had felt for you. And that, Marcella, was my betrayal to you." Brad ran his hand through his hair and walked over to the window. The silence in the room was broken only by Marcella's quiet sobs.

"Oh, Brad!" she stammered, "I am so sorry. I didn't know. Forgive me. Please, I am sorry."

"So am I," he said. He picked up his coat and hat and walked to the door leading to the front hall.

"Brad?" she cried. "Brad! Please say you forgive me. You can, can't you? Can't you understand what I thought? If only you had told me, I would have understood. Please tell me it is all right."

"Good night, Marcella."

"Brad, kiss me good-bye. Don't leave me like this. Please! It is so hard to be wrong. Stay with me! Brad—"

He kissed her cheek, and she clung to him. "Marcella . . . Marcella, let me go. I've got to leave. I can't think, and damn it, I can't stay. Not now. Not tonight.

Just let me go." He pulled free of her and swung the door open. She watched him run down the front steps and out into the street.

The next weeks were lonely ones for Marcella. Brad came and went, but he was like a visitor. The easy camaraderie, the openness, was gone. Scarborough stood between them like an invisible wall.

Then one day he didn't come at all. Late that afternoon a messenger came to the door and handed Marcella a thick envelope containing the deed, abstract, and history of Scarborough House. A note from Brad explained that he had decided to give it to her, not because he understood her feelings but because it was apparently important to her and that was enough for him to want her to have it. He asked that she give him time and that she not worry about him.

Marcella trembled as she sat down. He loved her enough to trust her with something this precious to him! She answered his letter immediately, telling him how happy she was and reminding him that he had not made out the paper for her to sign, promising that Nicholas would inherit the house at Brad'd death.

Days turned into weeks, and still Brad stayed away. In the beginning she thought nothing of it. He had asked for her patience and time for himself. Then Marcella began to hear stories about him. Gossips mixed fact with fiction. She heard about every woman he was supposed to be interested in, every smile he bestowed on any female.

She began to send him messages with greater frequency. Some he answered and some he ignored, but those that he did answer were not at all reassuring. There was in them a restraint, a wariness, that she had never known in Brad before. Slowly, her happiness turned to sorrow and remorse, then to self-pity, and finally to boredom, resentment, and restlessness.

Chapter Sixteen

When the War Between the States had begun, Charlotte's husband Martin Henderson had joined up immediately, believing wholeheartedly that he was battling for the right. His son, Martin, Jr., shared no such view and had steadfastly refused to volunteer. Not only did he think his father a fool, but in his private moments he believed that the South had a cause worth fighting for and that it had a perfect right to secede if it wished. As far as Martin, Jr. could see, the Southern way of life held a great deal more appeal than that of the North.

During the first years of the war, Charlotte's main concern had been to prevent a war between father and son. Then, in the last month of 1862, her husband was wounded. He died in one of the field hospitals, not of the musket ball, but of putrefaction of the relatively minor wound.

"Your father died a brave and honorable man," Charlotte said as she told her son of his father's death."

"He died a fool in a fool's cause," her son snapped. "Eulogize him if it makes you feel better, Mother, but the facts won't be altered."

Martin's position changed from one day to the next. Sometimes he spouted the words of Horatio Seymour, an advocate of compromise to avoid secession, and when that was no longer a possibility, he quoted an advocate of conciliation—peace at any cost. At other times Martin quoted Samuel Morse and Samuel Tilden, who declared that the South had a perfect right to do as it pleased. Martin had good company for his views, and he made use of all of them.

Already New York City was known as a center of Copperhead conspiracy, and it was to become worse. Some radicals even suggested that the city of New York, with its powerful port and business world, ought to secede and become a sovereign city. Charlotte's concern for her son increased. She had no idea how her son's hostility toward the War between the States might manifest itself.

"Tell me this, Mother," he sneered one evening. "Just how many blacks has Mr. Lincoln's Emancipation Proclamation freed? Tell me, Mother, should I go and die for something that isn't going to happen?"

"But, Martin, it all takes time! Mr. Lincoln only signed the Proclamation in January. One month, dear, is far too soon to judge."

He laughed. "A month is long enough." He walked slowly over to the serving cart and poured himself another tumbler of bourbon.

"You drink too much, dear."

"A month is enough," he repeated. "A month is too long, because Mr. Lincoln's Proclamation is just so much talk. It will never happen unless he brings out the troops and forces it to happen. No one gives a damn about the slaves. We care about slavery, the human condition—but slaves? Hah!" He smiled bitterly. "We care about commerce, railroads, raw materials, politics! We care about profits! North and South alike. Slaves? Soon we will all be slaves. There is going to be a conscription, Mother. Everyone says so. New York, by God, will be fighting it, and so will I. That's the army I will enter. I will fight only for my right not to fight."

Martin was right. March, 1863, brought the Enrollment and Conscription Act. The army offered a bounty to men who reenlisted for three more years. The term of enlistment was an admission that no one maintained the illusion that this would be a short war. It was going to go on and cost more than anyone had anticipated.

Horatio Seymour was reelected governor, mostly on the strength of his strong feelings about the Enrollment Act. Many of his speeches bordered on treason, and they stirred up large segments of the New York population to a fever pitch. On the Fourth of July, 1863, Seymour was back in the city, speaking out against the draft. The mood of the people was hostile and restless.

On Saturday, July 1, 1863, a hot, sultry day, the first names were taken from a lottery drum. The people who had crowded into the conscription office to hear the provost marshall call out the names seemed to take it all in good humor.

But on Sunday the day when the poor crowded into the bars and workingmen indulged in equal parts of spirits and talk, the people's mood changed.

The streets were filled with disgruntled men and women, and it seemed that that Sunday no one was to be pleased or satisfied. Governor Seymour, once again in the city to inspect the New York harbor fortifications, declared them inadequate and incapable of repelling any foray by the seaborne Confederate Commerce Raiders. He lodged his complaint and then left the city to take his vacation.

The complaints lodged by the people of the city, however, fell on deaf ears.

"It is a rich man's war!"

"A poor man's fight!"

It was true. Three hundred dollars could buy any man a substitute if his name were chosen in the lottery. Who had the three hundred dollars but the rich? Who needed it so badly that they would go to war to get it but the poor? The "dollar"—or East—Side of Manhattan became a symbol of all that the poor or the "shilling" West Side hated.

The cloying heat added to their resentment. As the day wore on, the sweat made their shirts stick to their backs; whiskey penetrated their minds and dissolved inhibitions. Hatred of the rich man's war became hatred of the authority that could force them to fight for a cause they neither understood nor believed in, and blistering hatred of the blacks, who, after all was said and done, were at the bottom of everything.

Sunday evening a report came into police headquarters that a down-and-out lawyer from Virginia was making an inflammatory anti-draft and anti-Negro speech to a crowd of people along Allen Street. No action was taken on the report. John Andrews was known to the police of the city. He had been in trouble before he came to the city in 1859, but he was known mostly for consorting with thieves and prostitutes.

Other reports came in, mostly of Negroes being beaten up in the Five Points areas. No one paid much attention; in Five Points, that was their way of life. As long as they kept it there, so much the better. An unusual number of fires was reported along the bottom of Carmine Street. Again no action was taken.

The city went to sleep in the heat; in the morning the second day of the draft lottery would begin.

Monday morning was just as hot as Sunday had been. The sky was overcast, and the air seemed as heavy and irritating as a heavy woolen blanket.

Just after sunrise people began to gather, moving out of the West Side, crossing Broadway and clustering along Eighth and Ninth avenues.

As usual, Charlotte had gone to her father's house first thing Monday morning to tend to the week's shopping list. From the moment she had left her own house, she had noticed something different in the air. It wasn't simply the penetrating heat; it was a sense of things stirring. She remembered that feeling from Five Points. It had always frightened her, just as it had excited Marcella.

She ran the last few steps to her father's house, feeling a little foolish about her fear. At the same time she didn't feel safe until she had closed and bolted her father's door behind her.

Within the hour, Charlotte went to the front door to answer a loud, persistent rapping. She opened the door a crack. A breathless, soot-covered messenger stood on the stoop, looking around him as if someone might jump him at any minute.

"What do you want?" Charlotte asked through the crack in the door.

"Telegram, ma'am. Please take it quick so I can get going again. All hell's breakin' loose out here. Excuse me, ma'am."

"Oh, yes, of course." Charlotte opened the door wide enough to take the envelope from the boy. He didn't wait for a tip but was off and running in a second.

With trembling hands, Charlotte opened the telegram. The last one she had received had reported her husband's death. What bad news did this one bring?

She read the message, read it again, and fled to the morning room, where she collapsed on the sofa. The telegram was from Leona Dowell, their cousin in Ohio, and it told her, as briefly as only a telegram could, that Jo and Terrance O'Connor, and their youngest child, Brian, had died the previous week of influenza. Leona was making efforts to place the surviving children in proper homes. Could Charlotte help with money?

Dear God, Charlotte thought, will it never end? Jo had been so happy. What would the children do? She would have to go to Ohio. How could she possibly leave New York at a time like this?

Her next thought was of Marcella. The only way she'll hear of all this is if I send her a message, she thought. She sat down and scribbled Marcella a note asking her to come to their father's house as quickly as possible. Sealing the envelope, Charlotte went to the front door and looked out.

Across the street she saw a young boy playing intently with a stick he used as a toy gun. She hailed him, put the envelope in his hand, and gave him a few coins with the instruction to dash over to the address on the envelope and see to it that the lady of the house took it from him personally. He doffed his cap and raced off. Unfortunately, he never reached Marcella's house. The city was already in chaos.

By early morning a mob consisting of two loosely formed groups had gathered along each of the avenues. They were armed with bludgeons, brickbats, sticks, and stones—a poor man's army, trained not by experts but by years of deprivation and hate.

They began to move north along Eighth and Ninth Avenues, recruiting others from the side streets. Few refused, and those who did were beaten and forced to join or left behind, much the worse for their refusal.

At police headquarters, Police Superintendent Kennedy was informed that an entire contractor's crew had failed to show up for work that morning. It was an unusual occurrence.

The mob stopped and rested for a time near Central Park, but within a half hour they were moving again, this time down Fifth and Sixth Avenues. The shouts and chants, louder and more hysterical as the march proceeded, defied

137

President Lincoln, the draft, the provost marshals, and the government in general. Waving placards protested: NO DRAFT.

Superintendent Kennedy sent the captain of the Nineteenth Precinct, with sixty patrolmen, to guard the Third Avenue Enrollment Office, and the Twenty-ninth Precinct force, with sixty-nine men, to guard the Broadway Enrollment Office.

There was no doubt as to the mob's destination, but neither did they seem in any hurry. So far they had done little but march and shout, wave their placards, and pass bottles of whiskey from one to another. Now they began to pull down the telegraph poles and cut the lines that were so important to police communications.

Several women were seen digging up the tracks of the Fourth Avenue Railway with heavy crowbars. Men broke into a hardware store and stole axes and hatchets and then once more went on their way. The fever of the crowd was mounting, and so was their arsenal of weapons.

So far the mob had done nothing directly to stop the draft or to interfere with the provost marshals. The sight of sixty policemen lined up in front of the Third Avenue Enrollment Office gave the vanguard of the mob pause. They hesitated, but the crush of people behind them made any rational decision irrelevant. The mob attacked.

Outnumbered and unprepared, the police sought refuge inside the office. The provost marshal gathered up his precious lists and hurried with his colleagues out the back entrance moments before the axes of the people outside broke through the front door. They ransacked the office, doused it with kerosene, and set it afire.

Superintendent Kennedy asked for military help and was sent a detachment of fifty troops from the Invalid Corps, men who had been wounded or were unable to fight at the front, and who had been assigned to secure civilian outposts.

Sent out now to curb the mob running wild in the streets of New York City, the soldiers confronted them on Third Avenue. When they called for the milling, shouting mass of people to retire and go home, the mob refused.

A warning volley was shot over their heads. The mob again began to surge toward the troops. The corps was ordered to shoot low into the crowd. Several fell. The others came on like a human tidal wave, screaming and battering the troops with their own weapons. Seizing their bayonets, the mob chased the terrified soldiers until they caught and punished them.

Since the telegraph wires were down, Superintendent Kennedy took his own one-horse carriage and went out to see firsthand what was happening. He was returned sometime later to the police station, badly slashed and beaten, more dead than alive. His men recognized him only by the jewelry he always wore.

New York began to blaze. Everything was out of control; the mob had turned into a pillaging, burning, looting, plundering, murdering throng, hungry with the fresh taste of blood and the scent of victory. They burned any house they thought might be hiding a policeman. They plundered and set fire to the Colored Orphan Asylum. Miraculously, all but one child was taken away safely. The mob also attacked and burned the Bull's Head Hotel at Forty-third Street, destroying it and the American Telegraph office it housed. Anyone well-dressed was in danger. Carriages were overturned, horses were turned loose to run wild in the streets.

That afternoon John Andrews, the lawyer from Virginia, once again addressed the crowd, congratulating them on what they had done. Behind him billows of smoke rose from burning buildings to which the people would not give the firemen access. Andrews himself volunteered to lead them on their path of destruction. The crowd roared its enthusiasm.

"Crush the draft!" they shouted and then went on to crush the city. One observer of the scene claimed: "Boys went through the streets, flourishing and firing off pistols, men brandished guns, and mad and hoarse with passion and bad spirits, cursed and swore and threatened everyone disagreeing with them in their excesses. Some threatened to kill every 'Black-Republican-nigger-wor-shipping son-of-a-bitch' and burn their houses."

With Superintendent Kennedy in Bellevue Hospital, the task of stopping the mob in the city fell to a depleted Metropolitan Board of Police Commissioners. One of them was away fighting in the war, another had the task of controlling Brooklyn and Staten Island, leaving only Thomas Acton to handle the fire-ridden island of Manhattan. His first decision was to gather his forces, concentrating them at headquarters, relying on the work of detectives to tell him where to deploy them.

They seemed to be needed everywhere. City Hall was being threatened; more important, the Armory at Second Avenue and Twenty-first Street was a target, along with the Union Steam Works, which had been converted into a factory to make army carbines. If the mob succeeded there, they would be well armed. People began to talk of rebellion, not riot. The authorities agreed that it had to be stopped—by whatever means—as quickly as possible.

The Armory was attacked, and while this signaled the bloodiest part of the four nightmare days, it also marked the beginning of the end. For the first time, police forces succeeded in routing the rioters, but at terrible cost. The Armory was set afire before the mob leaders could get the guns and ammunition out. The mob waiting outside was attacked by the police while those trapped inside began to jump from the burning building. The third floor of the building was a flaming mass of dying and injured; the streets were filled with the victims of police nightsticks.

Somewhere among the throngs on the street, Charlotte knew, was her son. While she doubted sincerely that Martin would actually take part in the looting and the riots, he sympathized with their cause. He was doing all he could to plan for the full and total destruction of the draft in New York.

On the second bloody day of the riots, Marcella made her way to Charlotte's house. A small, timid maid let her in, and as soon as Marcella was in the entry hall, replaced all the furniture that had been stacked against the door.

"I hope they don't attempt to burn the place down," Marcella muttered. "You'd never get out of here."

The girl's eyes were wild with fright. "Oh, my God! We are all going to die! They'll kill us all!"

"Be quiet, you simpleton! No one is going to kill you. You see me, and I just walked over here. There isn't a carriage on the road, not standing up, anyway. Take that clutter from in front of the door and take hold of yourself. Where is Mrs. Henderson?"

"She is in her bedroom, ma'am."

"Well, bring a tray up there and don't slop it all along the way. For heaven's sake, do stop trembling before you carry the tea. Hurry up!"

Charlotte's door was locked. At Marcella's authoritative rap, she called out, "Martin? Martin, is that you?" The door opened slightly, and Charlotte peeked out. "Oh, Marcella. You must have gotten my message. With all this commotion, I wasn't sure you would."

"What message?"

"Why, the one about Jo and Terrance. Marcella, I'm so sick about it—" She shook her head slowly.

"What about Jo?"

"Oh, Marcella, I'm so sorry," Charlotte sniffed. She reached for the handkerchief beside her and dabbed at her nose.

Marcella grasped her sister's sleeve. "Charlotte! *What about Jo?*"

"We got—we got—a telegram—from Leona Dowell," Charlotte stammered. "Just about the time the riots started. Marcella, Jo's dead. Jo and Terrance and their youngest, Brian. All of them. From influenza. Last week," she sputtered, rapidly losing control. "Oh, Marcella, our Jo, our little Jo—and all those children, without their mother or their father. Oh, Marcella, Marcella," she sobbed, crumpling into her chair. "They thought it was just a cold, but it wasn't. It was influenza, and—and—oh, Marcella—"

Stunned, Marcella stood up slowly, shaking her head as if to clear it. "Not Jo," she whispered, "please, dear God, not Jo. Not my Jo."

She walked across the room to the window and stood there, looking through the filmy white curtains, seeing nothing but a blur. Tears welled in her eyes and ran slowly down her cheeks. "Not Jo, not Jo, not Jo," she repeated numbly.

Behind her she heard Charlotte, still weeping. Suddenly she could not bear to be in the same room with her sister—with Charlotte, who had never really understood. It was almost obscene, she thought, that Charlotte should have known about Jo before her, before Marcella, who had raised Jo, who had been a mother to her.

"Marcella?" Charlotte whimpered. "Marcella?"

Marcella turned to look at her sister. Words of bitterness rang in her head, words she wanted to shout—at herself as much as at Charlotte. All these years, all that love—where were you? Where were you, Marcella?

What good would it do to shout at Charlotte, she thought. "I have to be by myself," she said aloud. "I must go home. I must go home."

Without another word, she gathered up her wrap and her bag and left the room and Charlotte behind.

That night a telegram was delivered to police headquarters on Mulberry Street from Edwin Stanton, the Secretary of War, in which Stanton assured Thomas Acton that five regiments were being returned to New York to restore order.

Wednesday the city experienced the hottest day of the year. The city sweltered and stank with the smell of burning buildings and wet ash. Weary to the bone, some New Yorkers fought off attack after attack by others in the still raging mob. The Negroes of the city were hunted through the hot, sultry nights like animals, hanged, beaten, and burned while crowds of rioters danced around their bodies, slashing at them with knives and sticks.

Thursday dawned, and the hottest day of New York's year ended. For all practical purposes, so did the riot. The Copperheads, intent on insurrection, had failed, and again the poor man had fought a senseless war. He had paid with his life and his property—and he had won nothing. The draft offices opened again under the protection of Federal troops, and names were called. Although relief funds were set up immediately for the families of the policemen and others who had suffered damage in the riots, none was set up for the poor.

The draft itself proved unsuccessful. It had no real supporters from the start, and in the end, the bounty that was payable to a substitute proved to be its undoing. Incompetents, drunkards, and riffraff filled the army's ranks and deserted at the first opportunity.

Marcella waited out the days of the draft riots and several weeks more, expecting Brad to appear at any time. He, of all people, was the one with whom she could have shared her grief. When he did not come, did not send any message, Marcella sank deeper into her depression.

For all practical purposes she remained a recluse. Only on Myrtle's afternoon off did she venture outside of the brownstone, and then only to wander up and down the street once or twice before climbing the front stoop and locking the door behind her.

The maelstrom of feelings, recriminations, and memories did not stop; from the morning, when she rose after a fitful sleep, until the evening, when she sat in her room alone, staring at the wall or the floor, the same questions besieged her again and again: Why? Why me? What have I done? What else could I do?

She relived scenes from her childhood, so many years—even decades—past, scenes with Jo, with Hilary, with her father, with Charlotte. Charlotte. How like her mother she had been—and still was, in so many ways. What a show of emotion she had put on that day in her barricaded house! What did she know of the pain Marcella felt?

Marcella resolved that, whatever else she discussed with her sister, she would never speak of Jo with her again. Her own memories were too sacred; they were some of the only beautiful things left in her life. No, Charlotte would never share them. And whatever news there was to learn of what was happening in Ohio, Marcella decided, she would try to get it from Leona Dowell directly. She would write as soon as she could manage to steel herself for another visit to Charlotte. Charlotte would have Leona's address.

She hadn't long to wait. Several days later, a messenger came to her door with a note from her sister, asking Marcella—rather meekly, Marcella thought—to come for tea the following afternoon. "I have just returned from Ohio," the note said. "There were some problems in placing the children in proper homes, but they have now been resolved. Dear Marcella, I know how difficult this time must be for you. If you'd prefer not to talk of Jo and Ohio, I, for one, would certainly understand." It was signed: "Your loving sister, Charlotte."

Marcella read the note again and then crumpled it into a ball and tossed it aside. "If you'd prefer not to talk of Jo. . ." She sighed. Perhaps Charlotte was not so insensitive after all. As long as she holds to her word, Marcella thought, I can talk with her about anything else.

The next day she woke feeling better than she had in days. It was a clear day—a day for resolving, for changing, Marcella thought, as she prepared to go to Charlotte's. Brad was very much on her mind.

Suddenly, she wanted more than anything else to see him. She shook her head. She had been too much beset by memories in the past few days. Everything seemed a bit confused. Perhaps the visit to Charlotte would set things right, bring her back to reality again.

She set off for Charlotte's house. When she arrived, Martin informed her Charlotte wasn't there. John Paxton, who had been caught by the mob and beaten on his way home from Wall Street during the riots, had not yet recovered, and Charlotte had gone back to the house on Eighth Avenue to care for him.

Marcella took an omnibus to her parents' house. She hadn't been there since Hilary's death. Jo was gone, and her father was but half his former self. Now that she was once again free to visit her family home, what was there left for her to visit?

Marcella knocked on the door of the house. She could have let herself in, but it still seemed important to her to have someone open the door and tell her that she was welcome.

Charlotte greeted her at the door. "Why, hello, Marcella. I wasn't sure you'd come. You didn't send back an answer yesterday, and I thought—"

Marcella smiled tentatively, surprised to find herself slightly embarrassed by the apologetic tone in Charlotte's voice. The two sisters stood at the door for a moment, awkward and formal.

"About Jo—" Charlotte began.

"Charlotte, please, let's talk of other things." Marcella smiled again, quickly, and looked past her sister into the house. "May I come in?"

Charlotte blushed. "Oh, my, yes, Marcella. I'm so sorry. I wasn't think-ing—I—" she mumbled, following Marcella through the front door. "Would you like some tea? Some cakes, perhaps?"

Marcella removed her wrap and hung it near the door. "Just as soon as I've said hello to Papa. I'll be down in a moment."

Charlotte bustled off to the kitchen, glad to be relieved of the initial strangeness of their reunion. She was pleased that Marcella seemed, if not happy, then at least more composed than she had expected her to be.

Ten minutes later, Marcella reappeared downstairs.

"Papa seems much better," she said cheerfully. "He told me you've been taking marvelous care of him. I'm so grateful, Charlotte, really I am."

Charlotte beamed as she carried the tea tray to the morning room. The two women sat down, and Charlotte poured their tea and offered Marcella a cake from the plate.

"You look very well yourself, Marcella," Charlotte began. "I mean, especially considering what's been happening lately—I mean, what we've been hearing about Brad and everything." She looked down at her teacup, suddenly afraid she had undone all the good feelings. "I'm sorry, Marcella. I didn't mean to—"

Marcella sighed. "On my way over here, I was thinking. Charlotte, when will I learn not to make such a mess of things? My whole life—I just seem to do everything wrong!"

"I assume you're talking about Brad."

Marcella tried to laugh. "At least *you* seem chipper."

Charlotte sighed deeply. "What a dreadful time this has been! I will never understand it at all." She looked at Marcella, seeking a response. Marcella's face remained impassive. "Thank God, Martin is at home again and safe," Charlotte hurried on. "I do worry about him. I really feel he is mixing with the wrong people, and Martin is such an impressionable young man. Of course, he has all the potential in the world. It is merely a matter of directing properly."

"Poor Charlotte. You always end up with everyone's problems."

"I just wish you would listen to me before things happen instead of coming to me after." She paused to refill her cup. "But what of you, Marcella? Do tell me."

Marcella put down the cake and the teacup. She was silent for a full min-ute before she began, as if debating whether to go into the whole thing with her sister. She looked up at Charlotte and plunged in, telling her all that had happened since the day she had first learned that Brad had gone to the Cats-kills.

Charlotte listened attentively until she finished. "Well, I must say, you got better than you deserved. If I have told you once, I have told you a hundred times, Marcella, you must curb that possessive, headstrong, and jealous nature of yours. You cannot keep the man on a leash. Why, if I had ever poked my nose into my husband's business when he was alive the way you do into Brad's, I am quite sure I would have found myself sitting on a street corner, homeless! He simply never would have tolerated it. I think it most admirable that Brad did not blacken your eyes for you."

"I rather wish he had. At least he would have had to be with me to do it. I never see him anymore."

"Be more pleasant, and perhaps you will," Charlotte suggested.

"Then you think it isn't so serious? I mean, it isn't so bad that I haven't seen him in so long?"

"I said no such thing!" Charlotte snorted. "He has done everything you asked—no, demanded—of him and obviously hated it and didn't understand why you wanted Scarborough House. I don't either. Under the circumstances you can hardly expect him to be overjoyed."

"I didn't expect roses, but he hasn't even come to see me. During the riots, he didn't so much as send a message to see if I was all right."

"If I know Brad Dalton, he knows that you are fine. I imagine a dozen different people have told him about you. But the point, Marcella, is that you have made the man prove that he loves you. You have asked for his trust and then in effect told him you didn't trust him. He still gave you that 'proof' you asked for. I don't know what you want of the man, Marcella. You have already taken more than you should."

Marcella fidgeted in her chair. "I do trust Brad, Charlotte. It's just that I love him so, and he could just leave anytime. There is nothing to keep him with me. I would rather not live than lose Brad."

"Then I suggest you change your ways radically, because you will lose him if you keep demanding proof of his fidelity. Imagine demanding a family estate from the man! It is like holding a hostage for the ransom of his love. Really, Marcella! No one can stand that kind of pressure and doubt being thrust at them. He will grow to loathe you if you persist. Start a new day with him and begin it by returning Scarborough to him."

"But I need that!"

"Bosh!"

"I do!" Marcella insisted. "It is all the security I have. Everything else you suggest, I will do. I'll be loving and sweet to him and trusting. I'll never ask for another thing—never! I promise."

"It isn't to me you must promise, Marcella. But there is no point in arguing with you. I can see by the look on your face that your mind is set and your ears closed. But I think you are wrong. The feeling I get is that things between you and Brad are very bad indeed. You seem cut off from one another."

"That I can take care of. That is no problem," Marcella said quickly.

"Then why are you here talking to me?"

Marcella looked up. "I don't know. I guess you were right. I was just blue and let it spread to everything. Things are much better than I thought! I can make Brad jealous so easily, and how he hates that! He is worse than I am." She paused for a moment, thinking. Suddenly a mischievous smile appeared on her face. "It just might do Bradford Dalton a world of good to know he is not the only man who finds me attractive. I think a little healthy competition for him is an excellent idea!"

She swept into a deep curtsy before her sister and then began to pace dramatically about the room. "Charlotte, you have made me feel so much better. I can see it all so clearly now!"

Charlotte was dumbfounded. "You talk like a fool and act worse! I don't believe you have heard a word I said."

"Oh, but I did listen—to every word. It was all so simple! Just the tiniest flirtation, and it will be like a thundershower to clear the air. Brad will grumble and be angry, and then we will make up, and everything will be like it was—no, better."

"When will you ever grow up?" Charlotte chided. "Don't tamper with that man. Let him be."

"You sound like an old woman," Marcella chuckled. "Brad would like it as much as I. We need a new start. It is so obvious."

"What can I say that you will heed, Marcella? Give him back the deed to Scarborough House, and trust him and love him as he is, not as you wish him to be."

Marcella laughed softly to herself. "Is that what you do with Martin?"

"Martin is different. He is my son."

Marcella glanced at her and glided toward the front hall. She took her bonnet from the stand and adjusted it on her head.

"Where are you going? I thought you would stay for a while."

"I couldn't stay now, not when I have so much to do!" She tossed her cloak around her shoulders, gave Charlotte a tiny wave of her fingers, and hurried out.

Charlotte watched her run down the street. It was useless to be angry with Marcella, but this time Charlotte had a feeling of foreboding. Hilary had always said Marcella would pay for the kind of life she led; this time Charlotte took her mother's prophecy seriously.

Chapter Seventeen

Eugene Timmins was a man Marcella had discouraged many times before. Very little redeemed him, as far as she was concerned, except that he was handsome, available, and was known to curry favor successfully with many smart but bored women of the city. They needed only to like flattery better than truth for Eugene to be at his best.

When Marcella visited him a few days later, he was only too willing to oblige. For once the tables were turned on him; he succumbed to his own obvious brand of flattery as it came from Marcella. He would be glad to escort her to the theater that evening, he said.

It wasn't often that Gene was seen with a woman like Marcella. He would enjoy ever minute of the evening—including the satisfaction of showing up Bradford Dalton.

Marcella and Eugene were a stunning couple, attracting the attention of everyone in the theater. Marcella, dressed in a brilliant green gown, was complimented repeatedly, always as a prelude to the real question on everyone's mind.

"Where is Brad?"

"Why, I don't know," she replied to one and all, flashing her dark eyes. "I haven't seen him for the longest time. Please do give him my best when you see him."

"Are you really finished with Dalton?" Gene asked her at the end of the evening.

She smiled sweetly. "Finished with him? What are you talking about?" If she had succeeded in fooling Gene, she knew, she had done as well or better with the other people she had seen that night.

She invited Eugene into the house when they returned from the theater, and he accepted, a bit puzzled by his apparent good luck. Before he left, very late that night, he elicited a promise from Marcella that she would accompany him to dinner the following evening.

When the door finally closed behind him, Marcella vented a long, satisfied sigh and sank happily into the nearest chair. She smiled to herself, anticipating the look on Brad's face when he appeared at her door.

She hadn't long to wait. Word of her previous night's appearance spread like a brushfire, and the following afternoon Brad was standing on the front stoop of her house, fumbling for his key. She opened the door just as he was trying to insert it into the lock.

"Well, Brad! How nice to see you. Wherever have you been keeping yourself?"

"What are you trying to do, Marcella?" He shoved her aside as he entered the house. "I have heard of nothing but your appearance in the theater last night. Every damned person I meet has some comment to make."

"Oh, really? I didn't know so many people had noticed me. What did you say to them?"

"What could I say? I don't know what's happening myself. What is going on? I sent the deed to you. What is it you want now?"

"We are being self-important, aren't we? I want nothing from you. I simply felt the need of some fun for a change. Is there anything wrong in that?"

"People are asking questions. They haven't talked about anything but you today. And why in the hell does it have to be a man like Timmins? What are you trying to do, Marcy?"

"Such melodrama!" she breathed. Suddenly she turned on him. "What am I doing to you?" she spat out. "That *is* funny, Brad. I haven't set eyes on you for—I don't even remember the last time. Did you even know I was alive? I could have been killed during the riots. This house could have been burned to the ground."

Shocked by her outburst, Brad muttered, "I was busy."

"Oh, you were busy! Well, I wasn't. I sat here and waited. Waited for you to come, to show some concern. Maybe you expected I'd sit here spinning fine linen until you decided I had been punished enough for you to come around again."

"I told you I needed time—time to think and sort things out."

Marcella did not let up. "Did you? Well, I needed entertainment. We have both got what we needed, have we not? You have had ample time in which to think, and now I have found a man who does not need time to decide whether he wants my company." She ran across the room to the window, and head bowed, began to weep silently, waiting for his response.

When she heard nothing, she looked back at him. He was staring at the empty fireplace. She went over to his side, placing her hand on his arm. "What is it, Brad? Why is everything all wrong?" Her voice was suddenly very subdued.

Brad shrugged but did not look up. "I don't know. I don't seem to know anything any longer. I suppose it had to come sooner or later. It is my fault, I'll admit that. But I never realized until these last few weeks just how much of my life is tied up in you, Marcella. When I don't understand you, I don't seem able to understand myself either. It is as if we had really become one person, and I just never thought of its ending. I certainly never thought it would end like this."

He looked up, his eyes full of sadness. "I have always thought of you and me as something that stretched out before me year after year, like a road showing me the way. Now I see women, and they aren't you. I have always . . . admired pretty women. Now I don't care. Maybe I am getting old, or maybe I am one of those people who never learn until the mistake is made. I certainly didn't see the indifference that Annette felt until long after we were married. And apparently I haven't seen your needs either. I don't know."

"Then you do love me?"

"I have always loved you."

She pressed herself against him. "I've wanted to hear that for so long. Tonight I can tell you mean it. Why haven't you said it before?"

"It isn't enough, or perhaps it is just too late. I could say it twice an hour and it wouldn't be enough for you now. I don't pretend to understand it, Marcella, I just know that is the way it is. We have lost that unity we once had. I don't know how, but we have."

"Brad," she whispered, burying her face in his jacket, "don't say things like that. It's me—all my fault. I am such a fool!"

"It wasn't you alone, Marcella. Shall we go out to dinner tonight? I will have to see about collecting some of my belongings here, but I really would rather start on it tomorrow. Today I just don't feel like facing it. All right?" He took her chin in his hand and raised her face.

"Brad. . . ."

"Don't say anything. There isn't any other way. I won't share you with any other man, not even for an evening's entertainment. And I won't be made a fool of in the eyes of people who see you and draw their own conclusions. You no longer feel about me as you did, and I don't like the feeling of not being loved by you."

147

"But I *do* love you! I do, Brad. What else can I say?"

"Nothing. You've said it already."

"But you don't really want to leave me, do you?"

"No."

"Then don't. Please don't. I was hurt and jealous. I couldn't help it. I am such a fool! I thought you had found someone else. I am getting so old, and everyone is talking. . . ."

"Who put that idea in your head?" He smiled a little and put his arms around her, resting his chin on the top of her head. "Your hair always smells so good, like a spring garden."

"Brad, I love you so."

"And I love you."

"Don't leave me. Don't ever leave me."

He kissed her softly and then took her hand and led her slowly to the stairs leading to her room. She wept in happiness and relief.

Sometime later, when dusk was falling, Brad turned on his side and looked down into her face. With the top of his finger he traced the contours of her face and upper body. Lazily she opened her eyes and smiled.

"I like you naked," he said and kissed her forehead.

"Is that what you were thinking about?"

"Umm, partly."

"What else? Tell me!"

He laughed. "Are you sure you can stand the truth?"

"Of course."

"I am starving. Let's go out and find the best chef in the whole city of New York." Marcella turned away from him suddenly, her body tense. "What's wrong? You're not angry, are you?"

"It isn't that."

"What, then?"

"I am afraid to tell you."

"None of that. If we are going to start anew, it will have to be honestly. Tell me."

"It's Eugene. I promised to go to dinner with him tonight. It was before—I didn't know you would come. I told him I would go last night. I didn't know this would happen." She began to cry again.

"Marcella, Marcella, don't take on so. I'm not an ogre. I understand. Look at me, Marcy, and smile. Remember—he cannot have you. You are all mine! Now, hurry up and get ready to go. I want you to look ravishing. Better than last night."

She threw herself into his arms, smothering him with kisses, and then leaped from the bed. He lay back and watched her as she bathed and prepared to dress for the evening.

Suddenly the doorbell sounded. Marcella grabbed for a towel and pressed it against her breasts. Her eyes were wide.

"It's him. It's Gene. What should I do? What can I say, Brad?"

"Don't do anything. Maybe he will go away."

"He'll just come back, or wait. I mean, he will assume I am dressing, won't he?"

"Probably. I have the perfect solution. I'll answer the door as I am. That should tell him all he needs to know."

"Bradford Dalton! You wouldn't dare. You'll cause a scandal for all time."

"But I would and I will! Who cares about scandal?" He jumped off the bed.

"Suppose it isn't Gene?" she called after him.

He popped his head back around the door. "Who else could it be?"

"I don't know. My dressmaker? You'd give poor Miss McCurdy an attack of palsy," she giggled.

"Maybe I would cure her."

"It might be one of the neighborhood children—or a messenger, or even the lady next door. It might be anyone." She laughed again. "Oh, go on and answer it as you are. It would be worth it just to see you standing there, naked as a baby jay, trying to explain yourself to someone. . . ."

He reached for his trousers. "Whoever it is, is impatient, and you know damned well it will be Timmins. You just want to spoil all my fun." He gave a final tug to his trousers and scowled at her. "Now are you happy, or must I wear a shirt as well?"

"No, your hairy chest is just darling."

He stuck his chest out and raised his eyebrows at her, and then hurried from the room. Marcella could not hear what was said between the two men, nor did she care. Brad was home with her. He could do as he liked with Eugene Timmins. That man had served his purpose.

"Is he gone?" she asked as Brad returned. He nodded grimly.

"What has turned you all sour?"

"He'll be back. You're going to have to talk to him yourself. I don't know what you told that man last night, or what you did, but he is not under the impression that last night was merely a night of entertainment."

"Brad, let's not talk about him. That is all in the past."

"He seems to think he has reason for being persistent. He is going to come back."

"Not Gene. You just don't know him."

"I am wondering how well *you* know him. Never mind, I shouldn't have said that. I don't want to spend the night discussing Eugene Timmins! Just make damned sure he knows I never want to see his pasty face near this house again." His voice was edged with anger.

Marcella looked up from what she was doing. "You have certainly fallen into an ugly mood, and I don't see why. You told me you understood."

"Perhaps I didn't quite know what I was agreeing to. You did give me the impression that last night was just a lark, that you wanted to go out."

"It was."

"That's not the idea I got from Timmins."

"Then you got the wrong idea."

"I don't want to argue with you. Just tell the m n never to come here again for any reason at any time. Is that clear?"

"Perfectly clear. And what's more, it sounds very much like an order, Brad."

"It is an order, and you damn well better see it carried out!"

"And just who are you to speak to me like that?" Marcella answered, unable to restrain the sudden flare of temper.

"The owner of this house, and don't you forget it. I say what does and does not go around here. Just be sure you do as I tell you, and do it soon."

He finished dressing and stood behind her, looking at himself over her head in her mirror. He checked his tie, adjusted it, and tugged at it until it met with his approval. "If I had had the good sense to be firm with you from the outset," he muttered, "we would not have had all this trouble. Can't you hurry? I am hungry, and it is getting late."

"Another order?"

"Yes, damn it!"

She began to dawdle, her mouth set in a firm line. She tilted her head this way and that. "I am just not pleased with my hair," she said, taking the pins out. Her long, thick hair fell around her shoulders. He stood motionless, his coat on his arm. "Don't you think it would look better swept back a little more?" she asked sweetly.

"I don't care what you do with it. I am going to get something to eat. Good-bye, Marcella. I hope you get your hair just right." He turned on his heel and marched out of the bedroom without looking back. Marcella picked up her hand mirror from the vanity and hurled it at the doorway. The sound of shattering glass covered the slamming of the front door.

"Oh! Why did I do that? A mirror broken. Why am I such a dolt? Brad! Brad, look what I have done. How do you cross out the ill luck that comes of a broken mirror? What do I do? Is it salt over the shoulder? No, that isn't it. Brad, tell me! What is it? What do I do about a broken mirror?"

It wasn't for some minutes and a few futile tears of superstitious fright that she realized she was alone in the house, and then its emptiness closed in on her all at once.

She clutched at her throat and stole through the rooms of the house, afraid to make a noise, afraid to be alone.

Finally she managed to calm herself. She returned to her room to finish fixing her hair. Then she went to the sitting room and waited for him to return for her. At ten o'clock she went to her pantry to get something to eat. It wasn't much, just enough to keep her from feeling so hungry, and not enough so that Brad would notice she hadn't a proper appetite. She imagined the midnight supper they would have, and the wine they would drink, how his eyes would look in the flickering candlelight, and how forgiving and loving she would be.

She went back to the sitting room again. By eleven o'clock she was tired and angry again. At one o'clock she suddenly recalled the sound of his voice as he had said good-bye to her.

When she got into bed she couldn't sleep. She rolled over and touched the pillow beside her, wondering if she would ever again see his head resting against it. By morning, her head hurt and her eyes ached with crying, but she had convinced herself that she didn't care what he did. He had lied to her and used her just as he had always used her, and he had left her just as he had always left her, running off to the safety of his wife and that pile of sanctity he called Scarborough.

She had made him sorry for the way he had treated her once, and she would do it again, but this time there would be no happy making up until she was good and ready! She shuddered as she remembered her pleading with him to stay, and how gratefully she had followed him into bed. Not this time!

When Gene came to the house late that afternoon, she welcomed him warmly. He acted hurt and insulted.

"Gene, must you look so pathetic? It can't have been as bad as all that."

"What do you think I went through when greeted at the door by that hairy-chested gorilla? I was appalled—crushed, Marcella. We had an appointment. What was I to think?"

"Why didn't you punch him in the nose, or did you expect me to do that for you?" Marcella snapped. "While you are bemoaning your own fate, have you considered at all what I might have done with him? Perhaps I could have beaten him off with a cudgel while protesting I had a dinner engagement with you. Surely if you were intimidated by him, Eugene, you can imagine what a poor helpless woman must have felt."

He looked at her warily but made no comment. As he made himself comfortable in one of the parlor chairs, Marcella smiled to herself, imagining yesterday's scene at the door. "Brad does have a primitive side to his nature," she said.

"I don't know why you permitted him into your house. You should know him by now."

"I have been wondering the same thing myself. Why did I let him in?"

They talked about Brad at some length. Marcella allowed Gene's animosity to bolster her own sense of hurt and confusion. She wanted to retaliate, and Gene wanted nothing more than to assist her. He was launching into another attack on Brad Dalton when the doorbell rang. Marcella excused herself hastily. "I am quite certain I know who *that* is, and this is one apology I want tendered on the doorstep before I let him in the house!"

She took the message the man was holding, and stood dumbly as he went down the steps, stopping long enough to mutter something about cheap people who didn't give tips.

Finally she looked at the thick envelope in her hand. She had no need to open it. She knew what it contained. She knew as soon as she saw the name of the law firm in the upper-left-hand corner. Brad was really finished with her.

She went back into the parlor.

"You have had bad news?" Gene asked. "Sit down. You look pale as a ghost. Are you all right?"

She waved him off but took the seat he offered her. In a few minutes she told him briefly what the envelope filled with legal papers meant.

"Are you going to lie back and take that kind of treatment from him?" Gene snarled. "Why, you mean no more to him than the rug he wipes his feet on. He has stained and dirtied you with his filth, and now he is going to cast you aside, and for a younger woman, I'll wager. I know his kind, they are all alike." He took hold of her arm roughly. "You can't let him do this to you!"

"What can I do?" she replied listlessly.

"No matter what he says, he does not own those properties. You do. They are in your name, don't you see? Verbal promises or agreements between you are meaningless. No one ever witnessed them."

"I gave my word."

"And what did you promise? Nothing, I'll wager. He used you! Can't you see him for what he is? He has been using you all along for his own career, and now he wants to go into politics. Well, no decent person is going to vote for a man with a wife and a child openly living with another woman, are they? So he is going to dump you. And you are going to stand by and let him get away with it. What's wrong with you? Don't you have any pride at all? Don't you deserve anything for all the years you have given him?"

Gene's voice pounded against her ears like surf on the shore. Suddenly he stopped, took in the blankness of her expression, and kissed her lightly on the forehead. "Promise me that after you have absorbed the shock of this a little better, you will think of what I have said to you."

"I will. I'll think about it, but it won't help. Even if all you say is true, it won't matter. I am just not strong enough to stand up to Brad. I couldn't."

"Well, give it some thought. I may have a plan that will serve very well."

"What?"

"Finally! I have captured your interest, and that's enough for now. I want you fresh and alert when I tell you. Get some rest, and maybe when I see you tomorrow we'll discuss it."

Marcella thought about little after Gene left. Her mind seemed to have gone numb. She made up her mind to go to Charlotte. Charlotte had been right all along. So had Hilary. She was no good, and what she did was bound to come out wrong because she had started wrong.

But when it came time to dress and go to Charlotte's house, she found she hadn't the energy to do it. She stayed in her room, not eating or thinking or sleeping. She lay on her bed, staring at the ceiling. From time to time she would stir herself, but only to wander aimlessly about the bedroom, looking out one window after another. The street behind the house was empty. It was little more than an alley. How ugly it is, she thought.

She felt no better in the morning and refused to come downstairs. Gene ignored the implied rebuke and had Myrtle usher him into Marcella's bedroom. She didn't seem surprised to see him, but neither was she pleased. He walked over to her and kissed her as if accustomed to the procedure. "You could at least pretend to be happy to see me."

"I am just not feeling up to much of anything right now."

"What is the point of feeling sorry for yourself all day? This is the time to cheer up. We have much to talk about, plans to make. You should know I wouldn't leave you all on your own at a time like this. Have you thought about what I told you yesterday?"

"Not really."

"But you must! Decisions have to be made quickly. I can see you haven't read the papers Dalton sent to you yesterday."

"I didn't need to. I knew what they were as soon as I saw the envelope." She blew her nose. "Gene, I don't mean to be rude, but would you mind? I would really like to be alone today. I don't want to think or make decisions. I don't even want to cheer up. I just want to be alone."

"You have no time to indulge yourself like this, Marcella. Even if I were inclined to do as you ask, you simply don't have the time. If you had read the particulars, as I did, you would know that Dalton's lawyers will have all the release forms, bills of sale, and deeds ready for your signature day after tomorrow. I don't suppose I need tell you what you'll get out of it all. We must make our move right away."

"Day after tomorrow," she repeated. "That is so like Brad. Once he has decided on something, he doesn't like to procrastinate. He is so sure and decisive and bold. I have always admired that in him."

Gene made no effort to hide his impatience. "Shall we get back to the subject and forget about admiring the man who is attempting to cheat you out of everything you own?"

"He wouldn't do that. Brad isn't that way. You simply don't like him, Gene, and after all, I do know him a little better than you."

"I am sure you do!" he snapped. "Perhaps you are right, the man is just trying to be kind to you. But explain to me, if you will, the nugget of pure charity in the fact that every deed—and I repeat, Marcella, *every* deed—you own is listed in this document, including the one to this house. He wants it all. Everything! Face it, Marcella, he is wiping the slate clean of all connection with you."

Marcella grabbed for the papers in Gene's hand. He pulled them back just out of her grasp, smiled triumphantly, and then handed her the list, pointing about two-thirds of the way down the paper.

"He can't! It's a mistake. He can't take this house away from me. He wouldn't!"

"That, my dear, is where you are wrong. He can and will ake it and anything else he can get. But remember this, Marcella, he can only do it if you allow him to. Wake up, for God's sake, Marcella! Fight for what is yours! And for the love of God, for once in your life open your eyes to what Dalton is."

"Why? Why would he do it? All those years... Didn't they mean anything to him? I loved him, Gene. We were together for so long ... it couldn't have been all pretense. I would have known, wouldn't I? I mean, your whole life can't be based on a lie without your knowing it, can it?" She looked up into Gene's face, pleading for reassurance.

"I don't know, Marcella. Perhaps it wasn't all pretense, but with a man like Dalton . . . Oh, Marcella, how can a man like Dalton truly care about anything? He is basically a ruthless man."

"No, he wasn't, Gene, not with me. He was always kind and fun-loving, and he did love me, I know he did. He had to!"

Gene shrugged and looked across the room at the far wall. "That is probably what his wife tells herself, and his son, too."

Marcella started to protest, but the words suddenly died on her lips. Annette had always been her rival. Marcella had attributed all of the problems between Brad and Annette to herself. She had never compared herself to Annette. But there must have been a time when Annette believed Brad loved her, and she must have believed and trusted in that love, too. But Brad had left her, for all practical purposes. Annette had had very little of Brad in these close to twenty years.

She stood up. "Let me get dressed, and then we can go downstairs and talk. I can't think properly, lounging here in this room. I keep thinking of—other things."

"Now we are getting somewhere!" He hugged her to him. She automatically drew back. He didn't mind. "I'll tell Myrtle to fix us something to eat. You must be famished after all your suffering martyrdom of the last few days."

"I'll be down in a few minutes, and believe me, I will no longer be looking like a martyr, suffering or otherwise."

When Marcella came downstairs, Eugene could sense the difference in her. She still looked tired from her sleeplessness, and her eyes remained puffy, but there was a new, angry light in them. She walked purposefully, all timidity and hesitancy banished.

Briefly Gene went over each of the papers Brad had sent with the messenger, and then he laid them neatly on the table. He leaned back in his chair and looked at Marcella.

"Everything is clear to you?"

"Clear? Yes, it is clear, much too clear. What do I do about it?"

"First, I want you to call a meeting with Dalton. I realize this will be the most painful part of the whole thing for you, but once you get past it, I am sure you will feel much better. Tell him you wish to discuss something with him."

"He'll think that I want him to come back."

"All right, tell him you want to discuss the inclusion of this house on the list. He'll probably be expecting that, anyway. I would guess the sole purpose for its being on the list in the first place is to force you to ask for it. He will be able to concede it graciously to you out of the generosity of his heart as payment for the rest. But once you have got him here, get him to offer to buy the property from you."

"Ask him to buy his property from me? He'll never agree to that."

"Tell him it is only just, after all you have done for him—furthering his career, acting as his hostess, whatever you can think of. Make it good, and above all, make sure you make him suspicious of your motives. We want him to offer on the low side."

"But why? If I am going to sell it to him, shouldn't I be asking for everything I can get?"

"Of course you should, my dear, but you are *not* going to sell it to him! You are going to allow him to think he can cheat you by buying everything cheaply, and then you and I, Marcella, are going to take him to court for fraud and sue him for every dirty penny he has taken from anyone. We'll let people see him for what he is, a man who preys upon the innocence and ignorance of those who cannot defend themselves against him."

"I can't do that! If I offered it to him, then I would set the price, and I couldn't claim later that he had cheated me."

"True. So what you must do is rely on your femininity, your lack of business acumen. He'll be expecting you to try something, so when you ask him the value of the property, he is very likely to set it low. You accept the figure he states, no matter what it is. Meanwhile I will know the exact market value. I have copied this list for myself, so that I can locate the information. The only thing that can possibly go wrong is that he will give you an honest figure. That would be a pity because we would simply have to take what we could get and forget the court case. But with this much money involved, the chances of that are small."

"You make him sound like a monster."

"Sometimes, Marcella, the appearance is as good as, or better than, the fact. Do you realize that people's sympathy often rides with a real monster, but an honest man accused and made to look bad while protesting his goodness will receive very little sympathy?"

"You are the most devious man I have ever met."

"I doubt that, but then we must all have our own ways of making a living in this world, and mine happens to be fleecing men who think they have a bit of God running in their veins. Brad Dalton has been a condescending, superior snob for years, and now my turn has come to look down on that insufferable son-of-a-bitch. This is one time victory will be sweet as well as profitable."

Chapter Eighteen

Marcella sent her message to Brad late that afternoon. When he came to the house, just as Gene had predicted he would, he was all business. Nowhere in his actions or manner did he betray his past feelings for Marcella—which made it easier for her to carry out her part of the plan, and much easier for her to believe the worst about Brad.

As soon as they were seated in the parlor, however, Brad began apologetically, "Marcella, I am sorry about the brownstone's being put on that list. It was a mistake, an overzealous clerk. I never intended it to be included with the others. This house is yours. I gave it to you with the intention of your having it, and I want you to have it."

"As payment for the rest?"

"That is up to you. Take it in whatever spirit you please."

"That is considerate of you, Brad, but I am afraid things are a bit more complicated than that. I cannot hope to survive with only the house. One does have to eat, be clothed, and pay bills. You leave me in a considerable amount of financial confusion, and I am afraid I haven't the knack for making money that you have."

"I realize that, and I will take care of you as I have in the past until you arrange to be independently situated."

"You are thinking I might become a seamstress, perhaps? Or maybe an old lady to tat Irish doilies by candlelight?"

"That wasn't what I had in mind," he said, looking away.

"I know full well what you had in mind. Just a simple change of occupancy. Your shoes removed from beneath my bed and Gene's put in their place. Well, if that is what you think—and I am sure it is—then I may never become financially independent. Gene is not as ambitious as you, nor is he as able to sniff out the possibilities of a deal."

"I will pay your normal bills for a period of three months after I regain the property, Marcella. After that, Timmins may support you in any way he can devise. But not with my money or sanction. I can't stop you, it seems, but I will not pay him to sleep with you!" He stood up and tugged at his waistcoat.

"There is no need for vulgarity. Sit down, Brad, and do try to be civil. Gene is always saying you put him in mind of one of the primates. I am beginning to see the resemblance myself."

"You bitch! How could I not have seen this side of you all those years we lived together. You are a rotten, conniving bitch."

"It is a recent accomplishment of mine," she said coolly. "I acquired it after I learned what a scoundrel you are. Now, do sit down. I have an offer to make you."

He glared at her. "Sign the papers, Marcella. On time and no bargains. In case you are wondering, that, too, is an order, and you'd better heed it."

"I'll not sign anything until you have listened to me. There will be a bargain, Brad, because you have little choice. I will sign nothing otherwise."

"What is it this time?"

"It seems to me that I should get something out of all this. I did help you a great deal, and for a very long time. You wouldn't be nearly as wealthy as you are if it hadn't been for me, not to mention the fact that it was I who encouraged you to try your hand at politics. From where I stand, the only thing I have got for my efforts is to be cast aside when I no longer fit into your new and now moral life."

"What do you want?"

"First I wish you would sit down. I can't talk if you lean over me in that threatening stance, and besides, I am getting a crick in my neck."

He moved back from her and glanced down at his tightly clenched fists. Flexing his fingers, he kept looking at them as though they belonged to someone else. He took the chair opposite her, pulling it close to hers. "Tell me what it is you have in mind."

"Just what is all this property worth? In money, I mean. You know I have never paid the slightest attention to what you put in my name. So, as always, I must rely on you, even at a time like this. Silly, isn't it?"

He eyed her suspiciously. "If you think it is of great value, you are mistaken."

"I was not thinking anything, Brad. I was asking. I never really thought you would put anything of great value in my name. It is just that it must be worth something."

"It is."

"How much?"

"Somewhere in the neighborhood of a hundred thousand, I think."

"That is quite a lot."

"It may be a little more. I would have to check to make certain."

"Well, I trust you, so that is of little matter. Since you say it isn't worth that much, would you consider buying it from me? That would take care of my money problems, and you would have your property back. That would be fair, wouldn't it?"

"Buy my own property twice over?" He managed a half smile.

"I realize that, but Brad, I do deserve something, don't I? And you would be naming the price. I certainly couldn't cheat you."

Soon thereafter, Brad left without giving her a definite answer. She knew he was considering it. She told Gene that evening she was sure Brad would accept the proposal.

At the end of the week she received a check from Brad and a letter. It was a partial payment, he explained, the rest to be paid when he received the papers and transferred deeds to his property. The total amount she was to receive was also listed. It was a little more than two thirds of what Gene had found the market value to be.

She cried when she read the letter. He said many of the things he hadn't been able to say when he saw her. And worst of all, he told her he loved her and always would, but that he wouldn't come back.

Gene was delighted, but Marcella was once again a mass of confusion and torn emotions.

After her meeting with Brad, Marcella found she had little more to do with the case. Gene handled everything. There were innumerable delays and postponements caused by Brad's lawyer, as well as by Marcella's, but it mattered little to Gene, who had been caught up in the game playing of the legal world.

157

Twice she accompanied him to the lawyer's offices; on both occasions they questioned her unmercifully. The last time they wrote down all she said to them about her life with Brad and their business arrangements. From that time on, she knew only what Gene told her, and that wasn't much. It depressed Marcella, and Gene risked nothing by telling her only the best of news.

She heard about Brad from time to time—where he was, who he was seen with—but she didn't see him herself. She often went to places that had been their favorites, but he was never there. She wondered how she had spent her time before. She had always seemed to be busy and interested; now the days were tedious.

Eventually she found herself seeking out Charlotte, as she always seemed to do when things got to be too much for her.

"I will be happy to talk with you, Marcella, and listen and do whatever I am able," Charlotte said even before she allowed Marcella to come into the entry hall, "but not before you go upstairs and visit with Papa. The doctor says he's not well at all." She looked at the floor, then hurried on. "He was very disappointed the last time you came and didn't so much as say hello to him. I won't let that happen this time."

"What's wrong? I thought he had recovered from the beating."

"He did, but he isn't young anymore, Marcella, and to be perfectly frank, I don't think he really wants to get well."

"I'll go see him," she said softly. She went up the staircase to the bedroom. As she stood in the doorway to her parents' bedroom, Marcella felt terribly strange, remembering vividly that Hilary wouldn't let her enter the room after Jo was born. She walked in and looked at the pale, wasted figure of her father lying on the bed he had once shared with Hilary. He was deep in sleep.

Marcella knelt beside his bed and touched his hand. He stirred but did not awaken. "Papa, Papa," she whispered softly. Now finally, she wept—for Jo, for her father, but most of all, for herself. "I need you, Papa. Get well. Please get well."

She had always been able to talk to her father, even through those terrible years when everything had gone awry, when no one else seemed to want to listen and care about what happened to her. Why did it have to come to this, she thought. Why you and Jo and me, like this?

She wiped her eyes on the bedspread and struggled to her feet. Leaning over to kiss her father, she saw how lined and full of pain his face was. Strange that he can sleep so deeply, she thought. For a brief moment, she wished she could trade places with him. This room was so clean, so quiet, so unlike her life.

Her sigh was almost a shudder. She left the room, walked down the stairs to the morning room where Charlotte still sat, waiting.

She slumped into a chair across from her sister. "Charlotte, I must talk with someone," she said, and began to tell her everything that had happened between her and Brad, sparing nothing and no one.

Charlotte remained silent until her sister had finished. "What will you do now?" she asked finally.

"I don't know. Go on living in the house, I suppose. You don't think there is any hope that Brad and I—that he will come back?"

"I don't know how you can even ask," Charlotte said. She sat silent for a long time. Then she looked up at her sister, studying her as she had many times in the past—the pretty face with the wide, child's eyes, and the mouth that spoke of innocence. Was there anyone less innocent than she? Was there anything left of which Marcella was not guilty—deception, adultery, and now, with this court case, slandering and stealing from a man, destroying his reputation and his business? And she claimed to love him.

Charlotte shuddered. "How could you do it? What possessed you? And to let a horrible creature like Eugene Timmins lead you to it!

"I have never approved of what you were doing with Brad. He was—is—a married man with a child, and you had no right to come between him and his wife. But at least I could understand your loving him. If not pardonable, that was at least understandable. But this! There is no reason, no purpose. It is far worse. What came over you?"

"I couldn't stand losing him," Marcella said in a low voice.

"You drove him away."

"No, I didn't, Charlotte. I know it looks like it, but I didn't. It was finished before Brad and I had our first argument. No matter what Eugene is, he is not entirely wrong about Brad. It ended when Brad went to Scarborough House that time when Annette was ill, and then took that trip to the Catskills. I don't know if it was Annette, or the people he was with, or what. But he changed."

"He did, or you did? You are the one who made it happen with that cockeyed plan to make him jealous. It is entirely your own fault."

"Maybe. Maybe it is. Something is gone from me. Maybe it is all my fault."

"I can guarantee you it is. And if you have a grain of sense left in you, you'll send that Timmins fellow packing. Stop the court thing right now, before it is too late. You are going to regret this for the rest of your life if you don't."

Marcella sat silent for several minutes. Then she nodded. "I will stop it. I don't want to win, anyway," she whispered.

"Thank heaven!"

"I will if I can, that is. I have paid no attention to what is happening. I don't even know how far it has progressed."

"How could you simply ignore something as important as this? You haven't testified, have you?"

"No."

"They will need you, I should think. It is your case. What could they prove without you?"

"I'll tell Gene to put a stop to it tonight." Marcella reached out for Charlotte's hand. "I am so selfish and wrapped up in myself, I didn't even ask you how you are or if Martin has straightened out his difficulties. Tell me."

"Martin is gambling. I am more than a little worried about him. He needs the firm hand of a father, I am afraid. Even though they didn't see eye to eye about many things, it was different when his father was alive. He simply won't listen to me." Charlotte looked over at Marcella. She wasn't paying attention but was staring sadly at the back of Charlotte's chair.

"It is the same as if Brad were dead," she muttered. "I can't touch him or call out to him. I miss so many little things I didn't even know were a part of him. Isn't it strange how the odd little things make the biggest difference? The way he awakened in the morning. He was so funny. I had forgotten how I liked to waken first so I could watch him go through all the stages and hear him say such ridiculous and silly things when he was half awake. Oh, Charlotte, how can I live without him?"

"The same way I live without my husband," Charlotte said coldly.

Marcella looked up, suddenly ashamed. "I'm sorry, Charlotte. That's all I seem to say to you. You started to tell me something about Martin. What was it?"

"It was nothing."

"Yes, it was. I do want to hear."

"I am just worried about his gambling, and several of his associations, one in particular."

"Who is the particular association? I assume it is a girl from the protective, maternal look on your face."

"What else!"

"Who is she?"

"Rhea Scott," Charlotte answered quickly.

"Surely not the same—"

"The same."

"But what of Nicholas Dalton? The last I heard, they were quite an item. What happened?"

"I know nothing, either. It seems to me that everytime I think of it, I do nothing but go in circles. Martin's gambling, which is bad enough, is not the worst of it. I know, though he hasn't told me himself, that he is getting himself into difficulty with those horrible, odious creatures who encourage him, and now the Scott girl. She is, if anything, worse than Martin. Never in my life have I met a woman so openly eager for money and notoriety." She stopped suddenly, as if she thought she had said too much.

Still, she went on. "Then, of course, there is Nicholas. For more reasons than one, I wish we could steer clear of the Daltons. It seems we trip over one or another of them at every turn. I am not sure how it all came about, but whatever happened, Nicholas and Martin are at one another's throats over this girl. And I'll swear she enjoys every minute of it. I don't think for a minute she will actually marry Martin, but the damage she can cause in the meantime I shudder to think of."

"Have you talked to Martin?"

"Of course I have. But what is a man of Martin's age going to listen to? He is sowing his wild oats. The cock of the walk. Certainly he isn't going to listen to his mother."

"Then I suppose it will all just have to run its course. Perhaps both Nicholas and Martin will see her for what she is, and neither of them will marry her."

"I think you are very optimistic. You obviously haven't seen Miss Scott. She is stunning and wild and—and alluring. You know how men are about those things. They never recognize—Well, as you said, there is little choice but to wait and see. There is simply nothing to do, but wouldn't it be nice if she were homely or something?"

"Oh, Charlotte, what a goose you are. Silly one, if she were even slightly homely, neither of them would have given her a second thought."

"How agreeable!"

"I would love to continue this, but I am going to have to leave if I am to see Gene tonight. He comes quite early, and I don't want to miss him. It will be a relief to be able to go to sleep tonight knowing all this ugliness is over and will soon be forgotten. You are absolutely right. I must have been a little mad to have brought Brad into court."

Charlotte got up and kissed her on the cheek. "Perhaps this will change everything for you. If you tend to be overly optimistic, I tend to be overly pessimistic. Maybe Brad will be softened by this. You never know. And he does love you. That I don't doubt in the least."

"I wish I could believe it, and I may just try to talk to Brad tomorrow. I've already lost everything important to me, so how can I go wrong? And as you said, there is always hope. I may as well use it until it, too, is gone. Maybe he is as miserable as I am."

When Marcella arrived back at her house, she saw immediately that she had missed Gene. He had left a note for her propped up in front of the mirror. Tomorrow the trial would be over, the note said. There would be no need for her to testify, as they intended to use the statement she had given in the lawyer's office weeks ago. It had been such a cut-and-dried case that the written testimony would suffice. "It will save you the discomfort of having to face him and the reporters who insist on interfering with everyone connected with the trial."

Gene had ended the informative little note by congratulating her in advance on becoming a wealthy woman. Marcella was amazed at the large sum of money involved. She had not thought about it before; when Gene had rattled on about a lot of money, she had nodded and smiled without ever considering what "a lot" might constitute. Now she stared dumbfounded at a figure over half a million dollars, the true value of the property and the damages that would be awarded to her.

She went to bed that night nervous and feeling guilty. Morning could not come soon enough for her to straighten out the mess she had allowed to happen.

As soon as she entered the courthouse, she was surrounded by reporters asking relentless, rapid-fire questions so fast and so loudly that she couldn't have understood them even if she had been inclined to respond.

She fought through the people and the reporters and began to walk along the confusing corridors, seeking directions. Finally she was rescued by a policeman who directed her to the proper courtroom.

Eugene Timmins, in the witness box, was looking up from the paper he had in his hand, explaining something to the judge on the bench. Marcella, who had never been in a courtroom before, was at first rather awed by the hush of the audience and the black garb of the judge. It was some minutes before she began to hear what Gene was reading. They were her words—her statement given in the lawyer's offices. She hurried up the aisle and leaned over the railing to whisper to the lawyer sitting at the table.

"You should not have come, Miss Paxton," he said. "Mr. Timmins was desirous of saving you this distasteful task. Why don't you take a seat, and as soon as Mr. Timmins has finished, he can take you home. It will all be over in a matter of minutes now, and you can have a grand celebration after that. Leave all this dirty business to us."

"You are not listening," she whispered urgently. "I want to stop this. I don't want to win the case, and I don't want the money or anything else. I want the whole thing ended right now!"

"That is impossible. You have won!"

"I simply want to tell the judge it is all over. I want to withdraw the suit. Now, are you my lawyer or not? If you are, then represent me as I want!"

The lawyer looked to Gene for guidance. Gene left the witness box, unexcused, and hurried to join Marcella and the lawyer. The gavel banged furiously, and the courtroom began to hum. Amidst the confusion, Marcella slipped away from them and walked to stand directly before the judge. Gene turned and saw her, darted forward to grab hold of her, but already it was too late. Marcella had put in her request, and Gene was ordered to sit down and behave himself or be expelled from the room.

Marcella was sworn in as a witness and was seated. Gene and the lawyer, with heads so close they nearly touched, had a hasty and heated conversation during which Marcella sat stiff and uncomfortable, her eyes tearing as she looked over at Brad. Even if Gene and her own lawyer had not told her so, she had only to look at his face to know the trial was going against him.

Was it because of the loss of the property and what that would mean to him, or because of the break between him and Marcella? She suspected the latter. He was just as lonely as she, and just as lost. She was anxious to get on with it, and Gene and the lawyer were equally anxious that this should not happen. She looked up at the black-robed judge, and then to her lawyer, who now stood in front of her.

"Miss Paxton, the statement that was being read by Mr. Timmins was one that you gave under oath at my law office. Did you give a truthful and accurate statement at that time?"

"Yes, of course I was truthful, but only about one part of it, one side."

"There is nothing in that statement that is untrue, is there, Miss Paxton?"

"That isn't what I meant. It just doesn't go far enough. What I want to say is—"

"We need no elaboration, Miss Paxton. As a matter of fact, it would merely be a waste of the court's precious time. There is sufficient evidence in what you have already offered. We all appreciate your desire to see justice done, but my dear lady, there is really no reason to go into all the sordid details."

162

"There are no sordid details. I want to tell—"

The entire courtroom was suddenly alive with catcalls and whistles, and Marcella's voice was drowned in the noise. The reporters' eyes gleamed with the promise of tabloid headlines. The spectators were out of their seats, craning to see and hear what was happening.

Brad's lawyer, sensing that whatever it was that Marcella wished to say would be in his client's interest, was on his feet, defending Marcella's right to say whatever she wished. The judge, looking more and more flustered, banged his gavel over and over. Marcella's lawyer was asking for a recess. The harried judge, unable to regain control, gave up and recessed the session for two hours.

Marcella rushed from the room and tried to make her way through the throng, but Brad always seemed to be just a little ahead of her. Just as she managed to get out into the main hall, Gene grabbed her arm.

"Let go of me! I can't talk to you now, Gene. I must get to Brad. I am sorry, I just can't go through with it. I'll explain later."

"We've won! You can't throw it all away now. He's beaten! Do you hear me, Marcella? He's beaten."

"No! I won't let it happen, and there is still time."

"Not this time. Not you or anyone else will take this from me. I've won. Yes, I am the one who did all this. It is my victory, and you are not going to spoil it."

"You're despicable! Let go of me, or I'll—"

"You'll what?" He held tighter to her arm, pinching the flesh until it hurt.

"Help!" she screamed, and turned to glare at him as the same policeman who had helped her earlier came to her rescue again.

"This man will not release his hold on me," she said. Gene's hand dropped to his side without a word from the policeman.

"I don't think he'll trouble you again, but if he does, give a holler. I'll come running."

Marcella thanked him and then ran down the corridor in search of Brad. She had lost sight of him when Gene had detained her and now had no idea of where to begin her search in the large building. She asked everyone she met if they had seen him or knew where he might be found.

Several times she was told she had just missed him, but most of the time she was given blank stares. Finally she located his lawyer, and told him of her intentions.

"I'll do everything I can to help you. You have no idea, Miss Paxton, what this will mean to him."

"I will do as I have said, regardless, Mr. Tussing, but there is one thing I would like to ask you. Will Brad be relieved because of the property or because of me?"

"The property is a consideration—particularly Scarborough House. But the answer is, it is you who have concerned him most. I have no idea how many times I have caught him staring blankly and saying, 'This is not Marcella. It is not Marcella's doing.' "

"That is what I had hoped. Now, can you tell me where I might find him?"

"I expect him in this office any minute. He just stepped out to get something to eat. Will you wait here?"

Marcella paced the room, occasionally looking out of the windows, hoping to see Brad returning. The people below looked small from that height. Nervously she straightened the papers on Tussing's desk. He looked up from his work.

"I am sorry," Marcella grinned. "I shall do my pacing and fussing in the hall."

"You needn't leave. Go ahead and make yourself comfortable until he comes."

"You are kind, but I shall go into the hall. I am sure we will both be happier if I do." She laughed as Tussing absentmindedly rearranged his papers.

She had been standing in the hall near the top of the stairs for about fifteen minutes when she heard the sound of footsteps. She ran to the head of the stairs and called Brad's name. She couldn't see him, but his voice answered her.

He began to run up the flight of stairs below her. His footsteps seemed to multiply and their voices sounded unnaturally loud as they echoed from the cold marble walls. Marcella began to run down the stairs to meet him. She had just turned to go down the second flight when she heard Gene's voice.

"Dalton!"

Brad's footsteps stopped. Marcella froze where she was, and then, panicking, she began to run faster, calling out Brad's name as she came.

"Stay back, Marcy! Don't come down. Stay back!"

She rounded the flight of steps on which he stood. Gene was at the bottom, pointing a small pearl-handled pistol at Brad. Brad stood against the wall, halfway up the flight of stairs.

"Gene! Put that gun down. Put it down," Marcella shouted. "You can't shoot him. I told you I wouldn't go through with it." She started forward again.

"Stay where you are, Marcella! Get back around the corner," Brad said, too calmly.

"I will not!" she shouted. "Give me that gun before I call that policeman again."

"Call him!" Gene screamed and fired the pistol.

Brad lurched forward and slowly began to tumble down the steps, bumping on each one. He didn't make a sound, coming to rest at Gene's feet.

"Call your policeman. You have use of him now," Gene said, looking up at Marcella. He put the gun back into his waistband, smoothed his coat, and walked unhurriedly to the steps leading to the first floor. No one stopped the well-dressed man leaving the building.

Brad Dalton was dead before Marcella was able to stumble down the remaining steps to his side. When people began to arrive, she was stretched out across Brad's chest, barely conscious.

After the initial confusion had died down, Marcella was taken home and Brad's lawyer was brought from upstairs in his quiet office to make the necessary decisions regarding the body. He immediately sent for Nicholas Dalton.

Brad's body had been moved to a small anteroom by the time Nicholas arrived. He had had little time to prepare himself, having heard the whole incoherent story from the messenger sent to fetch him from the country. He hadn't taken time to change, and now he stood, tall and out of place, in a pair of farmhand's trousers and an open-collared shirt, badly in need of a shave.

Tussing repeated to him what had happened, or as much of it as he knew.

"I assure you, Mr. Dalton, I had no suspicion of something like this happening when that woman came to my office. Nothing like this has ever happened to a client of mine before. She seemed such a nice person. Why, I even got the impression that she cared a great deal for your father."

"Why did you agree to let her see him?"

"I believed her. How could I have known the man was still with her?"

"He was with her in the lawsuit, wasn't he?"

"Yes, but she was going to change all that. Oh, I am sorry. I—" Words failed Tussing entirely at that point. He stared out of red-rimmed eyes and shook his head wearily.

Nicholas thought of nothing but his mother as he rode back to Scarborough House. He had always felt protective of her and resentful of Brad's treatment of her. It had been a marriage of empty years for Annette.

He thought, too, of the humiliation she must have suffered at Marcella's hands, and the hurt she would now suffer, in addition to the loss of her husband, when the scandal hit the newspapers.

At this time of the afternoon, Annette would be in her sitting room. She would have an elaborate tea service at her side, several cups with which to serve any of her friends who might drop in, and on her lap would be the eternal tapestry.

He walked into her room without knocking. She looked up at him and frowned immediately. "I will not have you coming in here looking like that, Nicholas. You look like a field hand and smell like horse. If you wish to have tea with me, I am afraid you will have to bathe and change. And must you continuously wear that scowl on your face?"

He ignored her little speech, proceeding to tell her as gently as he could all that had happened to his father that day, ending with the arrangements he had made for the funeral.

"I was assured, Mother, that he didn't suffer. The bullet went right into his heart. It was very quick."

"I see," she said quietly. She sat silently for a moment, looking more like a painting than a living woman. "I think you did everything as well as anyone could have, Nicholas. A simple funeral is fine. With all the publicity and notoriety that will be attached to this, it would look odd if we made a great fuss over his funeral service, wouldn't it?"

Nicholas waited.

"Well, dear, you'll have to excuse me. I must get dressed for dinner. I am attending a small dinner party at the Johnsons' tonight. I didn't expect you home, or I would have been certain you had an invitation as well. But Gert can fix something good for you."

Nicholas looked at his mother as if at someone deranged.

"That's all?" he whispered. "Just go to tell Gert what I want to eat, and you go to get ready for a dinner party? Mother, I don't think you have understood what happened today. Father is dead. He was shot and killed this afternoon."

"Oh, dear! I suppose you are right. The Johnsons are bound to have heard of it by now—"

"Don't you care about him? Don't you care at all?"

"Don't shout so, Nicholas. It is totally unnecessary. Your father and I have been virtual strangers for twenty years or more. I never did know him, really."

"You *don't* give a damn about him! You never did! All these years when I hated him for what he did, it wasn't him, it was you! My God! I hated him for what he had done to you, and it wasn't even his fault. What kind of a woman are you? No one can be that cold."

"Nicholas, don't speak to me that way. I am your mother, and I'll have your respect. And stop dramatizing something you know nothing about. I am sorry your father was shot, but something like this had to happen sooner or later, considering the life he led and the people he associated with, and I'll not be a hypocrite by pretending to be heartbroken."

Nicholas moaned, "Didn't you ever care about him, even at the beginning?" He took her hand and stroked it gently. She pulled her hand free.

"Leave me to dress, Nicholas. I will be late if you persist in this degrading show of emotion. I find it disgusting and unmanly. Unfortunately, it is one of the negative traits you inherited from your father. I have always considered that it was this animal drive of his that caused his downfall. How else could a woman of Marcella Paxton's type have tempted him?" Not even her eyes showed the slightest emotion.

Nicholas stood up, towering over her. He was a large man, broad-shouldered, taller than his father, and much huskier. Though his skin was smooth and olive like his mother's, he was far more forbidding and prepossessing than Brad had ever been.

"Nicholas, go away," she pleaded. "I want to get dressed. Let me alone."

"You're no better than a leech!" he shouted. "You and Marcella Paxton—both of you—you killed him. You used him, and you didn't care. You didn't care at all!" He backed away from his mother, moving toward the door. "Couldn't you have given him anything? What about me? Don't you care about me—love me—either?"

She heard him run down the stairs and out of the house. Slowly her pulse returned to normal, and she relaxed. She went into her dressing room, stood before the pier glass Brad had given her as a gift last year, and looked at herself. She made several faces, twisting her mouth this way and that. When she came back to the room she looked properly grief-stricken.

She rang for her maid. It was better, she thought, to send a messenger over to the Johnsons' and ask that they come to Scarborough to console her. While she waited, she picked out a black silk gown from her cupboard. She smiled; it was one of her most becoming ones.

Nicholas ran for the stable. He yelled at the startled hand to get Bender ready for him. Bender had always been Brad's horse, but the man knew better than to question Nicholas, his choice of horse, or anything else, when he was like this. Hurriedly he saddled and bridled the horse, and when he handed the reins to Nicholas, backed out of his path. Nicholas leaped into the saddle and rode at a reckless gallop down the drive of Scarborough House.

Nicholas, who under normal circumstances would never abuse a horse, pushed Bender to his limits tonight, riding into the city of New York as fast as Bender was able to carry him. He tethered the horse in front of Marcella's house, throwing the reins so they touched the post and then fell lankly to the ground.

Not bothering with the bell, he pounded furiously on the wooden panel of the door. The pain that had started in his chest as he spoke to Annette grew unbearable.

Inside the house, Myrtle rushed to the door and stood behind it, trembling, afraid to open it to whoever was outside, and afraid that if she did not, he would shatter the glass panels on either side of the door.

Nicholas was leaning against the door frame, his head pressed hard against the wood, when she finally summoned the courage to open it a crack.

"Who is it?" Myrtle's voice quavered.

Nicholas looked up, and the maid started. The man didn't look injured, but she was sure he must be. His face was drawn and haggard, as though he hadn't slept in days.

"Who are you?" she asked again. "What do you want?"

"I'm Nicholas Dalton. Nicholas Dalton, do you hear?" He choked and coughed, trying to catch his breath. "I want to see Marcella Paxton."

"Oh, no, sir, you can't see Miss Paxton, sir," Myrtle stammered. "She's not well, and you don't seem too good yourself, sir."

"I can and I will!" Nicholas screamed, pushing her aside and forcing his way into the hall. There he stood in a daze, not knowing where to go. Then he dashed toward the back of the house and up the stairs to Marcella's bedroom.

Marcella lay unconscious, drugged by laudanum, her face flushed and tearstained. As he stood in the doorway, he looked at her, beautiful in sleep, and tried to remember that this was the woman his father had loved.

"You bitch!" he sobbed. Everything boiled to the surface—pieces of the past, the coldness, the indifference of Annette that he had always thought was her sorrow, the hot passion of Marcella, and the needless death of his father, torn between these two women.

He thought of the wasted years, the torment he had felt when he couldn't approve of his father or be close to him without feeling he was betraying his mother, when he had been unable to reach his mother through that wall of ice. Suddenly he lunged at Marcella. Taking hold of her shoulders, he shook her violently. Her head lolled, bumping against the headboard.

Myrtle rushed into the room. "What you doin'! You're gonna kill her, you madman!" she screamed. "Get outta here. I'll call the coppers. Madman!"

He took a firmer grip on Marcella's shoulders and shook her again. "Wake up! Damn you, you can't sleep through it all. Wake up!"

"Let go of her! You're hurtin' her." Myrtle pummeled his back with her fists. With one hand Nicholas sent Myrtle cras'.ing into the vanity. She scuttled from the room, shouting, "I'll call the coppers!"

Nicholas crumpled, his hands cradling his head. "I wish you were dead," he cried. "God! Why can't I kill you? I want to. Oh God, I want to. You deserve it. All of you."

Myrtle ran back into the room. "They're comin'. I called them. Johnny'll be back with the coppers in a minute. They're gonna get you. Lock you up, they will. Madman!"

Nicholas stood up slowly. "I ought to kill you, too, you old harpy."

"You're mad! Mad dog, mad!"

Nicholas turned and took a step toward her. Myrtle jumped back away from him. She was terrified he might touch her, and she was sure she would die at that touch. She shivered in the corner to which he had driven her, muttering prayers to all the saints she could think of. Nicholas stood motionless for a moment, somehow sharing in her frantic prayers. His eyes glazed, and his face was wet with tears.

Myrtle didn't move until he had gone out, leaving her alone with her fright.

Chapter Nineteen

When Marcella awakened for the first time after the shooting, everything seemed hazy and dreamlike, a series of broken scenes and faces of people—Jo, Brad, Hilary, her father. She remembered little of what had taken place after she had heard Gene's gun go off.

Myrtle sat gnomelike in a chair at her bedside.

"He is gone," Marcella moaned. "I killed him. I killed him."

Myrtle put her hand on Marcella's forehead. She was still feverish. From the ewer at the side of the bed, Myrtle took a wet cloth, wrung it out, and applied it to Marcella's head, heightening the deep flush of Marcella's cheeks.

She pulled away from Myrtle. "Leave me alone. Just let me be. I don't want to be better. I don't want to live."

Myrtle had tried to find Charlotte but was told that Charlotte had gone to visit some friends upstate and was not due back in the city for several days.

Tired and frightened by the reporters who came to the door daily and by the possibility that Nicholas Dalton might reappear, Myrtle returned shakily to sit at Marcella's side day after day, praying that nothing more would happen until she could get help.

Three days later Marcella awakened without a fever. She got up from her bed that morning, tottering from lightheadedness but more herself in spirit. She began to show some interest in her appearance, luxuriating in a long, warm bath and then taking pains to dress her hair as she always had. She was combing out the tangles when Myrtle came to her room.

"Miss Marcella?" she asked hesitantly from the doorway. Marcella glanced at her and returned to working on her hair. "Thank the Lord. I was thinking I might never again see you comb your lovely hair. Shall I get you something to eat? Tea—tea and little sandwiches, just little ones, nice and light?"

Marcella gave an almost imperceptible nod and winced as the comb tangled once more in one of the snarls in her hair. "If I should ever fall ill again, remind me to shave all my hair off," she said, her eyes tearing as she forced the comb down.

Myrtle hurried off to her task and returned with the tray just as Marcella finished with her hair.

"Put it near the bed, Myrtle. I must be weaker than I thought. I am exhausted."

"Well, you just take it easy for a few days. Everything is going to be just fine now. You take it slow."

Marcella sat down and leaned back on the pillows Myrtle had stacked behind her. She nibbled quietly on the sandwiches. When Myrtle was sure she was calm, she told her about the final court decision and about Nicholas's midnight visit.

"So I won," Marcella said after a moment's silence. "After all that, I won. It is nice to be a winner, isn't that what everyone always says?"

"Oh, yes, indeed it is."

"What happened to Mr. Timmins? Do you know?"

"He was taken to jail. They got him in the saloon just down the street, braggin' about the whole thing, he was. It wasn't no trouble to know who it was after what he said and what you told the policemen. What a wicked man—doin' the devil's work, he was."

"I told the police about Mr. Timmins?" When did I do that? I don't remember a thing after. . . ." Her voice trailed off.

"I don't rightly know when it was you talked to them. It must have been over at the courthouse, right after it happened. You had to talk sometimes, 'cause that's how they knew who to look for."

"I suppose they will want me to testify against him."

"After what he's done, I s'pose you'll be wantin' to tell them all there is."

"No, Myrtle. I don't, and I won't. I don't really care what happens to him. Nothing will change what has happened. All I ever cared about was Brad." Marcella looked around her room. "You never really realize what you have until you have managed to destroy it, Myrtle.

"Brad and I really began with this house, this brownstone that I thought was a sign that Brad and I were meant for one another. His initials over the door of a stranger's house seemed a sign—that we were different, that we could live outside the boundaries and rules that held other people back. I was sure we were led together by some unseen hand—my dark star. I suppose you could say that was the day I really killed him."

"You shouldn't say things like that."

"It's true. But the difficulty with hindsight is that it can't change anything. Have you ever thought, Myrtle, what it would be like if someone had told you stories all your life, fairy tales about beautiful women and handsome men, and then told you that all of that could be yours? Told you that one day you could be a rich and famous lady, that you could have anything you wanted, and that you would marry the most wonderful man, have position, admiration, excitement? Have you ever wondered what it would be like?"

Myrtle blushed and wrung her hands self-consciously. "People like me ain't got the right to dream like that. It's a fool's dream—and who'd be tellin' me stories like that? I'm just Myrtle. No lady, no story, just Myrtle. I wouldn't know what to do like you do. Lordy me, think of it. Dressed up in finery. Why, think of it! What a fool I'd make of myself!"

Marcella looked at Myrtle. She had been young when she had first begun to work for Marcella. Now her hands were swollen from long hours of scrubbing, and her skin had begun to show the results of lack of care. Myrtle had once been attractive—she might even have been called pretty, dressed in a stylish gown and with her hair done.

Marcella's eyes played tricks with her as she thought of who and what she would have been, had she stayed in Five Points. She exchanged positions with Myrtle, saw her own hands red and swollen, her feet widened by long hours in rough-cut shoes. Was she any more a lady than Myrtle, or was she just the deluded fool that Myrtle had spoken of?

"You are a wise woman, Myrtle. Only a fool would try to be what she is not. In the end one winds up not knowing who one is at all. Perhaps trying to be something one is not should be ranked among the worst of mistakes. Somehow the baser nature will always slip out to destroy the pretense of the good."

Myrtle looked at her, perplexed. "I don't follow your meaning too good, Miss Marcella. That's what I was sayin', a body like me couldn't pretend. I wouldn't know what was goin' on."

Marcella sat in her parlor for a long time that afternoon, thinking about her life. She walked around the room several times, touching the furniture, running her hand across the back of the sofa where Brad used to sit, talking to her, laughing, teasing her.

"Do I own all the contested properties, Myrtle?" she asked as she went into the kitchen where the maid was preparing dinner.

"That's what I heard."

"Then I also own Scarborough House," she said softly.

"Dear me! How could I have forgotten. I was never so scared in all my life! I thought he'd kill you, I was that frightened. I called the coppers on him."

"Whom did you call the coppers on?"

"Mr. Dalton—I mean his son."

"Nicholas? But why? You said he came here, but why would you—? Perhaps you had better explain all of this to me. I think I have heard only a part of it."

"Well, like I told you earlier, he came here about midnight—you know, on that day. Half mad he was that night. He came in here lookin' like he'd keel over at the next step, and then all of a sudden he was wild, shakin' you and cursin' and cryin'. Mad he was, mad as he could be."

"And this was the night Brad was killed?"

"The same. The very same day."

"Poor Nicholas. What Brad and I have done to him. And it was all because of me and some stupid initials over a door."

"I wouldn't be knowing about no initials and such, but he don't look poor to me. Looks like they'd be lockin' folks like him away so they don't hurt nobody."

"Don't worry about him. He didn't hurt me, did he?"

"No, ma'am, but he sure bounced me off'n the vanity. I got a black-and-blue spot as big as his fist."

"He hit you?"

"No, ma'am, when I was beatin' on his back to stop him from shakin' you, he brushed me off like a fly."

"Well, then, it wasn't intentional. Believe me, Myrtle, if he didn't hurt me or you either that day, Nicholas Dalton is not likely to harm anyone. It was his father I killed, after all."

"I don't want to see him again. He's a devil! No better'n that Timmins fellow, if you ask me. All of these goin's-on puts me in mind of the day of reckoning. And I'm telling you, if it goes on much longer, I ain't gonna be here to watch no more."

"You needn't worry, Myrtle. I don't think anything more will happen."

As the weeks passed, Marcella spent more and more time in her room. It seemed to have become a kind of cocoon from which she emerged only with the greatest reluctance. For hours on end, she sat quite motionless, going over and over her life, sorting it all out.

Charlotte did visit her once, breaking precedent by coming to the brownstone. Their conversation, however, was awkward, and Marcella was glad when Charlotte stayed away after that once.

At last, when she had regained much of her physical energy and strength, she roused herself to action. One afternoon she called Myrtle to her room.

"Don't bother fixing supper tonight, Myrtle. I am going to give both of us a rest. I will want my small valise packed with only a few things. The least I can possibly manage with, one change of dress and my underclothes—and one nightgown. It will only be a short visit, so be frugal."

"So you're takin' a trip. Now that will be nice for you. Do you a world of good to get away for a while."

"I hope so."

Myrtle went to the wardrobe and pulled down a small suitcase. "Where will you be going?"

"Home, Myrtle. I am going home for a while."

"I always held that when there's trouble afoot, home is the best place to be. We need that from time to time, just to get the feeling of who we are."

Marcella smiled. "You are quite the philosopher, Myrtle. I agree with you. And that is exactly what I am going to do. Go back to where I began, and find out just who I really am."

"Mrs. Henderson will sure be glad to see you. She didn't look real happy when she was here before. This will give you two a nice long visit."

Marcella said nothing. She walked over to where Myrtle had her valise and dropped in her hairbrush. "I told you to be frugal," she said, removing a small jewelry case. "I shall certainly have no need of jewelry. And I won't need two pairs of shoes. The ones I am wearing are enough."

"You sure you don't want to change your mind and take your trunk? This is a battered old thing," Myrtle said, closing the case. "If you don't mind my sayin' so, it looks tacky for a fine lady like you to be carryin' something like this. I'll just go ahead and pack that nice shiny little trunk of yours. Leave this old thing behind."

"No, this is what I want," Marcella said, lifting the case off the bed.

Fifteen minutes later, Marcella was gone. She got a carriage and directed the driver to Five Points.

He refused to drive her all the way to Orange Street and charged double to go as far as he did. Marcella paid him and smiled. She was in no hurry. It was late afternoon, and the day had the odd coloration of early dusk when the weather promises to change quickly and harshly.

She stood at the edge of the district, looking down into the roiling streets. Somehow it seemed different from how she remembered it. The sounds refused to blend harmoniously. Here and there she saw a little girl, her back bent over, straining under the weight of a corn box strapped to her shoulders. The butter smelled good, and Marcella remembered the taste of the hot corn long ago. Somehow the memory cheered her, dispelling some of the strangeness.

Five Points had changed; it was poor, poorer than she remembered. There were still signs of the old familiar gangs, men on street corners and peering out of the groghouses, but the dirty streets were filled with odors foreign to her nose.

She thought of Lou and how he had picked her up and put her on his shoulder. Tough and disreputable as any of the Dead Rabbits, Lou still had had a kind of vitality that had fascinated her. She looked now at the faces around her—unsmiling, wrinkled, and encrusted with dirt in the folds of skin. Had it really been like this when she was growing up? She no longer wondered that Hilary had wanted her daughters far away from it. Thank God, Jo had never seen it!

She picked up the battered case and began to walk down into the heart of the Points. Orange Street was raucous as always. Music blared from the groghouses, and men squabbled out on the streets, spilled or thrown out the open doors.

Women called to one another from tenement to tenement; wet laundry hung on sagging ropes, dripping and flapping in the wind to dry and be called clean. Marcella remembered Hilary bent over a tub of brackish water, working for hours to get Charlotte's and her pinafores clean.

Marcella stopped in front of the tenement in which she had been born. Though five stories high, it was not as tall or as large as she remembered it, and it seemed to sag toward the rear. Momentarily she wondered what kept it standing.

A woman, half asleep or inebriated, sprawled in the doorway, muttering to herself. When Marcella said politely that she would like to pass, the woman let loose a flood of incoherent abuse. Marcella edged her way around the woman and entered the narrow passage that led to the dark, steep stairwell. She looked at it now and wondered why she hadn't broken her neck, running up and down those stairs as a child.

Carefully, she avoided the debris that littered them, and felt her way along in the darkness. The walls felt slimy to her touch, and the odors—fumes of the trapped gas and rot, sweet and deadly in the tunnel-like well—made her queasy. She began to hurry, vaguely aware that she was being followed.

She was out of breath and her head had begun to ache by the time she reached the old Paxton apartment. She wondered who she would find living there now. Would it be a lucky family, having the entire three rooms to themselves? She was almost afraid to find out.

She knocked on the door, softly at first and then boldly. In the face of the man who answered, all dreams of the past were banished. There was no family here, she knew immediately—at least not a family like hers had been. Whoever this man was, he was not fighting against Five Points. He had drowned in it long ago.

Surly and ugly, he bore the scars of many fights on his dirty, unwashed body. He smelled like the fetid gutters of the street below.

"Look what's standin' here." He threw the door wide open. Behind him Marcella could see a woman lying on a pallet of dirty straw and leaves on the floor against the far wall. The woman propped herself up on one elbow. "What's she want? What's she doin' here?"

"What d'ya want?" the man repeated to Marcella.

"I just wanted to see this apartment. I was born here, you see. Right here in this very room. I thought perhaps I could stay here just for a night or two, but I can see you have illness in your family, so perhaps—"

"Can you pay?"

"I had intended to, but as I said, it would not be—"

The man moved closer to Marcella. "Not so fast, sister." Marcella turned her face away, glancing down at the woman. The man dug at his scalp and extracted one of the creatures that inhabited it.

"You was born here?" he said as he squashed it between his fingers. His breath was foul.

Marcella coughed into her gloved hand. "Yes, I was."

"And you want to stay here a time?"

"Well I did, but—"

"How much?"

"How much?" she repeated. One of the men who had come up the steps behind her reached toward her, and she moved away.

"How much will you gimme if I let you stay?"

"What would you want?"

"Twenty."

"That is too much," she stammered, "and besides, I think perhaps that I no longer wish to spend the night." She edged toward the wall again, avoiding the hands that seemed all around her now.

"What about our bargain?"

"We have no bargain."

The man behind her now stood so near she could smell his breath.

"Gimme the twenty."

"Ten!" she cried. "Ten, and you must promise—promise you won't touch me. I mean, you'll keep the other men away?" Marcella gestured hesitantly at the group of men who had gathered to see what was going on. Several were now stroking the skirt of her dress and fumbling with the heavy layers of her petticoats. They touched her hair as she spoke, and talked to each other in languages she could not understand.

She began to realize that the people now in the Points were not like those she had lived with at all. It was worse, much worse. Five Points was dying of disease and decay. It was a dumping ground for each new wave of immigrants. The best had left and would continue to leave as they rose to the top like cream on fresh milk. What Marcella faced was the scum. They would never rise, these primitive men and women.

The man she had spoken to reached out, taking hold of her bodice. "You don't like me?" he grunted.

She gasped, backing away. "No! I mean, it isn't you. It's—I don't like men," she cried in desperation.

"She don't like men." He laughed and pushed his face into hers. "You weren't born down here, girlie. No one down here doesn't like it. It's all we got." He plunged his hand down her dress. She grabbed hold of his wrist, trying to take his hand away from her breast. He laughed and pulled her closer to him. "Hey, Georgie! Come on in here. Lookee what I got!"

A man emerged from the darkness of the room and staggered toward them.

"Says she was born here. Built good." Both men laughed, and the woman on the floor began to howl.

"Shut her up!" Georgie growled. Another man inside gave the woman a kick that set off a new bout of wailing.

"She don't shut up. She's goin' to die."

He turned to the woman on the floor, momentarily releasing Marcella, who began to move quietly toward the steps.

"Where you goin'?" he yelled, grabbing her and pulling her back to the doorway. "Bargain's a bargain. Ten bucks. Gimme the ten." He jerked at her arm and sent her flying into the room. She slammed into the opposite wall and froze where she was. He came over and stood before her. "Two days, twenty bucks."

Marcella didn't move. She looked frantically about the room, trying to see if there was any other way to escape.

"Gimme the twenty. Come on. Give it, or I'll get it myself. I know all the ladies' hiding places." He leaned forward, placing one filthy hand on the wall on either side of her head.

"You'll have to move, or I can't get it," she said as steadily as she could. "It's in my valise. I have to open it. I can't get it if you don't let me—"

He laughed again, breathing foul breath into her face. "What's you afraid of, girlie? 'Fraid I'll hurt ya again?" He grabbed at the front of her gown. Marcella cried out, and he released her.

Georgie danced around behind them, trying to see over the other man's shoulders. "Get the money first. Get it first!" he cried.

The man lifted one arm, and Marcella scuttled out from under his body. She grabbed the valise and took out a pouch. She tossed it across the room to him. "Here! Take it all. Take all of it and let me leave."

"She's got more, Dom. She's got more, damned if I can't smell it on her," Georgie said and took a couple of lurching steps toward her.

"No, I haven't. I haven't got any more! I gave it all to you. I haven't got any more!" she screamed. Georgie kicked the hall door shut as they both approached her. Marcella screamed into the dark room as their hands tore at her clothes in search of the money.

Later she sat quietly on the floor in the corner where they had left her, horrified and fascinated by the bugs and the vermin that crawled around on the floor, across her bare flesh, and onto the walls. She pulled back the tatters of her dress and began to scratch and pick at her hair.

Several times Marcella cried out to Charlotte, to God, to anyone, but the men paid no more attention to her agonies than they had to the miserable woman lying on the straw pallet. She had had all the absolution she wanted from Five Points. She wanted only to leave.

Each time she tried to go, she was stopped by the men in the room, now drunk with the liquor her money had bought. She waited vainly for them to pass out, or leave, or go to sleep—or even to kill her—anything that would end this nightmare. Whatever she was, she was not Five Points. Five Points was death.

It was three days before Marcella actually got out of the Points, before the liquor ran out and the men were finally convinced she hadn't a penny left to give them. They threw her out into the hall. As she picked herself up, everything became a sickening blur. There wasn't a part of her body that didn't hurt or that hadn't been abused by one of them. The revulsion she felt was so deep and degrading that nothing could force it out.

She wandered along the streets, clinging to the one untorn dress in her valise. She had no money, and in any event, no driver would stop his coach to take her as a passenger, looking as she did. Her head was buzzing, and she felt constantly nauseated. By the time she reached the better side of Manhattan, it was dark. Finally she reached the front stoop of her brownstone. She used the key she had always kept in a little niche cut in the lintel of the door for Brad, and managed to stumble into the house.

Myrtle began to scream when she saw her standing in the darkened hallway.

"Stop it, Myrtle! Myrtle, it's me. Oh, please stop! I need help." She slumped to her knees. "Help me, Myrtle. Help me."

In the end, Marcella got herself into bed. Myrtle wouldn't touch her. She was so tired she thought she might die before she could close her eyes in sleep. Her body seemed immobile and heavy; at the same time, there was a restlessness inside her. A hundred devils tortured her as the vermin bit at her; she felt the urge to be in motion and a horrible heaviness and hatred of that need to move.

The following morning, after a nearly sleepless night, she felt somewhat better and forced herself to go to the bathroom and scrub until she was sure there were no more of the horrid, biting creatures on her skin. Myrtle finally granted upon seeing her clean once again that she was indeed Marcella Paxton.

"What'd you do to yourself? Where you been? I'm gonna call the coppers. Who did this to you?"

"Don't call anyone! No one did anything."

"I'll get the doctor. You're all bitten up, and Lord, there ain't a piece of flesh left that ain't black and blue. What's happened to you?"

"Myrtle, don't call anyone. I'll get the doctor as soon as these bites go away."

"But you're sick! You need a doctor."

"I'm not sick. I feel much better this morning." She did. At least, the peculiar feeling she had been having was going away; surely that was a sign that she was getting better. All that was left was a dull pain in the small of her back. "Just don't tell anyone I am back," she told Myrtle. "Let them think I have extended my visit."

Myrtle scowled, but she took to having as little to do with Marcella as possible.

Daily Marcella scrutinized herself, expecting the insect bites to disappear. They didn't. It seemed to her that they were getting worse instead of better. They were larger, and while she couldn't be sure, it seemed that there were more of them.

By the fifth day they had whiteheads on them, and they hurt. She had gotten very hoarse, and her face was swollen. She thought she had noted some puffiness lately, but on that fifth morning, there was no doubt, her throat was badly swollen.

"Myrtle, get my sister. Please hurry. I need her!" Marcella called out from her dressing room, where she stood before the full-length mirror. Myrtle came to the door. "Don't come in! I don't want you to see me. Go get Mrs. Henderson now! Do as I say!"

"What's wrong with you?" Myrtle said, looking at the reflection of Marcella's back in the mirror.

"I don't know what's wrong. Go get Mrs. Henderson!" Marcella cried. "Myrtle, please. Get my sister. I am so frightened." Marcella lowered the robe she had been holding in front of her. "Look at my face! Look at it!"

"I'm not comin' back here. No matter what you say, I ain't steppin' foot in this house. No, sir! I don't know where you gone, or what you done to yourself, but I sure know *that* when I see it! I ain't comin' back."

"What? What is it?"

"Smallpox. How come you ain't been vaccinated? I should have knowed from the start, the way you was actin'. That's smallpox, Miss Paxton, that's what it is."

"No!"

"Yes, ma'am. I'll get you a doctor, and then I'm gettin' out of here."

"No, not the doctor! No one but Charlotte. Get Charlotte. Please promise me you won't tell anyone but Charlotte. Promise me, Myrtle!"

"You need a doctor."

"Charlotte will get me one. Oh, God, promise me, Myrtle. On your crucifix! Promise. Promise, Myrtle!"

Myrtle shrugged, kissed her crucifix, and went to gather her things from her room.

When she went to see Charlotte that day, she was told Charlotte was out for the afternoon. The maid told Myrtle they would be moving; Charlotte was selling her own house and preparing to move to her father's, which was larger. Myrtle might have left a note, but she had never learned to write, and she couldn't tell anyone else why she wanted Charlotte because of her promise to Marcella.

She went to see Charlotte the following day, but when she arrived, Charlotte was once again not home. After the second visit, Myrtle went to confession, was absolved, and went to Charlotte's house no more.

Marcella lay hour after hour, waiting for Charlotte to arrive. Her eyes swelled, and she could see little, sometimes nothing. She groped around her room when necessary, trying to find her way and crying out in pain as she touched or bumped into pieces of furniture.

Several days after Myrtle had left, Nicholas came to the house. He rang the bell, and receiving no answer, he was about to leave when he heard a sound from inside. He tried the door and found it unlocked. The house was dark, without a single lamp lit. He nearly walked into Marcella before he saw her. She stood there in the dusky half-light, saliva streaking from her ruined mouth. Her face was a mass of pea-sized pustules running with yellowish matter.

"Marcella," he whispered, taking a step back. He wanted to turn and run. "N'klish . . .N'klish. . . ."

He touched her, and she howled in pain. He drew his hand back. Picking up the sheet she had dropped, he tried to cover her with it. She cried out again.

"Marcella, what have I done?" He shook his head. "Stay where you are. I'll get the doctor. Don't move." He backed away from her, afraid. "I didn't mean—this. Not this. I would never have wished anything like this on you."

He brought both Charlotte and a doctor back with him. Marcella stood dumbly where Nicholas had left her over an hour before.

The doctor took her to her room and put her to bed. He left only a thin sheet covering her. "She will not be able to tolerate the pain, Mrs. Henderson," he told Charlotte. "Even the weight of a bed sheet can cause pain. We'll let her rest for now. There is little else we can do to help her at the moment."

"Can't I do anything? Surely there must be something—"

"Shall we do our talking downstairs?"

Charlotte led him down to the parlor. He shook his head sadly as they walked. "I don't understand how she got it. With the vaccine, this was one disease we thought was pretty well under control—except, of course, for places like the area of the Old Collect Pond, but your sister was not likely to have been there. That place is a pesthole for everything."

"Did you say the Collect Pond? Does that mean the cases you have had reported were in the Five Points area?"

"Most of them," the doctor replied. "We always have the most trouble from that area. It gets worse daily, and there seems to be no way to stop it. The place shouldn't be allowed to exist at all. Nothing but pestilence down there."

"I wished her dead." Nicholas's voice echoed in the silence of the room.

"Nicholas!"

"Come now, Mr. Dalton, we are far beyond the time when people believed that wishes could cause such things as smallpox."

"I wished her dead, and she is dying. She *is* dying, isn't she? Whatever you call it, she is dying!"

"I don't know that, Mr. Dalton, and neither do you. Her living or dying depends on good nursing and the will of God. Perhaps, Mr. Dalton, you'll find your wishes are not quite so powerful as His."

Nicholas stared at the floor. The doctor concentrated on Charlotte. "Give her cold water as often as she'll take it. Sweeten it a little, and perhaps something a little acid could be added, just to make it taste better."

"I'll get her fresh lemons every day," Nicholas offered.

"I think you have done enough already, Nicholas. We will do without your lemons."

"That would be very nice of you, Mr. Dalton. Mrs. Henderson, this is bad enough without promoting animosity between you and the young gentleman. I think you can see how remorseful he is. Now, if we can continue with the instructions—"

"Of course, Doctor."

"I will give you an ointment, Mrs. Henderson. It is simple, made from parsley. You may apply it with a soft swab. It will stop scarring if the disease is caught soon enough. In your sister's case, it is undoubtedly too late. I am sure she is too far advanced, but we will do it all the same, in the hope of minimizing the damage. There is little we can do at this stage but make her comfortable and hope for the best."

"Do you think she has a chance?" Nicholas asked.

"I certainly hope so, for her sake and yours, too, Mr. Dalton. You are very young, and the young like to suffer for their sins. As an old man, I could tell you that you had nothing whatever to do with Miss Paxton's condition, but at your age you think you know better, and never stop to listen to reason."

"Nicholas, I am sure Marcella will be all right." Charlotte still hadn't forgiven Nicholas for wishing Marcella ill, but neither was she going to allow the doctor to think her a grudging woman. She tried to smile.

"Is there anything I can do to be of help?" Nicholas asked.

"It would be best if you went home, Nicholas," Charlotte replied a little self-righteously. "Marcella needs a woman's care. Go home and see to your mother."

Nicholas looked at her. "My mother is no longer at Scarborough House. She has left."

"Oh, really? Where is she?"

"She left the week after Father was buried. She lives with her family in New Orleans."

"Oh, I am sorry. You are all alone, then."

"I prefer it that way," he said quietly.

The doctor mixed a generous supply of the parsley compound. "This should take care of her for the next few days, Mrs. Henderson. I shall stop in again tomorrow, and we'll see how she is. If this is too painful to her when you apply it, desist. As I said earlier, I think it is too late to have any great effect, so if it comes to a choice between possibly preventing scarring and her comfort, choose her comfort."

After Nicholas and the doctor had left, Charlotte slumped down in one of the soft chairs. It was hard to believe that Marcella's whole life had wound up in the horrible disfigurement Charlotte had seen today—and yet it seemed just.

Marcella was a fallen woman, she had lived in sin, sinned joyfully for years. Charlotte thought of the New Testament story of Martha and Mary and considered how well she fit Martha's role—the server, the competent woman ready to serve even a Mary as yet uncleansed. If God chose to cleanse through smallpox, who was Charlotte to deny His will?

Chapter Twenty

For the first couple of weeks while the disease raged, Charlotte never knew from one minute to the next if she would find Marcella dead or alive. Charlotte's days were filled with the kind of activity that easily lends itself to self-dramatization and therefore a kind of stimulating expenditure of energies.

Once Marcella was no longer in imminent danger of death, there was little for Charlotte to do, and she entered into the vague world of apprehensive boredom, a half life of nameless guilts, memories of unkind thoughts and words, helplessness to do anything, and frustration.

For Nicholas, time translated itself into a pattern. As a boy, when he was troubled, he had wandered on foot or horseback over Scarborough's acreage, stopping to look at the small streams that branched through the wild, uncultivated sections of the land.

This time, it was different. During those days long ago, his grandfather would eventually find him, and together they would sort out his problems. This time Nicholas was alone. His grandfather was dead; indeed, not another soul lived in Scarborough House with him but the servants. Perhaps for the first time, Nicholas Dalton felt the need to reach out to someone and knew there was no one to reach to.

Day after day, Marcella accepted Charlotte's care as she would the service of a hired woman. She rewarded Charlotte with no kind word, not so much as a smile. Marcella seemed to take notice of nothing.

"I am perfectly willing to work myself to the bone for you, Marcella," Charlotte told her one evening. "I have always been a devoted person when it came to my family, but the least you could do is make some attempt to cooperate. Dr. Bancroft told me you could begin to get up and about anytime now. You are perfectly well, if you want to be."

"He's dead, Charlotte. He's dead," Marcella moaned.

"I *know* he is dead! If I hear you say it once more to me, I shall scream. You cannot do a thing about that. You should have listened to good sense when you had the chance. You didn't, and you regretted it, just as I said you would. Now you must put this behind you and get on with your life."

Marcella didn't look at her. "I am so tired." She shut her eyes and feigned sleep.

"Ungrateful! That's what you are, ungrateful. Never so much as a 'thank you.'" Charlotte fussed about the room, straightening and dusting as she scolded Marcella.

"Charlotte, hand me the bottle of laudanum. I just can't seem to sleep, and my head is bothering me."

"You take too much of this," Charlotte muttered as she handed her sister the bottle and spoon.

"Dr. Bancroft told me to take it when necessary."

"Always is 'necessary' to you! You use it as an excuse so you don't have to face anything."

Marcella shut her eyes again.

As the days became weeks—and then months—Marcella continued to be unresponsive. Even the news of her father's death—he had never really recovered from his last illness, a bout with pneumonia—hardly touched her. Certainly she was incapable of attending the funeral, and she evinced absolutely no interest in the added burden Charlotte now carried.

More and more, Charlotte felt ill-used and unnecessary. Life was passing her by. Things she had never given a moment's thought before, now became important. The bustling city she lived in, the hurrying people, the omnibuses, coaches, and wagons—all began to invite her.

Always Charlotte had held what she considered the falsely alluring glitter of the city, its gaudy tinsel dreams, at arm's length, never permitting them to become a part of her. Now, as she seemed to stand still, she looked back at the lost years of her life, and she began to want what she had come to think the world owed to her.

There were so many people who owed her something for past kindnesses; somehow, all of that should be repaid to her. For the first time Charlotte felt a kinship with her son's desires for the riches of the world.

"Marcella, I have come to a decision," she told her sister one day. "There is no point in my remaining here in this house, caring for you, when anyone could do it. I have decided to hire a competent woman to come in daily. Martin needs my attention far more than you. It is high time I began to consider him, and to be honest, I am tired of being a drudge. It is time I did as I like, too."

Marcella tried to focus her eyes on Charlotte. "You are going to leave? Where would you go?"

"So! You *can* talk! I am leaving, Marcella. High time I did. I must get back to Martin. He needs me and appreciates me, and after all, he should come first. He is my son."

"Martin doesn't need you," Marcella whined. "He's a grown man. What would he need you for?"

"He needs me as any son needs a mother. He misses his father. He needs me now."

"*I* need you now!" Marcella cried.

"You have always needed someone! An audience is what you really want. I have done a lot of thinking these past weeks. All your life, you have cried out whenever things went wrong or you wanted attention, and there has always been someone there. You feed on other people's sympathies, Marcella, and now I am finished. I've done more than can be expected." Charlotte fussed with the ruffled neckline of her dress.

181

"You don't care what happens to me?"

"I have a life, too. Sometime someone has to think of me. And there is Martin. What am I going to do if he fritters his entire life away at some faro table? He is well on his way to losing every cent his father left."

When Charlotte looked down at her sister, Marcella was intently studying a piece of lint she had discovered on her quilt. "So I must go!" Charlotte added loudly.

"Where are you going?" Marcella asked, looking up as if the conversation had just begun.

"You're impossible. I am going home!"

"I need you. Who will take care of me?"

"You don't need me. Half the time you are not even aware I exist."

Marcella lay back against the pillow.

"Have you ever considered, Marcella, that of the three of us it was you who were given everything? Of course, you threw it all away and then asked for our sympathy and help. But it was you who had her fortune handed to her. You have money, you have this house, and of all of us, you were always the most beautiful and sought-after.

"What did Jo and I have? We were good. We didn't break the rules as you did. We led good lives and cared about our families, and what did we get for it? Look at you, Marcella! You had everything, and you threw it all away!"

Hearing Jo's name on Charlotte's lips, Marcella bristled. "Don't speak to me of Jo," she snapped.

"And why not? What did you ever do for her—or her poor, homeless children? *I* pay. Dear old reliable Charlotte. I've been paying for the care and housing of Jo's Kathleen. At the expense of my son's future and my own, I pay and pay gladly, so that my sister's child will be safe."

"No one ever told me about the children. No one asked me to help."

"They did, as a matter of fact. Cousin Leona told me she wrote to you. And even *I* mentioned it to you at the beginning. But I was the one to go to Ohio and see to their welfare."

Marcella said nothing.

"I don't know why I never realized how selfish and unfeeling you are!" Charlotte went on. "All these years and your eternal cries of 'Charlotte, I need you'! Never once have you stopped for a second to ask if any of us needed *you!* Even when Papa died, you couldn't be bothered."

Marcella groaned. "Oh, Charlotte, please. Why must you be so cruel? I was sick beyond hope when Papa died. How can you torment me by accusing me this way?"

Charlotte, suddenly remorseful, backed off. "I am sorry, Marcella. I didn't mean to say it that way." She fidgeted in her chair and then suddenly stood up. "Still," she said, a little more assertively, "it doesn't change anything. I really must leave. I have got to take hold of my own life."

Marcella struggled to sit up in bed. "Don't leave me, Charlotte. I do need you. I'll do whatever you ask." Her voice was pathetically small. "If it is money that worries you, I have plenty for both of us. Martin, too, if it comes to that. Just ask me."

"I'll not ask a thing! I am not the asking sort. I take care of my own problems."

"Then let me ask you. Let me help you as you've helped me. Will you stay with me now?"

"On the condition that you cooperate, Marcella. I cannot do this all alone. I tell you, when I see you lying there day after day, making no effort to help yourself, while I wait on you hand and foot, I could just scream in exasperation."

"I won't do that anymore. I will do as you say."

"Be thankful, Marcella, that I have been here for you. This time you would have died if I hadn't been here. Don't forget that."

"I won't. I won't forget, and I do want to repay you." Marcella moved to the edge of her bed, following Charlotte with her eyes as she paced. "I have no one but you, don't you see? No husband or children, no one to care about me or leave my things to when I die. I almost did die, and there was no one. Charlotte, that is so fearsome—to die and know there is no one. Sometimes I wanted it to happen so I would never have to think about it again—and other times I prayed God to let me come back long enough to make it all different. I do want it to be different."

"Do you really?"

"Yes. And I wish I had a child. Someone who would care. How lucky you are to have Martin."

"Huh! Martin. I am lucky, but it is not so simple. He—I don't know how to help him, really. If his father had lived, it would all have been so different. We would all have been secure. Martin would have had the money to start his own business, and there would have been none of this wretched desire to get rich quickly on a toss of the dice or the turn of a card."

"But there! Don't you see? That is where I can help you." Marcella thought for a moment. "Let me make Martin my heir. Who else have I got?"

"Would you—consider it?"

"Why not? There is no one else."

"It would amount to a great deal, Marcella. The money from that lawsuit and the properties was considerable."

"But who am I to leave it to?"

"Scarborough, too?"

"Not Scarborough. I promised Brad it would go to Nicholas. I gave my word."

"I'll have to talk it over with Martin. You do understand, if I agreed to this, it would be for his sake, his future?"

The conversation ended in an awkward silence. If Charlotte said one more word, she knew she would surely give away the enormous relief she felt at the prospect of an inheritance for her son.

The money Martin had used to finance his life of happy abandon had come primarily from Charlotte and from his own modest inheritance. He had easily persuaded his mother to sell her house, give him the proceeds, and move into the house she had grown up in, which her father had left to her. But it was clear to him, if not to his mother, that if he continued on the path he had set for himself, both he and Charlotte would be totally without funds before another year was out.

Charlotte knew she must not allow Marcella to know she had the upper hand, even temporarily. However weak and frightened Marcella was at the moment, she was basically a headstrong, independent woman. If Marcella's offer were to be taken, it would have to be taken quickly.

But Marcella was not really so meek as she appeared. It was true she was frightened, and she dreaded being alone after her recent experiences; at the same time, promising to make Martin her heir cost her nothing and assured her of a permanent family, should she need them. She had no doubt her offer would be accepted. Martin could and would get his mother to agree to anything in order to feed his craving for money. Money was his passport to gambling, and for Martin Henderson, gambling was an obsession to the point of disease. He would jump at the chance to have his future debts insured, Marcella knew. She lay back on the pillows, shut her eyes, and fell asleep.

Once Charlotte and her son had agreed to accept Marcella's offer, Charlotte's good humor and reservoir of patience returned. Marcella was permitted to slump comfortably back into her depression and self-pity. Again she filled the bedroom with melancholy sighs and proclamations of grief, now more habit than anything else.

"Charlotte, I cannot bear to live without him. Nothing is left now that Brad is gone. It would have been more merciful to let me die. That is all I want now—death. Death and peace."

Charlotte bustled around the room, straightening clothing and furniture. "You don't mean a word of it, Marcella. I am going to need some money for the household this month, and then"—she paused in her work and looked down at her dress—"I do need some new dresses. The ones I wear are so out of style."

"Order some made, or go to Stewart's. They have some very nice things."

"Perhaps I shall, at least I will look," her sister replied absently. "Oh, Marcella, dear, have you given any further thought to including Scarborough House in Martin's inheritance? It would make all the difference in the world to him. Already, I feel he is turning over a new leaf. I haven't heard him complain about needing money in ever so long, and he has said that if he had a place like that to call home, he would be absolutely dedicated to it."

"No, I haven't." Marcella turned her head to the wall.

Charlotte looked at her sister. It was terribly strange, she thought, that Marcella hadn't shown the slightest interest in her appearance. She had made no attempt to look into a mirror, nor did she seem to notice the pockmarks that pitted her hands, arms, and legs. It was as if she didn't see them at all, or perhaps she refused to admit to seeing them.

Late the next afternoon, Charlotte came into the bedroom bearing a tea tray. "I thought you might enjoy sharing tea with me. I have found a marvelous little pastry shop just around the corner. Aren't these lovely? Wait until you taste them." She held the tray out in front of Marcella. "I have told Martin to stop by, if he has the time. I am hoping he will get here in time to enjoy these with us."

"I haven't seen Martin in quite a while."

"I wouldn't allow him to come when you were so ill, and since then you have not been exactly willing to talk to guests. You've hardly spoken to me."

She stood up suddenly and said, "You haven't said anything about my new dress. Don't you like it?" She circled slowly, modeling an overly ornate afternoon dress of a heavy, dark-green material.

Marcella quickly picked up one of the cream puffs, and in an entirely indifferent voice, said, "It is very nice, Charlotte. Did you get it at Stewart's?"

"Yes, it is a nice store, and large. Shall I get you a nice bed jacket from your cupboard? And perhaps some hair ribbons? We can both show off a bit for Martin."

"I suppose if I am to have my first guest this afternoon, I should look good, shouldn't I?"

"Neat will be enough," Charlotte said, rummaging through Marcella's clothes. "You do have some very nice things. I have always admired your mode of dressing, Marcella."

"Fuss with those things later, Charlotte. I would like my mirror and hairbursh, please. You are right, I have lain around too long, and this is a good time to change all that. I will dress today."

Charlotte stopped what she was doing and silently cursed herself. To Marcella she said, "You don't need to do all that. Just put the bed jacket on. Martin will be pleased just to see you well enough to greet him. You are still too tired and weak for anything more."

"You have done nothing but nag at me to take an interest in myself again," Marcella pouted. "Well, I am ready to do so. Bring me the brush and mirror."

"Not today. There isn't time," Charlotte said sharply. "Martin should be here at any moment."

"Then he can wait," Marcella snapped. "Men are used to waiting on ladies to complete their toilette. They expect it."

"Not today!"

"Charlotte, why won't you give the mirror to me? That's it, isn't it? You don't want me to look in the mirror."

"I don't want you upset. Not today. Let him see you at your best—at least this first time."

Marcella threw her blanket off. She pulled up her long nightgown and looked at her bare legs. She touched the scars and then examined her hands and arms. "My face is like this also?"

Charlotte nodded, unable to speak. She hurried back to her task of searching through Marcella's clothes, hastily putting away the bed jacket she had already taken out. The longer the silence lasted, the more frantically Charlotte rummaged through the clothes in the cupboard.

"Turn the mirrors to the wall, Charlotte," Marcella said softly. "If it is that bad, perhaps I don't want to see—ever." Charlotte did as she was asked. The mirrors strained at the twisted wires that held them facing against the walls.

"It isn't as bad as you think, I am sure. In the beginning it will seem the worst," Charlotte said soothingly. Marcella reamined seated on the edge of her bed, moving her fingertips over the scars. She touched her face. "My face hurt very badly. I remember in the beginning—the horrible red spots and the swelling—" She grimaced.

"You'll come to accept it in time."

"What you are really saying, Charlotte, is that it is worse than I am imagining, not better. My mouth—"

"Put this little gown on, Marcella. Don't think about it anymore now. Think about Martin's visit. I am sure he will cheer you up. That is one thing I can always say about Martin—"

"He has never had to comfort a ghoul before."

"Marcella! What a thing to say!"

"Oh, for pity's sake, stop lying to me, Charlotte. If I had any hope before, I don't now, after all your sugary talk."

Spurred by her anger, Marcella got up from her bed and walked over to the wall mirror that Charlotte had just turned around. She touched it hesitantly at first.

"It would soon break the cord and fall anyway, if we left it this way for long," she said and began to turn it back, being careful not to look into it. "I have already broken one mirror this year, and see what has happened. Imagine what might befall me if another should fall and break!"

"Marcella, I do wish you wouldn't do this. You're not acting right. You frighten me in this mood."

Marcella chuckled. "That is very funny, Charlotte. After all these years, I should think you would know me well enough to know I am always 'in this mood' when I am about to do something stupid and willful."

She looked directly into the mirror and gasped, but she didn't turn away. For a full minute, she didn't move a muscle, nor did she speak.

Charlotte hurried around to see her face. Marcella's eyes were tightly shut. When Charlotte touched her shoulder, Marcella opened her eyes and shrugged off Charlotte's hand. "I am all right."

"Let me help you back to bed. I told you this was too much for one day."

"I said I am all right," Marcella growled. "I'll drink my tea alone today. I want to be left alone. Completely alone, Charlotte!"

Charlotte brought her a cup and began to pour the light-greenish liquid. Marcella glared at her. "I won't drink this. I want my good, strong brand of tea—and I want my gin."

"Marcella, don't please. You have been doing so well lately. Don't drink that stuff anymore. Dr. Bancroft said it wasn't good for you."

"Dr. Bancroft can go to hell. Today I need it, and I'll have it. Get it for me. I want the gin, and don't water it down, either."

"You'll not get it from me! I thought that was all behind us."

"Things change. Are you going to get it for me?"

"No."

"Bring it, or I'll get up and get it myself."

"You'll have to. You know I disapprove of spirits other than for medicinal purposes."

Charlotte followed her sister out into the hallway, where Marcella left her standing as she went downstairs to get her bottle of gin and her pot of strong tea. Returning moments later, she tossed her head at Charlotte and strode back into her bedroom. Deliberately, she poured the gin into a glass and the tea into the cup, and took a long drink from each.

"I don't like them mixed in the glass," she said pleasantly, and then walked over to shut her door in Charlotte's disapproving face. Charlotte snatched at the door handle and flung the door open before Marcella had had time to get back into bed.

"If you continue to behave like this, I won't stay with you!" Charlotte yelled at her.

"Ask your son about that, Charlotte! See if he wants you to leave now."

"How can you say that!" Charlotte sputtered. "Ingrate! Ingrate! Martin will always serve my best interests first."

"Hah!"

Martin Henderson, Jr.'s, idea of the good life had always been a bone of contention between himself and his parents, especially his father. Martin, Sr., had not been a wealthy man by anyone's standards—nor had he been, as far as his son was concerned, either ambitious or very smart. To the sin of failure he had added the sin of not recognizing his failure.

As far as Martin had ever been able to see, his father had taken on every conceivable burden of menial work and servile responsibility and had enjoyed not a whit of reward or fun for his efforts. Martin had always been ashamed of his father and determined that his life would be different—and better, much better.

Even in the years since his father's death, Martin had been unable to summon up regard for his memory. In fact, the only thing Martin seemed to have regard for was his quest to get what he wanted from life, which, he had persuaded himself, owed him something for his trouble.

The key, as far as he was concerned, was to cultivate the appearance of style long enough to have people part with their secrets, social and financial.

He proceeded on that premise, taking pains to appear where he thought it would do him the most good for the least effort. No one was better dressed than he or gave a more resplendent impression of monied refinement. Whatever errors of judgment he made in good taste or style were for the most part unnoticed or ignored by the men and women he knew, who, like Martin, were on their way to what they considered the top in post–Civil War New York City.

Nothing could have suited Martin better. He joined in the trend, trading his shallow loyalty to the South's leisurely, genteel grace and romance for the vital, throbbing energy of the new North. It had a different kind of romance to it, and its own special allure, promising a taste of the fruit from a forbidden tree. A code of manners and grace had given way to a code of pleasure, success, and excess.

It was easy to fall in love with the world of the Flash Age; it pulsated and beat to a new rhythm of expansion and promised greatness. Martin held in awe the men who moved this new world. They were manipulators with a kind of arrogance and a well developed ability to exercise raw, unrefined power that Martin admired.

Trying to look the part of one of the new breed, Martin moved along the outskirts of their circles. Though men like Jay Gould and Jim Fisk had never said more than hello to him, he nonetheless could and did eat at the same restaurants as they. He could and did rub elbows with them at the Oyster Bar, and he listened, as did others, as these two plotted their moneymaking schemes.

By 1869, Martin had gained a reputation as a gambler and a small-time speculator. While others missed the similarity, Martin could see a resemblance between his small career and that of Gould or the Prince of Erie. Martin's face and notes were known all along Ann Street, and on Greene Street, where John Morrisey ran his gambling house. Surrounded by the decorations of white marble columns and glittering chandeliers, Morrisey's patrons were encouraged to spin the wheel just one more time.

While Martin spent much of his time—and more of his money—at the gaming tables, others spent theirs in gold speculation. At a time when everything went to the bold, the manipulator, the speculator, the fortunes of an entire country were no exception.

Fisk and Gould dipped their hands into the gold market in a grand and daring way, bringing about one of the most spectacular and disastrous gold speculations in the history of the market. Many men lost their fortunes overnight; companies were destroyed, credit was broken, the nation was plunged into economic disgrace.

As money became tighter, Martin began to gamble more heavily than before. Where once he had moved along the tables for fun, he now came in earnest. As always, winning was reserved for winners, and Martin was far too desperate to be in a winning frame of mind. He was too preoccupied with pennies to be shrewd with dollars. At each turn, his financial situation seemed to worsen.

At the moment, Martin was in the midst of an especially bad losing streak. It would be simple enough for him to use both Marcella's fears and Charlotte's maternal concerns for his own benefit.

When, on his arrival, Charlotte discussed Marcella's behavior with her son and suggested that even an estate was not worth the misery of having to put up with her, Martin listened patiently. To Charlotte's chagrin, however, it seemed that Marcella was right about Martin's motives.

"You are upset, Mother," Martin purred. "This is no time to make a hasty decision. Surely you can see that. Why, you'd be foolish to leave now. We will be set up for life, and you would be near your own sister. You've always cared about your family. And aside from her vile disposition, you have no real difficulty with Aunt Marcella, have you?"

Charlotte looked at her son. His handsome, broad-planed face showed nothing but filial concern. She smiled and smoothed out her dress. "That Marcella! She can plant devious thoughts in anyone's mind—even mine. You are entirely right, Martin. Of course I will stay, for your sake. After all, what are mothers for? Marcella is such a—devious person. Do you know what she had me asking myself just now?"

Martin grinned, leaning forward and taking his mother's hands in his own. "What awful thought did she put in your head?"

"She suggested that you would encourage me to stay here only so you could inherit her money. With no regard for me or my feelings, mind you! Now if Marcella can get me to consider a preposterous idea like that about my own son, what can't she do?"

Martin patted his mother's hand and smiled sympathetically. "You are just tired, Mother. Perhaps I was wrong. Perhaps it *is* too much for you. You are not as young as you once were, and Aunt Marcella—well, maybe you are just not up to it."

"You make me feel as if I have one foot in the grave."

He laughed and chucked her under the chin. "You know full well I meant no such thing. I really think you are upset and distraught because you are unaccustomed to such depraved behavior as you see in Aunt Marcella."

"But, dear, I don't think Marcella is depraved. Mischievous and devious, surely, but not depraved."

"You are far too good, and that is the problem. She is depraved, and always has been. Put up with her, ignore what she says, and you'll have no problems. And if you should, then by all means leave, and don't worry about me. I'll get by. I always do, don't I?"

Charlotte sighed. "I don't know why I allow her to upset me so. Well, dear, shall we go ahead and have our tea?" She picked up a cup from the tray and then paused, looking up at Martin. "I should have been more tolerant. I have been anticipating this day for weeks. Now here it is, and all my good intentions to be understanding and patient have gone right out the window."

"Tell you what, Mother, I'll go up and say hello to her now. Maybe I can cheer her up a bit. Not a woman alive can fail to respond to me if I put my mind to it."

Charlotte blushed. "Oh, Martin! What conceit."

"Conceit!" he laughed. "How can you say such a thing? Truth—truth of the purest sort." He strutted out of the room and went up the back stairs to Marcella's room.

He knocked at the door. "Aunt Marcella!"

"Go away."

He opened the door and stepped quickly inside, shutting it quietly behind him. "Why wouldn't you join us? I have come all this way, given up an afternoon of fun and frivolity to see you, and you hide away in your room."

"I didn't ask you to come."

"I came to cheer you and to enjoy a pleasant afternoon with two of my favorite ladies."

"Since when have I been a favorite of yours?"

"Why, Aunt Marcella," he said in mock surprise. "You pain me. Since you made me your heir, of course."

"I expect it to be worth my while, Martin, not an act of generosity."

Martin sat down on the edge of Marcella's bed. "You are a tough old woman, Aunt Marcella."

"I am neither old, nor am I tough. And I am most certainly not stupid. I know why you are here, and I resent your pretense that it is otherwise."

Martin shrugged. "As you like. I am here because I want your money and I want the property. Speaking of which, I could use a little pocket money right now. I happen to be a little short, and there is a lovely young lady who has a fondness for gifts."

"Might that be Rhea Scott?"

"The same. A very beautiful woman, if I do say so."

"She is in love with Nicholas Dalton, from all I have heard. Why should I give you anything to woo her, when she isn't even interested in you?"

"Several reasons, the first being that I want to woo her. Secondly, you are mistaken. Nicholas has turned quite strange since his father was shot. I don't know what happened to the dear boy, but he is not the same at all. From all I have heard, he is very nearly a recluse. And last of all, Aunt Marcella, if you do not give me what I need from time to time, I shall find it increasingly difficult to convince Mother she should stay with you." He smiled, showing his small, evenly spaced white teeth.

Marcella looked at him for a moment and then shook her head. "How did my sister ever give birth to a child like you?"

"Now, Aunt Marcella, don't be like that. You of all people can hardly fault me for wanting a better life. We should be natural allies."

"Have you ever considered working for this better life?"

"I think if you would just fill out a bank draft, it would serve best. Your bankers might as well get accustomed to seeing me, anyway. And then there is Mother. She worries so about my debts. The less she knows, the better. Don't you agree, it is best we both keep Mother as happy as we can?"

He handed Marcella the necessary equipment to fill out the draft. "Oh, and since summer is so near, we might begin to think about moving to our country house."

"What country house?"

"Scarborough, of course. Surely you aren't planning to let it stand empty and fall to ruin? Or perhaps it slipped your mind? You really should cut down on that stuff you drink, Aunty." He took the signed bank draft from her hand. "Well, I'll be on my way now. It's been a pleasant visit, Aunt Marcella, and don't forget about Scarborough House. Talk it over with Mother, and when you ladies have made your plans, I'll see to making the necessary arrangements."

"Martin—"

"I have to go now, Aunty. Business, you know!" He saluted her with the bank draft and slipped it into his breast pocket.

Marcella, upset by the entire conversation, took her laudanum and slept the day through.

As it turned out, it became unnecessary for her to face Martin's troubling proposals about Scarborough House. The next day, Nicholas came to visit, bringing a proposal of his own.

"I think I owe you something, Marcella," he told her. "I would like you to spend the summer at Scarborough. I would feel much better if you would accept the invitation."

"You owe me nothing, Nicholas," she replied slowly, a little puzzled by his sudden generosity.

"Perhaps not. But what does it matter? I am still offering you the use of the house. You'll be more comfortable there."

"What about your mother?"

"I am alone there, except for the servants. I roll around that house like a loose marble in a box. I'd be grateful if you would allow me to do something for you."

"You had nothing to do with what happened to me, Nicholas. It was my own fault. If you need a superstitious reason, I shall tell you that I broke a mirror the night your father left me. As a matter of fact, I broke it in the attempt to throw it at him. No matter how you look at it, natural or supernatural, the fault is mine."

Nicholas looked down at his hands. "I know it wasn't the mirror, or my wishing either, but I did wish—"

"For my death? I don't blame you for that. Why wouldn't you, after what I had done?"

"I don't know. Maybe that is really why I am asking you to come to Scarborough. I don't seem to understand anything these days. Why did all this happen? Whose fault was it? I dream about it, think about it. My God, I don't seem to think about anything else." He sighed deeply.

Marcella gestured for him to sit down on the edge of the bed. "So do I, Nicholas," she said, laying her pockmarked hand on his arm. "And I ask the same questions you ask. I never meant to hurt your father. Why did I do it? Why?"

Nicholas looked up. "Then say you'll come. Papa always did want us to know one another, and somehow we never did."

"There were good reasons for that, too." She smiled sadly. "I will talk to Charlotte about it, Nicholas."

"There is plenty of room. Even if Charlotte doesn't want to accompany you, there is no problem. I can get someone to care for you."

Nicholas left with Marcella's promise to think about coming to Scarborough House. She had given Brad her word that she would never set foot in that house or in any way try to control it. Now Nicholas offered it to her as if it were his. Didn't he realize it had been awarded to her along with Brad's other property? Or was he counting on her promise to Brad that Nicholas would, in fact, inherit the house at Brad's death? She didn't know.

What she did know was that Nicholas was offering her an alternative to needing Charlotte, or more accurately, to having to put up with Martin's growing demands for money.

The only thing that gave Marcella any pause was that she dreaded being alone. In spite of her independence, she had always relied on Charlotte, and Charlotte had always been there for her. If she were to back out of their agreement now, Charlotte would never forgive her. Marcella would be cutting the last link she had with her family.

One day Nicholas would marry and raise his own family at Scarborough. Where would Marcella Paxton fit into the scheme of things then? Whatever she did, Marcella decided, she needed Charlotte. And she needed to begin to lead as normal a life as she was able.

Marcella did not mention the move to Scarborough until she was once again on her feet and feeling fairly well. When she was sure she wanted to go and had planned how she would manage it, she told Charlotte of her decision. Charlotte was given to understand that the move would be made with Martin's interests in mind. To Nicholas, Marcella said simply that she would accept his kind generosity.

For the first time since Marcella had dealt with Eugene Timmins, she felt dirty and cheap. She knew she was deceiving everyone concerned, but at least she would be safe this way. Charlotte would stay with her as long as Marcella needed her, and Nicholas would trust her to return Scarborough to him, just as his father had trusted her before.

That night, for the first time in a week, Marcella returned to her drinking and her laudanum. She didn't like what she had done, nor did she like admitting what she hadn't done. She had not told Nicholas that Martin would be coming to live at the house along with Charlotte and herself.

Marcella reached for the bottle of laudanum that stood beside her bed and took another dose. It made things easier, not so sharp-edged. Charlotte could handle the explanation of Martin's presence. Charlotte could handle anything.

Everything would be fine. Marcella smiled drowsily and fell asleep.

Chapter Twenty-one

The day they left for Scarborough House, Marcella was drugged with her sleeping potion and numbed by her intake of spirits. She jostled against the hard panel of the coach wall, oblivious to the beauty of the Hudson Valley she had always loved when she was young. Green, grassy areas gave way to trees and forest and then to the sheer, multihued Palisades that rose far above the river.

As much as she might have regretted missing the scenery, she would certainly have been pleased to know she had also missed all Charlotte's efforts to pacify Martin each time he swore he would dump Marcella out on the road rather than let another person see him in her company.

It was just as well that Charlotte convinced him of the merit of kindness before they arrived at the house, for things were only to get worse as the day progressed. As they drove up the long driveway to Scarborough House, Martin turned to his mother. "How big a place is this, do you know?" He looked through a break in the trees to the open, rolling land, and beyond it, to what appeared to be an orchard.

"I am not sure, Martin. Not large, I think. I believe Marcella once told me that most of the farmland had been sold to the tenants long ago. If I am correct, Scarborough consists of the land the house sits on and whatever land they need for the home farm."

Martin shook his head. "Pity."

Suddenly the carriage gave a jolt that sent Marcella sprawling into her sister's lap. Charlotte shoved her back against the wall of the carriage and propped her carpet bag against Marcella's side to prevent her from rolling in that direction again.

As they came up the last stretch of the drive, the house suddenly appeared before them. Martin slowed the horses.

"Now this is more what I expected." He looked up at the house. "That is a house a man could be proud of owning."

"Please move along, Martin, we can look at the house all summer. I do want to get out of this vehicle. I fear I am becoming a bit queasy."

"Move away from Aunt Marcella. Her breath will do you in, Mother," he laughed.

"I hardly think it a laughing matter. There doesn't seem to be anyone about, does there? I wonder how we shall get into the house."

"Don't you have a key? Surely Aunt Marcella— Mother! If you have dragged me all the way out here and now can't get into this house, I promise you I'll leave her here. I won't take that old sot back to town. Why in hell don't you check on these things?"

Charlotte cringed. "Nicholas will be there, I think," she stammered, "and —and surely he has servants of some sort. He couldn't manage a place like this on his own."

"What is Nicholas doing here?"

"Why, he lives here, dear. You knew that."

"No, Mother, I knew he *lived* here. How are we to stay here with him living right under our noses? Can't I trust anything to you and have it done properly?"

"Well, perhaps he's gone. After all, Marcella did tell him we were all coming, and I don't suppose he is any fonder of us than we are of him."

"Did you hear her tell him?"

"She told me she did."

Martin stopped the horse and carriage under the portico.

"I have a feeling this is a day begun badly and ending even more badly," he muttered. "Keep an eye on Sleeping Beauty, and I'll go find someone to assist us."

He walked up the steps and knocked sharply on the front door. As he stood waiting, he looked around. The lower section of the house, which in a lesser house might have been a cellar, provided space for the kitchen and quarters for the servants in this house. Around it and under the porch on which Martin stood, was a walkway enclosed by latticework.

Impatiently, Martin walked around to the corner of the house. Finding no one, he returned to the front door and hammered on it again.

Charlotte began to get out of the carriage. "Perhaps there is no one there, Martin. Why don't you try the door? It may not be locked."

"Stay where you are, Mother," Martin said irritably. "Stay with Aunt Marcella."

"I beg your pardon, sir?" said a strange voice from behind Martin. He whirled to face a very old man dressed in the uniform of a butler.

"It's about time you answered this door! Get someone to come out here and help this lady into the house right away," Martin ordered. He started back toward the carriage.

"Whom did you wish to see, sir?" the man asked, unperturbed.

"Look, you old geezer, I don't want to see anyone! I live here, and I want help now!"

"What in hell is all the racket, Carlisle? What's going on?" Nicholas called from inside the house. A moment later he appeared at the door, looking rumpled, as if he had been in bed. "What the— What are you doing here, Henderson?"

"What are *you* doing here? This is my aunt's house, and I would appreciate it if you would make this old fossil understand that I want someone to help me get her out of the carriage."

Nicholas ran his hand across his chin. "What are you talking about? What aunt? What do you want?"

Martin shifted his weight to one foot, lit a cigar, and looked back to Nicholas. "You are expecting Marcella Paxton?"

194

"Yes," Nicholas said with a yawn. "Next week sometime."

"She's here now. I'm her nephew, and I am here now. So get someone to haul her into the house!"

Nicholas took a couple of steps onto the porch, blinking sleepily into the sun. "Why can't she come in herself? What's wrong with her?"

Martin sniggered and tossed the cigar away. "She's having one of her spells."

"Marcella isn't well, Mr. Dalton," Charlotte said from inside the carriage.

"Hello, Mrs. Henderson. I didn't see you."

"Wake up, man! Get someone to take her into the house," Martin repeated.

"Yes, of course. Come on. I don't know what Marcella told you, but— Well, never mind for now, we'll talk it out later."

He turned to Carlisle. "Go tell Joe to help Miss Marcella into the house. He may need another man to help him." Then he turned back to Martin. "I'll be with you in a moment. I think I'd better clean up a bit."

Nicholas left them waiting for Joe and hurried back inside the house. "I have a feeling," he muttered to himself as he climbed the stairs, "that I am going to need my wits." Neither he nor the house was ready for Marcella. And, he thought to himself, he'd never be ready for Martin to be a guest—not after the whole business with Rhea Scott and Martin. . . .

Nicholas hadn't seen Rhea since the last time he had gone to a ball held at the Abbey, a social club. Although he had once been a regular at the Abbey, his visits in the year since his father's death had been sporadic and generally unsatisfying.

People he had once enjoyed there had become intolerable. Some bent his ear, explaining that everything had happened for the best and it would all be well in time. How many times had he sat and listened to them and wondered how it could ever be for the best when a man died as his father had?

Others were drawn to him apparently because of the scandal and the violence that had touched his life. Those voices he couldn't bear, for they sounded too much like the echoes of sins committed by neglect and then forgotten.

The last time he had been there, he had asked himself over and over why he had come. To make things worse, it was the first time he had seen Rhea Scott with Martin Henderson. He had gone directly to Rhea, ignoring Martin.

"I thought you said you were too busy to come out this evening."

"I am," she said without a trace of embarrassment.

Nicholas, who was seldom ill at ease, was suddenly speechless. He cleared his throat abruptly and glared at Martin. "I see."

"There is nothing to be gained in not coming to the point, Nicholas. I don't want to spend my life bemoaning the fate of the Daltons, nor do I want to watch you do it. You have changed completely, and I neither understand you nor enjoy seeing you change from someone gay and lively into an introspective bore."

Martin had put his arm around Rhea's shoulders. "In other words, old man, you are no longer welcome at the lady's door." He had smiled patronizingly at Nicholas and steered Rhea toward the dance floor. Someone had placed a glass into Nicholas's hand as he watched Rhea walking away from him.

Richard Burns, a long-time friend, had stood at his side. "Better snap out of it, Nick," he had counseled. "She is too pretty to bore."

Nicholas had left the Abbey feeling only slightly emptier than he had before he had entered. The music, the people, the activity—nothing had seemed able to snap him out of the lethargy that had taken hold of him.

Now, not a year later, he still felt like a man only half awake, too tired to be moved by anything. He sighed, walked over to his shaving stand, and looked into the tiny mirror. Nicholas Dalton. A pair of wide-set gray eyes, giving off no spark, no excitement. A beard, heavy and dark from two days' growth. What did anyone care?

He shaved and dressed in clean but informal clothes before going downstairs once again to see Martin and find out what was happening to him this time. He wondered if he would care. Did anything really make a difference? Wasn't it better to sit back and let what would be, be?

Why was it, he wondered, that Marcella's life always seemed so tied up with his own? No matter what he did or where he turned, she was there, influencing him, twisting everything out of shape and making it into something he couldn't control.

He walked slowly down the steps and turned down the large hallway that ran the length of the house.

Martin was standing in the open doorway of the front parlor. "There you are! Mother and I thought perhaps you had gone back to sleep."

"Has Carlisle seen to all your needs?" Nicholas asked as he passed Martin and entered the room. Mother and son both said they had been shown to their rooms, and Charlotte added that Marcella was settled and sleeping comfortably.

Charlotte tried valiantly to keep up a stream of bright chatter, but Nicholas had to fight the urge, as he listened to her, to run from the house and mount his horse, leaving all of them to do as they pleased with the house.

Finally, Charlotte ran out of things to say. Nicholas sighed and leaned back in his chair. "Would you care to explain to me what is taking place, Mrs. Henderson? I invited Miss Paxton to use the house as a place of recuperation and to bring you with her if she wished. I felt I owed her that. But I invited no one else, and Miss Paxton said nothing about bringing anyone else with her."

Martin stood up, shoving his hands into the pockets of his waistcoat. "Aunt Marcella," he said acidly, "has a habit of saying only as much as is convenient for her at the time."

"Well, this time I am afraid she has made an error. You are welcome for the night, but I am not prepared for guests, and quite frankly, I don't care to have any. I am sorry you have been inconvenienced, but that is the way it must be."

Martin laughed out loud. He walked over to a liquor cabinet and poured himself a drink. "Would you care for something, Mother? I see some sherry and—yes, a bottle of claret and one of port."

"You know I never drink, Martin." She began to twist her handkerchief.

"I thought perhaps after the long trip . . . What about you, Nick? What can I get for you?"

"Nothing, thank you. It's nice to see you feel at home, Martin."

Martin drank the glass empty and then looked up. "Why not? It is my home."

Nicholas shifted in his seat. "I have been laboring under the idea that it is my home."

"Sorry, old man, but you've been working too hard. You *used* to live here. I live here now. The roles of guest and host have been reversed, or have you not kept up with the events of the last year? Surely you have heard of the great court battle and ensuing tragedy of Bradford Dalton and Marcella Paxton? Well, that Miss Paxton happens to be my aunt, and she, dear boy, has won the ownership of this house."

"Martin!" Charlotte gasped.

"By the way, what is the name of that butler?" Martin asked, ignoring Charlotte.

Nicholas sat motionless, struggling to keep his composure. "Carlisle," he muttered without thinking. "What is all of this, Mrs. Henderson? I don't mean to seem rude, but—"

Charlotte cleared her throat. "The only one who can answer that is my sister. I think Marcella has told each of us what she thought we wanted to hear. She does that, you know." She tried to smile at Nicholas, without much success. "I can see she has placed you in a completely untenable position. I shall try to clarify if I can. At least I can tell you what she told us.

"We came because Marcella informed us we would be living here from now on. She does own Scarborough House, as you know, but what I think you do not know is that she has made my son her heir. When she dies, Scarborough will be Martin's."

Nicholas's face drained of color. "She can't! She has no right!" he began to shout, and then stopped abruptly, as if he were behaving foolishly. "Excuse me. I must speak to Marcella."

Nicholas ran from the room and up the stairs two at a time, looking in one room after another until he found Marcella, asleep.

He shook her, gently at first, then more roughly. She mumbled and turned but wouldn't waken. He gave up in frustration and stormed from the room, seeking the refuge of his grandfather's study.

He hurried into the long, rectangular room and closed the door behind him. His hand still on the doorknob, he leaned his head against the cool, dark wood, fighting down the urge to scream in anger. He turned around, surveying the room as if to reassure himself that at least in this place all was as he expected it to be.

He walked to the oversized fireplace and slumped down in one of the leather chairs that flanked it. How many warm, joy-filled hours he had spent here with his grandfather! He leaned his head back, looking at the snowy-white ceiling high above, covered with clusters of flowers and fruit in relief. What would old Nicholas do if he were here now?

He looked across the room at the collection of model ships on the shelf. Old Nicholas had started it for his son when Brad was a tiny boy, and had continued it for his grandson. Each year he had added one; there were ferries, barges, whalers, ships with sails, ships with boilers.

Nicholas felt tears welling up. He put his head in his hands, rocking it back and forth, moaning in anger and grief. "Oh, Grandpa, what am I to do? What am I to do?"

Abruptly he stood and walked over to his desk. He gave a vicious pull on the delicate petitpoint bell.

Carlisle answered the call immediately. "Yes, sir?"

Nicholas cleared his throat authoritatively. "For the next day or so, you and the others are likely to hear anything. Until I get this situation under control, try to ignore, without appearing to, the more outrageous instructions you may be given by our guests. Run the house as we always have. And I would appreciate it if you could manage some control over the inevitable gossiping that will come from the maids and the kitchen. Things will be bad enough around here without adding rumor and gossip to it."

"I understand, sir. You can count on me to do my best, but as to the talk, sir, I just don't know. There are—er—questions, sir."

"Including your own, Carlisle?"

"Well, sir, I would like to know who *does* own the house. Your granddaddy would be mighty upset to hear anyone claim this isn't Dalton land."

"You needn't remind me."

"Mr. Henderson talked to me just before you rang the bell. He said this is his property, and if I want to keep my job, I should be listening to him and not you."

Nicholas ran his hand through his hair. "When and if Mr. Henderson begins to pay you your wages, Carlisle, obey him, obey him fully. For now, I suggest you do as I say. One thing you can count on, Carlisle, is that whoever does own this house, it is not Martin Henderson. At least not yet."

"That comes as a great relief, sir."

Nicholas nodded. "That's all, Carlisle, and tell Gert I will eat dinner in here tonight."

Nicholas sat alone in the study, uncomfortably aware that the elegant dining room of Scarborough House was filled with light and voices, brought back to life by people unwelcome, wrong for this house.

How often, he wondered, had he seen his grandfather lean back, draw deeply on his pipe, smell the fragrance in the air before he spoke? "No Dalton will ever be beaten, Nick, as long as he clings to the strength of his own kind," he had said. "Take a bundle of sticks and separate them. One by one you can break them with ease. Keep them bound together, Nick, and it takes a mighty force to break them then. Remember that, boy. That is where strength lies."

Nicholas had listened and believed. But what would happen now that he no longer had his grandfather's support? From whom would he draw strength? All the Daltons except him were gone, as if they had never been.

He ate little from the dinner tray Gert brought.

"You didn't eat enough to keep a bird alive!" she scolded as she came back to clean up.

"I wasn't as hungry as I thought."

"Bosh! Big man like you? You gotta be hungry. I know you, Mr. Nick. You're moonin', and a fine lot of good that's going to do you. Your granddaddy wouldn't think much of this."

"Why does everyone remind me of what Grandfather would think?"

"He was a good man, that's why. We do miss him sorely."

"We do. We do miss him," Nicholas said softly.

"You didn't light your fire in the grate either. What's come over you, Mr. Nick? I'll just go and light it for you, but you have got to pull yourself together. Joe tells me that horse of yours needs a good working out. All you do is talk and wish. Aren't you gonna do nothin' no more?"

Smarting from her impertinence, Nicholas stood up. He thrust his hands deep into his pockets and walked to the window looking out over the sloping lawn. If he followed that path, crossing the open area down the slope, he would finally come to the willow pond. He hadn't gone there much in the past year. It was probably overgrown because of his neglect.

"Will you be wanting anything else now?" Gert asked his back.

"Nothing, Gert. Good night."

Somehow it surprised him that the house had settled down as it always did in the evening. In spite of the new people, the house was as calm on the surface as it had ever been.

It was not so the following morning.

Chapter Twenty-two

When Marcella awakened late the following morning, she was ravenously hungry. Her first thought was to shout at Charlotte for neglecting to give her her meals. Her head throbbed, and her stomach was churning. She rolled over, burying her face in the pillows, softly groaning and promising herself she wouldn't be tempted to use spirits or laudanum again.

Suddenly she stopped moving and lay still. The scent of roses—the scent she had on all her linens—was missing. She lifted her head, sniffed the pillow slip again. It was a fresh, clean odor—lavender, she thought—but definitely not roses. Forgetting her pounding head, she whirled around in the bed and looked about the strange room. There was a fireplace—but it was different from the fireplace in her room in the brownstone. She glanced at the window. Everything was strange.

"Charlotte! Charlotte!" she screamed.

Charlotte rushed into the room. "What is it? What's wrong? Marcella! What's happened?"

"Oh, you're here! You're really here! I thought you had had me put somewhere. I thought— Where am I?" Marcella sat up and looked around the room again, clutching at Charlotte's hand. "What is this place? Where are we? Why am I here?"

"Calm down, Marcella. You are at Scarborough House. We came yesterday afternoon. My dear, you must learn not to scream so. You gave me the fright of my life. I thought something awful had happened."

"So did I! I thought you had got rid of me."

"How could I possibly have got rid of you? Honestly, Marcella, you can say the worst things."

"Well, why didn't you tell me we were coming here? Haven't I any say in what I do anymore?"

"You are the one who decided to come here. I suppose you don't remember."

"I remember everything! I never said I would come here. You must have tricked me. How did you force me into this? I gave my word to Brad that I would never come here. You must have tricked me. Did you drug me? Is that it? It is! I can see it in your face. That is why I have this wretched head."

"Now stop it! I have heard entirely too much."

"I want to know. How did you get me here? It was duplicity. Martin did it! I know he did. It is his kind of thing."

"Martin carried you from the house, Marcella, because you had drunk yourself into insensibility, and then you finished the job by dosing yourself with laudanum. The doctor never gave that to you to be used as you do. One of these days you'll kill youself that way."

"That would please your precious son. All he wants is my money," Marcella spat out.

"Marcella! How you talk! He has tolerated abuse from you, been humiliated by you beyond endurance, and still he tries to help you."

"I bought his tolerance. He should help me. I pay him enough."

Charlotte was incensed. "If you weren't ill, I'd slap you for that," she gasped. "I'll not hear this talk of Martin, Marcella, I warn you. I am the one who wanted to insure his future. If it were left to him, he would not take a cent from you."

"Hah! I may be as drunk and befuddled as you say, but thank God I am not blind or stupid. Martin, my dear sister, would slit your precious throat if he thought your blood of any monetary value. That man is and has always been a slave to his passions and ambitions," she went on, warming to the subject. "What he does not need is a doting, blind mother. He needs to work, to straighten out. If he does not, the men to whom he is constantly in debt will do it for him. By then, Charlotte, it will be too late. You give in to Martin far too much. Always have. He has always been your one blind spot."

Charlotte made a visible effort to speak calmly. "I think you are still under the influence of the unholy stuff you pour into yourself, Marcella. For that reason alone, I shall forgive you what you say." She turned away from Marcella and left the room.

As soon as she had gone, Marcella rang the bell. Gert appeared a few minutes later.

"I am hungry. Why has no one brought me anything?"

"We didn't know you were awake, ma'am."

"What's your name?"

"Gert, ma'am. If you'll tell me what you'd like, I'll fix it for you."

Marcella squinted at Gert, plain and too healthy for her purposes. "Doesn't Nicholas have a cook? Surely you're not the cook!"

"I do some of the cooking, ma'am. If there is something special you have a taste for, I'm sure we can get it for you."

"Who else cooks?"

"Mrs. Barth, ma'am."

"Is that all she does—just cooks?"

"Yes, ma'am." Gert looked puzzled. "Can I get something for you? Strawberries? Mr. Nick loves them, so we get them special whenever we can. We have some now."

Marcella wrinkled her nose. "You let Mr. Nicholas enjoy his strawberries. Send Mrs. Barth along to me."

"But she only cooks. She doesn't—"

"Send her to me!"

"Yes, ma'am."

Marcella had a short chat with Mrs. Barth when Gert sent her up. One look at her veined nose and face convinced Marcella that she had found her partner in crime—and a source for any kind of spirits that tempted her. As soon as Mrs. Barth had returned to her pots and pans, Marcella snuggled down in the large four-poster bed to take a nap.

She had had barely enough time to get comfortable when a knock came at her door. She listened to the sound. What if it were Martin?—Martin, who, she told herself, made her drink and indulge in laudanum. She felt a sudden flood of revulsion and guilt, blamed Martin, the alcohol, the laudanum, and herself—in that order—for her misery.

That hand knocking on the door, asking entrance to her room, was an accuser, an observer of her failure. She pulled the blanket up close under her chin and willed the demon that made her want to drink, and the demon who begged entrance to her room, both to leave her in peace. Neither left.

Sighing, she gave up. "Who is it?"

Nicholas, not Martin, appeared. "Oh! It's you," she breathed. "I was just about to take a nap." She leaned forward as he adjusted the pillows behind her back. "What brings you to my room?"

"You need ask?" He raised an eyebrow. "Your entire family moves in on me, unannounced and uninvited, and you wonder why I come to see you. Dear God, Marcella, what's going on?"

"Well, it was hot and uncomfortable in the city—"

"Marcella, Martin has as much as asked me to leave here. According to him, this is not my house, but his. You are giving it to him. Just like that! He has become your heir and will own Scarborough as a consequence. Is it too much to ask you for an explanation?"

"You take Martin far too seriously. Ignore him. He is so blown up at the moment, filled to overflowing with his good fortune and self-importance, he is likely to say anything."

"I am only interested in one thing he said. Is it true that you are giving him this house?"

"Oh, I am sure he thinks it is," she said, dismissing the suggestion with a wave of her hand. "Nicholas, would you happen to have a drop of—of sherry? I am so dry."

"I am not carrying it with me at the moment," he said and looked away. He cleared his throat and went on. "Then Martin's claim to Scarborough is not well founded? You will remain firm to your word?"

"It was a promise I made to Brad," she said. Nicholas sat back in his chair. "Is that all you wanted, Nicholas?"

"I want him to leave the house. He can't stay here, Marcella. The whole thing is impossible."

"There is nothing to be so upset about. It is a big house. You needn't even see him if you don't care to."

"Marcella, do you have any idea what you're saying? Aside from the fact that I have no intention of skulking around my own home trying to avoid someone I don't like, there are—things between Martin and me. I don't want him here. If you want your sister near you, I understand, but not Martin. My God, Marcella, he hasn't been here a day, and already he has tried to fire my butler, disrupted the kitchen, rearranged rooms to suit himself, and for the love of God, you can't pretend you don't know about him and Rhea Scott."

"But you don't care for her anymore, do you?"

"What has that to do with it?"

"She was never your kind of woman."

He moaned and shook his head. "My God, you are impossible! What do you know about how I feel and how I don't?"

"You remind me of your father. Perhaps that is how I know. Let Martin have Rhea. They deserve each other."

Nicholas folded his hands and looked directly at Marcella. "You have steered me completely away from what I came here to talk about. I will not live in the same house with Martin Henderson, and I sure as hell don't want to live in the same house as Rhea—not while she is someone else's wife. He will have to leave! I am simply telling you so you won't be upset when I have him put out."

"Be reasonable! I need Charlotte, and she won't stay without Martin. And really, Nicholas, while I don't like to bring this up, in spite of whatever promises I made to your father, this *is* my house, and both you and Martin are my guests."

"Nothing changes you, does it, Marcella? You still claw and cheat and lie to get your own way. I wondered how my father was taken in by you. It's easy. You play on everything a man can feel—hope, emotions, guilt. You twist everything around until it is to your advantage, and then you snap the trap shut. My father was a fool—he loved you. I am worse—I never even had that excuse."

"That little speech was uncalled for, Nicholas. We were having a pleasant talk."

He laughed bitterly. "What do you expect? Shall I wait humbly, Marcella, as my father did? Is that what you want?"

"Nicholas!"

"Go ahead. I've watched you destroy, kill, suck the life from others. So, go on, Marcella, I'm the last one."

"The last one, indeed. You disgust me. You're not a Dalton. You've become a whiner, a sniveler. No spirit. No fight and pride!"

"All gone, Marcella. All eaten up."

"Get out! Get out of here! I don't want to look at you any longer." Marcella clutched the blanket and pulled it up close. "Go away, Nicholas, before I forget entirely that you are Brad's son, before you or I say something neither of us will be able to forgive or forget."

The anger drained from his face and was replaced by quiet despair. "I don't want to lose Scarborough, Marcella. It has been in this family since before this land was a nation. It is us. It is the Daltons. I can't lose it now."

"Nicholas, I am very tired."

He said no more.

Marcella was left to wrestle with her memories—the promises she had made to Brad, the failings of her life. Somehow Hilary crowded into all the memories and taunted her, telling her over and over that she had been born evil, that no matter what she did she would somehow go wrong. Marcella shuddered as she thought of Nicholas's sad voice accusing her and mingling with all the other voices of the past, reminding her that she had failed time and time again.

Nicholas hated her, she decided. She didn't begrudge him that. What she did mind was that he had been kind to her. Though the house hadn't been his to offer, he had thought of it as his. She minded greatly that by trusting her he had placed on her shoulders the responsibility for what happened to him as well as what had happened to his father.

"And I didn't even see Papa when he died," she cried into her pillow, suddenly thinking of her own father. "I am worthless. I am bad. Oh, Mama! Why—why is it so?"

At that moment Mrs. Barth hurried into the room, looking like a conspirator, checking to her left and right for fear some sneaky teetotaler like Charlotte would discover the treasure she carried in her carpetbag.

When she had left, Marcella stared down at the bottle that now rested on her lap. She loathed the thought of its smell and its taste, but she took it, and took it gladly, hurrying so it would have its effect before Hilary, Brad, Papa, Eugene, and so many other ghosts returned. She drank until she was washed clean of memory and doubt and fear.

Chapter Twenty-three

After his first show of authority, Martin wanted none of the worries of the household thrust upon him. He was perfectly content and somewhat relieved to return to Nicholas's hands the task of running the estate.

For the first time in his life Martin was certain nothing could go wrong for him again. He had managed the impossible when he had come to Scarborough House.

Now that he was firmly ensconced there, he had only two problems left. One was to get Marcella to continue giving him enough money to cover his current debts. In the beginning she had given it to him readily, but the stronger she became, the more reluctant she was to hand over whatever sum he designated.

His other problem was that he already owed a great deal of money to some men of unsavory reputation and character, men who had threatened him with violence if he failed to pay up quickly. While he hadn't taken them seriously, the thought had sickened him.

Just days after he had come to Scarborough House, two beefy men arrived at the front door.

Charlotte tried to peer around Martin to get a closer look at the men standing on the porch. "Why don't you invite your friends in?" she asked. "I am always so pleased to meet Martin's friends. Won't you come in and join us in some coffee and after-dinner talk?"

She reached toward the door. Martin grasped her hand harshly. "No Mother! They don't want to come in. It is—it is a small business matter. Go sit down. I'll join you in a minute."

"You are not being very gracious, Martin. You gentlemen could use the morning room, or perhaps Nicholas would allow you to use the study, if this is a business matter."

Martin shifted his weight uneasily from one foot to the other. He longed to wipe the perspiration from his brow, but he dared not let go of his mother's arm or the door. The visitors were getting impaient. "Mother, please, go on into the parlor. I will join you soon."

"He is just gonna take a nice little ride with us, ma'am. Thanks for the offer an' all. Good night, ma'am."

"Are you going out, Martin? You said—"

Martin looked at his mother and said softly, "I won't be long."

When they had gone, Charlotte stood for a moment at the door. She couldn't think why, but something had just not seemed right. They had not sounded at all like gentlemen, and besides, what sort of business would anyone be conducting at this time of night? She watched the carriage drive away.

Martin was sandwiched uncomfortably between the two men. "This invasion of my home was unnecessary and distasteful. I always pay my debts. John knows that."

"Mr. Munroe says we take you to show you what happens if you wait too long to pay," one of the men said.

"Take me to John Munroe. I'll show you what the man says."

"We already know what he said. We gotta show you. Mr. Munroe don't feel like talkin' no more. No more notes, no more talk."

"You'll do as I say! Driver! Take me—"

The man put his hand firmly over Martin's mouth. "No more talk, Mr. Henderson. I'm supposed to treat you nice and polite. Be quiet and let me do my job, or we're both gonna be sorry."

Martin nodded and looked warily from one man to the other. The man on his left smiled. "That's the way it is, Mr. Henderson."

Martin sat back and watched as they drove into the city. Each block took them closer and closer to the slums and their weather-worn tenements, empty streets, and occasional bums and drunks. The carriage stopped in front of a large and apparently abandoned building.

"Just step out of the carriage, Mr. Henderson, but don't try to go noplace. We'd just have to go and get you."

Martin did as he was instructed. He stood at the side of the carriage, flanked by both men. "Look," he said, "if you are going to do something, do it now or forget it. I'm going home, and you can tell Mr. Munroe I'll pay him when I can. If he wants his money, he'll have to leave me alone."

He stepped away from the carriage. One of the men grabbed his arm and twisted it sharply behind his back. Martin gasped with the sudden and unexpected pain. The man kept up the pressure until Martin was on his knees on the pavement.

"Stop!" he whimpered. "Stop! I won't move. I won't."

The man forced him down further, until he was bent double, his face inches from the filthy walk. Suddenly the man released his arm; it fell limply. Martin stayed on his knees, hugging the arm to his side.

"Get up, Mr. Henderson. Your show is about to begin."

"You've broken my arm. I can't move it."

"It ain't broken, Mr. Henderson. Get up on your feet, or we'll have to help you."

Immediately Martin scrambled to his feet and leaned heavily against the carriage. Shadows moved around the ground floor of the darkened building. A wavering light—a torch from somewhere inside—showed the building to be no more than a gutted ruin. There were sounds of scuffling and a man's terrified voice begging for mercy.

Martin shivered. "What's going on? What kind of place is this?"

"It's called the House of Blazes. Some come here for fun. Some for—other reasons."

Martin looked warily at the heavy man beside him. "Why are we here?" he asked.

Suddenly a scream penetrated the darkness. Martin could see a man racing around frantically inside the lighted interior of the building, the shadows surrounding him, his clothes a blazing mass. His tormenters chased him around and then fled into the darkness from which they had come, leaving him screaming and rolling on the ground.

Martin leaped forward, but the other two grabbed him and dragged him back to the side of the carriage.

"Easy there, Mr. Henderson. This ain't your business."

"But that man! My God, you can't just stand by and—"

"Get back in the carriage, Mr. Henderson. We got one more stop."

"Dear Jesus, you're not—I mean, you're not going to do that to *me*? You wouldn't!" He ended on a whisper.

"That's up to you. Mr. Munroe just said we should show you."

"John Munroe is responsible for that?"

"No one said that, Mr. Henderson. You mustn't jump to conclusions. It's bad for everyone. We got one more stop, and then we'll take you home, and you can think it all out."

Martin clutched his arm and stifled a sob. "Where are we going now?"

"Just a couple more blocks. You're an impatient man, Mr. Henderson."

"Look, I've gotten the message—honestly. Take me home, please. Or just let me out here. Let me go. I'll pay you whatever you ask. Please, let me go. What do you say?"

The carriage stopped before the man could answer, and Martin looked quickly to see where they had brought him. "Please!" he cried, grabbing the coat of the man on his right. "For God's sake, please. Don't do anything. I'll pay. Tell John I'll pay him this week. I swear it! On my mother's head, I swear!"

The man pried Martin's fingers loose. "Step down from the carriage, Mr. Henderson, and you wait right here with Arnie. Don't try to run this time. You don't want that arm broken."

"What is this? What are you going to do?"

"No need to get all upset, Mr. Henderson." Arnie's voice was chilling.

Martin giggled pathetically. "Are you going to kill me? Are you?"

"We already told you, Mr. Henderson. You are safe tonight. We don't kill anybody, anyway, Mr. Henderson. I don't know who gave you these ideas."

"What are you going to do?"

"Well, this guy's owed Mr. Munroe for a long, long time. Made promises to pay and such, just like you, Mr. Henderson, but he's never come through. Mr Munroe gave him a lot of credit, just like you got, but like I say, this guy just never did come up with the money."

The man turned Martin toward a lopsided frame tenement. Both men watched as Arnie's colleague came around the side of the building carrying another man like a sack of potatoes. He dumped him in the street in front of Martin.

"Oh, my God!" Martin sobbed. The man was no more than pulp.

"He didn't play honest with us," the man said, shaking his head sadly. "Now nobody wins. Mr. Munroe don't like that. He always says he likes everyone to be a winner."

"His face. I'll tell the police what you have done! I'll tell them. Don't touch me! Don't come near me!"

Arnie laughed and shoved Martin into a puddle of muck. As he slammed against the carriage, the horses shifted, throwing Martin further off-balance. Arnie whistled sharply, and an undersized urchin came out of the tenement. He handed the child a coin and a scrap of paper. "Always help the needy, son." The child left him at a dogtrot.

The man ordered Martin into the carriage, got in himself, and told the driver to get moving. "Well, that's that, Mr. Henderson. The fellow's wife will be informed her husband has had a mishap. Don't worry yourself. Mr. Munroe likes you. He wanted you to see what accidents can happen to people. Your poor mother won't have to worry herself, long's you're cautious. Nice of Mr. Munroe to warn you. He don't do that for all his customers."

"Yeah, you're sure a lucky man," Arnie agreed. Both men laughed.

"We better get you back home. Your mama is gonna be worried about you, sittin' there all alone waitin' for her coffee and after-dinner chat."

Martin shivered.

"You cold, Mr. Henderson? See if we got a blanket to put around him, Arnie." Arnie reached down to the floor of the carriage, picked up a moth-eaten lap robe, and tossed it over Martin.

On the ride back to Scarborough, Arnie seemed to be sleeping. The other man chewed on a ragged stogie and drummed his fingers. Martin fought down nausea caused by the odor of the blanket and the recurring vison of what he had seen this night.

When they let him out of the carriage at the foot of the driveway to the house, he ran up the drive, not daring to look back. He stumbled into the house and leaned against the front door, gasping and sobbing into the sleeve of his coat.

The door to the study opened. "Who's there?" someone asked.

Martin turned and saw Nicholas silhouetted in the bright light from the study behind him.

"It's me. I just came in. It's all right. I'm locking up," Martin stammered.

Nicholas took several steps forward, squinting in the darkness of the hallway. "Are you all right?"

"Leave me alone! I'm all right, now get the hell out of here!"

Nicholas stood still for a moment and then turned and stalked back into the study, slamming the door behind him. The hall was plunged into darkness again.

*   *   *

The following morning, Martin, bedraggled and pale, shaken to his boot-straps by the previous night, went to Charlotte and confessed his entire involvement with John Munroe, begging her to help him.

At first she looked puzzled. "But the money I gave you—the money from the sale of the house . . . What about your business? What did you do with the money?"

"I'll promise anything you want. Anything, Mother. I'll never go near another gambling game as long as I live. I've been such a fool. Oh, God, what a fool. You were right. These people are awful. It's a sin. Gambling is a sin. I beg forgiveness." His face shone with perspiration and fear.

"But what happened to the business? The money? I don't understand, did you fail?"

He nodded. "I failed. Forgive me. I—I never started in business. You never asked what it was, it was always just 'the business.' I never invested in anything."

"Nothing?"

"Nothing. Forgive me, please. I have learned. I need you, Mother. I need help."

Charlotte reached out and touched Martin's damp hair, smoothing it from his face. "Money isn't the most important thing in the world, Martin. That I can easily forgive, but what of you?"

"I'll never go near those men again. Never!"

"Then it has all been worth it. You'll see, dear, working at a regular job is the best. Everything will be all right now. Oh, Martin, I have waited so long for the day when you would see the folly of that kind of life. I've worried so about you."

"I need money, Mother. I have to have it," he whispered. "Aunt Marcella won't give it to me. I've asked her. What am I going to do? You've got to talk to her, Mother. Make her see! Make her give it to me. Oh, God, I don't want to die! Not like that!"

Charlotte put her arms around him and pressed him gently to her. "No one is going to die, Martin. You have worked yourself into a state. There is no need for that, child."

He pushed away from her. "You don't know!" he cried. "You just don't know. They will kill me if I don't pay them."

"But you *will* pay them, dear. You'll pay them and then never again degrade yourself by having to see them or talk to them. Now that you know what despicable people they are, you'll never go near them again. I do have your word on that, don't I, Martin?"

"Yes, yes! Anything. Mother—"

Charlotte smiled as she extracted a small account book from the bottom of her sewing basket. "I was saving this to give to you as a wedding gift, but I don't suppose you'll be needing that now, with Scarborough and all. God does take care of everything—"

"You have money? How much?" Martin's eyes lit up. Charlotte looked down at the book. "I've saved this for a long, long time," she sighed. "And what better use could I put it to than to give my son a new life?"

Martin took the book, fumbled, and dropped it. He bent down and retrieved it, thumbing through to the final entry. He squeezed his eyes shut in relief when he saw the amount.

Two days after he had been taken on the night ride, Martin walked into John Munroe's saloon. He went into Munroe's office and handed the man an envelope containing a check for his debts, taking in return a handful of notes he had signed at one time or another.

John Munroe smiled up at him from behind his large, inlaid desk as he examined the check. "Good to have you back, Marty," he said heartily and reached across the desk to shake Martin's hand. "Feel like playing tonight? There are a couple out there just askin' to be relieved of weighty pockets. Maybe the wheel?"

"No, thank you. I have finished with all this, John. You succeeded in forcing me to pay you a bit earlier than I would have, but no more of this for me. Your tactics are a bit out of my line. You knew I'd pay. I always have. I don't like being threatened, John."

"Well, it worked, didn't it? Here you are, and everyone is happy," Munroe said mildly. "And I doubt, Marty, that you took that too seriously. The boys were just having a little fun with you, I think you know that."

"Fun? I watched two men die that night and nearly had my arm broken."

"Your arm wasn't broken. And no one died. You are wrong about that, Marty, completely wrong. No one died. No one died," he said slowly. "I wouldn't do a thing like that. Surely you realized the poor man was someone Mig had found beaten and left in the street behind the tenement?"

"Found him, huh?"

"We all know these things go on. None of us are naive, so Mig took advantage of common knowledge and let you see what might befall you, had you been in with the wrong sort of man—someone not so patient as I."

"I can see there is no arguing with you, but at least grant me some respect for my intelligence by not asking that I accept what you say. Good-bye, John." Martin stood up and replaced his wallet in his breast pocket.

"Never 'good-bye,' Marty. My house is your house. Sit down and have a drink with me. No hard feelings between us." Munroe signaled to a man standing at the side of the room, who returned momentarily, bearing a tray with glasses and whiskey.

"The best in the house!" Munroe said and lifted his full glass in a toast. Martin took the seat offered to him, and the glass. An hour later he left the office room with three twenty-dollar gold pieces.

"Even if you never use them," Munroe called after him, "take them and remember John Munroe gave them to you. Good luck, friend."

Martin stopped several times on his way out of the saloon. Several women came up to him, glad to see him. He bought one a drink. He stood behind a poker table, watching as the player won one hand, then two.

He stared at the big, whirling wheels until he was dizzy; the sound of rolling dice beat against his ears like a favorite tune. Over and over, he fingered the three gold coins in his pocket. He strolled around the outer perimeter of the saloon one more time, and then he walked out into the misty night.

As he headed back to Scarborough, he thought, If I'd stayed tonight, I would have won. He was lucky that night. He could feel it. He could have put John Munroe right out of business that night. Halfway to Scarborough he turned his horse around and rode at top speed back to Munroe's.

Munroe slapped him on the back as he entered. "Welcome home, Marty!"

"Watch out tonight, old man!" Martin laughed. "Drinks still on the house?"

Munroe nodded. The woman with whom Martin had had a drink earlier appeared, glass in hand. Martin went to the tables, the taste of whiskey in his mouth and the smell of her perfume in his nostrils. Never had he felt so charmed a man as he was that night. He could do no wrong.

The following night he walked out of Munroe's a little unsteadily, very late, and very conscious that he now had nearly as much cash in his pocket as Charlotte's bank draft had amounted to. Twenty-four hours—and what a difference! Looking up at the lightening sky, Martin took in deep breaths and stretched his arms wide. He could not recall when he had felt any better. He laughed aloud and let out a whoop in the quiet streets.

Chapter Twenty-four

Perhaps John Munroe himself was surprised by the winning streak that began for Martin Henderson that night. He had never seen anything like it. Martin's success didn't stop at the gaming tables, either. Everything he touched seemed to turn to gold—including his faltering relationship with Rhea Scott.

A year before, Nicholas Dalton had had the inside track with Rhea, while Martin had looked on longingly but with little hope. Now, with his incredible streak of good fortune, he could afford to woo her in the style to which he thought she was accustomed. He never forgot to bring her flowers and usually brought a present as well, sometimes of little, sometimes of great value.

"Martin Henderson, I swear, you must be the richest man in the entire world or the greatest fool!" she cried out one night when he produced a velvet-covered box containing a gold bracelet.

Martin bowed in mock gallantry. "I am both. One for you, and the other about you. Do you like it?"

She put it on her wrist and turned it to the light. "It is lovely. You do think of everything."

"You are by far more beautiful." He leaned over and kissed her on the cheek. "Let's go to the ball tomorrow night and have a grand old time. Let me show you off. Show your favorite man a good time and make the world jealous of me."

That next night, and many nights thereafter, they went out. Rhea showed off the gifts, and Martin showed off Rhea. Her affections were on the auction block, and despite Martin's previous financial shortcomings, he had calculated down to the halfpenny the proper price for Rhea Scott.

Less than two months later, he asked her to be his wife. She hesitated. An occasional gift was fine, but not enough for life, she sniffed. Grandly he told her of his prospects—including Scarborough House.

"Surely you don't expect me of all people to believe that!" she scoffed. "It is the Daltons' family estate. What a fool you must think me."

She turned and glared at him. "And I don't think it the least bit gentlemanly of you to throw it in my face that way. You know very well there was a time I expected to be the mistress of that house. It is a low, mean trick that you have played."

"It would be—if it were a trick," Martin said sympathetically. He slid onto the couch beside her and moved closer to her, forcing her to lie back. "But as it happens, there is no trick. When have I ever treated you unfairly? Have I ever shown you anything but love? Scarborough is yours, my love. Anything on earth you desire, I'll get for you."

"You're mocking me. Martin don't—"

"Scarborough is mine and therefore yours—or will be at my aunt's death."

"But Nicholas—"

"Nicholas what? When I say something to you, I expect to be believed. Nicholas nothing. Scarborough is mine! Believe it or not, as you please."

Rhea stopped struggling. She put her arms around his neck and let him kiss her as she lay back. "I believe you. It seems impossible, but I believe you. Everyone has said as much, but I thought it was mere talk. And you live there?"

"I live there."

"But how?"

"Aunt Marcella. Remember the court case that started the whole Dalton mess? Aunt Marcella won that suit. Scarborough was a part of that. She already had the deed, but when she won the suit against Brad Dalton, Scarborough was hers. And when she's gone, it'll be mine."

Rhea was convinced. "We can have parties—and Martin, please, let's be married on the lawn, right outside the house. We can dance and—and—Martin, it will be wonderful, won't it? I mean, we won't be like so many married couples. We'll do things and have fun and travel, won't we?"

After that night, all that remained was to inform Charlotte that they intended to be married. Martin had realized for some time that Charlotte would object to any woman who became his wife, but he had no doubt that he could handle his mother. The decision had been made, and Charlotte would have to resign herself to that decision. He was sure his mother would be as easy to deal with as Rhea's maiden aunt had been. With her, it had scarcely been a matter of asking Rhea's hand in marriage; rather, it had been a matter of telling her their plans.

Martin waited for what he thought was the right time to tell his mother. They went for a pleasant afternoon ride—something he didn't do often—and she was flattered and happy he wanted to be with her. When they returned and were having tea, he told her about Rhea.

"Are you sure, dear? You are so young, and Miss Scott does have a—a reputation of sorts, you know." This was as close as Charlotte could come to expressing her true feelings about Rhea.

"Mother, you are going to change your mind about her as soon as you get to know her, mark my words. As to her so-called reputation, it is grossly unfair. She isn't bad, she is spirited. She likes excitement." He rose from his chair, unable to sit still. "I can't believe my good fortune. Think of it! Not a year ago I had nothing. My God, I thought I had hit bottom. I could see nothing—no hope and no Rhea. I could never have asked her to marry me then. I could never have asked her to marry me without your help. You got me started again. Look at me, Mother, look at me! I'm a king. A king, Mother."

"Perhaps. To my ears, you sound more like a court jester," Charlotte said, a bit put off.

Martin walked over to his mother and put a hand on her shoulder. "Don't be like that," he said. "If I can't be happy over my wedding, when can I be? Be happy for me, Mother."

She took his hand in hers and put it to her cheek. "You are a thoughtful man when you choose to be, Martin. Rhea has a good man in you. I only hope that you have been as fortunate in your choice."

"I have been. You'll see. Things will be different from now on. I'll take care of you. Everything will go well for us."

Charlotte plunged into the task of planning an engagement ball with as much zest and energy as she could manage. It took a great deal out of her, for she had to contend both with Rhea's extravagant desires and Marcella's interference. At least, Charlotte thought, Nicholas has left us to our own devices.

Marcella, as far as Charlotte was concerned, added insult to injury by insisting that she be invited to join the guests at the ball. After a few halfhearted objections, Charlotte gave up trying to prevent her sister from making an appearance. She simply hadn't the energy to cope with another tongue-lashing from Marcella. Besides, Marcella had stayed sober enough to encourage Charlotte to believe she wouldn't make a spectacle of herself on that score.

On the evening of the ball, Marcella concocted a cosmetic paste she was certain would hide the smallpox scars on her face and neck. Meticulously, she spread it on herself, then did her hair, dressed, and went downstairs. The music had started, and Rhea's and Martin's friends were dancing or standing in small groups, talking.

Reaching the foot of the stairs, Marcella dramatically dropped her ostrich-feather fan from in front of her face. Even Charlotte stopped what she was doing to stand and stare at what at first seemed to be Marcella renewed. Only as her sister approached could Charlotte—and the others—see the tiny cracks forming in the drying cosmetic paste. Little bits of it fell onto her vivid green gown like tiny flakes of dandruff, becoming more noticeable each time Marcella turned her head or smiled.

Charlotte hurried to her side and tried to get her to return to her room. She was the center of attention, dressed like a queen and made up like a clown. People began to titter and whisper among themselves.

Marcella shook Charlotte's hand from her arm. "Am I not welcome?" she demanded. "After you've used my house and my money, am I to be unwelcome at the party?" She rapped at Charlotte with her fan.

No one would ever have described most of the people Martin and Rhea knew and enjoyed as especially kind or considerate. Now, some of the guests laughed discreetly; a few lifted their glasses to Marcella. Others turned away, embarrassed, and moved to isolated corners to talk of more pleasant things. They had all heard of Marcella Paxton, but who would ever have expected this?

As the makeup dried and flaked from her skin, Marcella, oblivious to the cause of her sudden popularity, beamed at everyone around her.

Seeing what was happening, Charlotte called for the orchestra to begin playing. "Never mind what you have planned! Play! Play immediately, something merry—anything—but gay and fast and—"

The leader nodded, and the room suddenly filled with the sound of an old but fast reel. Charlotte hurried back across the crowded floor, jostled this way and that on her way to Marcella. She saw her sister, looking tired and unsteady on her feet, reach out to take the arm of a young man who had put his name on her dance card. The room was filled with dancing couples; with each step, Charlotte seemed farther away from Marcella. Near to tears, she gave up and went in search of Martin.

"She's all right," he said when Charlotte found him. "Let her be. Whatever harm could be done, has already been done. You might as well leave her alone." He swallowed what was left of his champagne.

"Martin, please. They're making fun of her. Marcella isn't stupid. It won't be long before she sees."

"You worry far too much. She isn't going to see anything. Before long, I'll be carrying her up to her room, and that will be the end of that." He winked at Rhea, who stood at his side.

"Let's go join her! Come on, Martin, it would be fun. Let's go," Rhea laughed.

"Martin, you go," Charlotte pleaded. "Dance with her. Take her off the floor and get her back to her room. Please, dear. Dance her to the hall, and then I'll be able to take her upstairs. Just do that."

213

Martin shrugged. "I'll dance with her in just a moment. First I want one moment to dance with Rhea." He gave Charlotte's hand a quick pat and disappeared into the crowd with Rhea.

Charlotte went out into the hall to wait. She wrung her hands as the orchestra played one tune after another, but she saw neither Martin nor Marcella. Gert passed her, bearing a tray of food to replenish the ones in the dining room.

"Gert, wait here for a moment," she said. "If you see my son bringing Miss Marcella this way, take her upstairs right away, please. I am going to go in to see what is taking so long. Mr. Martin should have brought her here to me by now."

"Miss Marcella's not in there, ma'am."

"Oh, yes, she is! And making a fool of herself."

"No, ma'am. I don't like to contradict, but Miss Marcella passed through the kitchen five minutes ago. I saw her myself. She said she was going out for a walk."

"Kitchen? What would Marcella be doing in the kitchen? Why wouldn't she use the front door if she wanted to go out?"

"I don't know, ma'am. All I know is that Miss Marcella came down to the kitchen and went on outside."

"But where could she have gone?"

"I don't know, ma'am. She said she was going for a walk. I 'spect that's just what she did." Gert excused herself and carried the tray into the dining room. Charlotte hurried off to find Martin again. "Marcella is gone!" she told him.

"Good, then you can enjoy the party again. Who took her upstairs?"

"Martin, listen to me. I said *gone*. I don't know where she is."

"Mother, for the love of heaven! This is my engagement party. Will you stop worrying about Aunt Marcella? Wherever she is, she'll be back in a few minutes." He put his arms around Rhea and whirled with her toward the middle of the room. Charlotte tried to keep up with him. "She left the house. Please come and find her."

"No. I am not trudging around the grounds looking for her. Send one of the servants."

Charlotte stood watching them for a moment and then hurried once more into the hall. Suddenly a man appeared from around the corner.

"Oh, Nicholas! You frightened me!"

"Sorry, Charlotte. I was just coming out to see a bit of the merriment." He looked at her closely. "Is something wrong?"

"Marcella, she's gone. I must find her. She came down and made a fool of herself. It was—well, I couldn't do anything with her, and now she has left the house. She is outside somewhere." At this point, Charlotte seemed considerably more annoyed than concerned about her sister.

"How long ago did she leave?"

"I don't know. Fifteen minutes, at the least. Gert told me she'd gone."

"Go on back to your guests, Charlotte. I'll find Marcella."

"Nicholas, you understand, I can't ask Martin tonight. It is such an important night for him."

"You go back. I'll take care of it."

Charlotte hesitated.

"Hurry up now, or you are going to be missed." He made a small bow and walked toward the kitchen stairs. "Gert! Gert, where are you? Mrs. Henderson said Miss Marcella had come through here. Did you see where she went?"

"Last I saw, she was standin' right outside the windows there. Out there in the walkway lookin' out at the lawn through the latticework. After that I didn't see her, but she did say she was goin' to take a walk."

Nicholas hurried down the walk that circled the house, but Marcella was no longer there. On his way back, he passed the bright windows of the kitchen and then went out to the side of the house. It would be just like Marcella to conceal herself among the weeping branches and watch him chase about, hunting for her.

She was not there.

He stood for a moment, feeling a twinge of anxiety about her. Whatever she was doing, it was not a joke. He looked out across the Scarborough lawns, to the willows, and then toward the orchard. She might be anywhere.

He went back to the kitchen. "Show me where she was when you last saw her, Gert."

Gert walked out onto the walkway with him. "She was standin' here. Right here outside this window."

"She wasn't walking past? She was just standing there?"

He leaned against the lattice, trying to think what she would have done. He looked across the way directly into the orchard. The moonlight had turned it a soft, silvery green, muted and inviting. To the far side he could see the garden path that led to his grandfather's favorite haunt, the willow pond.

He stood for several minutes and then decided to follow the light of the moon up into the orchard. After he had walked a hundred feet or so, he suddenly turned back and headed for the stables.

Again he began the trip to the orchard, this time astride Night Wind. Soon he was deep among the trees. There he dismounted and for the first time called her name. She didn't answer him, but he was sure she was there. He heard her crying and found her slumped at the foot of a peach tree. He sat down beside her on the damp ground.

"You followed the moon trail," he said softly.

"Go away, Nicholas. I came out here to die."

"And I came to keep you company." He crossed his arms over his knees and gazed out across the orchard.

She placed her hand on his arm. "I had forgotten. This is not a good night for you either. But still—that is no reason to keep me company. I tell you, you are fortunate she is marrying Martin."

"You may be right. Now that you have my life straightened out, what is amiss with yours? What is it you must give up tonight, Marcella?"

215

"Ah, you are a clever man, Nicholas Dalton, but not that clever. I have nothing to free myself of. I have nothing left. That's what they said, all those young people with their pretty faces and fancy manners. They said I was an old woman someone had forgotten to bury. A mummy. Well, I'll let them bury me!"

"No one is going to bury you, Marcella. Not for a very long time yet."

"They should. I am angry, Nick, but even I can't fool myself all of the time. They were cruel tonight, just as I would have been when I was younger, but they didn't lie." She looked earnestly at him, playing with a bit of grass as she talked. "What do I have to live for? Shall I spend the rest of my days hiding? I was never one to do the 'proper' things ladies do. I can't sew worth anything, and I can't play the piano or paint. I am of no use to anyone."

"I can't sew, either," he chuckled. "Come along, Marcella. I have had enough of this death-and-desolation talk, and so have you. You and I may not like our lots in life, but neither of us wants to die." He pointed to the full skirt of her gown. "Can you ride in that outfit?"

"Ride?"

"Just back to the stable. We'll take Night Wind back and hitch up the cart. You and I are going to take a good look at the Hudson with the moon riding on its back."

"The Hudson!" Marcella breathed. "I met your father on the Hudson." She struggled to her feet. Nicholas helped her onto Night Wind and jumped up behind her. The horse shied at the added weight and then headed for home.

Less than a half hour later, Joe was on his way into the house to tell Charlotte all was well and Marcella was with Nicholas.

Marcella clung to the side of the light cart as they made their way across the lawns. As he often did, Nicholas ignored the roads. They jogged and swayed in the cart, laughing as they bumped against one another.

"Is there no road?" she cried out after one jolt had threatened to overturn them.

"You said you never did anything properly. What do we need a road for? I used to ride across this lawn in a cart like this when I was no bigger than your baby finger. I'll admit it didn't seem as bumpy then as it does tonight."

The Hudson was a lovely sight that night. Marcella drank in its beauty. "I have always loved this river. I haven't any idea why. I loved it as a child when I had no reason to."

"So have I," Nicholas replied. "I don't suppose I'll ever leave it. Another silly notion. That is the problem with being a romantic, I suppose. You let too many things tie you in, and you can never break away from them."

"Why should you?"

"I have never figured that out. Perhaps that is why I haven't. My grandfather was the same way. He loved it. I have him to thank for my attachment to this place. He raised me on this river, or the idea of it, making me feel its tempo, making it seem alive, making it a part of our lives."

"Brad used to speak of your grandfather the same way you do. I wish I could have met him. What a confusion life becomes. So many things go awry."

"They straighten out again somehow—or so I've been told."

"Now you are thinking *those* kinds of thoughts again."

"Guilty! Scarborough and other things. I think too often about—them. Have you decided what you are going to do about Scarborough? Martin seems to think he can count on it." He stopped for a moment and looked out across the river. "Don't ever give it to Martin, Marcella. It belongs to the Daltons."

"Brad made that very clear to me," she said, apparently annoyed at just how clear he had made it. She got out of the cart and walked to the river's edge. "Why must they clutter this beautiful river with all those hideous buildings?"

"What about Scarborough?"

"I think we had better be getting back to it. You have been a dear, and I feel much better. As long as it is good and dark, I feel like the Marcella of old."

But by the time they had got back to the house, Marcella was once more depressed and moody. She went up to her bedroom alone.

Nicholas met Charlotte in the hall. "She is feeling put upon and annoyed, but she has gone upstairs and is all right."

On his way up to his own room, he was stopped at the landing by Rhea on her way down from the powder room. "Why Nicholas! Nicholas Dalton!" He gave her a crooked grin and waited for her to go on. "Where have you been hiding? All the ladies will be so upset when I tell them you have been here all along and have ignored us all."

"I have not been here," he said quietly. "I have just now come in."

"Aren't you going to dance with me? Not even one dance? And no congratulations, Nicholas? What a way to behave. People will think there are hard feelings between us. Come, dance with me, Nick. Just once."

"You look lovely, Rhea, and I would like nothing better than to dance with you, but I am very tired and not dressed for the occasion. I wish you happiness. Marriage will become you, as does everything." He stepped away from her.

She put her hands on his chest. "No dance? You never used to be so reluctant."

"You never used to be engaged. Good night, Rhea."

"Such a mean little man you have become! But never mind, Nick, there will be other times, and nights when you'll wish you had put your arms around me when you had the chance. You haven't forgotten."

"I haven't forgotten, Rhea, but neither do I want to repeat myself. Nor do I want to follow in Martin's footsteps. I prefer a fresh path to follow."

"Well! You have become sarcastic as well. But I don't mind that, either. Good night, Nick. Sleep well." She brushed her lips against his and flounced down the stairs.

Nicholas went to bed rather happy that it would be Martin's lot, not his own, to keep track of Rhea. She was pretty and she was tantalizing, but he was very pleased he no longer had any desire to think of her as his wife.

*   *   *

217

Charlotte was exhausted the following day—not surprisingly, since the ball had gone on until just before dawn and she had insisted on staying up until she had seen the last departing guest to the door.

An afternoon nap did her no good whatever. She could not possibly manage Martin's wedding, she decided, not with the elaborate schemes that seemed to appeal to both Rhea and Martin.

"You'll have to make other arrangements," she told Martin. "I simply cannot go through all of that again." She looked around her at the wreckage of last night's ball. "I do not have the strength for all of it, Martin. I am sorry. You'll have to have Rhea's family take care of it. They should, in any case."

Martin, much the worse for wear, had no patience to spare for his mother. "You know perfectly well she has no real family. She lives with a maiden aunt. You can't expect an old woman like that to do this up right. You wouldn't want that kind of a wedding for me."

"I cannot do this alone, Martin!"

"Then get help."

"Think of the cost, Martin! Marcella is generous, but my dear, we must use some discretion. If I hadn't all the responsibility—I mean, if I didn't have to look after Marcella and the house and all—it might be a different matter. If I could concentrate only on the wedding, then perhaps—but someone must care for Marcella."

"Aunt Marcella can tend to herself for a time. She is not half so feeble as she pretends. You saw her last night. When she wants something, she is perfectly capable. Take away her drink and her sleeping potion for a spell, and she'll be fine."

"That is not the point," Charlotte fretted. "We agreed we would care for her when we came here. The reason she has given us this home and has been exceedingly generous is that she wants her family around her. If Marcella thinks she needs me, whatever her reasons, I must give her that care."

Martin exploded. "I don't care what you do, Mother! Care for her or don't. Hold her hand twenty-four hours a day if you must, but I am not going to let that old harpy ruin my life. I want to be married here. And Rhea wants a very big wedding. Get someone to care for Marcella or hire help to do the wedding for you."

"But who? Where would I find someone Marcella would accept?"

"There must be someone," Martin muttered, thoroughly disgusted with his mother. "Some distant relative. I daresay she hasn't any friends, distant or otherwise."

Charlotte had caught only part of what Martin had said. "Some distant relative," she repeated. "I wonder. . . ."

"You wonder what, Mother?"

"I was just thinking about Kathleen O'Connor. My sister Jo's daughter in Ohio. I wonder if she would consider coming."

"Don't give her a choice. Tell her you need her and expect her here to take care of her ailing aunt. She's family. She'll understand. Especially after everything you have done for her over the years. Just tell her to come."

"But Martin, dear, I can't hire her like any common servant. She is my sister's child, one of the family."

"For the love of God," he snapped, "will you stop arguing with me? She'll probably be glad to come. She can't have much where she is, and what can she be looking forward to?"

Charlotte thought for a moment. "She might even be glad of the opportunity," she said, looking up at her son. "And we could introduce her to some nice young men. It might work out, mightn't it? We could see to her future here. I mean, we could provide her with opportunities she'd never have there."

"I told you! I was right. Coming here will be the best thing that ever happened to her, and Aunt Marcella should be pleased with that arrangement as well. Wasn't Aunt Marcella particularly close to Aunt Jo at one time?"

"Marcella very nearly raised Jo. She loved her very much. Always loved her, but then—" Charlotte shook her head slowly. "Well, after Jo turned her back as she did on Marcella, maybe she won't want Kathleen around her after all. Maybe it's not such a good idea, Martin. We really don't know the girl."

Martin slapped his head dramatically. "Now you're making excuses! Just write to her. The sooner the better. And for pity's sake, don't go talking this over with Aunt Marcella. She'll make a mess of it all."

Before Martin left her, he placed writing paper and a quill by her side. Charlotte tried to balance the misgivings she had about asking her sister's child to be no more than a nursemaid against all the advantages she was sure would be Kathleen's by coming to Scarborough. She decided to do as Martin had suggested.

Having dealt with her qualms of conscience, she began to feel much better. Marcella's care had weighed heavily upon her, mostly because Charlotte had never really understood her sister. Whatever it was that had kept Marcella weak, dependent on her medicines, and forever cantankerous, was not ill health. Charlotte was enormously relieved, knowing that soon someone else would have to grapple with Marcella.

Marcella and Nicholas were not informed of the decision until Kathleen had written that she would come. Neither was given a chance to object.

Several days afterward, Nicholas visited Marcella in her room. "I hear you are to have a new nursemaid."

Marcella looked up. "Did you? I was told I was to have a surprise. That Charlotte never could keep a secret for long. She told me my sister's daughter would be coming out to Scarborough."

"I wonder what the young lady thinks she is to be. Nursemaid or niece?" Nicholas plunged his hands into his pockets as he paced about the room. "This place is fast becoming a circus. It is like a boardinghouse of oddities."

"Are you still annoyed about Martin and that Scott woman? I thought you had finally put all that behind you."

"Rhea is only part of it. Of course I don't like the idea of her living here right under this roof as his wife. But that isn't all. . . ."

"You know, Nicholas, for all of your dislike of the things I have done, there is one thing I can say for myself. What happened to your father and me happened because I loved him. I grant you that I was stupid and foolish and jealous. We both paid for that. Rhea Scott doesn't love anyone but herself. You must never let someone like that twist your life. However badly it turned out for Brad and me, our love was worth something."

"Was it? It brought an awful lot of unhappiness, and not just to you and Father."

"I have admitted that we were wrong—"

"Well," Nicholas interrupted, "it is nothing to worry about, since I am not the one who's going to marry Rhea. But let's forget Rhea. Tell me about your niece."

Marcella smiled and let him change the subject. "She is my youngest sister's child. Jo went to live in Ohio because she wanted to be as far away from me as possible, after I got involved with Brad." She sighed. "I seem to leave a trail of people behind me with all my misdeeds."

"Everyone has regrets. It won't do you any good to hole up in this room and brood about them."

"You brood."

He took a deep breath and sat down. "It doesn't do me any good, either. Perhaps I should take some of my own advice. I have been thinking of leaving here for a while. There is an entire world out there that I have never seen."

"Are you serious?"

"I am not sure. I have the feeling that if I leave now, I'll never come back. I don't want all this lost to me."

"Then stay and fight for it, if this is what you want. Martin hasn't got it yet."

"*You* have it, Marcella. Why all this teasing with it? If you want Martin to have it, tell both of us. If you are going to pass it on to me, then tell us both so that we can all get on with our lives."

"I am not really teasing, Nick. You say you want Scarborough, and in the next breath you talk of leaving."

"Marcella, I believe in nothing but the land. Nothing."

"Someone once told me that Brad and I would do more damage to you than to anyone else. I can see she was right. I have been wrong about you. I've worried about you and Rhea Scott, but you don't regret losing her and you've never tried to get her back."

Nicholas said nothing.

"Someday you'll have to face all these things you have decided to look away from. I may be a lonely old woman now, Nick, but I have a full life to look back on. What have you? You're how old? Twenty-eight? Thirty? And what have you got to remember? You trust nothing. You are making a sad life for yourself, Nicholas Dalton. An empty life."

She stared at him for several seconds, watching the light in his gray eyes change. "No one can stand in one place forever," she said softly.

"They can if there is noplace they want to go."

"Say that when you are an old man with rheumatism and great-grandchildren."

"I am not likely to be a great-grandfather."

"Do you want me to accept blame for that as well?"

"I am blaming no one. It is the way things are."

"Bosh! An excuse. You are a coward, young man."

He squared his shoulders and stood up. "Many faults I admit readily. Cowardice is not among them."

"Oh, stop your strutting! I don't mean physical cowardice. You are no coward, but you are a fearful man, Nicholas. Martin would run if I threatened him with my hatpin, whereas you would merely walk up and take it from my hand. But then Martin would take a chance on anything, and you, Nicholas, would walk away from any chance. Your father was not like that."

"No, he wasn't, was he? He jumped right in—with both feet—and look what it got him. A wife who didn't give a damn when he died, a grieving mistress who had led him to his death. He lost everything he had ever had—family, property, his life, and any dignity he might have had left. And you, too. You were the same. You didn't hesitate, did you, Marcella? What do you have that anyone would want or care about?"

"Scarborough House."

Nicholas stalked out the door, slamming it behind him.

Marcella thought of Jo—the little girl with the red hair who had clung to her hand in the dark, who had begged for one last bedtime story, even when her eyes were heavy with sleep. Would Kathleen look like Jo? Could Kathleen fill the void Jo had left in Marcella's life so long ago?

She conjured up a hundred faces for her niece. All of them looked like Jo.

"Charlotte!" she yelled, not bothering with the bellpull. She yelled twice more before her sister appeared, breathless from running up the stairs.

"I want you to write to Kathleen. Tell her I don't want her. You'll neglect me completely as soon as she comes. I won't have her here."

"Marcella, it is too late. I can't tell her now. She will be here in three weeks. I will keep my word to you, you know that."

"You won't."

"All right, Marcella. If you insist, I shall send the girl home. I shall tell her that she is here for a visit and send her back after a week."

"Never mind. What is done is done."

"It can be undone."

"Not now. You have made your bed, lie in it. Kathleen shall stay. And you will regret it!"

Charlotte left the room perplexed and worried. She no longer knew what Marcella wanted; often she wondered whether Marcella herself knew. She would be happy when Kathleen arrived, even if she stayed only the week. Anything would help.

BOOK THREE

Chapter Twenty-five

Kathleen O'Connor loved to get mail. She sat curled up in her favorite overstuffed chair, relishing the prospect of opening the two envelopes lying in her lap.

"This one must be from Aunt Charlotte." She hefted it, held it up to the light, and put it aside. "Aunt Charlotte usually has all manner of news and gossip about the people in New York." She opened the other and made a face at Minerva Shaw, her guardian, who sat across the room, sewing. "Nothing. An excursion announcement," she said, tossing it into the wastebasket.

She opened Charlotte's letter and began to read it silently. Suddenly she bounced out of the chair, tossing back her long black hair.

"Minerva, look at this!" She handed the letter to the other woman. "I am to come to work for Aunt Charlotte, it seems. Not a by-your-leave or a would-you-please in the entire letter. Just 'get there'!"

Minerva skimmed the letter for a moment. "What will you do?"

"I don't see I've been left much choice, do you? She is obviously calling due my debt to her."

"Then you will be going."

Kathleen chewed her bottom lip. "How much money have we saved from Grandpa's legacy, Minerva?"

"Not enough to repay your Aunt Charlotte, if that is what you have in mind."

"Then I have no choice but to do as she asks."

Minerva read the letter through once again. "She's mighty sure of herself."

"Like the carnival barker says, Minerva, you pays your money and you takes your choice. She paid, and I'm the choice."

Minerva sniffed. "I just don't know, Miss Kat—"

"Who knows, Minerva, it may turn out not to be so bad as we think. Aunt Marcella sounds as if she could stand some care. Besides, I have never been to New York. And when you come right down to it, I haven't any real reason for disliking Aunt Charlotte. Only bits and pieces of things Mother said years ago and—"

"And the fact that she was perfectly willing to pawn you off to anyone who would take you when you had no home."

"Yes, but I did end up with a home, the very one I would have chosen for myself, had I been able. I had no complaints about that, Minerva. I wanted to be with you, and I have been very happy."

"No thanks to her," Minerva muttered.

Kathleen hurried from the room in search of pen and paper.

"No need to be in such a hurry about things," Minerva called after her.

"Putting it off won't change it," Kathleen replied from the next room.

That same afternoon she sent off a curt, businesslike reply to Charlotte. "That should tell her we mean business every bit as much as she," she laughed, showing Minerva what she had written. "I wonder what this Scarborough House is. This is not Aunt Charlotte's old address. She must have moved in with Aunt Marcella, but I had the impression Aunt Marcella lived in the city. Oh, well, I suppose we'll find out soon enough."

They spent the rest of the day making lists of things Kathleen would have to take care of before she left, chattering about what New York must be like. Neither of them had ever been there; it seemed a foreign country to them both.

Whatever qualms Minerva had, she kept them to herself; she had no desire to dampen Kathleen's girlish enthusiasm. Don't borrow trouble, she thought to herself—it will crop up soon enough.

Around suppertime, as they straightened the room, Kathleen began humming an Irish tune. It had been one of her father's favorites.

Minerva paused and turned to look at her. "I think you really *want* to go," she said a little sadly. She held up a much-used and -mended petticoat. "You sure can't take this with you, Miss Kat. Looks more like a rag than a petticoat."

"Oh, just toss it in with the others," Kathleen sang out. "I'll use it for walking and whatnot. They must have a park or a woods or something nearby where I can take hikes. I wonder if there might be a horse I can ride. Anyway, who is going to be peeking at my petticoats?"

Minerva balled up the petticoat and tossed it aside. "Nobody's going to get the chance to see you in a rag like that!"

"Don't be such a fusspot!" Kathleen giggled, dropping into her chair. Suddenly she was serious. "Minerva, what's been bothering you all afternoon?"

The older woman sighed and shook her head. She, too, sat down and thought for a moment before she spoke. "This whole thing smells of 'poor relation' to me, Miss Kat—I can't help it. So don't go getting your hopes up about this trip. You're going to work for your Aunt Charlotte, make no mistake about that, and don't you let her put any pretty name on the truth. She should pay you, for one thing. See that she does! Just as soon as you've repaid your debt to her, we're going to get right out of there."

"You see, Minerva, there was something bothering you all along." She frowned thoughtfully. "You sound as if you don't approve of Aunt Charlotte."

"It's got nothing to do with approving of or not approving of," Minerva grumbled. "She let you down once, or tried to. That lady didn't bat an eyelash when you were wandering around with noplace to go. She was all set to see you grow up in a convent or one of those homes for children. She didn't want you then. What do you suppose she wants from you now? I'll tell you, my girl—work! Cheap work, that's what."

Kathleen refused to be discouraged. "Oh, Minerva! It might actually be fun. And she must have some good in her. She is caring for Aunt Marcella, after all—"

"I don't rightly know, Miss Kat." Minerva shook her head, as if to clear it.

"Anyway, just see to it that you get it straight from the start. Get a fair wage and days off. Maybe I should go with you right away, instead of staying here for a while. Maybe you'll need more looking after than either Miss Aggie or Mr. Terry."

"I'll be fine, Minerva. After all, I have had you for all these years, and surely Aunt Charlotte can't be a harder taskmistress than you! Besides, Aggie isn't half as brave as she puts on. That sister of mine will need you when the baby's born. I'll be all right, really I will. And I promise I'll write and tell you everything."

"Well, all right, Miss Kat. But if anything goes awry, I'll just have to straighten it out when I get there."

For all their conversation, neither Kathleen nor Minerva was quite sure what to make of Charlotte's request and Kathleen's imminent trip to New York. After Kathleen's parents had died, Charlotte had sent rent money to her and Minerva each month at precisely the same time and in the same amount. But aside from twice-a-year letters—one at Christmas and one at Easter—Charlotte had had very little to say to her "distant relative" in Ohio.

For Kathleen's part, as soon as she was old enough, she had written to her aunt once a month, thanking her for the money and telling her whatever news she might have. She could seldom think of anything that might interest her aunt, so Charlotte knew little of what her niece had experienced since her parents' death.

After the death of their parents, Kathleen, Agatha, and the three remaining O'Connor brothers had found that the world they lived in, a world they had always accepted unthinkingly as a free and permanent gift of God, was no more real and permanent than the tales their father had told them of fairies and trolls. Those stories, like the days and nights they lived through, had beginnings and endings that changed with the mood of the storyteller. Nothing was the same, nothing was as it once had been.

Terrance O'Connor had had all the charm, ingenuity, and wit his Irish heritage afforded, and he had used it well, winning the hand of Kathleen's mother, Josephine Paxton. The O'Connors, newly married, had left New York City and settled in Columbus, Ohio, where Jo had begun raising the children and Terrance had begun his life's work.

A successful man, he did with his hard-earned wealth what many Irishmen did—he sent the money to others, so that they could come to this country and begin a new life. He provided them with passage and a home, and they took from him the opportunity for an unharried life, without the biting poverty and uncertainty of the old country.

Sometimes Terrance was repaid, most often he was not. It was an endless drain into which he poured his time and his money year after year. There was always someone in need, and together, Jo and Terrance decided time after time to help.

Most people admired Terrance. Some mocked him, called him softheaded;

others disliked him for his religion and his Irishness. Regardless of their personal feelings about him, however, members of the Columbus community respected and trusted him. Terrance O'Connor owned and ran an honest store. His prices were fair, and he was never quick with a bill when someone was having a hard time. Generally people would lend him money to finance his charity, or they would extend his mortgage, for they knew he would always pay them back. He was a man of his word.

In the early spring of 1863, all the O'Connors caught what they first thought were colds. As in most large families, it spread from one member to another. By the time Agatha, Kathleen, and the three oldest boys had recovered, Terrance, Jo, and the baby, Brian, were ill. As a rule, they were a robust family, so no one worried much about their being a little under the weather.

Still, little Kathleen fidgeted in the enforced quiet of the O'Connor home. She was not permitted to run or play normally in the house, and she had been barred from her parents' room.

Kathleen pestered her sister Agatha for the fifteenth time that day. "Why can't I go see Mama and Papa, Aggie? If they're not really sick, why must I be so quiet? Papa doesn't like quiet children. He says children should be happy."

Agatha was sitting on the window seat at the stair landing, looking at the snow falling in heavy, wet flakes. Last week it had been so warm she hadn't needed to wear a coat. Today it was snowing, but it was still strangely warm. The small, wavery pane of glass in the leaded windows made the melting flakes turn all the colors of the rainbow as they touched and melted.

"It won't last," Agatha said absently. "Nothing ever lasts." She turned and jumped down from the window seat.

"Maybe if it melts and gets warm again, Mama and Papa and Brian will feel better again. I am getting awfully tired of being quiet. When can I go see them, Aggie?" Kathleen persisted. "Aggie?"

"Questions, questions, questions! All you do is ask me over and over again. I keep telling you, *I don't know!* Why don't you go play with your dolls, or go ask Gracie to comb out your hair. It looks awful. And I hope she pulls all the tangles. It would serve you right! Go away and leave me alone!"

"Gracie will not pull my hair. It's your frizzy hair that gets tangles."

"Girls!" Minerva seemed to appear from nowhere. "Miss Kat! Miss Agatha! You know better than to carry on like this. Miss Agatha, I expect more of a big girl like you. What's come over you two? Mercy!"

Minerva Shaw was a giant of a woman, making even Terrance seem to shrink in size when she stood beside him. None of Kathleen's brothers disobeyed her; it was far too humiliating to risk. When they had, she had been known to pick up the largest of them, tuck the offender under her arm, and move off at march time to the woodshed for a good thrashing with her seldom-used hickory stick. As a result, people said the O'Connor children were the best behaved in the city.

For the moment Minerva towered over the girls. Finally Agatha spoke. "She won't let me be, Minerva. She asks questions, questions, and more questions."

When Minerva looked over at Kathleen, Agatha stuck her tongue out and made a face at her sister.

"Miss Kat, get on with you now. Go play with your dolls. That new house your papa built for you is just sitting there waiting for some nice little girl to put her dolls inside. Why don't you do that?"

Kathleen's brilliant blue eyes flashed. "I no longer play with dolls," she announced, raising her finely shaped little chin. "If Agatha is too old, then so am I. Agatha isn't the only one getting to be a lady. I am, too."

"Well, I never!" Minerva hooted. "Will you listen to this? Too big for dolls, are you? Too big for your bloomers is more like it. I suppose you think you're too big to be baking bread with me, then."

"Me?" Kathleen squealed.

"You. Come along, Miss Big Britches. We'll bake bread and keep your troublesome little nose out of trouble for an afternoon." She grinned at her favorite and took Kathleen's tiny hand in her own.

"Can't I come, too?" Agatha called after them.

"Just me, isn't that right, Minerva?"

"Because you're such a little angel," Minerva added. Behind Kathleen's back she motioned for Agatha to come along.

"Yes, because I am good and very grown-up."

Minerva whacked her on her behind and chased her down the stairs. Agatha followed more sedately.

Temperamentally, the two girls couldn't have been more different. Agatha, though she had her mother's red hair, lacked the bravado and dash to carry it off. Kathleen, who had her father's curling black hair and his blue eyes, also shared his fun-loving, impish nature. It was understandable she was his favorite.

That afternoon Minerva managed to turn the girls' minds completely away from the quiet seriousness that had come over the house in recent days. It was no mean success. For in spite of the antics, the laughter, the flour and dough everywhere, when it was over, the same nameless feeling of dread returned.

As a rule, Kathleen and Agatha were seldom permitted in the kitchen, but from that day on, Minerva invited them to help with one or another of the household projects. Neither Kathleen nor Agatha saw in Minerva's actions anything but great fun.

During the next few days, what seemed to Kathleen to be streams of people came to the house and left again, like a great train of ants.

"Who are all these men?" she asked Minerva.

"Vultures, Miss Kat. Nothing but vultures," Minerva growled, wiping her hands on her apron.

However much Kathleen dared pester Agatha with her questions, she knew better than to try it with Minerva. So she left Minerva in the hallway and sought out her sister in the third-floor playroom.

With her was their oldest brother, Terry. If Minerva's rare bad humor hadn't told her something was wrong, the sight of Terry in the playroom did. At seventeen, he scorned anything that smacked of playing and childhood.

Kathleen thought he looked silly sitting on one of the small chairs, facing Agatha. "What are you doing here, Terry?"

"We're just talking, Kat. Come on in."

"Don't say anything to her about—you know what," Agatha whispered to Terry, glancing over at Kathleen.

"What, Aggie? What, Terry? Tell me, tell me!" She looked from one to the other, and getting no satisfaction, began to stamp her feet.

"Kathleen, why must you always be like this? There's no secret! You really are a brat. You are making everything seem horrible!"

"You're hateful, Agatha. There *is* a secret! I heard you."

"Stop it! Both of you," Terry said sternly. "There is no secret, Kathleen. I am going to tell her, Agatha. What difference if she knows now? Minerva was going to tell her tonight, anyway. She has to know."

"Oh, tell me, Terry! What is it?" Kathleen danced over to him, her face glowing with curiosity.

Agatha groaned. "I told you not to say anything. Look at her. She thinks it is some kind of game."

"You made her think it!" Terry shot back. He sat Kathleen down on the chair he had vacated and squatted in front of her. "It isn't a secret, Kat," he said softly. "It is about Mama and Papa—and Brian. They are—" He paused.

"What about them?"

"Nothing. Nothing about them." He stood up. "Minerva will tell you."

"You can't stop now, Terry! You've already started. Tell her," Agatha said. Kathleen began to look worried.

Terry began again. "Kat, Mama and Papa are. . . ."

"Say it, Terry. They're dying," Agatha said and burst into tears. "I heard the doctor say so."

"Brian died early this morning," Terry added and walked quickly to the far end of the room.

"Well, maybe they won't," Kathleen said. She looked at Terry for confirmation. He didn't turn around. Agatha was still crying. Kathleen beat her fists against her knees. "You're lying! Brian didn't die. He didn't, he didn't, he didn't!"

"Do something with her, Agatha!"

"I don't know what to do," Agatha sobbed.

Terry moved slowly toward Kathleen and then sank to his knees. She lunged for him, wrapping her arms around his neck and crying brokenheartedly as he gently rocked her. Agatha got up and went from the room to get Minerva.

Minerva came on the run, scooped Kathleen into her arms, and carried her back down the steps to her bedroom.

She knew Kathleen still had not learned the extent of their tragedy that day. She would learn it slowly over the next few days as it unfolded piece by piece. Two days after Brian's death, Jo died, and the doctor repeated his pronouncement that he doubted Terrance would pull through. He had pneumonia.

But Terrance clung to life. Nothing anyone said could shake Kathleen's belief that her father would get well and come to romp and play with her again.

"He's my papa, too, Kat, but he isn't going to get better," Agatha told her. "The doctor said you will get sick, too, if you don't believe that."

"You're lying."

"I'm not," Agatha said, her small voice filled with tears. "We are in an awful fix. They are going to take away everything Papa had, and we won't have anything."

"Those men that come here are Papa's friends. They will take care of everything until Papa is better."

"Kathleen, they're not! They are going to take the roof right off our heads. I heard them. Papa owed them a lot of money, and now they want it, and Papa is sick and can't give it to them. So they are going to take everything else."

"Well, they can't. We'll just have to give them their money for Papa."

"We don't have any! All we have is another funeral this afternoon, and poor Mama is going to be put into a pauper's grave because we can't give her a proper burial."

"Oh, we can't let that happen. Papa would never stand for it!"

"It's all Papa's fault! I heard them say so. Papa gave all his money away, and now we don't have any."

"You shouldn't talk that way about Papa."

"I'll talk the way I want. You are just too young and stupid to understand anything!"

"And you're a frizzle-haired redhead with freckles and spots all over you!"

They parted, glaring at each other, to dress for their mother's funeral.

Kathleen's frock was of good silk. Her bonnet and her shoes were new, and her gloves had come from France, because her father had always liked to see her looking her best.

When she finished dressing, she looked at herself in the long mirror. Terrance had put one in each of the girls' rooms. He said he liked them to see what the Lord had blessed them with. "Two beautiful girls He has given to me. Never deny it, never hide it, and never let it rule you," he had said often. "If you have been given beauty, it is to be used to make beauty known. If you have been given forgiveness, it is your part to forgive."

Poor Papa, she thought, he wouldn't even be told what was happening to Mama. Maybe what Agatha had said about the money was true. Papa might be buried in the same graveyard. She wondered if they would be near to one another.

Kathleen came out of her room at the same time Agatha emerged from hers. Animosity forgotten, she automatically moved close to Agatha.

Kathleen had not had an opportunity to say good-bye to her mother. She hadn't been permitted in the room. She made a solemn promise to herself as she walked to the carriage that she would see her father. No one was going to keep her away from him.

That night, she tiptoed down the corridor to his room after everyone was asleep. When she came to his bedside and spoke to him, he didn't answer, nor did he open his eyes. Kathleen had only to listen to him breathe, or touch his hand, or watch him, to know that he was very ill.

She began to talk to him, to talk about all of the things of her life. He had always liked to hear her talk. When she ran out of things she thought might interest him, she repeated the recipe Minerva had used to cure the drunkenness of Mr. Marshall, when he had staggered up to their back door. She knew that if her father did not respond to that, he would respond to nothing. He did not respond.

She cried and told him about her mother's funeral. He said nothing and did nothing. Kathleen wished she hadn't come to the room, but once there she couldn't bring herself to leave him. She began to pray—all the childish prayers that he and Mama had taught her and said with her each night. She repeated them until they became a litany. Finally she fell asleep on the floor beside his bed, unaware that Terrance O'Connor was dead.

Nothing was ever the same after that night. They had not even got Terrance properly buried before the creditors began to arrive in earnest. Terrance's estate would never cover all he owed. He had been as deeply in debt when he died as any honorable man who planned to live to a ripe old age would have dared to be. For the creditors it would be first come, first served.

For several days Minerva stood like a great bronzed Amazon on the front porch, threatening them with her rolling pin. But she knew it was only a matter of time before they would come back, more likely with the sheriff. Minerva sent Terry to get Malcolm Adams, the family lawyer and a longtime friend.

She ordered the rest of the children upstairs. "I don't want you down here when these vultures come back again. They may have their rights, but they don't need to get a free look as well."

"What's a vulture?" Lawrence wanted to know.

"Get on upstairs! I don't have time for your questions today. Hurry up! Miss Agatha, take charge of them like a good girl. And see if you can explain to Mr. Lawrence what a vulture is."

They all began to walk slowly up the stairs, looking back to the door. The younger ones hoped they might get to see Minerva swinging her rolling pin again. They were not disappointed. She shook her rolling pin at them and watched them scatter, laughing and squealing, toward the safety of the playroom.

When Terry returned from his errand, he found Minerva sitting near the door, waiting. He reported that Mr. Adams was busy but would be there as soon as he could get away.

"I was hoping he'd come back with you," she said, shaking her head. "But we can wait. Now you go on up to the others in the playroom."

He didn't move. "I am the man of the house now, Minerva. If there is going to be trouble, I ought to be here."

Minerva smiled. When she had first come to work for the O'Connors, he had been a small child, no bigger than Brian. How quickly he had grown into this young man standing before her, solemn and ready to take on heavy responsibilities.

"Yes, sir," she replied without a trace of mockery in her voice.

He grinned. "It sounds funny to hear you say that—to me."

"No, sir. You are right. You are the man of the house, and I've always called the man of the house 'sir.' " She straightened her apron and turned toward the kitchen. "You just ring if you need anything, Mr. Terry, sir." This time she emphasized the word and smiled at him.

Minutes later the door chimes rang. Gracie hurried to answer the door. The caller was one of the more persistent creditors.

"What shall I do, Mr. Terry? He won't leave, and he says if Minerva comes near him again, he'll have the sheriff at our door within the hour. What'll I do?"

"Tell him— No, just show him in here. Bring him to me."

She looked doubtful for a moment and then moved to obey him. "Yes, sir. I'll show him in here."

Terry sat down and tried one or two poses he thought would indicate dignity. He was still adjusting himself when a tall, burly man entered the room. Instantly, Terry was on his feet, showing respect to his elders.

The man walked over to Terry and thrust an impressive sheaf of papers into his hands. "It's all there."

Terry looked blankly from the man to the papers and back again.

"What are you going to do about it?" the man asked, his voice less belligerent than before. "I can't sustain the loss this represents to me."

Terry hadn't the slightest idea what the man was talking about. As he listened to the older man go on about his financial straits and about Terrance's habit of giving everything away to those who didn't deserve it, he became more and more confused.

Fortunately, Malcolm Adams arrived just in time to save Terry from having to reply.

"Patrick Casey! I haven't seen you in town for a coon's age," he said, tossing his coat over a chair. "What are you doing here at this time of grief for the family?"

"Hello, you old shyster. You know damned well why I'm here."

"My dear man, the poor soul is not yet in his grave. Couldn't it wait for a day or so? Come to my office, Casey."

"No need of that. I only want my due, or equal value. I've known you for a long time, Mal, and I want to know from you, can Terrance O'Connor's estate meet his just debts? If you say it can, I'll take your word for it, but the word is that it can't."

"We've not had time to begin to look into Terrance's affairs. His death came as a great shock to all of us. A young man like that. I still can't believe it. Terrance was healthy—in the prime of his life. Who could have foreseen something like this happening—and both of them going at one time?"

"It happens." Casey shrugged apologetically. "And he hasn't left the wherewithal to pay his debts."

233

"Mr. Adams, why do we owe Mr. Casey money" Terry's voice startled the two older men.

"A farm, Terry—a farm of your father's. He bought it at the wrong time, and it is mortgaged to the hilt."

"I didn't know we owned a farm."

"You don't!" Casey laughed shortly. "You own the deed, and I own the mortgage on the worthless land, which I shall no doubt get returned to me."

"I don't understand."

"He means he will foreclose if we cannot make the payments." Malcolm Adams looked at Casey. "Lord knows why you should have a penny. That farm was worthless, and if you hadn't fed Terrance a cock-and-bull story about needing money, he never would have bought it."

Casey shrugged. "This isn't much of a mortgage."

"It's enough." Adams shuffled the mortgage papers for a moment. "Look, Casey, I give you my word," he said finally. "We'll do the best we can on it. Terrance was an honorable man, you know that. He'd pay you if he could, and so will his son. But we do need time. You will be the first debtor officially recognized by me as executor of Terrance's estate. Will that satisfy you?"

"You're going to say that to every man who comes to you, Mal. Still, I don't see that it matters or that I've got a choice." He tipped his hat to Terry. "Good day to you, Mr. O'Connor. My sympathies to you and your family."

When he had left, Adams sank down into a chair and cradled his head in both hands.

"Are you all right, sir?"

"No, I'm not all right, and neither are you," he muttered. "Your father couldn't have left things in a worse mess if he had planned it."

"Just how bad is that?"

"How bad do you think it could be?"

"Not so bad that we can't manage. We have the store, this house, and the farm—if we meet the payments. We could work that farm. Lawrence and William are old enough to help out now. I know they couldn't do much, but they could help."

"I wish I could tell you you'll get the chance, but you won't."

"Why not?"

"Because your father has left nothing."

"Look, Mr. Adams, I know we have never been wealthy, but then we aren't exactly poor either. Papa always provided well for us. He had to have something in order to do that."

"He did. He would have again. I'm telling you this happened at the wrong time. That farm of Casey's—your father bought that to give to some family he was bringing over here. They're not the only ones he's helped. He always said it would all come back. Most of the time he was right, but it took time. Those people had to have time to set themselves up.

"Well, this time it just won't come back. Your father was in a bad way financially, and with his passing, you aren't going to get the chance to— Oh, what's the use. Just face it. There is nothing, and there is nothing you can do about it unless you know where a miracle is."

"Maybe some of those people Papa helped could pay back some of it."

"Don't count on it. I don't think they have it to give. Of course, you might be able to take their farms or stores away from them—"

"Papa wouldn't do that. I won't either. What else can we do?"

"I'll have to find a home for you. You children will have to be sent somewhere. There's no adult to care for you."

"Why can't we stay here? I'm an adult, and Agatha is old enough. Minerva would stay with us, too."

"Terry, I am not going to lie to you. You aren't going to have this house for long. It will only be a short time before everything you do own is sold to pay for other things. We need to find you a home."

Terry struggled to take in what Adams was telling him. "But these people—they were Papa's friends. They wouldn't put us out."

Adams closed his eyes and rubbed the bridge of his nose. "Terry, there're five of you to feed, shelter, clothe. How can you hold off a list of creditors? It was one thing when Terrance was alive. Everyone knew him, had faith in him. But they won't take payment of pennies a week from you, and that is what it would be—pennies—or you would all starve."

Terry's voice was very small when he spoke again. "You keep saying I can't. Tell me what I *can* do. What's to keep us from starving if I don't work, Mr. Adams?"

"I have already told you. I shall have to find homes for all of you."

"Like a pack of homeless orphans?"

"You are orphans, damn it! I don't like it any better than you do. You'll be damned lucky if I can find a place for all of you."

"We won't be separated."

"The devil you won't! You'll take whatever I can find and be glad of it." He got up to leave. "You'd better tell the rest of the family how things are. Once your father is laid to rest, there will be no holding things back."

Adams left Terry baffled and heartsick. What could he say to his brothers and sisters? Ashamed and angry that things were as they were, he knew full well that whatever he felt now was nothing compared to what he and the others would be feeling in the days to come.

What would it be like when the house they had all grown up in was dismantled and parceled out piece by piece? How could he tell his brothers and sisters that they were now orphans dependent on the whims of strangers, that they would be looked over and judged as to whether they would be worthy additions to a stranger's household?

He picked up a delicate figurine of a shepherdess, one of his mother's favorites, and smashed it against the hearth.

"What was that?" Minerva burst into the room and stopped immediately. Terry whirled around. The guilty expression on his face dissolved immediately into listlessness as he stared down at the shattered pieces of china at his feet.

"I just wanted to do it, Minerva. I just wanted it to be mine. They shouldn't have Mama's things. I just wanted to—" He slumped into a chair and buried his face in his hands.

Minerva picked up another of Jo's statuettes and dropped it to the floor, where it thudded against a chair and broke. "I know just what you mean. I know just exactly what you mean, and there are some things in this house they aren't going to get!"

Terry looked up. "What would life be like without you, Minerva? You hold us all together."

"You'll have to talk to the others soon. It can't be put off. You're going to have to tell them right away."

"I know."

"But not until we've had a good dinner. A good, special dinner! We're going to eat like royalty for as long as we can. Come along there, Your Majesty!" She took him by the hand as she had when he was very small. "Call those other whippersnappers while I get Gracie to help me put this feast on the table."

By the time the children had washed their faces and hands and arrived in the dining room, Minerva and Gracie had completed laying out the dinner.

"Oh, Minerva!" William exclaimed. "It's like a holiday!"

"It isn't right with Papa lying over there in the other room," Agatha said solemnly.

"Hush yourself, girl. I've known your papa a lot longer than you have, and he'd be the first one to approve." Minerva sat her down and pulled out a chair for Kathleen, patting her on the shoulder. "You eat a good dinner, Miss Kat. I don't want any more moping from you."

"Cheer up, everyone, and that is an order," Terry declared from the head of the table. "Minerva made me king for the night, and all my subjects must obey." He raised his glass. "To the O'Connors! Come on, everyone, drink to us."

They hardly knew where to begin. Minerva had turkey, ham, and chops piled on the meat platter, green corn and lima beans fresh from the garden, carrots and turnips, and fruit. She waited by the side of the table, arms folded over her stomach, as they chattered, joked, and ate with a maximum of relish and a minimum of ceremony.

After dinner, when Terry told them what had happened, Kathleen felt small and alone and frightened. As she lay in bed that night, she was sure she heard her papa's voice telling her all she needed to know—that he loved her. She kept hearing sounds she knew couldn't be real. She strained harder and harder to hear the voice that was not really there.

In the days that followed, Malcolm Adams searched for homes for the five children. He had started out well. All three boys could go to Patrick Casey. Together they would work the farm that Casey was unable to manage alone.

Leona Dowell, the only relative of the family Adams knew about, agreed to take Agatha as her companion and personal maid. Agatha had an agreeable nature and was old enough to be useful and worth her keep.

Kathleen was another matter. She was too young to be helpful, and headstrong. Everywhere Adams turned in the attempt to place Kathleen, he was thwarted. Finally he packed her up and sent her to Leona's house by coach, thinking that the lady would surely not turn her out.

By five o'clock the same day, Kathleen was making her way back across town alone. Leona Dowell had told her to go back to her own house and tell Malcolm Adams that he would have to make other arrangements. "I may be a Good Samaritan," she had said, "but I am not a nursemaid. I cannot manage both of you."

No one had expected the house to be closed up so soon. Minerva, instructed to close the house as quickly as possible, had done it in record time, and had followed the boys, as planned, to the Casey farm.

It seemed to Kathleen that it took much longer to get home than it had to get to Miss Dowell's. No matter, she thought, I'd rather go back home, anyway. She hadn't liked Miss Dowell at all.

"Minerva! Minerva! I'm back! I'm home!" She leaped up the last two steps to the front porch and reached for the doorknob. It wouldn't turn. Kathleen, still too excited about being home to be alarmed, beat lustily on the door panels. She made a terrible racket, pounding alternately on the doors and the windows that faced out on the porch.

"Mercy, what noise! Kathleen? What are you doing back here?" It was Mrs. Harrison from next door.

"Where is Minerva?"

"Why, she is gone, child. They've all gone, and so should you be. What are you doing back here?"

"I came home. Why is the door locked?"

"Does anyone know you are here?" Kathleen shook her head. "You ran away, didn't you?"

"I just came home."

"Well, miss, it's locked up tight, and no one is there. Everyone's gone. Now you just get on back where you belong. You always were a handful. Go on! Get back before you are missed. Imagine running off like that. Go along! Scat! Hurry off."

Mrs. Harrison walked hastily back to her garden, clucking in disapproval.

Kathleen began to knock on the front door again, softly and hopelessly. "Minerva, please be there. Hail, Mary, full of grace, make Minerva be there."

Before long, it began to grow dark. Kathleen wandered about the outside of the house, avoiding Mrs. Harrison and searching for a way to get in. For a while she huddled in the swing at the side of the house.

She was hungry, and there were disturbing noises she had never noticed before. She had never really been alone in her entire life. There had always been her brothers and sisters nearby and loving arms to enfold her.

Finally, she left the house and hurried toward the downtown section of the city, thinking vaguely that someone would take her to Mr. Adams. She didn't know exactly where she was going, but she had come this way other times with

237

her mother. Then, suddenly, she looked around, and the buildings in the dark no longer looked familiar. Store windows were blackened and shuttered. Everything was closed. She sat down on the stoop of Webster's Grocery Store, frightened as she had never been before, and she cried.

Fortunately, the Websters' daughter, who was out back feeding her mother's prize chickens, heard Kathleen. She took her inside, where amidst murmurs of "poor child" and blessedly few questions, Kathleen was fed and put to bed.

The next day, they took Kathleen back to Leona Dowell's house. For the second time, Leona refused to allow Kathleen to stay. Mrs. Webster persisted, however, until Leona relented. She would take Kathleen in temporarily and wire Charlotte for help.

A little more than a month later, Charlotte came to Columbus, and together Leona and Charlotte decided that the best place for Kathleen would be the county home or a convent school, whichever could accommodate her first.

Both women wanted the problem solved quickly. Charlotte, anxious to return to New York as quickly as she could, told Leona that only the strongest sense of family duty could have brought her west to deal with Kathleen. Her son, she complained, was involved in all sorts of activities she didn't understand, her father had been ill, and it was simply no time for her to be away from home.

For her part, Leona was anxious to be rid of her talkative and nervous houseguest and to begin living an orderly, uncomplicated life once more. Neither woman had thought that Agatha would hear what they had to say or dare to take exception to their high-handed decisions regarding Kathleen's life. But Agatha, who had been listening, went directly to the Casey farm and Minerva.

"You did right to come to me, Miss Aggie. It's never disloyal to protect your own. I couldn't be prouder of you if you were my own daughter!" Minerva hugged Agatha to her. "I just didn't know it was possible to miss anyone like I miss my two girls."

"Oh, Minerva, I've missed you, too!"

"You? My tough little Miss Aggie? Maybe when we get things all settled you can come live with Kathleen at your Aunt Charlotte's. And you mark my words, that Aunt Charlotte is going to do right by our Miss Kat, or I'll know the reason why!"

"Oh, that's why I came here. I knew you could do something."

Minerva listened to all Agatha had to say, and then she went to see Charlotte Henderson. Faced with an angry, righteous Minerva dressed in her Sunday best, Charlotte was fairly overwhelmed. When Minerva emerged from their visit, she was Kathleen O'Connor's guardian.

Chapter Twenty-six

The arrival of Charlotte's summons that summer—so many years since the last time Charlotte had expressed any personal interest in Kathleen's life—had been thoroughly unexpected. Nonetheless, for Kathleen, by now a beautiful and exceedingly capable young woman, it represented a kind of adventure she had planned countless times in her imagination.

After she had posted her letter to Charlotte, announcing that she would arrive at Scarborough in a month, her life became a whirlwind of real plans. She and Minerva decided that Kathleen would go ahead, and Minerva would follow as soon as she had visited each of the other O'Connors.

Agatha, married the year before, was expecting her first child and could certainly use Minerva's wise and practical advice in setting up her household. Terry, now grown, married, and the father of three small children, would never forgive Minerva if she left for New York without spending a few days with his family.

Lawrence was fortunate enough to have been sent to college, while William was going to take over the Casey farm, and no doubt marry the youngest Casey daughter, with whom he had grown up.

So, her family settled and secure, Kathleen could leave Ohio with no qualms at all. As she prepared to make the trip to New York—her first trip anywhere alone—the prospect became more and more exciting.

She took the train from Columbus. At first the landscape was a blur, making her feel dizzy. Soon, however, she learned to focus her eyes to accommodate the changing speed.

On an adventure, Kathleen suffered none of the monotony or boredom that the other travelers seemed to. Her dress got just as sooty, and the seat in which she rode was just as hard as anyone else's, but for her the excitement overrode any discomfort.

With each mile that passed, she grew more aware of her freedom. She was heading into a new world and a new life that seemed more tempting and more challenging the nearer she came to it. Minerva was probably right about Charlotte. Kathleen was prepared for Charlotte to expect her to be a retiring, grateful relation, willing to work her fingers to the nub. She smiled, thinking how shocked her aunt would be. Well, Charlotte would simply have to take her as she was.

Kathleen's only moment of anxiety came when she arrived in New York City. She had never seen anything like it—throngs of people, miles of buildings. Was there such a thing as an empty doorway in New York? How was one to cross a street without being cut down by carriages?

The entire city seemed to be in motion, admitting and then spewing out one body after another from the dark doorways of innumerable shops and restaurants. One day soon, Kathleen decided, she would return to the city and walk through it, street by street.

She hailed a cab and asked the driver to drive her to the train that would take her north out of the city. Her enthusiasm about her trip engaged the attention of the driver, who suggested she travel the last segment of her journey by water.

He drove her to the pier, where she boarded a steamship headed north on the Hudson. The joys of the train paled, replaced by those of the river. Kathleen held fast to the deck rail and leaned out as far as she dared, letting the ship and the air and the water take hold of her imagination.

She looked from one side of the wide river to the other, loath to miss anything—the Palisades, the hills, the green lawns, the great houses on either side of the river. Several times she wondered whether this house or that could be Scarborough.

Kathleen laughed to herself. Aunt Charlotte could never live in one of those mansions; no ordinary person could.

When the steamer put in near her destination, Kathleen sought out an open carriage to take her the rest of the way.

"Do you know the way to Scarborough House?" she asked the first driver she saw.

He touched his cap. "I know the way." He helped her into the carriage, put her two bags in with her, and set off along a winding road that led up and away from the river.

The carriage wound through narrow roadways until, to Kathleen's surprise, the driver turned up a long, grand driveway, apparently the approach to one of the magnificent homes she had seen from the river.

She held her breath, not daring to believe her eyes. At the last turn in the drive, the trees gave way to the open space of lawn, and suddenly she saw the house itself. That is not a house, she thought. It might be a painting, or a monument, or a palace—but never a mere house.

She called to the driver to stop, and taking her two valises, she paid the driver and got out of the carriage before he could take her the rest of the way up the drive. Scratching his head and counting his money twice, he left her standing on the lawn, the two valises by her side, staring wide-eyed at the mansion ahead.

She walked the last few yards to the front of the house. Only as she looked at the huge knocker on the front door did she begin to think again of Charlotte and Marcella, but they were afterthoughts and unimportant beside the fact that she had immediately fallen in love with a river and a house.

She stood in front of the door several minutes, trying to reorganize her thoughts. When she finally raised the knocker and let it fall, she wore the face of a serious, determined young woman who bore no resemblance to the moonstruck girl of moments before.

Carlisle answered the door. He blinked at her, his eyes watering a bit as the bright light hit his eyes.

"I have come to see Mrs. Henderson," Kathleen said.

Carlisle looked down and saw her two valises. "Who shall I say is calling, miss?"

"Miss Kathleen O'Connor. I am her niece. She is expecting me." She followed him into the hall.

"If you'll sit down and be comfortable, miss, I'll fetch Mrs. Henderson directly. Miss O'Connor, you say?"

"That is correct." Kathleen looked down the long hallway that ran the length of the house. The door at the other end was open, and she could see another porch like the one at the front of the house. Beyond it was another lawn rising upward to a hill.

She turned at the sound of footsteps. About midway down the hall she saw a man coming toward her. He was definitely not Carlisle. He wasn't particularly tall, but he was well proportioned and quite handsome. He looked at her for a moment, not exactly smiling, but with a look of amusement that she rather liked.

"Are you Miss O'Connor? Carlisle said Miss O'Connor had come, but surely you cannot be she." He pushed back a lock of straight brown hair from his forehead.

Kathleen sat straight in her chair. "I am she. I am here to see Mrs. Henderson, my aunt."

"So you *are* Kathleen. The poor child with no prospects in her poor life." He laughed and looked her over from head to toe. "There seem to have been a number of misconceptions where you are concerned."

Kathleen, momentarily flustered by his manner, frowned deeply. "I'm afraid I do not know what you are talking about. Who are you?" she asked. "Is Mrs. Henderson in, or isn't she?"

"She is in. As to who I am—I am your cousin Martin. Martin Henderson. I am very happy to meet you, Kathleen, and doubly pleased to have you turn out to be a pretty, charming young woman."

. "I am pleased to meet you as well," she said, less certain than he. "I would like to see Aunt Charlotte now, if I might. I have had a long trip, and I'd like to get to the business that brought me here."

"There is no hurry. After all, it's only a family matter, and we have many years to make up for. Mother will be coming downstairs for tea in a short while. She takes a nap about this time every afternoon—or tries to. In the meantime, I will have Gert show you to your room, and let you freshen up." He gestured toward the stairs and picked up one valise.

She smiled. "I think I have half the dust of the universe on me. I would like nothing better than to have time to change into clean clothes."

"Gert will get whatever you need," he said as they moved down the hall. "You'll find that Gert practically runs the entire house single-handedly. If you ever need anything, just ask her."

As they moved toward the staircase, Kathleen stumbled, trying to see into the room they were passing.

Martin caught her arm. "It's the dining room," he chuckled.

She blushed and looked to the other side of the hall. "The parlor?"

"There are two adjoining parlors. They can easily be opened to make one large room. Had you come sooner, you would have seen them opened and all decked out for my engagement ball."

"You are to be married soon?"

"Very soon."

"Hmm," she said, half listening. She paused at the staircase and nodded toward a room farther down the hall. "Is that the kitchen?"

"No, that is Nicholas Dalton's study. On the other side is the music room."

"And where is the kitchen?"

"The kitchen and the laundry are downstairs."

She smiled a little apologetically. "It will take some doing to become accustomed to this house. It is so large."

"Oh, you'll get used to it soon enough," Martin said as they started up the stairs. "And I am sure you will have many willing helpers. You have one already."

"You? That is nice of you to say." Suddenly Kathleen remembered she had meant to be all business. "But I think I shall be far too busy to have much time for any of that. I had best familiarize myself with it quickly so that I can find my way around and perform my duties."

Martin laughed out loud. "Don't be so stiff about it. You're with family."

"Nonetheless, I am here to work, and I had best keep it firmly in mind. I was not invited here as a cousin. I was asked to come in order to care for Aunt Marcella. Quite a different matter." She glanced up at him. "And I shall do just that."

"I have the feeling you are nothing at all like what my mother is expecting."

"It wouldn't surprise me if you were right. What did you say before? 'A poor child with no prospects'?"

"I had the impression that you were a forlorn little creature, homely and not terribly likable. You have the singular honor of being the first person who has put me in total error."

"I see. Perhaps as we get to know each other better, I can correct other mistaken impressions."

"No. I have the magic touch of the gods. I am seldom, if ever, wrong." He laughed. "At least when I am, I do not admit it, and I work very hard to correct myself before anyone else has a chance to."

"Such nonsense. I think you are an unmerciful tease. How many people live here? Surely not just you and Aunt Charlotte and Aunt Marcella."

"Just about. There are only four of us besides the servants. Five, now that you have come."

"But it is such a large house. What a shame it is not filled with children and noise and activity. It seems as though it should be. Don't you think it feels like that kind of house?"

"I'll do my best to remedy it. After I am married, perhaps you shall hear sounds more to your liking." He paused at the top of the stairs and looked at Kathleen. "It *is* a shame Mother took so long in asking you to come here. . . ."

"Please, Martin," she said, a little embarrassed, "where shall I find Gert? I would like to see my room."

"Of course, my dear, of course." He walked a little way down the second-floor hall and pushed the door open. "This is your room." He let her walk past him into the room. Without speaking again, he tugged the bellpull in the corner and waited for Gert to answer it.

Kathleen moved around the room, pulling back the heavy draperies and opening the windows. She didn't hear Gert come in. She turned only as Martin spoke.

"I'll leave you to Gert for now, Kathleen. Take Miss O'Connor through this floor, Gert, so she will be familiar with it, and then bring her to the parlor for tea when she is ready."

Kathleen thanked Martin and followed Gert out the door to tour the rest of the floor.

"I shall become lost in here," Kathleen said cheerily as they walked down the hall. "It is so large and beautiful. You must love to awaken here each morning."

"Yes, miss." Gert's voice told her nothing.

Kathleen considered Gert's solid back as she walked ahead, methodically opening doors along the corridor. "Have you been here long, Gert?"

"Yes, miss."

"Is that all you say? 'Yes, miss?' If it is, there isn't much point in talking to you."

Gert turned to face her. "Mr. Henderson doesn't approve of servants talking to the family in a familiar way, miss," she said quietly.

"Mr. Henderson? My cousin Martin?"

"Yes, miss."

"Huh! He must have a family skeleton to hide. But never mind. I am not Mr. Henderson, and I love to talk."

"Yes, miss," Gert answered and opened another door. "This is Mrs. Henderson's sitting room. I believe she is napping, so we shall not look into her bedroom, but it is right behind that door."

"Yes, Gert," Kathleen said and grinned at her. Startled, Gert returned her smile.

"I'll take you back to your room and let you get settled a bit before tea."

They walked back to Kathleen's sitting room, a room larger than the parlor she had shared with Minerva in Columbus. She stood in the middle of the room, hands on hips, as she examined the high, ornate ceiling, the chandelier, and the inviting fireplace that graced one wall. "Oh, bookcases!" She hurried over to them as if the empty shelves might hold a secret treasure.

"I am glad you like it, miss. This room once belonged to Mr. Nicholas's grandmother. Actually, it is a suite of four rooms connecting, but now we have closed it off into two rooms each."

"Who is Nicholas? Mr. Henderson mentioned his name, but I cannot place him. He is not another cousin?"

"No, miss. It was his family that built Scarborough. This was all theirs until Mr. Brad had his misfortunes and lost it all."

"How could he have lost it? How could anyone lose a place like Scarborough? And what happened to Nicholas?"

"He lives here still. As to Mr. Bradford's troubles, I cannot tell you that. It isn't my place, but your aunt will tell you. She'd know all about it."

"Aunt Marcella?" Kathleen said.

"That's right, miss."

"Where is Aunt Marcella's room? We haven't passed by it, have we?"

"It is just down the hall, miss. I will show you when we go down to the parlor. If you will follow me now, I'll show you where your bathing room is."

Kathleen gaped at the sumptuous room with its glistening marble walls and turned again to Gert, her eyes shining with pleasure.

"What was he like?" she asked.

"Mr. Nicholas?"

"No, the man who built all of this. What was he like?"

"That was another Mr. Nicholas. The young man's grandfather, miss. He built it for his wife and his family. Of course, the family owned Scarborough before he built the house. There was an old house on the land then, a frame one, I think, but he built this one for his wife. Nothing has ever been quite the same since he passed on."

Kathleen put a hand on Gert's arm. "Gert, thank you for talking to me. I won't tell Cousin Martin that you have."

"No need, Miss Kathleen. I guess I expected you to be more like your cousin, but I decided some minutes ago I would be wagging my tongue with you."

"Well, I guess I had better stop the tongue-wagging for now, or I'll be late. I don't imagine Cousin Martin would like that, either. It is strange, but when I met him just before you came in, he didn't seem to be the kind of man who would be so particular."

"I believe he has many things on his mind, Miss Kathleen."

"Oh, by the way Gert, Minerva—she is the lady who raised me—has always called me Miss Kat. So did my family—Kat, I mean, not Miss Kat. Anyway, I would like that much better."

"Very well, Miss Kat."

Kathleen hurried to wash away the dust from her trip. It was worse than she had imagined; when she looked into the mirror, she saw a face streaked and smudged with dirt. Laughing to herself, she dabbed at the dust-covered face until she had made a clown's mask of herself. She poked her head out the door and made a face at Gert. Both giggled.

Then Kathleen got down to the practical business of making herself presentable. In twenty mintues she again faced Gert, this time sober-faced and dressed in a tidy plain dress of gray cotton gabardine.

"I am ready now."

Gert went with her back through the hall and down the staircase.

"Oh, my dear, how lovely you are!" Charlotte exclaimed as soon as she saw Kathleen. "Stand back and let me see you. Oh, Martin, isn't she lovely? This is your cousin, Jo's daughter."

"We've met, Mother."

"It is so good of you to come, and such a pleasure to see you again. My, how the years do fly! Can you forgive your aunt for neglecting you so terribly all these years?" Charlotte hugged Kathleen awkwardly.

"There is nothing to forgive, Aunt Charlotte. I have been grateful to you, and I am anxious to be able to repay your kindness." She paused to clear her throat. "As you know, I have no money of my own to speak of, and I must think of the future. So if it is convenient, I would like to discuss the arrangements of my employment—and it must be employment, Aunt Charlotte. I don't expect much, but as I said, I do have to consider my future."

"Employment!" Charlotte gasped. "Whatever gave you such a thought! I have no intention of employing you. You are my niece, my own sister's flesh."

"But am I not here to care for Aunt Marcella?"

"Yes, but—"

"Then I shall expect a suitable salary so that I may be able to repay you for the years you have taken care of me. Besides, it will simplify matters for both of us."

"But I don't want to be paying you. Oh, what shall I do? Martin! Martin, did you hear her? She expects to be an employee."

"I am sure there are some arrangements to be made," Martin soothed. "But we need not discuss this standing up and wringing our hands, Mother." He took Charlotte by the arm and led her back toward the center of the room. He looked back at Kathleen. "I told you no one was prepared for you."

Kathleen followed Charlotte and Martin to the sofas on either side of the fireplace. Already seated on one of the sofas was a striking blond woman. Kathleen could not resist the impulse to stare. Rhea Scott returned her appraising look coolly.

Kathleen broke away first and looked around at the rest of the room. At the far end were double doors curtained with translucent hangings and opening into what appeared to be a conservatory. For a moment, a man's face appeared at the edge of those curtains, and then disappeared.

"This is my fiancée, Miss Rhea Scott," Martin was saying. Kathleen's attention was drawn back to the woman. Rhea seemed very sure of herself, she thought, sitting far back, almost lounging, her hair piled high on her head in a fashion few women could wear. In spite of her air of assurance, which Kathleen rather grudgingly admired, she was disturbed by Rhea's blue eyes; they seemed to hold no emotion whatever.

"Is this the girl you mentioned, Martin?" Rhea asked. She was not rude, only completely disinterested. "She is to take care of your Aunt Marcella? Well, that will be a relief."

"Oh, no, my dear," Charlotte chirped, once more all aflutter and wringing her hands. "Kathleen is my sister's child. She is my niece, a part of the family. Martin, I do wish you would try to understand and help me out in this. Kathleen cannot be a servant in this house."

"I was under the impression that that was why she had come."

"That is true," Kathleen said firmly before either Charlotte or Martin could speak. "That is my sole reason for being here, Miss Scott."

"You mustn't feel that way," Charlotte declared. "You really mustn't. This is all unsuitable. I didn't plan this at all. Oh, you do distress me so." Charlotte glanced down at the tea tray. "You pour, Rhea. I simply cannot manage it, and everything is getting cold. The sandwiches are soggy, too."

She put a small square of bread back down on her plate. "You have not even mentioned your family, Kathleen. All you've talked of is wages and duties. What am I to think? Am I not your closest relation? Do unbend and tell me the news I long to hear. What of your brothers? And what of Agatha? Cousin Leona wrote some time ago and told me that Agatha had been married. I was terribly hurt. I didn't receive so much as a note from her telling me of the marriage."

Kathleen settled back into her chair, pleased that her teacup didn't clank against the saucer as she took it from Rhea's incredibly steady hand.

"Minerva will be helping Agatha for a time, and then she will follow me here. I do hope that is suitable. You can be certain Minerva will be a great help."

"Is this Minerva person also a relative?" Rhea asked.

"No. She was the O'Connors' housekeeper, wasn't she, Kathleen?" Martin said, looking to Kathleen for verification.

Rhea raised her eyebrow. "And you simply decided to bring her here on your own?"

"Yes, I did." Kathleen smiled sweetly. "And I do think it is time I got on with the task I came here to do. I would like to meet Aunt Marcella now, please."

Charlotte became agitated. "Not today, Kathleen. Marcella is having one of her spells at the moment. It doesn't happen often, mind you, but occasionally she becomes very melancholy, and it is very bad for her when that happens. It would be far better for you to wait to meet her tomorrow or the next day. Take a few days. Accustom yourself to the house, and let us have a chance to enjoy you. There is no hurry—you could help me with the wedding plans in the meantime. That would be entertaining for you, wouldn't it?"

"Mother—" Martin began, giving her a warning look.

"I just want her to feel at home, Martin."

"I would feel much better if I could get on with the task for which I came," Kathleen offered. "I didn't come here for a vacation, Aunt Charlotte, and even though I appreciate your concern, believe me, I am happy to be able to help you and Aunt Marcella."

Martin stood. "She is absolutely right, Mother. Let her find her own way of being at home. You have all you can manage for now."

Charlotte looked from one face to another, then nodded her head in agreement. "Very well," she said finally. "I'll take you to Marcella's room. But I do wish you would listen to me." She began to stand up and then looked at Kathleen. "You really must not become too headstrong, Kathleen. It would not be seemly. Men don't like too much of that in a woman, you know."

"I shall be careful in the future, Aunt Charlotte," Kathleen said and kissed her aunt's cheek. "Now you stay right where you are and finish your tea. There is no need for you to accompany me. Gert showed me which room Aunt Marcella is in, and I shall have no difficulty finding my way there. You were right, Martin, Gert is very capable. I shall be calling on her often, as you suggested."

Kathleen left the room and stood in the hallway for a moment, tempted to go outside and walk around the grounds. As she turned to go to the staircase, she saw the man who had glanced through the conservatory curtains earlier, standing at the entrance to the room Martin had referred to as Nicholas's study. He appeared to be reading a newspaper.

She supposed he was Nicholas Dalton; but this man was young, and she had thought Nicholas would be older—a gray-haired man, romantic, well situated, with an aura of sadness and greatness about him. The man she looked at hardly fit her image.

He glanced up from the paper in his hand and stared back at her. Finally she gave a little nod and hurried up the stairs. She wished she had stayed to see if he would acknowledge her.

"Oh, Minerva," she thought as she rushed up the last of the flight of stairs. "Wait until you see him. You will go goofy trying to marry me off to him."

She sauntered to Marcella's room, looking again at the decor and peering from the windows at the grounds and gardens.

Charlotte's letter had informed her niece about her sister's condition—the disfigurement and Marcella's sensitivity to other people's reactions—but had not told her what had caused it. Kathleen had supposed it had been fire. Too many women had been severely burned by candles, stoves, or kerosene or oil lamps. Kathleen was therefore prepared to be sympathetic to Marcella's occasional bouts of melancholia. The dear Lord knew she had reason enough, with her illness and disfigurement, to be unhappy.

What Kathleen was not prepared for was the drunken, snoring woman who lay on the couch in Marcella's room. At first she thought the woman was one of the housemaids caught in her cups, but on closer inspection she was sure it was her aunt.

"Aunt Marcella," she said. There was no response. "Aunt Marcella!" she said, more loudly. She shook Marcella by the shoulders, patted her cheeks, cooled her brow with very cold water. Marcella barely stirred. Kathleen's first feeling, revulsion, changed to a strange kind of sympathy and then to anger—anger at those in this house and elsewhere who had let this happen, and who had let her walk into it thoroughly unprepared. Obviously Marcella was more ill than Kathleen had been led to believe.

"Spell, indeed!" Kathleen said aloud. She began to tidy up the room. She washed Marcella's comb and brush and again felt angry that they had been neglected for so long.

Marcella had still not awakened when she was finished. Kathleen stood at the side of the couch, looking at her; she was grateful now that their first meeting had happened without Marcella's participation. She would never have been able to hide the shock the first sight of Marcella elicited from her. No fire had caused this damage.

She went back to her room, discouraged, and began a letter to Minerva. Before long she found herself writing down her fantasies of the old man who had built Scarborough House. She put down her pen and stared into the empty fireplace. His name had been mentioned only once, and yet here she was, thinking of him and feeling certain that she would have cared for him the same way she did about this house and the land it sat on. Perhaps she had tangled her thoughts about the architecture of the house with the man who had built it, or perhaps it was that she was to sleep in the room of the woman for whom this house had been bulit.

She tore up the letter to Minerva and began again, telling Minerva about her trip, the river, her handsome cousin, and the dark-haired man she assumed was Nicholas Dalton.

Chapter Twenty-seven

After Kathleen had finished the letter, she went back downstairs. She had intended to walk around the outside of the house and look more closely at the gardens, but the more she thought about Marcella—and Charlotte's curious reluctance to discuss what was really wrong with her—the angrier she got.

Instead of goimg outside, she sought out Charlotte. "You did not tell me that Aunt Marcella—that she imbibed!" she said when she finally located Charlotte in the small ladies' parlor.

Charlotte looked up from the book resting on her lap. "No," she said softly. "It isn't something one likes to speak of."

"How can I be expected to help if you keep such things a secret from me?"

Charlotte flushed, a little startled by her niece's forthrightness. "It doesn't happen often. It is a part of her illness."

"Bosh! It is pure intemperance. What other things are going to come as a surprise to me? Will you tell me what caused her to be in this condition? Or at least tell me precisely what her condition is?"

"There isn't any condition. The doctor says it is all a matter of Marcella's not wanting to be like she is. She has simply never been able to regain her—her will to live since she fell ill."

"Then she had smallpox?"

248

"Who told you that?"

"What else would leave scars like that?" Kathleen sat down uninvited. "And why should you wish to keep it a secret?"

She pressed the matter until Charlotte, to stop her questions, told her niece the story of Marcella.

"Well, that explains a great deal," Kathleen said matter-of-factly when Charlotte had finished.

"One must feel terribly sorry for her. Such a tragic life, and in spite of her imprudence, one wonders if such dire punishment was due her." Charlotte sounded terribly self-righteous.

"I don't know. But I do know that the past belongs in the past, and sorrowing over it will change nothing. At the moment the future is our concern."

"You are a very hard young lady!"

"Perhaps I have had a need to be hard in the past."

"But I thought you liked Mrs. Shaw. I did my best for you."

"I am not belittling what you did for me, Aunt Charlotte. I love Minerva. She is a wonderful and kind woman, and she has been both mother and father to me. But that doesn't change the fact that I have learned to make my own way in the world. Living with the past as though it were an open sore will do no good, and Aunt Marcella will have to learn that, too. I did."

"I don't know," Charlotte said uncertainly. "It was all her fault, you know. Maybe we aren't meant to forget our guilts and sins. Look at what she has done to so many around her. Your own mother left home because of her. Who is to say Jo wouldn't be alive today if she had stayed in New York? And look at my life—"

Kathleen interrupted her before she could go on. "Earlier, Aunt Charlotte, you said that what happened to Aunt Marcella was tragic. Now you sound as if she should be a penitent, flagellating herself forever. Whether she forgets it or not, it seems to me the best thing for everyone is to help her live a more normal life. In any case, she certainly should not drink as she does now. Quite frankly, I believe she has had more than just spirits."

Charlotte sighed and shook her head. "It is her laudanum. She promised she wouldn't touch it after the doctor said she didn't need it any longer. . . ." Her voice trailed off. "That was so long ago, so very long, it seems."

"Well, it is clear something must be done." Kathleen got up from her seat. "One thing, Aunt Charlotte. If I am unable to help Aunt Marcella, I will not stay here."

Kathleen actually met Marcella for the first time the next morning.

Marcella was standing by her window, looking out across the hills to the Hudson. Only a small portion of her face could be seen from the way she stood, but she looked old and spent. Marcella stood motionless, as though giving Kathleen time to observe her. Traces of red remained in her graying hair; it was clear she had once been a magnificent beauty.

Her stillness made her seem isolated and remote. When she showed no sign that she was aware of another person in the room, Kathleen gave the still-open door a push and let it slam shut.

Marcella turned, looking blank for a moment. She plucked at the front of her soiled dressing gown.

"Who're you?" she asked. Before Kathleen could answer, she said, "You're Kathleen! You're my niece. Jo's daughter." Her voice dropped as did her initial look of pleasure. "You don't look like her," she grumbled. "You don't look a bit like Jo. You're all Terrance. Just like Terrance."

"I have always been told I look like my father, but then I have also been told from time to time that I have a bit of you in me."

"I had red hair." Marcella touched the graying strands of hair that peeped from beneath her nightcap. "Did she like you?"

"Did who like me?"

"Jo. She didn't, did she? She didn't like you at all."

"Mama? Of course she liked me. Why do you say such a thing?"

Marcella shrugged her shoulders and swept her hand across her face. She was still feeling very fuzzy and unclear. "You're not like me," she said tonelessly. "Not a bit! You wouldn't be here if you were. I would never have locked myself away, caring for an old woman."

"You said that to anger me, Aunt Marcella, but it won't work for two reasons. First, I know it isn't true. When you were my age, you stayed at home and took care of Mama. She told me that. And secondly, I am not here by choice, and if I had been given a choice, I would not have come. Puzzle that one out!" Kathleen congratulated herself on her little sermon.

Marcella snorted. "We all make our own choices."

"Not always. But since I am here, I intend to get on with the job. We are going to get you back on your feet and able to care for yourself."

"I can care for myself whenever I feel like it."

"And you feel like it except when you have your bad spells?"

"That's right!"

"From what I have been told, there is no reason why you must succumb to these 'spells' of yours at all. Once we have straightened that out, Aunt Marcella, I, too, shall go out and live and make my own choices."

Marcella squinted at her from across the room. "Come a little closer. My eyes aren't what they once were. Brad always told me I had the eyes of a hawk, but that was a long time ago. Come along, I won't bite you."

Kathleen moved closer. "I didn't expect you would."

Marcella peered at her and then frowned. "Well, perhaps the shape of your brow is somewhat like mine." She turned to look out her window again. "It must be the brow that caused others to think you resembled me."

Kathleen said nothing, but smiled and allowed herself to become interested in the scene outside the window. The Hudson was visible through the trees, and a barge passed as the two women watched.

"Do you like the river?" Marcella asked.

"Who could help but like it?"

"I suppose Charlotte has already introduced you to everyone in the house?"

"Yes. When I first came."

"What do you think of them?"

Kathleen looked directly at Marcella. "I don't know anyone here well enough to have an opinion," she answered cautiously.

"Everyone has an opinion!"

"Aunt Charlotte seemed pleased to see me. I found her to be kind and pleasant. Martin, too. He is handsome, and I met his fiancée. She matches him well. She is very pretty."

"And?"

"That was all. Oh, and I liked Gert very much."

"You haven't mentioned Nicholas. Haven't you met him, or don't you like him?"

"He wasn't around. I have been told about him, though, and I believe it was he I saw standing in the hallway last evening, but I haven't actually met him. He didn't seem very friendly, in any case."

"Not friendly? He didn't insult you, did he?"

"Oh, no. I doubt that he wanted to speak to me at all. From the little I saw of him he is a very intent type. His newspaper had all his attention. He just stood there all sort of dark and brooding." She laughed. "You realize I am jesting, Aunt Marcella. All he was doing was reading a newspaper, and he happened to glance up as I passed. I really have no opinion of him at all."

"Well, you will before long. He lives here, too, you know."

"So I have been told. But he is not the problem at hand, is he? Have you had your breakfast yet?"

Marcella made a face. "I am never hungry in the morning."

Kathleen had breakfast sent up for both of them, and they ate it together in Marcella's room.

"I believe in a good breakfast," Kathleen said between bites of food. "And from now on, we shall have breakfast every morning. But not here. We shall eat downstairs with the others. So you must be ready to go down on time."

Kathleen spent those first few days getting to know her aunt. She urged Marcella to talk about whatever she wished. Whenever she could, Kathleen coaxed and bullied her about living a more active life. Things were progressing beautifully, to Kathleen's way of thinking, until one day Marcella stopped talking and looked sullenly at Kathleen.

"You know, you are nothing but an interfering little busybody. Why do you keep asking me questions? And why do you force me to do what I do not want to do? Who are you to be my judge?"

"I am not judging you, Aunt Marcella!"

"Why, then, do you ask me about every little thing?"

"It seems the only way anyone will tell me anything. I thought Aunt Charlotte had explained everything to me, but I was wrong. There are so many secrets, it seems. I swear, Aunt Marcella, all of you would keep the dinner hour secret from one another if you could!"

Marcella smiled and patted Kathleen's hand. "You'll get used to us in time. We aren't as bad as we seem, even with our secrets. All you have to do is ask me, and I'll tell you anything."

Before Kathleen could open her mouth to protest, Marcella went on. "We are all quite average, I think, really. Perhaps we all have an excess of greed, but then that can be found anywhere these days, can't it?"

Kathleen was thoroughly puzzled. "Greed? What has greed to do with it? I'd call it rudeness."

"No, dear, it is greed. You just haven't asked enough questions yet, but you will know soon enough. We all want something, and we need each other to get it, so you see, we all keep our secrets so the others won't find out what we want and then not give it to us."

"Aunt Marcella, that is pure gibberish. It must be all that vile stuff you take to sleep. It is addling your mind."

"Nonsense, I am perfectly clear. I haven't had any of my sleeping draft for two days. You are confused, I am not."

Kathleen put her hands up in surrender. "I do not know what to do about you. Most of the time I feel as though I am the butt of an enormous joke of which everyone is aware but me."

Marcella nodded. "Good Samaritans often find themselves the butts of enormous jokes. Most lack the stamina to have the last laugh. Everyone in this house thinks I am their Good Samaritan, but then I have the stamina to have the last laugh. I wonder about you, Kathleen."

"The last laugh is not among my life's ambitions. Whoever wants it is welcome to it."

"That's too bad. You could have added to the fun around here, but if you give up so easily . . . Run along now. I don't feel like talking to you any longer." She waved a hand toward the door.

"I am supposed to be taking care of you, not indulging you in these games of yours. I spend more time uselessly arguing with you than anything else."

"It is your own fault," Marcella answered, disappearing into her bedroom. "Now run along and leave me alone." She waved imperiously and slammed the door behind her.

Kathleen leaped to her feet. "Aunt Marcella!" she shouted at the door. "Aunt Marcella, come out of there at once! Aunt Marcella, I shall come in and get you if you don't come out yourself."

Marcella opened the door only enough to peek through. "What do you want?"

"I want this nonsense stopped. I am not Aunt Charlotte by a long chalk, so get out here. I don't know how I ever let you buffalo me in the first place."

Marcella laughed. "What if I refuse?"

Kathleen quickly took hold of the doorknob and pulled the door open. "Now, come out of there."

"So, you do have some spunk," Marcella chuckled. "That's better." She swept into the sitting room and curtsied deeply. "Here I am. What are we going to do?" She tried unsuccessfully to suppress a smirk.

"You *are* impossible!" Kathleen looked her over from top to bottom, making a face at Marcella's tattered dressing gown. "And you are a disgrace. You were once a beautiful woman. Did you wear clothes until they were fit for nothing then? The first thing we are going to do is burn that dirty old dressing gown. No excuses, now."

With a stubborn look, Marcella folded her arms across her chest. "I like this gown. Brad gave it to me."

"So might I, if it were cleaned and mended. Perhaps we can wash it if we are careful. Now come along while I draw your bath water, and then we'll see what can be done with your hair. There must be a more becoming style than that."

Marcella had been tending to her hair by cutting out any snarl that proved too difficult to comb through. Washing it and trimming it into shape was no mean task. Fortunately, Marcella was uncharacteristically compliant through the whole ordeal.

Kathleen stood back to evaluate the job. "What a difference!" she said, pleased with herself. "For a woman who was once proud of her beauty, you certainly did allow things to get into a mess. Here, take a look at yourself." She handed Marcella the hand mirror.

"I don't like mirrors."

"No spunk?" Kathleen remarked, putting the mirror back into the bureau drawer. "All right, I won't force you."

"Give me that mirror!"

Marcella made a pleased little sound in her throat but then turned to glare at Kathleen. "Nothing makes a bit of difference. And if you think you can win my gratitude by making me slightly less ugly, you can begin to think again."

Kathleen was unruffled. "Winning your gratitude has nothing to do with it. Now come over here and help me straighten out these drawers. Honestly, Aunt Marcella, I do believe you are part pack rat."

"Do it yourself. You're being paid. Probably more than you're worth."

"As you like." Kathleen began to dump the papers and magazines out of the drawers into a waste receptacle.

"What are you doing? I want those things."

"Then come over here and arrange this drawer as you like—as long as it is neat and orderly."

Together, they sorted through the clothing and papers. Marcella gathered up several letters, and with a scowl at Kathleen, put them in a neat stack and bound them with a ribbon. Before long, both Marcella and Kathleen were engrossed in what they were doing.

Neither of them heard Nicholas knock on the door, nor did they notice when he entered the room. Kathleen touched Marcella's arm when she glanced up and saw him standing in the doorway, looking around at the disarray with obvious distaste.

"Oh, dear, he is in one of his grumbling moods," Marcella breathed to Kathleen.

Nicholas's eyes scanned the two of them sitting on the floor amidst Marcella's things. He looked straight at Marcella. "I would like to talk with you, Marcella. Alone."

Marcella stood up slowly, unbending stiffened limbs. "Oh, I am indeed too old for all of this."

"Marcella, I want to talk with you *now*," he repeated impatiently.

"Alone?"

"Alone."

Katheleen stood and brushed a bit of dust from her skirt. "I don't mind, Aunt Marcella. I'll just go into the other room and begin some of this mending."

"*I* mind, Kathleen. I don't want to talk to you alone, Nicholas. Particularly not when you are in one of these moods. Now do be sweet for a change and let me introduce you to my niece. I am told you two have not officially met."

"How do you do, Miss O'Connor?" he said, not paying the slightest attention to Kathleen. "Can we talk, Marcella?"

"Oh, you are rude! I can sympathize now with Kathleen's opinion of you. You are not even civil."

Nicholas looked from Marcella to Kathleen and back again. "What was it that you said about me, Miss O'Connor?" he asked.

Kathleen threw a hateful glance at Marcella for having gotten her into this predicament. "I said I hadn't met you, and that I had no opinion of you personally, but that generally this household was the coldest and rudest I have ever been in."

"As long as I am not included in the general category of people in this house, I would agree with you. I might even be more specific and say that the Paxton clan and all its offshoots are the coldest, most grasping people I have ever met—"

"I," Kathleen interrupted, "am part of the Paxton family, Mr. Dalton."

"I am aware of that, Miss O'Connor. The only difference between you and the rest of your family is that I have not yet been told what it is you want."

Kathleen bristled. "You have proved yourself quite as rude as anyone else in this house, Mr. Dalton. Perhaps I had no opinion of you moments ago, but I definitely do now."

"Perhaps if you were someone else," he replied, "I would have made certain your opinion of me was a good one, but as matters stand, we are both better off having the sides drawn firmly from the outset."

"Mr. Dalton, whatever side you are on, I can assure you I will always be on the opposite side. Now, if you will excuse me, I prefer to darn stockings rather than remain in your presence." She turned on her heel and left the room.

Marcella began to laugh. "I do believe she has you, Nicholas. If she were not my sister's child, I might think she was my own."

Nicholas's face was flushed from his exchange with Kathleen. "She is ill-tempered, dark, and small." He glared at the door through which Kathleen had passed and then left the room abruptly.

Marcella, relieved that he seemed to have forgotten what he had wanted to discuss with her, let him go without a word. The longer she could put off dealing with the question of what she wanted to do with Scarborough House, the better.

Nicholas had changed, and Marcella wondered whether Brad himself would have recognized his son. Nicholas seemed to be falling into the habit of choleric temper and cynicism. How much of that attitude was real and how much was pose, Marcella could not tell. Perhaps he wanted Scarborough for a mammoth tomb in which he could spend his life, alone and wallowing in self-pity and indifference.

The door to her bedroom opened, and Kathleen looked out. "Is he gone?"

"Yes. He left—forgot entirely what he came for. That is not like him. He is usually most persistent when he has something on his mind." Marcella looked at her niece. "Kathleen! Of course! He was taken with you. Why, my dear child, he likes you."

"Does he? Imagine how surly he might have been if he hadn't," she said acidly.

"I *am* glad you have come," Marcella said. "I am so glad. You don't know it yet, but in many ways it is as if you had begun my life all over again. Jo's child, and here you are handing to this old shell of a woman a new chance, a second—oh, no—a fourth or a fifth chance, at least. I have been so wrong so many times. Pray God I am not this time."

"Aunt Marcella, you're doing it again. You're talking on and on, and I don't know what you are talking about."

Marcella rushed on, ignoring Kathleen's comment. "Not once have you looked away from me, do you realize that? It is difficult to explain what that means to me. You have never known me any way but the way I am now, but there was a time when I was a very beautiful woman. Men liked to look at me, and I liked it, too. Now even I find it difficult to look at myself in a mirror, the change is so great. But you—you have been kind, Kathleen, and it has been the best kindness. It was natural. Do you understand what I am trying to tell you?"

"In part. I am sorry about your face, but there are worse things, and I'm sure that with a little thought and effort you could be much more attractive."

"I am sure you are right about both matters. The way I have led my life, though, I am more than certain to encounter all those 'worse things' before I die."

Together they knelt down and picked up the remaining items from the floor, stuffing them back into the drawers. "We'll get back to this tomorrow or the next day," Marcella said. "I feel like taking a nice, long walk. What about you?"

Chapter Twenty-eight

Marcella's momentary good humor was short-lived, much to Kathleen's chagrin. Her aunt's moods, she discovered, changed unpredictably, sometimes from one day to the next, sometimes from moment to moment. Each time Kathleen was sure they had made real progress, everything would come crashing down again, often for no reason Kathleen could determine.

Charlotte told Kathleen that Marcella had always been extreme in her emotions, had always reacted strongly to her surroundings and people she knew.

"You have only to think of the life she has led to know what I say is true," she told her niece. "I mean, running off with a married man. All she ever said was that she loved him. How, I ask you, can any decent person call lust love and get away with it? You need only look at how it all ended."

Kathleen had no reply for Charlotte. Although she could offer no defense for what Marcella had done, neither could she believe Marcella's past choices had been based on mere lust. All Kathleen knew for a certainty was that when Marcella was brooding and depressed, she drank constantly and relied on her laudanum to put her to sleep. Wasn't that at least as bad as her original mistake had been? Charlotte said no. It was fair punishment and self-inflicted. No one could do anything to alter that.

Kathleen had decided she would try—and she was not about to give up now. With all the fervor of a young, still-idealistic social worker, she plunged again into the task of keeping Marcella active every waking minute of the day.

Marcella insisted—as she often did—that she was interested in nothing. As Kathleen tested one thing after another, Marcella went along halfheartedly, usually out of curiosity. They invaded Mrs. Barth's domain, the kitchen. Marcella showed no interest whatever in baking or cooking, to Mrs. Barth's great relief. She bade them a thankful farewell and cleaned up the mess they had left behind.

When they had exhausted all the possibilities of normal housekeeping tasks, from the care of the silver to the inventory of possessions, Kathleen decided to try the conservatory as a last resort. She hadn't been anxious to try this, for like the study, the conservatory seemed to be Nicholas's domain, and she did not want to cross paths with him unless it was absolutely necessary. Since it did appear to be necessary, she went to his study to ask his permission.

She tapped on the door and entered. He was bent over his desk, concentrating on the figures in a ledger before him. She knew immediately that it was the wrong time to ask him anything. He slammed the ledger shut and looked up, annoyed, expecting it to be Gert.

"Don't come in here without knocking!" he snapped and then looked again. "Miss O'Connor. I'm sorry, I thought you were someone else."

"I did knock, Mr. Dalton. Apparently you didn't hear. I have come to ask you permission for Aunt Marcella and me to work in the conservatory in the mornings. If that won't upset your own schedule, I'd appreciate it." She stared at the top of his desk as she spoke.

"Miss O'Connor, I am sorry I spoke to you as I did. I—"

"How you speak is no concern of mine, Mr. Dalton. May we use the conservatory?"

He put both hands flat on the desktop, sighing. "Use it whenever you wish."

"Thank you, Mr. Dalton," she said and left the room as quickly as she could.

Whatever the encounter had cost her in pride—she hated having to ask Nicholas for anything—it succeeded in interesting Marcella for a time. During the mornings they spent with the plants in the conservatory, her niece began to see glimpses of the woman Marcella had once been. Kathleen came to look forward to their shared moments of laughter and occasional seriousness.

She still found the other side of Marcella frightening and inexplicable. In the many letters she wrote to Minerva, she went over and over again the problems she encountered with Marcella—and with Charlotte. Minerva's advice was always the same—to learn as much as she could about Marcella and see if she couldn't discover some pattern.

In time, Kathleen did begin to see a pattern—Marcella's spells always seemed to come shortly after she had been with Martin, Charlotte, and occasionally, Nicholas. She finally confronted Marcella directly with her hypothesis. About Martin and Nicholas, Marcella said little, but about Charlotte she said much that made things clearer for Kathleen.

"It is difficult for Charlotte to be around me," she mused. "I know I ought to tell her to leave—to go wherever she wants. She has tried to save me from myself ever since we were children." She touched her face. "She thinks I deserve all this."

Kathleen began to protest, but Marcella interrupted. "No, Kathleen, Charlotte is a very good woman. She always was. Charlotte did everything right. Mama used to be so proud of her."

"And of you?"

"Oh, God, no. Mama worried about me right from the start. She always did say we were different, or that I was. . . ." Her voice trailed off, and Kathleen knew further conversation with her would be pointless. Marcella would not be in fit condition to talk or do anything until she had gotten over this new bout of melancholia.

Kathleen wandered, troubled and aimless, downstairs and went into the large library. It was a warm, paneled room, smelling of leather and the slightly dusty odor of old books. At the far side of the room the bookshelves held a collection of miniature ships, all built to scale. She walked directly over to them, reached out, and touched a steamship model.

"That is the *Clermont*, Miss O'Connor, the first of Mr. Fulton's steamships to travel on the Hudson. It is named for a mansion—the Livingstons' home."

Kathleen, startled, whirled around. Nicholas was standing behind her on the opposite side of his desk. "Is there something you wanted in here, Miss O'Connor?"

"I am sorry," she said, moving back toward the door. "I had forgotten that you don't like anyone to enter this room. It's so inviting and comfortable."

Nicholas looked closely at her troubled face. "No, wait, just for a moment. Something is wrong. Tell me if I can help you."

Kathleen shook her head. "It is nothing, Mr. Dalton. I am preoccupied."

"I may be cold and rude, as you put it, Miss O'Connor, but I am not entirely insensitive. If this is not of a personal nature, perhaps I can assist you."

Kathleen laughed shortly. "You would not help me personally, Mr. Dalton? And yet you tell me how sensitive you are. I must remember that in case I ever do need help."

"I merely meant I did not want to pry. Is it Marcella?"

"Why, yes," Kathleen replied, genuinely astonished. "It *is* Aunt Marcella. I simply don't know what to do." She looked at Nicholas as if to ask: "Do you?"

He motioned to her to sit down on one of the large leather chairs next to the fireplace. She sighed, looked at him, felt some reservations about discussing the whole matter with him, but decided to plunge in anyway.

Nicholas listened attentively, not interrupting her until she had finished. He even managed to stay silent when she included his name among Marcella's tormentors. "I am aware," he said finally, "of why my visits to her occasionally upset her. While I do not feel inclined to discuss the matter with you, I assure you I will do my best not to disturb her unduly. However, it happens to concern a matter that is important to me.

"As to Martin, I know why Martin goes to see her, but as she is aware of it also, I don't know why it should upset her. Martin goes to Marcella for money, pure and simple. Your cousin is a gambler—not a very good one—and she has put herself in the position of having to give him what he asks for."

"I find that hard to believe. Aunt Marcella doesn't give in so easily—and besides, she is more aware than most people I've talked to of things like money. She always amazes me, the way she talks about the stock market and business trends. She seems to be abreast of everything that concerns the city—the whole country, I guess. It must be those radical newspapers she subscribes to. It doesn't fit that she should condone Martin's living a life of idle leisure."

Nicholas smiled. "Well, perhaps she won't for much longer. Now that she has an ally in the house, and all those radical newspapers to read, she may get her back up and put an end to the whole thing."

"I wish she would. Martin seems to be a very bad influence on her."

"And you seem to be a very good one."

Kathleen looked up suddenly and smiled. "That couldn't possibly be a compliment coming from you, could it, Mr. Dalton?"

"A compliment and an apology," he said. "Will you accept that?"

"Gladly. I never meant to get off on the wrong foot with you, or anyone else for that matter. I guess I didn't come here in the proper frame of mind. I rather felt as though I were being ordered here, and quite honestly, Mr. Dalton, I am not fond of being ordered about."

Nicholas looked at her intently for a moment. "Do you think, Miss O'Connor, that you could call me Nicholas?"

Kathleen accepted Nicholas's implied offer of friendship cautiously. Scarborough House was too subject to changes in the weather, she thought, to accept anything—least of all friendship—unconditionally. Within days, she discovered that her caution was warranted.

She and Marcella were busy in the conservatory. They had started several flats of new plants from clippings from the old ones, and Kathleen had turned her attention to two overgrown ferns.

"Do you know how to propagate these, Aunt Marcella?"

"Mr dear child, I know nothing whatever about anything. Why don't we just cut their heads off and hope they grow back?"

"How awful! But I'll bet that I can take them out of these old pots and divide their roots in half, or maybe three parts, and they will be all right. Don't you think that would work?"

"Try it. What have we to lose but two ferns?" Marcella said and returned her attention to a flat of jade plant cuttings.

Kathleen struggled with the large fern pots, trying to dislodge the plants. When she finally managed to get them out, the resulting mess covered one whole end of the room. She divided the first of the plants and was working on the second, when Nicholas came into the room. He greeted Marcella near the door, pausing when he saw what Kathleen was doing at the far end.

"What are you going?" he cried, taking the fern from her. "Look at this! What the hell are you trying to do?"

"Well, you needn't be so angry!"

"You'll kill these plants. If you don't know what you're doing, leave them alone."

"I was dividing them. They're overgrown."

"You don't rip a plant apart."

"I didn't!"

"You did, I was watching you."

Fuming, Kathleen wiped her muddy hands on her apron. "Then, Mr. Dalton, I suggest you fix your plants yourself. I hope they wilt!" She hurried from the room, dragging Marcella with her.

"Why don't you just ask him to show you how to do the ferns, Kathleen?" Marcella said as she followed her niece up the stairs. "You do want to know, don't you?"

"I wouldn't ask *him* anything."

In Marcella's room, Kathleen sat down. "I don't know why I ever thought he could be pleasant. He can't."

Marcella remained silent.

"Well, why don't you say something?" Kathleen snapped.

Marcella grinned. "I wouldn't dare."

★   ★   ★

The following week was one of Marcella's worst, and Kathleen struggled to maintain whatever patience she could summon up. Nothing she did seemed to satisfy her aunt. One day, in utter exasperation, she simply fled from Marcella's room without a word.

She went to the music room, which housed an admirable art collection of scenes of the river and the Catskills, mostly by Hudson River artists.

"Are you an art lover?"

She jumped at the sound of Nicholas's voice. He stood not a foot away from her, resting his weight on the back of a chair.

"I know little about it," she said slowly, determined not to let his ill humor worsen her mood. "I cannot judge from knowledge, but from personal pleasure alone."

He looked down at the tapestry back of the chair he leaned on. It was one of Annette's. He moved his hands so that his fingers wouldn't touch the tapestry. Finally he looked up at Kathleen. "I suppose I should be kind and educate you."

"Thank you very much, Mr. Dalton, but I think not. You have the disposition of an adder. I am sure I would never survive your instruction." She looked at him defiantly; then she lowered her voice and said, "I don't really know why you find it difficult to be charitable when you speak to me."

"I?" He began to laugh. "I can't think why I should find it difficult to be charitable to you, either. After all, you are just a sweet child."

She looked away. "I knew you could say nothing nice."

He stopped smiling and moved out from behind the chair. "I really had intended to speak to you in a most pleasant way. I have no idea why I always seem to be angry with you. I never mean to be. In fact, I came in here for the express purpose of apologizing to you for the way I spoke the last time I saw you, and now I have compounded my offense."

"Thank you, Mr. Dalton."

They stood looking at each other until both became uncomfortable. She wondered why he didn't leave. His eyes scanned the room, stopping at the paintings. "Would you like to know about them?"

"I'd prefer to know about the study. Why were you so upset when I came in the other day? Was I intruding?"

He shook his head and moved a few steps away. Suddenly he looked back at her. "Miss O'Connor, would you like to take a walk? I don't seem able to stand still at the moment."

"Mr. Dalton, you are free to go at any time. I don't wish to make you uncomfortable, nor will I ask you anything else about that room, if that is what is upsetting you."

He blushed in spite of himself. "I don't believe it is the room that is upsetting me," he said. "I have no logical reason for keeping the room closed to everyone but myself. I feel rather foolish now. Let us say that it is not on purpose that I keep it closed off, but from personal prejudice alone. Will you accept that?"

She smiled at him as if at a small boy. "I will accept that as among the best of reasons, Mr. Dalton. Now—I would like to take a walk with you, if you meant the invitation."

His relief was visible. "I did."

They started for the door. "Where is everyone?" Kathleen asked. "I haven't heard a sound since I left Aunt Marcella's room."

"Martin is out. I think I heard him say he was going to the Abbey. I believe Charlotte went to the city for the afternoon."

"This house is so big, often I cannot tell if I am alone or not. That must sound ridiculous to you. I suppose you are so accustomed to it that you don't notice the size."

"Does it bother you?"

"Not really. Well, yes, it does, in a strange way. I like being alone, but I don't like thinking I am and then finding I am not. It gives me the strange feeling that someone is looking over my shoulder. Does that make sense to you?"

He held open the front door for her. "But you have already mentioned Marcella, and you know I am here. You were never alone."

"Oh, but I was . . . What I mean is—"

"We do not interfere with your peace of mind, and you can be solitary and yet, at the same time, feel comfortable knowing that there are others around you?"

She touched his arm gratefully. "That is it exactly. How did you know?"

"As you said, I am used to the house. And maybe that same feeling is what led me to apologize in the first place. I chased you away and then could think of nothing else. You stole my peace of mind, so I had little choice but to restore it."

"You are a very unusual man, Mr. Dalton." She laughed. "Nicholas."

"Kathleen." He offered his hand for her to take. When she obliged, he smiled gratefully. "Would you like to see the willow pond, or have you already found it?"

"The willow pond?"

"Come, I'll show you."

She held fast to his hand as he led her down the path to the pond.

Behind Scarborough House, the land fell away in terraces until it reached the flat bed of the valley lawn. They walked across that valley and came into an allee of trees that formed a tunnel of shadow and emerald.

Kathleen looked at the heavy undergrowth crowded between the trunks of the trees, a profusion of rhododendron and wild roses.

"No one told me about this path."

"It was a secret. No one comes here but me."

"Then why are you bringing me?"

"I haven't any idea. I'll probably regret it."

"Then why are you doing it?"

"Will you please stop asking?"

"Now you are angry again. I don't understand you at all."

"So much the better. You are an infuriating woman. Watch where you are going, or you'll trip." He grabbed for her as she stumbled over a small root hidden by the tall grass. "Now pay attention to where you are going. I won't catch you the next time."

"I wouldn't have fallen! And I'll walk where I please."

"Do as you wish," he muttered, annoyed.

She stopped walking. He went on a few steps and then stopped, refusing to look back to where she waited.

"I'll not go a step further until you tell me why you are acting this way. What have I done?"

He turned slowly and looked at her. As she stood waiting for him to say something, the noise in the brush seemed to die away. The trees closed in and isolated them; the air was still and quiet. Nicholas looked at her intently and then began to move toward her.

She saw the expression on his face, glanced around quickly, and then ran toward him like a frightened deer, darting to the side before he could reach out for her. She raced down the path, her skirts gathered above her knees, running until her side hurt and she had no breath left.

The opening in the dark greenery was sudden. A gentle bend and the allee disappeared. Kathleen found herself staring out into a clearing surrounded by hemlock, spruce, and pine. A good-sized pond, its surface momentarily smooth as glass, lay in the center, guarded by three huge weeping willows. On a small peninsula of land jutting out into the pond perched a summerhouse. At first glance it appeared to be floating on the surface of the pond.

As Kathleen stared, Nicholas came up behind her and placed his hands on her shoulders. "It was built for my grandmother. She is the only woman who has ever been here—except you."

The walked across a small wooden footbridge to the summerhouse on the water. An old oak swing still hung from the roof. She sat down on the swing, thinking about her own home, and the swing her father had built there, large enough to hold all eight O'Connors. Then she looked at Nicholas and realized that when she had thought of her father and her swing at home, she had seen Terrance with Nicholas's face.

"Why did you bring me here?"

"When I saw you, I thought of this place. You seemed to fit—to belong here. I wanted you here. Why do you ask so many questions? God alone knows why it is you." He looked away and then he turned back, almost angrily, took her in his arms, and kissed her.

That night, Kathleen wrote to Minerva: "He is a man who has everything a person could desire, and yet I don't believe I have ever met another person quite so alone or lonely as he."

She had a strange premonition that she might lose something precious before she had had the opportunity to taste it.

Chapter Twenty-nine

The following afternoon Nicholas invited her to go riding.

As they walked down toward the stables, he asked Kathleen, "You are very fond of Marcella, aren't you?"

"Of course I am," she replied, looking up at him. "Why do you ask?"

Nicholas said nothing. He studied the ground ahead of them as they continued to walk. When they got to the stable door, Kathleen put a hand on his arm. "Nicholas, why did you ask me that?"

He refused to look at her. "She isn't the only one," he answered, nudging a stone out of the soil with the toe of his boot, "who would like a friend and ally."

Kathleen smiled and tugged at the sleeve of his jacket. "Come on, Nicholas. Let's ride. I think you know how I feel about being your friend."

He blushed, slightly embarrassed by her forthrightness, and helped her up onto the horse the stable hand brought out for her. Mounting his own horse, he reined it around abruptly and tore out of the stable yard and across the lawns.

Kathleen chuckled to herself as she watched. How like a little boy he was at times. She prodded her own horse forward, following the direction Nicholas had taken.

From the house, Gert and the other servants looked on, delighted to see Nicholas ride for the sheer pleasure of it. It had been a long time, they agreed, since he had done anything with such obvious relish.

For the first few days Kathleen was content to follow Nicholas at a distance as she adjusted to riding again. Thereafter, however, she began to become restless and annoyed that she could not follow his lead. She felt constained by her heavy riding habit and by being forced to ride sidesaddle. She longed for the freedom she had enjoyed as a child when her father had taken her riding, but if she abandoned the conventional dress and saddle, she knew, she would scandalize Charlotte and probably Nicholas as well.

Only Marcella urged her on. "Oh, do go on! Ride with him."

"Aunt Marcella! You have never even seen me ride. I might break my neck. Before I knew it, that ridiculous skirt would be tangled all about my legs."

"Well, if you were not so old-fashioned, you would not even be wearing that dress to ride in. You'd have breeches on!"

"You will make a scandal of me yet."

"You know you are dying to go out there and show him a thing or two. We'll have the dressmaker in. Perhaps if she modeled the outfit after the bloomer—with modifications, of course—that would do."

Kathleen looked at her for a moment. "Do you really think I should?"

"I would."

"Shall we both have riding costumes made?"

"I am afraid of horses, Kathleen! I said I would, but that is, if I were you. Fortunately, I am not."

"But you are no more afraid of horses than I."

Marcella shrugged. Kathleen was quiet for a moment. "When I rode with Papa," she began, "when Papa took us to the country, I wore breeches. Let's call the dressmaker."

"That's more like it!"

Kathleen's eyes shone. "I would love to beat him just one time. He would be so amazed."

"Race Nicholas? I am not so sure of that, dear. You had best be careful. I think Nicholas was born half horse. You might very well break your neck trying that."

"Oh, I can! I know I can. Especially if he doesn't know about it ahead of time."

In the afternoons that followed, Kathleen rode with Nicholas every day when he was not in town on business, keeping her ladylike pace behind him, admiring and complimenting him on his horsemanship. In the mornings and after she had had her ride with Nicholas, she hurried back to Marcella's room, where she designed the new riding outfit and listened to Marcella tell her of her new "career."

"A career? You are embarking on a career?"

"I have decided you have been right all along. I mustn't keep dwelling on all these things that are long past."

From under her bed Marcella hauled out piles of papers, old copies of magazines, and newspapers she had saved. The one she selected to show Kathleen was a copy of the *Mirror*.

"Have you ever heard of a lady called Jenny June?"

"Yes. She writes a column in the Sunday *Times* called 'Parlor and Sidewalk Gossip.' I have often read it."

"Well, she is a remarkable lady, and I am a firm supporter of hers. She is quite a fighter for the rights and betterment of women."

"Aunt Marcella! You are not going to become one of the suffragettes, surely?"

"Oh, no, dear, they are far too impractical for me and call too much down on their heads. I want to make progress, not acquire a headache."

"That is a relief."

"No, what I was thinking about was writing a letter to Mrs. Croly. Now she is a suffragist. There is quite a difference, you know. Suffragists are far more practical and Mrs. Croly's a practical woman in all respects. Croly is Jenny June's true name. I was thinking perhaps I could ask her if she could use another woman's help in her work. After all, I have been in a man's world most of my life and have had a hand in many careers. Not directly, mind you—it was always Brad's name that was in the foreground—but every now and then it was I who decided that we should buy a particular piece of land or sell a stock. Perhaps I could advise them on investments. I could certainly do as well as Victoria Woodhull, and she has done quite well, I think."

"You are going to fight for women's rights?" Kathleen asked, as though testing out the sound of it before committing herself one way or another.

"I am thinking about it." Marcella looked at her niece, soliciting Kathleen's reaction.

"I think it's a marvelous idea. But Aunt Charlotte will be mortified."

"There is no reason why she should find out—at least, not at this point. You aren't going to tell her, are you?"

"I won't say a word," Kathleen promised and left it at that. When the subject was not brought up again, she decided it was just another of Marcella's passing fancies.

A few days later, the dressmaker brought the riding costume to the house. Kathleen went to the stables and made arrangements with Joe for the next day's ride. She asked that he give her some faulty piece of equipment so that she could return to the stable after she and Nicholas had started out. Joe would have her favorite horse, Derry Dell, ready to ride, with a regular English saddle.

"You mustn't let Mr. Nicholas know anything about this. Promise me you won't say anything to him."

Joe hesitated.

"If Mr. Nicholas is angry, I will take full blame," she added. "I'll tell him you didn't want to do as I asked, but that I insisted."

All the next morning, Marcella could not hold her niece's attention for five minutes running. Finally she stopped what she was doing and looked over at Kathleen. "Why don't you go on down to the library and tell Nicholas I am tired this morning. Tell him I want to take a nap, and then go out riding now. You are worth nothing to me at all."

Kathleen looked chagrined. "Do you mean it?"

Marcella sighed. "Yes, I mean it. But do be careful. I'll watch from my window."

Kathleen hurried to her room and put on the new riding outfit. She put the skirt of the old habit over the new, sucking in her stomach to make it fit. She could barely breathe, but it would only be for a short time.

When she went to Nicholas in the study to ask if he would like to ride early that day, he was quick to agree.

"Indeed I would," he said, shuffling papers together. "I have to go to Albany later this afternoon. I thought we wouldn't be able to go out at all today."

She had on the same ridiculously decorative bonnet she always wore, and Nicholas noticed nothing unusual about her as they walked together toward the stables. Kathleen looked apprehensively toward Joe, who gave her a slight nod as he helped her into the sidesaddle.

As they rode out together, Nicholas stayed by her side. For a moment she thought he was going to be content with jogging along beside her instead of racing off and coming back to her as he normally did. Night Wind pranced, tossing his head impatiently.

"Why don't you go on and give him a good run? I think my girth is not as tight as it should be. I am going to go back and have Joe see to it."

Frowning, Nicholas looked at her horse's side, but Kathleen's voluminous skirts hid anything he might have seen. "I'll go back with you," he said.

"That is silly. Night Wind is dying to run, and I can't keep up with you, anyway. You go on. I'll meet you as soon as this is corrected." She turned her horse around and began to move slowly back to the stables. Nicholas sat motionless on Night Wind, seemingly undecided. She waved cheerfully and breathed a sigh of relief when he rode off.

"Is Derry Dell ready, Joe?" she asked once she was in the safety of the stables. She ran into Night Wind's empty stall and took off her skirt.

She heard Joe's gasp. "What you doin' there, Miss Kat? You can't go ridin' in your bloomers!"

She laughed. "Not bloomers, see?"

"Oh, Lord. You be careful."

"Look out and see where Mr. Nicholas is."

Joe trotted to the door of the stables. "He's ridin' this way, miss. I think he's comin' here. What you gonna do?"

Kathleen took hold of Derry Dell and swung up into the saddle unassisted. She moved the horse toward the entrance. As soon as Nicholas came near, she asked Joe to call to him to say she would be right there. Nicholas waved to show that he had understood and turned Night Wind back to face the open lawn.

Kathleen leaned forward, dug in with her knees, and gave the eager horse a swat. She had very nearly caught up to Nicholas before he turned to look. As she flashed by him, she could see the look of utter astonishment on his face.

Kathleen directed the horse to the first jump Nicholas had taken with Night Wind. Fortunately, Derry Dell was a good jumper. Both horse and rider were having a wonderful time. Kathleen's hair had come free when the hat with the plume had fallen off at the beginning of her ride.

Derry Dell was very fast, but she lacked the stamina of Night Wind, and soon Nicholas pulled up next to her. Allowing the horse to slow to a more reasonable gait, and finally to a walk, Kathleen looked over to him. Her face was red from the wind, and her eyes bright with excitement and victory.

She threw her head back and laughed. "I beat you!"

Nicholas laughed with her and agreed wholeheartedly.

When they came back up the stairs of the house to the porch, Charlotte was waiting for them.

"You might have been killed!" she exclaimed, wringing her hands. "And look at you, wearing pants like—like a man. Nicholas, you shouldn't have let her do that. You, at least, should have better sense."

"I have just been beaten in a race by a tiny lady I did not even know could ride like that," he said with mock indignation, "let alone that she would dare to wear pants! It is *I* who am scandalized, mortified, and humiliated in the bargain. You are her aunt. Why don't you do something?"

Charlotte flushed. "Mocking me and making light of this situation will not undo what has been done. Kathleen, as your aunt and guardian, I am responsible for you. I will not have this kind of behavior from you."

"Aunt Marcella gave me permission. In fact, she had this outfit made for me."

"I might have surmised Marcella would be behind this," Charlotte sniffed. "It is just like her to encourage irresponsible behavior in you. Well, I shall have a talk with my sister. In the meantime, get rid of that shocking outfit and dress yourself properly." Charlotte did not wait for a reply but hurried into the house, leaving Kathleen and Nicholas smiling after her.

Nicholas chuckled. "Do you want to go upstairs and protect Marcella from the tirade?"

"No. With something like this, Aunt Marcella is perfectly capable of talking for herself. If anyone needs protecting, it may be Aunt Charlotte."

He took her hand and led her back down the steps from the porch. "Tell me where you learned to ride like that."

"Papa taught me. He used to race with the neighboring men on Sundays, and I rode for the fun of it and to give him a bit of token opposition. Papa loved a good run on the flats."

"Apparently his daughter does, too."

"Were you really surprised?"

"Very much. I didn't know what was happening, and then you flew by and—"

"I've been dying to do that for the last week or so."

"Of course you cheated," he laughed.

"I had to. I couldn't have beaten you otherwise, and that was the whole point."

"You are certain that Marcella won't need your help with Charlotte?"

"No, she is prepared. In fact, she is looking forward to it. We both knew Aunt Charlotte would be horrified if she saw me. Aunt Marcella was practically licking her lips at the prospect. And that isn't the only thing Aunt Marcella is looking forward to telling Aunt Charlotte about."

"What else?"

"Aunt Marcella has decided to join something called Sorosis."

"Sorosis? Sounds like a disease."

"No, silly. It's a women's organization."

"She is not going to become a suffragette, is she?"

"I asked her the same thing." Kathleen looked up at him. "No, this is a club that sponsors the emergence of women into man's world. They refer to themselves as suffragists. Mrs. Croly is the president, and Madame Nell Demorest is also a great backer of the movement. They urge women to be educated, to read, to exercise, and to have hobbies that are fulfilling and useful.

They are not nearly so radical as the suffragettes, but they seem to be quite a large group. Aunt Marcella wants to take up her pen and write for them. She is thinking of taking a more active part later on."

"I believe she will do it, too," he said. "She'll turn this whole damned house upside down in the process, but she'll do it."

"You don't approve?"

"Of course I approve. Now that you have told me about it, it amazes me that she didn't think of it long ago. It is a natural for Marcella. According to most of what you have told me, and what I've read about this organization, it is what Marcella has believed in and done all of her life."

"That is exactly what she said!"

"But Marcella won't go into it calmly. She'll manage to stir up trouble. Wait and see."

"How could she cause trouble? There is no one to object to what she wants to do. You don't and I don't, and Aunt Charlotte will say her two cents' worth and then forget it. In the end Aunt Marcella always comes out having her own way with Aunt Charlotte."

"What of Martin and Rhea?"

"What about them? It's none of Martin's business and even less of Miss Scott's."

"We'll see," he said as they walked into the orchard. From one of the trees he broke off a delicate sprig covered with peach blossoms and handed it to her. "To emancipated ladies," he said and bowed deeply.

"I think you are making fun of Marcella—and of me, too."

"Oh, so you're a believer, too?"

"Well," Kathleen said, "there is a great deal in what she says that appeals to me. I have to think about it some more. Why, Nicholas? Are you against it?"

"No. If that is what you want, then I want it for you."

"But you don't really like it?"

"I have to ask what it is you wish to be emancipated from, and I don't find answers. For myself, I think I prefer the idea of a woman for my home and myself."

"And would you be willing to be a man only for her and your home?"

"That isn't the question. There is a matter of earning a living and providing the necessities."

"This organization of Aunt Marcella's has no quarrel with your views, it means only to expand on them a bit. A woman can and should do more than sit idly at home."

"Like ride wearing men's pants?"

Kathleen made a face at him.

Suddenly Nicholas was serious. "I will be going to Albany this afternoon and then into New York. Will you miss these afternoon rides?"

"No!"

"You are a liar."

"I will miss you," she said quickly and looked away. When she looked back

268

at him, he was smiling. Kathleen flashed a mischievous grin at him and took off, running through the trees.

He followed, darting in and out among the blossom-laden trees, peering in all directions to catch a glimpse of her bright blue outfit. When he caught up with her, she was lying on the ground, breathless from running, and laughing. He lay down beside her and kissed her.

Suddenly he sat up again and looked away. "I am sorry. I shouldn't have done that," he said.

"Such a waste to be sorry. I quite enjoyed it, but then Aunt Marcella did tell me you were brooding and standoffish about women, so if you feel better being sorry, that is all right. I understand."

He laughed. "Is there nothing about you that follows an ordinary code?"

"Very little. At least I hope that it is little. Why is it that you do not like women? Aunt Marcella said you didn't. Why don't you?"

"I don't believe I ever said I don't like women. That's your Aunt Marcella talking. She exaggerates nearly everything." He shook his head. "I think I had better take you back to the house."

She held her hands out for him to take. He pulled her to her feet.

"Once, Nicholas, you said I was a Paxton, and like all Paxtons, before long I would find myself wanting something. You were right. I do." She looked at him for a long time, then released his hands so they could slide around her waist.

He held her close, murmuring her name. Finally he pulled away from her. She touched his face—the prominent cheekbones, the high-bridged nose, the wide, firm-lipped mouth.

"Miss Kat," he said softly. "That is what Gert keeps calling you. Now I know why. It fits you."

"Shall I be your Miss Kat, Nicholas?"

"My Miss Kat."

Chapter Thirty

Nicholas decided to postpone his departure a few days. That evening he took Kathleen in the dog cart down along the river. They watched in silence as the barges passed, going in both directions.

He pointed to one travel-worn barge. "That's coming from Argentina." It was loaded with animal hides to be taken to the tanneries up the river, where huge forests of hemlock would be stripped of their bark to process the leather.

All along the river, the vast wealth of the land was being exploited. Lime deposits along the Hudson's banks made the best cement, and men left great caves in the sides of those hills when they took the lime away. At night the eerie light of the kilns in the brickyards burned against the darkness, glowing red and hot.

As the last of the day's light faded away, and they could no longer see any barges, Nicholas led her back to the cart and turned the horse back toward home.

"How long will you be gone?" she asked.

"I am not sure, perhaps a week—ten days at the most. I don't know exactly. Marcella has asked me to talk with her broker. I have some papers to deliver to her lawyer for her, and I have business of my own to see to." He turned and smiled at her in the darkness. "I should be back just about the time the wedding is over."

"There was something once between you and Rhea, wasn't there?" Kathleen asked softly. "Do you think often of her?"

"I think about her, but only in the sense that I wonder why things happen as they do."

"And what is that supposed to mean?"

He flicked the whip lightly on the horse's back. "I only meant that I am one of those who seem to be consistently wrong where women are concerned. I frankly don't believe I have ever judged one correctly in my life. I still haven't any idea what Marcella is really like. She seems to me to be simple and direct, but considering what has happened, she is hardly that. I used to feel sorry for my mother. I thought she was pining away because my father had discarded her for Marcella. I tried to comfort her when he died. I don't believe she even cared.

"Then came Rhea. I might very well have married her, I suppose. I thought she cared, but then she couldn't have. . . ." His voice trailed off and then picked up again. "I am afraid my grandfather managed to spoil my judgment entirely."

"I would have liked your grandfather, I think. Even the first day I came here, I thought that. Gert told me a little about him, and it was as if I could sense his being there."

"He built this house for my grandmother."

"Gert told me." She was silent for a moment. "Nicholas, do you—I mean, you are not still in love with Rhea, are you?"

He looked at her sitting straight on her seat, her back erect. She was looking ahead. "You seem to have but one thing on your mind tonight," he muttered.

"I wish you would answer me."

"I shouldn't think you'd have to ask. I doubt that I was ever in love with Rhea. I was simply mistaken about her. I told you I am a man out of step with womankind. I wasn't being bitter, I meant that."

She said nothing, and they returned to the house in silence.

She knew there was a part of him that was glad to be leaving. What tormented her was that she didn't know why. She didn't believe it had anything to do with Rhea. Whatever had once been between Rhea and Nicholas, she did not think it was love. She thought of Rhea, and of the aura of cool invitation —or challenge—that Rhea exuded. Kathleen thought she knew very well what kind of affection Nicholas had had for Rhea, and perhaps still did.

That forbidden subject was one of the mysteries of men that repulsed and titillated her. How much did that unspoken attraction of a woman count with a man? Would it outweigh faithfulness, compassion, tenderness, concern—all the things she thought of when she thought about loving a man? Or were these simply excuses used by women who wanted to be thought virtuous and tolerated by men for whom they were phantoms of unattained desires?

Kathleen had never spoken these thoughts to anyone, nor would she, although since her arrival at Scarborough they had plagued her more than usual. She had thought that Marcella might be the one person with whom she could talk of these matters, but she could not do that, either. Marcella, even with all of her worldliness and tolerance, might think Kathleen unnaturally forward.

Did Nicholas know or suspect how much she loved him? Would he be horrified if he did know? Was it that that kept him from her?

For his part, Nicholas was just as perplexed about his feelings as she. He had no idea what it was he felt when she was near; his powers of concentration fragmented like so many shards of an exploded bottle. He was far too conscious of her and himself, not in the lusty, sexual way as with Rhea, but in a subtler, more concentrated passion that was rather fearsome to him. He would be glad to leave, but he knew before he had gone through the outer gates of Scarborough House he would be longing to return.

The following morning Kathleen hurried to the stables, hoping Nicholas would have time to ride with her. When he didn't come, she rode alone.

It was still early when she returned to the house, but already the day promised to be hectic. Charlotte, busy with the last-minute details for the wedding, was barely able to carry on a coherent conversation.

Instead, each time she saw Kathleen, she seemed a little more annoyed. "Honestly, Kathleen," she snapped as she passed her niece on the stairway, "I wish you would stay out of my way. Both you and Marcella are causing me nothing but additional confusion—something I simply cannot cope with at a time like this."

Kathleen, astonished at her aunt's outburst, began to protest.

"I am sorry, my dear," Charlotte interrupted, "but I simply cannot have you underfoot like this. Why, every time I turn around, either you or Marcella is in the way. Now, please, would you be so kind—" And she bustled on down the stairs.

Kathleen stood where she was for a full minute, wondering what she could possibly have done to elicit such a fit of temper. Had Marcella said something to Charlotte to make her angry?

She proceeded slowly up the stairs, recalling a conversation she had overheard between Charlotte and Marcella the day before. When Marcella had asked her sister about the wedding arrangements, Charlotte had made it quite clear that she could and would manage them herself—even though Marcella would be picking up the bill for the festivities.

Kathleen stopped at the top of the stairs. She heard Charlotte hurrying around below, issuing orders to Gert and the other servants. Suddenly Kathleen wondered why she hadn't realized it before—Scarborough House was in effect Charlotte's domain, which she intended to hold secure for her son.

It all seemed so clear. Marcella—and to a lesser extent, Nicholas—were being used and then discarded as though they were nothing of consequence. Kathleen ran to Marcella's room and burst in.

"I don't see why you put up with it, Aunt Marcella! You are being treated as if—as if you didn't matter at all."

"Oh, for pity's sake, you frightened me, rushing in like that. Sit down and catch your breath. Stop talking in riddles and tell me what is bothering you."

"Aunt Charlotte is keeping you out of everything, and she is doing it on purpose. She is using you—you and Nicholas."

Marcella chuckled. "Is that all? I could have told you that, dear. I am the woman in the attic. The only reason she doesn't lock Nicholas in with me is that Charlotte's ideas of sin won't permit it. You are only allowed one Dalton per lifetime. I have had mine. But it doesn't really matter, and besides, it isn't all Charlotte's fault. I want this wedding as much as Martin or Charlotte. Even as much as Rhea."

She smiled to herself and then looked at Kathleen. "After the wedding, I may have a few things to say that will please you and give Charlotte a bit to think about. Now run along and visit with Nicholas. He will be leaving soon, and you won't be seeing each other for a time."

Kathleen, still fuming, was reluctant to leave. "He mentioned he had some things to do for you."

"Yes, but never mind that. You go on and see him. He'll be looking for you." She touched Kathleen's arm. "You have made a great difference in Nicholas, Kathleen. I thought all the fun and nonsense had vanished from him for good. But it hasn't. It makes me feel very good to see you two together."

"I don't know, Aunt Marcella. I know Nicholas cares for me, but I have the strangest feeling that he would rather not. Don't laugh at me. I mean it. When we are together, everything is fine, but as soon as he is away from me, it is as if he is relieved not to have to think of me. Like this trip. I know it is necessary, and he must tend to business, but—"

Marcella considered for a moment. "The whole country is in terrible shape, Kathleen. It has been for some time. What kind of businessman would he be if he simply ignored the trends?"

"I know that and respect it, but that isn't what I meant, and you know it."

"But you don't understand, dear, or you wouldn't say that. Men are losing everything these days. Business is very precarious, and one simply cannot count on the stock market at all. Nicholas could lose just as well as the next man if he were not cautious. So could I. Nicholas tends to all of my holdings now, too, and he is making this trip for me as well as himself."

"Nicholas manages your money?"

"Surely you didn't think I would turn it over to Martin! Martin could ruin us. He thinks anything with odds is suitable."

"Martin can't be all that bad."

"As a matter of fact, I rather like Martin in spite of himself, but he is a foolish man. He is still waiting for his fairy godmother to give him his big chance."

"Maybe Rhea and his marriage will change that. He'll have responsibilities."

"Oh, the poor fool. She'll do nothing for him. That one will go her own way, and it will be an extravagant way." Marcella walked to the window and looked out across the lawns. "People have always assumed I was that sort, but I never was. I never used any man. I like having money, but it wasn't that that kept me with Brad, and it wasn't money that brought me to him in the first place."

By the time Kathleen left Marcella's room to find Nicholas, she was ready to accept Marcella's version of his preoccupation. It was business. She should have listened to Marcella sooner, she decided; she would have saved herself a lot of worry.

When she went to the study, she found him uncommunicative, absorbed in his work. She left quietly. If he wanted to see her, he would have to find her himself. Avoiding Charlotte, she went back to Marcella's room.

"It seems no one wants our company, Aunt Marcella," she said. "Would you like to go for a walk?"

They went out to the formal garden, an enclosed area of privet hedges laid out so that each path within the garden was isolated and hidden from the others. Marcella liked to sit there in the afternoon sun, thinking and sometimes talking, as she seemed inclined to do this afternoon.

"Women are silly creatures, Kathleen," she said as they sat down. "Why do you suppose we allow ourselves to be left behind and forgotten when men go out into the world and make it change and grow? They say they do it for us. Why do you suppose they bother? Why should a man go out to work just to house and clothe and keep a woman he allows to do nothing but bear him children—who turn out to be, for the most part, useless and ungrateful?" She fell silent, staring up into the branches of the tree that towered above the privet hedge. "Women should understand and be sympathetic to a man's world."

Ordinarily Kathleen liked listening to Marcella. Today, however, everything she said brought Nicholas to mind. "I wouldn't want to be part of a man's world," Kathleen said absently.

"Neither would I."

Kathleen looked up, suddenly attentive. "But you just said—"

"You didn't listen. Your mind is elsewhere today. What I said was that a woman should understand, not become. Women are far too adept and needed in their own world to bother with the mechanics of the male world. The question is not whether a woman should attempt to enter the man's realm, but rather, what are the limitations of a woman's world, and are they just? Tell me, is medicine—and caring for the ill—not very much in a woman's nature?"

"It is, but—"

"But nothing," Marcella interrupted, warming to the subject. "There are no women doctors to speak of—and why not? And justice—is there a woman alive who has not meted out justice every day of her life in her own family and with her servants? And the design of houses. Who, may I ask, runs those houses, lives her entire life in them? A woman. But do women design them?"

Kathleen was about to say something when she noticed Marcella smile and look at something else. Nicholas was standing at the edge of the path, grinning and shaking his head.

"Before we know it, Marcella, you will be standing alongside Miss Woodhull, advocating free love and women in politics."

"I might at that. She might have done better if she had had a woman vice-presidential candidate to run with her. One never knows what might have happened had we both tried." She smiled broadly. "I doubt if Miss Woodhull would have much use for me now. She is far too young and beautiful to want an old lady advocating her cause. I believe I am more in line with Nell Demorest and Mrs. Croly."

"Well, whatever you do, don't talk this one"—he gestured toward Kathleen—"into taking to the streets with placards and causes. Leave me one woman with an apron and broom."

Marcella put her hands on her hips in mock indignation. "Such gibberish, Nicholas Dalton! I'll never see the day when any wife of yours will be wearing an apron and wielding a broom. As far as I can surmise, you would much prefer to kill her on horseback, racing and jumping over everything in sight. Now take her with you and say no more."

"Yes, ma'am." He grinned and put his hand out to Kathleen.

Marcella sat back comfortably and watched them leave the garden. Not so long ago, her entire world had seemed hopeless and bleak. She had thought she could not get along without Charlotte. Every day when she had seen Nicholas, she had been reminded of what a terrible mistake her life had been. But if Nicholas was as happy as he seemed to be, had it all been a mistake after all?

Poor Charlotte, she thought. She had seldom paid Charlotte any attention unless she was frightened and needed Charlotte's support. Now Kathleen was here, and with her coming, the emptiness and the fear had gone, along with her liking and need for Charlotte.

Her final thoughts that afternoon were reserved entirely for herself. She had a future, a future that had risen up out of all that darkness and despair. She had already written to Jenny June—a letter that had taken Marcella a long time to gather the courage to write. Mrs. Croly and Mme. Demorest, after all, were known to be ladies, and she had not been at all sure how they would receive someone as notorious as she had once been.

They had written back, urging her to join the women's club. Mrs. Croly's letter had included a quote from one of her speeches: "We shall live—live to see the women's club the conservator of public morality, the uprooter of social evils, the defender of women against women as well as men, the preserver of the sanctities of domestic life, the synonym of the brave, true, and noble in women."

She could not have chosen her words better, thought Marcella.

When she got up from her seat, it was dusk. The sky had lost its radiant

color, and the eerie evening blue hovered in the eastern horizon. She straightened up, stretching her arms. She touched her face, felt the slight double chin she
had developed, touched her stomach, and looked down at herself.

"What I need is less food and more walking," she said aloud. She walked
briskly back to the house, composing in her mind an article she wanted to write
and send to Jenny June—an article on the value of an active body.

The following morning Marcella got out an old croquet set she had found in
the back of the barn. After wiping off the cobwebs and dust, she went to the
front lawn with it and set up three wickets. A bit of practice would help before
she tried to play a game. She stood five feet from the first wicket and whacked
each of the croquet balls.

Hearing her name called, she looked toward the house. Charlotte stood on
the porch, waving frantically. Marcella waved back and returned to her
croquet. Moments later Charlotte ran up, panting.

"You need exercise, Charlotte," Marcella said. A clod of soil dislodged as she
hit the last of her croquet balls. "You are short-winded."

"Marcella, stop this!" Charlotte gasped. "Look what you are doing. There
are great holes in the lawn already. It will look awful for the wedding."

"You'll simply have to get accustomed to having gouges in the lawn until I
become more proficient at this, Charlotte. I am to have my exercise every day."

"Is this another of Kathleen's ideas?"

"No, I thought up this particular venture myself. Will you join me?"

Charlotte was beside herself. "If you must do this, can't you at least do it at
the back of the house? Perhaps in the orchard? Anywhere but here. Think of
how this will look when all of the wedding guests come up here."

"Tell them one of the horses broke loose and trampled everything up,"
Marcella replied, taking careful aim with her mallet. "It does look rather like
that, doesn't it?"

"Marcella, have you been drinking again?"

"Not a drop all day. You know, Kathleen is quite bright. She told me I
would feel much better if I didn't use all those medicines. I do."

Charlotte sputtered but said nothing for a moment. "Marcella," she began,
making an obvious attempt to remain calm against impossible odds, "the sun is
hot. You'll get freckles standing out here like this."

Marcella looked at her blankly and then touched her pocked face. "Do you
really think it will matter?"

Nonplussed, Charlotte stammered, "At least you should wear a hat."

"Well, if you won't play, send Gert out here. She can use some fresh air and
exercise, too."

"I can't spare Gert! She is busy making pastries for the wedding supper."
Charlotte looked around. "Where is Kathleen? She is being paid to look after
you. Why isn't she here?"

"She is with Nicholas, and you leave her alone. He leaves tomorrow, and she
should be with him."

"Tomorrow? He was supposed to leave this morning."

"Well, something happened to change his mind. Ha!" Marcella said and chased after the ball.

"Marcella Paxton, you come back here. What is going on? You haven't encouraged that girl to go off with him—alone?"

"I have."

"I suppose you call it wise!"

"That would depend on the outcome, but I think it most probably was wise. He will bring her to no harm, certainly, and anything else, I believe, she would find most agreeable."

Charlotte gasped. "You never change! After all that has happened to you—and now you are leading a perfectly innocent child along the very same primrose path you followed. Shame! God will punish you for your wickedness."

Marcella stopped long enough to look up at her sister and grimace. "You should have become a preacher, Charlotte. Fire and brimstone absolutely erupt from you."

"If you won't look after her welfare and good name, if you care nothing whatever for decency, I suppose as usual I shall have to see to it." She began walking toward the house. Marcella's voice, booming behind her, stopped her forward progress.

"You'll do nothing of the kind! Go inside and tend to your own son's wedding. We'll never get him married if you don't begin to mind your own business. Kathleen is my keeper, not yours, and I pay her, not you. Now scat, Charlotte, or I'll show you how well I can aim these croquet balls. Scat!" She hissed and threw up her arms.

Charlotte jumped back a pace and stood there, lips pursed tight. "I don't know what has come over you, Marcella Paxton! And this time you are playing with an innocent young girl's life. Nicholas is no better than his father. He'll use her just as Brad used you, and he'll take a wife just like Annette. Someone with background and family—"

"Is that why Martin is marrying Rhea—family and all that?" Marcella interrupted, a twinkle in her eye.

"Yes, it is, you know that. Martin has a position to think of."

"Then you had better inform him that Rhea's father was a good-for-nothing carpetbagger who walked his way back North after he got in trouble in the South. Last I heard, he had gone west. Gold-rush fever, about twenty years too late."

"I don't think you have a nice bone in you!" This time Charlotte was determined to get back to the house.

"Don't forget to tell Gert to come out here to play this game with me," Marcella called and slammed into the croquet ball, sending a chunk of grass up into the air. "I just don't seem to have the knack."

Chapter Thirty-one

The day before the wedding, the entire house hummed with activity. Marcella and Kathleen watched with pleasure as the flowers and potted plants were placed in every room, from the top of the house to the front hall. They had taken the conservatory as their own project, and these decorations represented many hours of their work.

For the most part, their presence on the main floor of the house during the final wedding preparations had been barely tolerated by Charlotte. But Kathleen had insisted that they participate—at least to this extent—in the wedding arrangements. Marcella had complied enthusiastically.

Kathleen and Marcella joined Charlotte, Martin, and Rhea—who had come for the afternoon—for lunch. Sitting down, Marcella looked directly at Charlotte and announced that she would be delighted to attend the wedding ceremony and reception.

Charlotte exchanged glances with Martin, who was obviously shocked by Marcella's pronouncement. Flushing in embarrassment, Charlotte looked back at her sister. "I thought it was all decided, Marcella. After what happened the night of the engagement party, I can scarcely believe you wish to see those same people again."

Pulling her chair up, Marcella replied, calmly and quietly, that she would attend the wedding or the house would be closed. "And don't think for a minute, Charlotte, Martin, and you as well, Rhea, that I won't do it. I am not dead yet, so if you want to spend my money, you'll have to suffer my watching it be spent."

"Aunt Marcella"—Martin's voice was patronizing—"what is all of this? No one has said anything that you need defend youself against. We hesitated to ask you to be present, that is all. You've had one very bad experience lately, and there will be a great many people here. All of us are aware and sympathetic to your sensitivity to being seen in public. But if you have really recovered from that aversion, by all means, we will be delighted to see you at the wedding. You know that."

Marcella touched the side of her face. "Do you really think people would stare?"

"No, of course not," he said smoothly. "Well, perhaps a few, but what would they matter?"

"Then you think, for my own peace of mind, that I would be better off not being seen."

"Need you ask?" Charlotte said.

"I asked Martin," Marcella said, returning her attention to her nephew.

Martin's face was very serious, as though he were struggling to find just the right words.

Kathleen put her napkin down. "Why are you trying to frighten her, Martin?" she snapped. "You are doing it deliberately, and it is cruel."

Marcella bumped her fork off the table, bent down to retrieve it, and gave her niece a pinch on the thigh as she came up.

"He is trying to look after my welfare," she hissed at Kathleen.

Martin smiled triumphantly. "I am, indeed. And before you call me cruel, think of what you yourself are doing. You seem perfectly willing to expose her to the eyes of the curious. Either you don't know or have forgotten that Aunt Marcella was involved in quite a notorious scandal some years ago—"

"How long will it be," Kathleen fairly shouted, "before you stop reminding her constantly of what happened?"

Rhea coughed discreetly and dabbed at her mough with her napkin. "You know nothing of this, Kathleen. Martin happens to be telling the truth." She sounded like a teacher speaking to a recalcitrant child. "If anything, he has minimized things. Public opinion regarding the Dalton affair was high, and remained so. Your aunt was not the one to whom their sympathy was given. She was merely the fallen woman, while Bradford Dalton became a sort of romanticized martyr." Rhea picked up her fork and began eating again.

Kathleen remained silent, staring at Rhea. "How long," she asked finally, "do you suggest Aunt Marcella hide herself away?"

Rhea's mouth turned down at the corners. "When one suggests you use a bit of common sense, Kathleen, one does not mean you need dramatize the entire situation. Aunt Marcella is not in a prison. She may do as she wishes. I suggest discretion. Nothing more."

"I wonder," Kathleen muttered.

Martin shifted uneasily in his seat. "Let's not bicker. Aunt Marcella, do whatever you wish about coming to the wedding. Rhea and I will be pleased to have you if you choose to come."

Rhea looked up at Marcella. "You know how grateful Martin and I are for all you have done for us, and will be doing. It is only you we are thinking of. After all, it isn't as if I am a stranger any longer. By this time tomorrow, I will be a part of this family, too. Another niece."

Marcella made no comment but turned to Kathleen and asked her to take her back to her room. Marcella smiled wanly at Martin and Rhea and leaned heavily on Kathleen's arm as they went out.

By the time Kathleen and Marcella had reached the staircase, well out of sight and earshot of the others, Marcella was laughing.

"Why, you aren't upset at all!" Kathleen was genuinely astonished. "What, may I ask, was that pinch for?"

Marcella started up the stairs. "I wanted to hear what they were going to say, and you, my dear, were all primed to do battle for me. Isn't it comforting how they both think of my welfare?"

"You are awful. You led them on."

"If they had a grain of sense between them, they would know better than to be so obvious. But I have a few surprises for them."

"I am beginning to understand what Aunt Charlotte means when she says she can sense you're up to something."

"I'll tell you when I tell the others. You'll approve, I think."

"You're not going to tell me now?"

"No."

"I don't suppose my coaxing would change your mind."

"Not in the least."

Kathleen stopped at the top of the stairs. "Well, if you think I am going to beg, you will be disappointed. I won't. So, are you going to the wedding? Or did you let them talk you out of it?"

"Of course I am going," Marcella laughed. "Come along, and we'll see what I can wear that will make me look less awful than usual. If I wore a high-necked dress, perhaps with a ruff of lace at the throat? What do you think?"

"It sounds very nice."

"Good. We'll need to do some altering, and I think I have some very nice lace we can add to a mauve-colored gown I have."

The rest of the afternoon was spent outfitting Marcella. By evening both were tired but pleased with their efforts. Marcella was looking forward to going downstairs the following morning.

"It will be like a trial run, Kathleen. Martin was right when he said I am sensitive to people looking at me. But some people are born ugly. I suppose there must be a point at which you learn to use other qualities. Now we shall find out if I can begin again."

When Marcella appeared in Kathleen's doorway early the following day, dressed in her remade gown, she looked like a new woman. And as they walked down the stairs, she exuded a kind of vibrant dignity that made up for her lost fairness of face.

She had not corrected all of her habits of dependency, but she had made significant headway, Kathleen decided. For one thing, Marcella had attacked the problem of her drinking with determination and now had it within bounds of moderation as long as she was not upset or depressed. Her laudanum was used only to aid her on sleepless nights and to relieve the headaches that continued to plague her. But Marcella Paxton was no longer a woman resigned to wasting away in the blur of alcohol and drugs.

The entire afternoon of the wedding day was a tribute to Marcella's new beginning. Not an unkind word was spoken to her, and she had no lack of admirers. Perhaps they stood at her side for different reasons than they once had, but nonetheless they were there, and they listened and watched as she spoke about her new causes.

By the time she was ready to return to her room for a rest, Marcella was tired and showing the strain, but she was also happy and radiant, buoyed up by her success. She had taken particular delight in walking up to Rhea and Martin after the ceremony and congratulating them. She had nearly been regal, Kathleen thought.

Rhea and Martin left on their wedding trip to New Orleans that evening, and Scarborough House was emptied of its guests. Nicholas arrived home very late the night of the wedding.

He was at the breakfast table the following morning when Kathleen came down.

She ran to him. "When did you get back?"

"Last night. Why weren't you there when I came home?"

"But I didn't know—"

"That is no excuse." He grinned. "Are you busy this morning?"

"Yes, and you'll never guess why!"

"I give up."

"Far too easily. Aunt Marcella is going into the city. Alone! She won't hear of anyone's accompanying her. She says this is her great test, and she will do it herself or not at all. So I am to help her get ready this morning."

"I wonder what it is she wants to do in the city."

"I haven't the slightest idea. It might be something to do with this women's club she has joined. She is very excited about that, and she has talked about little else. Even yesterday at the wedding, everyone else was talking about the bride and groom. Aunt Marcella was going on about reform and the slums."

She pulled out a chair and sat down. "Nicholas, you will not believe what a difference there is in her. Even in the few days you have been gone. She has had me sewing and remaking her clothes. Perhaps it is my imagination, or maybe I am used to her now, but the scars don't seem half so noticeable. I think she is going to be perfectly well again, Nicholas. I really do."

"I wonder what she is up to."

Kathleen glanced at the door, then she looked back at him. "So do I. She has as much as told me she has something in mind, but I can't get her to tell me what it is. She acts very mysterious and then tells me I will learn of it when the others do."

He wiped his mouth with his napkin and looked toward the window. "It is going to rain later. Try not to be too long with Marcella."

"You are a pessimist. It is not a bad day today."

"I am never wrong about these things. The wind can come up in this valley and change the entire outlook in minutes."

"All right. I'll hurry as much as I can, but I do have to wait until she is ready to go. This is a big day for her, and I do so want it to go well."

By late morning Marcella was ready to go. She had found a small carpetbag in the attic, which she had filled with papers—articles she had written and the mysterious plans she had talked of.

Dressed in a forest-green traveling suit, Marcella was an arresting figure. She smiled happily at Kathleen as she prepared to go out the front door to the waiting carriage. She stood at the top of the porch steps and took a deep breath, looking around at the profusion of green grass and trees. She turned back for a moment and faced her niece.

"It is so good not to be afraid anymore."

Kathleen waited on the porch until her carriage was no longer in sight, and then went in search of Nicholas. She went to the study first and found it empty. Nicholas was nowhere to be found. She looked everywhere and asked both Gert and Carlisle. No one knew where he was.

She went outside and began to walk toward the path to the willow pond. As she neared the end of the allee, she realized how disappointed she would be if he were not there.

She walked slowly under the shelter of the trees, hesitant and yet consumed with anticipation. When she came into the clearing, she scanned the pond, the bridge, and the summerhouse. No one. She felt miserably disappointed.

She walked around the perimeter of the enclosure, concentrating on the ground at her feet. The first sounds of thunder rumbled from the distant mountains, and the changing wind rippled the smooth surface of the pond. Kathleen looked up to the sky; it was as if the entire coloring of the world were changing suddenly.

The breeze grew stronger and became a wind beating at her skirts and brushing color into her cheeks. The first drops of rain spattered on her upturned face. She smiled and threw her arms out wide. Thunder rolled and rumbled as the storm moved closer. The sky, eerie with its muted colors of storm and sun mixed, brightened with flashes of distant lightning.

She spun around, looking up into the sky, blinking away raindrops. Losing her balance, she reached out to steady herself and looked straight ahead. Nicholas stood just to her right in the shelter of the trees and heavy underbrush.

"You'll be soaked to the skin," he said. Kathleen thought his voice sounded very strange—a bit too detached for Nicholas. "You had better go into the summerhouse. It won't keep you dry, but it will be of some help."

He stepped into the clearing, took her by the hand, and began to run toward the footbridge and the summerhouse beyond. "You'll have to stay here now. The storm will be on us before you are halfway to the house."

"Nicholas, I haven't said anything about going back to the house."

"You can't," he said, looking out at the pond. "You'll have to wait for the storm to pass."

Kathleen sighed. "All right, Nicholas. I'll wait for the storm to pass. Would you tell me, please, why you were not at the house when I came down to see you? You told me to be there after Marcella left. Why weren't you there?"

"I didn't think you were coming," he snapped. "You said you'd be there early."

"I said I would try. You knew I would be there as soon as I could be. Why didn't you wait?"

"I didn't feel like it." He turned to look at her where she stood just inside the entry to the shelter. "You can't stand there. It is going to pour any minute."

"You haven't answered me, Nicholas. If you won't apologize, give me an answer."

"I wanted to see what you would do and where you would go. Does that satisfy you?" he grumbled. He took her to the swing and waited until she sat down. Then he walked back out into the pouring rain and stood on the far side of the bridge, looking back at her.

"You aren't leaving, are you?"

He leaned down to rest his elbows on the railing of the bridge. "I just wanted to look at you sitting there."

"I don't know what has come over you. You've lost your mind. Come in here. You are getting all wet!"

"I have been wet before, but I have never seen you here like this before."

"If you don't come in here out of the rain, I shall have to come out there. We shall both catch cold. Then I would feel awful."

Nicholas chuckled. "I probably would, too—at least for a few days. But you needn't worry. I never catch colds or chills."

"Please come in."

In four long strides he crossed the bridge. In another, he was standing before her, his clothing wet and clinging to him. Little rivulets of water streamed from his legs onto the floor. He felt like laughing, like smiling and laughing aloud.

Kathleen's hair was heavy with moisture and coming loose. He took one pin that had worked its way loose and put it on the small table, then he took out the others one by one and watched the masses of silky black hair tumble down over her shoulders. He touched her hair, letting it run across his long, slender fingers and slip off the edge of his hand. He put both of his hands deep into it, looking at it as though he had never seen a woman's hair before. Slowly his hands moved down her back and he held her against him.

"Did you ever come here when I was gone?"

"Never. Only when you were here."

He looked out to the pond as the rain spattered on its surface. "It won't last much longer," he said wistfully. "The Heer is not favoring me."

"Who is the Heer. *What* is the Heer?"

"Ah—the Heer! The Heer of Dunderberg, and all of his little imps control the storms and winds hereabouts."

"Oh Nicholas, you are such a fool." She laughed. "Who told you that story? Your grandfather?"

"Who else? Too bad his stories weren't true. I could use a friendly Heer to keep the rain coming for a time. But there is no Heer. The rain will end and you will go back to the house too soon," he said and held her close.

In fact the storm passed as quickly as it had come, leaving the deep grass vividly green and the air smelling of dew and flowers. Reluctantly, Nicholas picked up the hairpins from the table and handed them to her one by one as she set about refastening her hair.

He sighed and looked out across the clearing. "I don't want to leave. It is so quiet and peaceful here. Grandfather never allowed anyone to come here when Grandmother was alive, except the two of them. He was a smart man."

"I think your grandmother was a very lucky woman." She looked over at him. His face was flushed, and his eyes bright. "Nicholas, you don't look well. Are you all right?"

"I am fine. A little chilly."

"I do believe you have just caught the chill you claim never to catch. We had better go back to the house immediately."

They ran nearly all the way back to the house, but by the time they got there, he was shivering. At dinner, between forkfuls of food and the few comments he made, he sneezed.

The following morning he did not appear for breakfast. Kathleen went to the kitchen to prepare a tray for him, including a posset for his cold. As she left the kitchen, Gert warned Kathleen that Nicholas had a nasty mood to match his cold.

"What are you doing in here?" he asked through his handkerchief as she entered the room, balancing the tray and kicking the door closed behind her. "I don't want anything to eat. I'm not hungry, and I'll be damned if you're going to pour that steaming bilge down me."

"If you want to be damned, Mr. Dalton, so be it. But drink all of this as quickly as you can. It will soothe you and help with your fever. Minerva always gave this to me when I had a cold, and it works very well." She rested the tray on his lap and put the hot cup in his hand.

He looked over the lip of the cup. "What's all that stuff in there?" he asked, poking at a piece of cinnamon.

"Cloves, cinnamon, carraway, balm, and several other things. Drink it now, please."

He sneezed, nearly overturning the tray and its contents. "I don't want it," he gasped through the handkerchief.

With exaggerated patience, she took the tray from his lap and went into the bathing room, returning with a wet cloth.

"What are you doing now? Get out of here. I don't want to be taken care of. Leave me alone."

"Do you really want to be left alone?"

"Yes," he replied and leaned back on the pillows so she could wash his face. His forehead was hot, and his eyes more beautiful than ever in the shining brilliance the fever lent them. When she finished, she again left him momentarily.

"What do you think you are going to do with that?" he asked when she returned, carrying fresh linen.

"Sit up and drink the posset, or it will no longer be hot enough, and I shall have to go downstairs and reheat it."

She took the pillows from behind him as soon as he leaned forward to obey her, stripped them of the damp cases, and put clean ones on. Then she pulled out a fresh nightshirt.

"Now, pull the old shirt over your head, and we can slip this one down." Seeing the look on his face, she began to laugh. "I would never have suspected you of such modesty, Nicholas."

"Nor I you of such immodesty! I suppose this is the way you bullied Marcella," he muttered, struggling with the exchange of nightshirts.

"I am far worse with Aunt Marcella."

"Some people prefer to be left alone in their misery, not to be pestered by your well-intentioned ministrations."

"I have no doubt, but then I don't provide many with them. Only a select and special few," she said cheerily.

He leaned back on the pillow and glared at her. "Anyone in this house who was ill would receive your attention. Who they happened to be would make no difference to you at all. Everyone wants a hold on someone else. This is your way." Kathleen was startled by the cruelty of his words. "What will you want from me in return for your kindness? Flowers? Perhaps a small trinket?"

"I want nothing from you, Nicholas Dalton. Nothing."

"I don't believe you."

"Believe what you please. That is all you would believe, in any case. You suffer from the worst sort of conceit! If one is to exercise power over another to extract an attachment, the object to be gained must be worth the effort. What gives you the idea you are worth that much to me?"

"You came to the pond looking for me. You came in here with your little bag of cure-alls."

"I should have let you get good and hungry before I came in here, you ungrateful clod! And I will before I come again!"

"You are going to come back?"

"Of course I am. Whatever you think I want from you, I will not let you lie up here and be neglected. You were right. I would do it for anyone. Anyone at all."

He began to eat what she had placed on the tray. Before long, he had devoured every scrap of food and drunk the rest of the posset right down to the dregs. She took the tray without saying anything and walked to the door of his room.

"Miss Kat!"

"Yes?"

He picked up the washcloth she had left at the side of the bed. "My head is awfully hot."

"Is it, now? You can suddenly bear my touch, can you?"

He grinned. "I think I am coming to like your bag of cure-alls. You wouldn't really do all this for just anyone, would you?" He reached out as she came near and took her hand. She bent down and kissed his forehead.

"Not exactly this."

"You'll catch my cold," he said softly, stroking her hair. He began to pull out the pins. "I don't like your hair up. It's prettier when it is down."

"You'd have me running about the house with my hair flying like a Gypsy's."

"Kat," he whispered, "will you always put up with me?"

284

She pulled away from him. "What a question! Shall I answer 'No' and have you angry with me again? Or shall I answer 'Yes' and have you do your worst to prove me truthless? You shall have to find out for yourself." She began to pin her hair up again.

"Leave it down. Just for a time."

"Don't be ridiculous. I have work to do."

"Stay awhile. Kiss me again."

"I'll catch your cold."

"You see, I knew you wanted something from me. Women always want something."

"How fortunate you are to have found one who wants something as inexpensive as the sniffles." She wiped his face gently with the cloth. He took it from her hand and dropped it into his water jug; then he pulled her toward him until she rested on his chest. "Lie down beside me," he whispered softly, kissing her ear. "I don't need a nurse, Kathleen."

"When you love me enough to trust me with yourself, Nicholas, I'll lie down beside you."

"You're extracting payment again."

"I'll not settle for a part of the whole—a kiss today, a night with you tomorrow, a day's loneliness, a stolen embrace, a moment wondering, when you have gone, if you shall ever return, and when you do, wondering why you are really there. You were right about me. I do want something, and I'll not take less."

"This time, I'd rather have you prove me wrong."

"If you really feel that way, then I am wrong."

He said nothing but lay still.

"Are you angry?" she asked.

"No."

"What, then?"

"I was thinking."

"About what?"

"What it would be like being married to you—on your terms. You ask a great deal, and at the moment it all seems quite reasonable. I think my fever must be going up."

"It must be. You would never think these thoughts otherwise." She buried her face in his chest.

Nicholas remembered another night. They had gone to the willow pond, and he had begun to make love to Kathleen. She had lain back in his arms and allowed him to unfasten the bodice of her dress.

All of a sudden, it had all seemed to overwhelm her, and she had sat up and cried out, "Nicholas, I can't." She had pulled the dress closed. "I can't do this. You are tearing me apart. I love you, but I can't give myself to you in bits and pieces."

"I want you," he had said.

"Not as I mean."

"No one loves like that, Kathleen. No one. It is a dream, a fairy tale, no more real than the mythical Heer of Dunderburg."

"It must be real. It has to be."

"You're cold and shivering," he had said, pulling his jacket tight around her shoulders. He had wondered why he stayed there with her, why he came back to her over and over again when it was so clear to him that he could never be what she wanted.

She had wept silently by his side that night, while he had stared out into the darkness, not wanting to give in and look at her. He had thought about the night and the seasons and love, and how alike they were, how transitory.

He had looked down at her then and had said softly, "If it were only marriage you wanted, Kat, I'd give you that gladly. But that isn't what you want, is it?"

"No!" she had said, blowing her nose violently. "I would not even think of marrying you now. I don't want what you have or what you choose to give me. I want you."

They had never mentioned that night, that conversation, again, for there was nothing more to say about it.

As he lay in bed now, with his cold, he looked at her again, thinking of what had happened that night. He touched her hair and tangled his hands in it.

"I've been meaning to tell you something," he said. "I have met the Heer of Dunderburg. Not only does he exist, but he wears a sugarloaf hat and Dutch trousers just as reported. It seems all manner of things are true that I never suspected."

Chapter Thirty-two

The remainder of the month during which Rhea and Martin were gone made a great, and for the most part, happy difference in those left in Scarborough House, especially in Nicholas. The study that he had kept entirely to himself became a place where they all gathered. Soon Charlotte was more a part of their family and their lives than she had ever been. Together, she and Nicholas functioned as the best of managers of a large house.

Closets were aired, seldom-used silver was polished, accounts that had been neglected were examined and straightened out. Marcella's room was redecorated.

Nicholas himself, seemingly awakened from a long sleep, became interested in the coming harvest of the home farm and the concerns of the smaller farms around him. He seemed to be everywhere, generally in a good and expansive humor, always in a hurry.

"Aren't you ready yet?" he asked cheerfully one morning as he burst in on Kathleen, Charlotte, and Marcella.

Marcella put down the newspaper she had been reading to the others. "What are we to be ready for? Where are we going? Has something been planned that I know nothing about?"

"I have to go into the city this afternoon. I thought perhaps you ladies would like to join me. We'll take the steamboat in and then have dinner—perhaps at Delmonico's, if that suits you."

"And we could shop while you are busy. Oh, that would be nice." Marcella looked over at Kathleen. "I want to take you to Demorest's while we are there. She does have the most beautiful styles. She does them herself."

Kathleen stood up to go upstairs and get ready. "Aunt Charlotte, you have said nothing. In fact you have been very quiet all morning."

Charlotte looked down at her hands. "I don't think I'll go. I have some things I want to tend to. You two go and have a good time."

"Charlotte, you are lying through your teeth," Marcella scolded, cheerfully. "You haven't a thing to do all afternoon. Kathleen's right, you have been mooning all morning long. What is it?" She reached over and picked up a letter from Charlotte's lap. "It is this, isn't it? Must be bad news. Will you give me permission to read it, or must I be rude and read it anyway?" Not waiting for a reply, she began to open the letter. "Oh, it is from Martin. Why, then, the long face? You should be pleased."

"I am. He and Rhea seem to be having a good time, and they plan to come north soon. They will be staying an extra week in New York City before returning to Scarborough."

"Well?"

Charlotte glanced at Nicholas, lounging in the doorway. "If you prefer to talk without my presence," he said, "I can wait for you in the study. I have some papers to prepare, in any case."

Charlotte sighed. "You may as well hear it, too, Nicholas. You'll all know soon enough. He is gambling again, having the time of his life, he says."

"He has always been a gambler," Marcella observed. "That is nothing new. Why should it upset you now?"

"After all those promises he made to me! Marcella, he swore he'd never do it again, and here he is—on his honeymoon! He'll be in trouble again. Before he knows it, everything will be just as it was before. It frightens me. Martin told me those horrible people he had gotten involved with had actually threatened him."

Nicholas walked to Charlotte's chair and put his hand on her shoulder. "Perhaps it isn't as bad as it seems, Charlotte. Apparently he isn't losing. If he were, he wouldn't claim to be having the time of his life."

"You do make a great fuss about things, Charlotte. You always have," Marcella added. "In any event, you cannot do a thing about it today, so you might as well come along with us. We'll all buy something new and feel much better for it."

Nicholas pulled his watch from his pocket. "You'd better hurry, then, or none of us will get anything done. Can you be ready to leave in half an hour?"

"Half an hour!" Marcella shrieked.

"We can be ready," Kathleen grinned. "Aunt Charlotte, too."

The trip to the city was a huge success. Nicholas, with admirable foresight, hired a man and his cart to follow them and carry their purchases. They went through Stewart's and Demorest's, laughing and buying anything that caught their fancy. To all intents and purposes, Marcella seemed to have forgotten the financial worries she had mentioned to Kathleen. It was quite a shopping trip.

"I haven't done this for ages!" Marcella exclaimed, picking up one pair of gloves after another at the counter. She turned a pair of English five-button thread gloves over and over. "These thread gloves are supposed to take the place of kid, but I wouldn't feel properly dressed without my kid gloves. They do dye them so nicely to match any gown, though. Look at these, Charlotte. What do you think of them?"

"Marcella, how would I know? I have never been as conscious of these things as you have been. They both look elegant to me."

"Perhaps we should get a pair of each. With these new fashions, one never knows how long they will last. But kid, kid will always be right."

Marcella bought yards of Aberdeen woolsey and an equal amount of silk.

"Marcella, why must we buy so much of one color?" Charlotte complained, infected at last with her sister's shopping bug. "We'll all look like duplicates of one another. Shall we not take more variety and less quantity?" Marcella agreed and went off to look at fichus.

She bought two—one trimmed with a puff and lace around the neck, the other in velvet, blue plaid, and satin, high at the neck, with a plaiting of lace, and finished with a bow. She thought momentarily of days gone by, when she would have avoided high necks and camouflaging laces, and then took her two fichus and came back to where Charlotte was still looking through the yard goods.

Kathleen, a little way off from her two aunts, was looking at a bolt of primrose silk, trying to figure out if she could afford to buy it for herself.

Marcella hurried over to her side. "Is that what you prefer, dear? It is lovely, but have you seen the blue that Charlotte unearthed over here? It was just made for you!"

Kathleen protested, and Marcella bought.

They finally went out of the store happy, leaving in their wake an exhausted salesclerk and considerable stock to be put away. The man with the cart looked on aghast as the salesclerk came out of the store and loaded his cart with bundles.

He smiled and shook his head. "Where to next, ma'am?"

Charlotte sighed. "Let's go somewhere and sit down. I am exhausted."

"Don't you want to look in Tiffany's windows?"

"Marcella! It is no wonder we have had hard times. While you were ill, half of the national income disappeared. We can afford to spend no more."

"You spend more than I. And anyway, I only want to look."

"You have never just looked, and this won't be a first time," Charlotte muttered. "We can at least take a cab."

"But Kathleen has never ridden on a Red Bird."

"What is that?" Kathleen asked.

Marcella pointed to a great yellow horse-drawn bus. "It is like that one, except that it is red."

"If Aunt Charlotte is tired, what does it matter how we ride? Why don't we just take the first vehicle we can?"

"I've always been partial to Red Birds," Marcella said wistfully, then told the man to meet them at Tiffany's. She hurried to the edge of the street and hailed a taxi. A carriage pulled through the congested street and they boarded it.

That evening, they had a lovely dinner. Nicholas listened patiently as Marcella and Charlotte discussed and squabbled over the things they had bought that afternoon.

By the time they boarded the steamship and settled themselves comfortably in the lounge, Charlotte's head was nodding. Marcella, sitting beside her, nudged her in the ribs each time someone passed by. Kathleen and Nicholas watched the two older women, laughing from time to time.

Kathleen poked Nicholas and nodded toward Marcella "She is a bundle of energy, isn't she? No wonder Aunt Charlotte is exhausted. Nicholas, you cannot imagine all the places we went. Most of the time we had to walk, because Aunt Marcella wanted to breathe air—good city air with soot in it, she said—and she had to look at each of the new buildings going up. She told us about all the old houses and buildings that had been torn down.

"Poor Aunt Charlotte. It must seem strange to her to be the one who is tired and sleepy. For so long it has been Aunt Marcella who could do nothing."

Kathleen, Charlotte, and Marcella spent the next few days sorting out all they had bought, while Nicholas was out of the house most of the time, preparing for haymaking.

"I just don't remember when I had so much fun!" Marcella exclaimed from time to time, plunging into yet another package. "It is quite like opening Christmas gifts. We must have the dressmaker here this very week. In spite of all the new ready-made stuff, I still prefer the dressmaker. I must be old-fashioned."

Kathleen looked up from a stack of dress patterns. "We could make some of these ourselves, Aunt Marcella."

"Don't be ridiculous. I could never manage that sewing machine. I only bought it because Madame Demorest said women should become more useful. Dear heaven, I'd have my bodice attached to my hemline before I knew it."

"Madame Demorest did not encourage women to simply buy sewing machines," Kathleen said sweetly. "She said women should make their own clothes. What would she think if she knew what you had done with your sewing machine?"

Marcella sighed. "Well, then, ask Nicholas to bring it back down from the attic. We might try a few, but only the simplest. If truth be known, I have a horror of that machine. It goes so fast with that needle."

"We shall each do a part," Kathleen chuckled. "You cut the patterns, Aunt Charlotte will do the fitting, and I shall do the sewing."

During the next two weeks, Kathleen and Marcella were caught up in a frenzy of sewing projects. Only Charlotte seemed preoccupied, uncomfortably aware of how quickly the time was passing.

She had received several letters from Martin. The first came from New Orleans. Martin was in high spirits—the letter was long and informative. The other two letters came from New York. In the last one, he had not asked her to send him money or even hinted that his luck was changing, but she knew it would.

She had not answered that letter; she hadn't known what to say, how to tell him how disappointed in him she was. He would only have accused her of nagging and irritating him. So she had said nothing.

There was a time she would have been pleased to get his letters, would have carried them with her, telling friends about her son and his wedding trip. Now she looked at the letters, written in Martin's bold, childish scrawl, and sensed that underneath the words, Martin took her for a naive fool who was blind to his faults. He would never listen to her. For him she functioned only as an anchor to which he could cling when things went wrong.

The world had played a nasty trick on her, she thought. During Martin's absence, Scarborough House seemed to hum with activity. She watched Nicholas busy and happy, planning his harvest and glorying in his love for Kathleen.

There had been a time when Charlotte had compared herself to Nicholas. Both of them, she had thought, had lived their lives being needed by other people and yet not really being wanted. Now, as she stood back on the sidelines, she watched him begin to come alive with Kathleen. In a strange way, she believed she was seeing what she herself might have been if anyone had ever cared that much about her.

She heard them squabbling and fighting; she heard them laugh and mock one another when the storm had passed. She heard them apologize for their anger and make up, first teasing and then loving. She had seen them in moments when they thought they were alone—the look in Nicholas's eyes, his strong workman's hands suddenly tender as he held Kathleen.

There had never been any doubt in Charlotte's mind that Kathleen was in love. It was Nicholas she marveled at. She had never really liked him. He had always seemed a shell of a man, competent and bright, but an actor for all that. She had thought him far too much like her to have liked him. But then, did she even know what she was really like? And dear God, was there anyone on earth who cared?

As Charlotte grew quieter and more introspective, Marcella began to grow concerned about her moodiness.

"You are brooding again!" she teased. Charlotte turned away quickly. Immediately Marcella was sympathetic. "I am sorry, dear. You really are worried about something. What is it, Charlotte?"

"Everything I do seems to be worthless," she sniffed.

"That isn't so. I wouldn't be alive today if it weren't for you. I would never have recovered without you, and now look what I have done! You're tired and worn out, and it is all my fault."

"It isn't your fault. Besides, it was Kathleen who got you back on your feet. All I did was drive you to drink and make you want to hide yourself. I meant well, but I was—"

Marcella would not listen to her sister's objections. "You are the one who brought Kathleen to me, as well. Oh, Charlotte, don't look back to those awful times. Look ahead. Martin is married, and he and his wife will be living right here with you. And look at Kathleen and Nicholas. It wouldn't surprise me in the least if we had another wedding at Scarborough before long. Why, Charlotte, you might well be a grandmother soon!"

Charlotte smiled a little. "I do hope they wait a bit," she whimpered. "I am still tired from the engagement party and Martin's wedding."

"Oh, but this time I can help. In fact you couldn't keep me from it. But you still have not told me what is worrying you."

Charlotte pointed to her letter. "It's Martin. Isn't it always? I can't help him, and Rhea is not the kind of woman who will. I don't think she knows how. My son is buying his wife anything she wants. And what is he using to pay for it?"

"You haven't given him any more money, have you?"

"I haven't got it. He is gambling again, and I gather he is winning at the moment. But you know as well as I do that that won't last for long. In his last two letters, he hasn't been very specific, and he hasn't asked for anything, but—I don't know, Marcella. I just don't know what to think anymore."

Later that evening Marcella went to the study to see Nicholas.

"Charlotte doesn't know this," she said, "and I don't want her to, but I received this from Martin today." She handed Nicholas a note. "He says he needs money, and asks me for a loan. Is there any way you can find out just what is happening with him, Nick?"

Nicholas frowned. "I think I can. I am familiar with a few men who would know who owes what to whom."

"I am reluctant to give him another penny, but Charlotte is very concerned about him, and she is feeling very low at the moment. If Martin is in deep trouble, as Charlotte seems to think, then I will help him, if only for her sake. But I hope there is still time to prevent it."

"I see. Well, I have been thinking up excuses as to why I need not make a trip on business. You've provided me with a good reason to go. I'll be off to Albany for a couple of days, and then I'll go into New York, tend to things there, and find out about Martin at the same time. When are he and Rhea coming back?"

"The end of the week. Friday, I think Charlotte said."

291

"If I leave here on Thursday, I can be back by the following Tuesday. Would that suit you?"

"That would be fine. Why don't you and Kathleen go somewhere tomorrow? I don't need her bustling about me like a mother hen anymore, and your hay will wait a day for you. Charlotte and I can take care of one another for once. I may even have another go at trying to get her to play croquet." Nicholas winced. "Out back, near the barn."

Nicholas spent the following day with Kathleen. They went far up the river on horseback, with no particular destination in mind. Both of them loved to wander and enjoy the scenery and the rock formations they passed from time to time. They picnicked in a grassy field belonging to a farmer Nicholas knew.

If Nicholas occasionally questioned the permanency of love, he no longer had any doubts about Kathleen. Whatever lay in the future, he knew he didn't want to spend it without her. That day he asked Kathleen to marry him, and she accepted. They decided to be married at the beginning of the new year.

Four months seemed like an eternity to him, but she had told him she wanted a new year to begin in. How strange, he thought, that she should have chosen the dead of winter to look upon as a new start, when he had always thought of it as an ending. But somehow it seemed appropriate that she should change his thinking. So he would begin again in the wintertime, at the start of a new year, the year of his country's hundredth birthday.

The following day, when Nicholas had left for Albany, Kathleen hurried to Marcella's room to tell her of their plans to be married. Marcella, as Kathleen had expected, was delighted. After her burst of enthusiasm, however, Kathleen noticed that her aunt was not as animated as usual.

"Do you feel all right, Aunt Marcella? You look terribly pale."

Marcella sat down on the edge of her bed. "I think I have done a bit too much lately, that is all. Charlotte is right. We are getting old. I keep forgetting. Now, I don't want you to be upset or jump to conclusions, but I am going to take my medications for a time—just until I am well rested again."

"The laudanum?"

"I don't seem to be sleeping well. But don't you worry. I am going to be fit as a fiddle for your wedding. You and I will go to the city and find a wedding gown and dresses and whatever else you'll need. We'll have a good time before you become Mrs. Dalton."

"And not after?"

"Oh, then I expect you to be busy. I am looking forward to seeing Jo's and Brad's grandchildren. Do you know what that will mean to me? I have never loved two people more than those two, and now their children are marrying, and I am here to see their grandchildren. So don't you worry about me. I am just tired, and that is all."

"I believe you, but wouldn't it be better to call a doctor and have him see you?"

"He'd tell me what I already know, and so do you. I wouldn't listen to him, anyway." She smiled at Kathleen. "I need rest. I will get it and be on my way again. I haven't told you, but I am going to help Madame Demorest with her exhibit in Philadelphia for the Centennial celebration."

"You'll be leaving here?"

"For a time. I have never been to Philadelphia before. It is about time I did some traveling. I'd like to go to Ohio, too. You know I have never met your brothers and sisters?"

"They know about you, though. I write to them about everything that goes on here." She got up to leave. "I'd better let you rest," she said.

"Just a moment, Kathleen. I want to ask something of you, dear. A favor. . . ."

"Of course."

"Would you please not say anything to Charlotte or Martin about your wedding for a while? Not so much Charlotte—I'm sure she has guessed already—but still, I would rather have her just guessing it than actually knowing."

"But why, Aunt Marcella? I want to tell everyone."

"It would only be for a little while. I have something I must do, and if they know ahead of time, then it will look as though I have been scheming. It is important that both Charlotte and Martin understand what I am doing and accept it as the best I can do for everyone concerned. Can you do that for me?"

"You know I will. But aren't you even going to tell me what it is about?"

"After Martin and Rhea return, I shall tell all of you."

When Martin and Rhea arrived late that afternoon, Martin was in very bad spirits. He and Rhea had an argument in their bedroom less than half an hour after they returned, and Martin stormed out of the house immediately thereafter.

Charlotte went upstairs to see her daughter-in-law.

"What do you want!" Rhea snapped as Charlotte walked into the room. "What did you come here for?"

Charlotte looked at her helplessly. "I just wanted to be certain you were all right. Is there anything I can do to help?"

"A little late for that, isn't it? The damage has been done. I'm married now," Rhea spat back.

Charlotte listened to her berate Martin for several minutes and then went downstairs to the music room. Marcella sat at the piano, playing simple tunes—and not very well, at that—and Kathleen was puzzling over her embroidery.

"He has taken her jewels to pawn," Charlotte said without preamble. Neither of the other women said anything. Charlotte walked to one of the large chairs and sat down heavily. "I don't know what to do. They have been married only a matter of weeks, and already she is screaming that she won't remain with him. I can't talk to her. She is accusing him of marrying her under false pretenses, and who knows what all else. She called me a liar and a number of other things."

Marcella turned all the way around on the piano bench. "Perhaps there is something I can do."

Charlotte shook her head slowly. "No. No more money. It is of no use. Even I am ready to face the fact that with Martin, there will always be a next time. He isn't going to change. It is in his blood."

"But if he is in trouble—"

"It won't help. He promised me the last time that he would stop. Believe me, it isn't something I like to face. I didn't for a long time." She sighed pathetically. "But what am I going to do? He is still my son. I love him."

"Charlotte, you don't mean half of what you say."

"But I do mean it. Martin would have been far better off if I hadn't doted on him. He had such potential, Marcella. You remember him when he was growing up. Such a bright boy." She sniffled into her handkerchief. "I thought he would find himself as he grew older. I was so sure of it."

Marcella got up and walked over to her sister. "It isn't too late yet," she said, not really believing her own words. "Martin is still a young man. He has plenty of time to change."

"It is too late for me. I can do nothing for him." Charlotte leaned her head back against the chair and closed her eyes.

Chapter Thirty-three

With the return of the newly married Hendersons, much of the gaiety that had become a normal part of the household disappeared, to be replaced by loud, daily arguments between Rhea and Martin.

Rhea stayed in her room when she wasn't fighting with Martin or going out to a party. Occasionally she could badger Martin into escorting her, but more often than not, she went without her husband. Martin, looking tired and harried, was often gone from the house.

Kathleen worried about all of them, but particularly about Marcella and Nicholas. Her aunt, though not depressed or melancholy, seemed to be chronically tired and preoccupied. Kathleen worried, too, about Nicholas, who had come home several days after Rhea's and Martin's return.

The house was quiet when he arrived. Marcella and Charlotte were both in their rooms resting, and Rhea and Martin were out. Kathleen stood halfway down the dark hall, waiting for Carlisle to let Nicholas in.

But Nicholas used his own key, bumping his luggage against the frame of the door as he maneuvered to manage everything with his free hand. She smiled when he looked up and saw her.

"You missed me?"

"I missed you," he said, reaching out to her with his free hand. She led him down the hall to the study.

"Did you have a good trip?" she asked, closing the door behind them.

"No. I couldn't keep my mind on anything." He took her in his arms and kissed her. "January is so far off."

"Not so long. Welcome home, Nicholas."

He hugged her to him. "If you were just a bit smaller, I could put you in my coat pocket and take you everywhere with me."

"Oh, I would like that. I am so glad to have you back home. It has been miserable without you."

That night Nicholas went to Marcella's room.

"Welcome home, Nicholas. Sit down." She gestured toward a chair. "What did you find out about Martin? How bad is it?"

"I am not sure," he said thoughtfully. "He apparently owes quite a lot of money, and to several people rather than just one. That might help a bit. The one man who may mean trouble is John Munroe. From what I've been told, Martin is in debt to him now—and was once before—pretty heavily."

"Did you find out what he owes this man?"

"Not exactly. The talk is that he owes close to three thousand, but apparently he is gambling for larger stakes than usual. To win it back, I suppose."

Marcella walked to the window and looked out. "You were fortunate to have been gone these last few days."

"Why? What's been happening?"

"It's Martin and Rhea, Nick."

"Things are bad between them already?"

"I can't say how bad, but most definitely loud. I have never heard a woman who could shout like Rhea." She shook her head. "But enough of that. What of the rest of your trip? Are we still afloat, or are we in the same financial difficulty as the rest of the country?"

"We are doing reasonably well. We have a few weak spots, but there is no cause for alarm at the moment. I'll show you the reports I have brought back. I am sorry I wasn't able to get more information for you on Martin."

"I think you have provided me with enough. But let me ask you one final question. Do you think that Martin has time in which to pay his debts, or do you think he has reached the point at which they are demanding immediate payment?"

Nicholas thought for a moment. "Ordinarily, I'd say he has time. But because he owes this John Munroe and because this is not the first time, I am not sure. It depends on Munroe. Generally he is a pretty amiable fellow, from what I hear, but then he also has a reputation for using a delinquent customer as an example to others." He got up to leave. "I just don't know, Marcella. I can tell you this. If I were Martin, I'd make damned sure I paid that particular debt back fast. I wouldn't gamble on John Munroe's charity."

During the next few days, both Marcella and Nicholas were very busy.

Nicholas began to reorganize the haymaking. When his grandfather was alive, the haymakers had all gathered at Scarborough for an annual autumn party after their work was complete. But since Rhea's and Martin's return, Nicholas had changed his mind and was now busy convincing a neighborhood group of farmers that they should combine their efforts and have one large group to harvest all their fields and a party for everyone afterward at the church instead of at Scarborough House.

Marcella went to the city several times. She said her trips concerned Sorosis, but Kathleen doubted that. She continued to worry about Marcella. Her aunt still looked pale, and she tired far too easily. Martin was seldom at home, and when he was, he was gloomy and uncommunicative. Kathleen found herself with a great deal of time on her hands and no one with whom she could share it.

As far as Kathleen was concerned, the situation at Scarborough House was totally unsatisfactory and promised to get much worse. Come January, she and Nicholas would be married, and though she had kept her promise to Marcella not to say anything about their plans until Marcella had made her still-mysterious announcement, she was becoming more and more impatient.

Obviously, both Nicholas and Martin could not run the place. One would eventually have to go. As usual, it all came back to Marcella. She would have to make up her mind once and for all as to what she intended to do with the house. On several occasions Kathleen had wondered if this was what Marcella was being so mysterious about. So far, Marcella had done nothing about telling everyone.

At one point, Kathleen tried to befriend Rhea. One afternoon, when Kathleen was on her way outside, she saw Rhea sitting alone in the parlor.

"Would you like to come for a walk with me?" she asked. Rhea shrugged but got up and walked with Kathleen out of the house. It was near the end of autumn, but still warm, and the leaves were brilliantly colored. Kathleen glanced up at one of the tulip trees.

"What a tenacious creature it is!" she said. "Their leaves always cling to the very last."

Rhea looked around to see what she was talking about. "The tree?"

"Yes, the tulip tree. We had one in our backyard at home, and when all the other leaves had been raked and burned, the tulip tree was still golden. Just when we children thought the raking was over, the tulip tree would let the leaves fall, and we would have to rake again."

"How fascinating."

"I guess it isn't. But I like to remember it. I don't suppose you were raised the same as I."

"Hardly."

"But don't you enjoy thinking of silly things you did as a child that seemed so important and big then?"

"Not really."

Kathleen was silent, not knowing what to say. "Did you enjoy New Orleans?" she asked finally.

"It was hot and muggy, but I did enjoy it. Something goes on all the time, so at least we were never bored. And the men—the men, my dear, are incomparable. It is like visiting a whole new world. They are raised as men should be raised. That is a place where you are made to know you are a woman every minute of the day and the night. Such gallantry and grace."

"And Martin liked it as well?"

"Martin likes nearly everything as long as there is a deck of cards nearby. What difference does it make to him where he is? One smoky room is as good as another."

"I was really thinking more of the places you went together," Kathleen stammered, trying to back away.

Rhea whirled on her. "Together! The only thing we do together is—" She stopped abruptly. When she resumed, her voice was very low and, Kathleen thought, very threatening. "I would never have married him if I had known the truth. All of you knew he lived off that old harpy aunt of his, and not one of you said a word to me. Fine bunch you all are!"

Kathleen and Rhea turned back to the house in silent agreement that they had nothing whatever to say to one another.

The following Sunday, Marcella asked that everyone be present at late-afternoon supper. Martin didn't want to come, and Marcella had to put it in the form of a demand before he would. Rhea also refused.

"I prefer to eat alone in my room. I want nothing to do with any of you."

Marcella raised an eyebrow. "I don't care if you are present or not, as a matter of fact." At that, Rhea decided to come, too.

At dinner, everyone was unnaturally quiet. Before long, everyone but Marcella was uncomfortable.

Finally Martin slammed his soup spoon down beside his dish. "What in hell are we all gathered here for? It's like a wake without a corpse."

Marcella rang the bell for Gert and Mrs. Barth to clear and serve the rest of the dinner. "Shall we eat first, Martin? Then I'll tell you why I have asked you all to be here."

"You eat. I have to be in town." He began to get up from his seat.

"In that case, perhaps I had better say what is on my mind right now. I suggest you sit down, Martin. This concerns you as much as anyone."

Martin seemed undecided. Charlotte leaned over and put her hand on his arm. "Sit down, Martin. She's not going to say anything until you do."

Once Martin had sat down, all eyes turned to Marcella. She stood up, looking at each one of them before she spoke.

"I have been unfair in the past—"

"Amen," Martin said and angrily brushed aside Charlotte's restraining hand.

"I have been unfair in the past," Marcella repeated slowly. "I promised Brad that I would keep this house only until it was time to pass it on to his son. That time has already passed, and all I have given to Nicholas are vague assurances that I would honor my original promise to his father. I have been equally vague about my intentions to Charlotte and Martin."

She looked at her sister. "Charlotte, we all know your desires. As usual, they do not have as much to do with yourself as with your son. You have always wanted his place in life secured, and I recognize that. I have also taken advantage of that wish. I forced you to stay with me and care for me when I was ill, by promising Martin would be my heir. He assumed—and naturally, you believed—that he would also inherit Scarborough House at my death. While I did not verify that fact, I did not deny it. Quite frankly, I was perfectly content to permit each of you to think what you chose. It made things simpler for me."

"Marcella, there is no need to go into all of this," Charlotte said, flushing.

Martin fidgeted. "Come to the point, if there is one. I have an appointment."

"I shall, Martin. The point is simply this. I have never told you what I have in mind for Scarborough House. Today I shall.

"Nicholas, your father never intended that Scarborough become the means by which you could hide yourself away from responsibilities—to yourself or to the future. I shall never hand it over to you for that purpose."

Martin sniggered. Marcella turned to him immediately.

"As for you, Martin, before you smile so confidently, you had better listen to what I have to say. You shall not have Scarborough either. Scarborough House will be left to Nicholas Dalton's firstborn, should he marry and sire a son or a daughter.

"Should you, Nicholas, decide to remain unmarried and relinquish your duties as head of this family and house, Scarborough House shall be put to much better use. This house and all of its property will be given, with an adequate sum of money to maintain and run it, to Sorosis for the purpose of housing and caring for young women who are in the unfortunate circumstance of being with child and without spouse."

"My God!" Martin screamed. "You have gone mad! What do you think you are doing?" He leaped from his seat, bumping the table and overturning the coffee.

"I haven't finished yet, Martin," Marcella said, calmly waiting for his outburst to subside. "Sit down and hear me out. You still have no cause to cheer." He remained standing, shaking his head in utter disbelief.

"Marcella, please don't make fun," Charlotte said weakly. "Not now. Just finish."

Kathleen glanced over at Nicholas. He was playing with his napkin, twisting it and then smoothing it out, folding and refolding it. Kathleen was relieved; his face revealed no bitterness, no disappointment—only concentration. She turned back to look at her aunt.

"Charlotte," Marcella went on, "you and I are going to do whatever we please. We are old enough to be free to enjoy ourselves. I am going to travel. I'd welcome your company, but I'll not demand it of you. For once, I want to be the means by which you do as you please."

Then Marcella looked over at Kathleen. "To you, Kathleen, my will shall leave nothing. You must blame yourself for that, dear. It is no lack of love that prompted that decision. It was the talks between us late at night in my room. How often have you told me that there is nothing on this earth that you want except the kind of love you saw between your mother and father? That would require a man—a very special kind of man—and unfortunately I haven't one to leave you. As it is, I can leave you only my trust and my belief in you. Know this, Kathleen, that if I did not believe that you will find exactly what you desire, I would not be so brave as to do what I have done. Naturally, you will have a home here for as long as the fate of Scarborough House is in question." She took Kathleen's hand in her own, squeezed it affectionately, then let it go.

"And now, back to you for a moment, Nicholas. I suppose I have managed to interfere in your life more than in anyone else's. I don't seem able to avoid it. It will continue that way. I have asked that you care for all of my holdings, which you have done with great ability. I want you to manage my estate after my death as well, including Scarborough House, whether it belongs to your child or to Sorosis.

"And I have one more burden to hand you. I promised Martin he would be my heir, and so he shall. Martin, you will be given a business—a good, sound business—to run. It shall be of your choosing, Nicholas. I also ask that you include Martin in your handling of my fortune. Consult with him, make him a part of it, and perhaps, if he is man enough, Martin can still make his way in this world."

Martin's face had gone from scarlet to white. "You can't," he stammered. "You gave your word."

"I am keeping my word, Martin."

"My God, don't you see what you are doing to me? You can't—you can't do this! I don't want a business! You don't understand."

"Oh, but I do, Martin. Have I made everything clear to everyone?"

All nodded, except Martin.

"I assume," said Nicholas, "that Martin and I are coexecutors of your estate."

"More or less, Nicholas. Naturally, I couldn't put in all the conditions I have stated here. On paper you stand as sole executor, with Martin second in line. Of course, you are now in the same position as I was with your father. He trusted me to keep my word and carry out his wishes. I am asking you to do the same."

Nicholas nodded. "As to the house—" He grinned sheepishly. "I don't know how to phrase this tactfully."

"Plunge on!" Marcella said.

"Are you saying that I must marry and have an heir before your death?"

"Oh, my, no. Who knows what might happen? Your child might pass away before reaching maturity. Any number of things could happen. And in spite of my allegiance to Sorosis, I certainly will not go so far as to say I trust or even respect all of the women in it. No. Sorosis will not be able to touch this house for ten full years after my death. So even if I should be cut down by a runaway horse tomorrow, you would still have ten years to produce an heir. That should be sufficient time, don't you think?"

He grinned at her and glanced over at Kathleen. "I think it should be adequate."

"But don't be too hasty. I have a good deal to do and a lot of country to see before I give up the ghost. I am merely telling you now, because Martin needs the information, and so does his mother.

"All of us are aware of your difficulties, Martin. But you will now be assured of a steady income, a respectable position, and a means of doing as much or as little with your life as you choose. Charlotte, I hope this plan of mine, in some way, repays you for the moments of difficulty I have given you in the past."

"Martin, did you hear?" Charlotte said softly, turning to her son. "It's a new life—a new beginning, Martin, free from all the things that have troubled you. You can begin afresh, you and Rhea. Have your own home and—"

"Mother, for God's sake, will you shut up! What about the money? You gave your word! What about the money? Does *he* get all that, too?" he shrieked at Marcella. "You said I'd be your heir. You gave your word!"

"You are my heir, Martin, I have told you that. In time you shall inherit quite a bit. But I will tell you one more thing, Martin. Your inheritance depends entirely on what you make of your life. My lawyers are best equipped to explain how that works to you. I will be happy to make an appointment for you and Nicholas whenever it is convenient. I have not broken my word to you. I have merely put conditions on it."

"But I need money now!" He moved several steps toward Marcella, then stopped abruptly

"Martin!" Charlotte began. He glared at her and turned back to Marcella.

"You can't do this!" he whispered.

"I think you are mistaken. In any case, I am not dead yet. So even if I had not taken the steps I did, and had not written this will, there would be no question of your getting money now."

"But I could have borrowed against my inheritance! I could have—"

"You may *work* for it, Martin. That is the point of this whole thing. That is precisely why I have chosen to tell you what I have in mind. Neither you nor Nicholas has lived up to your potential. Neither of you has given much thought to your own responsibilities. If you choose to continue as you are, that is entirely up to the two of you, but I shall not reward either of you for it. What I am endeavoring to do is to hand to each of you an opportunity to begin again. If you don't want it, throw it away. I have no claim on you, and thank God, I no longer want one."

Martin didn't say another word. He shoved his chair toward the table and stalked out of the room. Charlotte looked down at the white damask tablecloth with the spreading coffee stain on it and counted the seconds before the front door slammed shut.

Marcella walked over to her sister. "Charlotte, you look exhausted, and I feel it. Why don't we old ladies go up to my room and have a cup of tea and perhaps a glass of port before retiring? Kathleen, would you ask Gert to send up a tray of light food a little later? It doesn't look as though anyone has an appetite now, but we'll be hungry later."

She looked over at Rhea, who was sitting very still.

"Will you join us, Rhea? I think perhaps you wish to talk."

Like Charlotte, Rhea seemed incapable of speech. She nodded.

Nicholas cleared his throat and stood up. "Kathleen and I are going for a ride. It won't be long before snow is on the ground, Marcella, and then we'll all go in the sleigh."

Marcella smiled. "I don't believe I have done that since I was a young girl. We'll look forward to that, Nicholas," she said, looking at Charlotte.

Charlotte made an effort to smile. "Oh, indeed. Something to look forward to."

"He has sold every jewel he has ever given me," Rhea said to no one. "Everything—he's sold everything."

"Shall we go upstairs?" Marcella said gently. "We'll all be more comfortable in my sitting room, I think. Nicholas, why don't you and Kathleen go ahead?"

Kathleen hurried off to tell Gert about the tray of food for Marcella and to get her coat. Rhea and Charlotte started up the stairs, and Marcella lingered behind, waiting for Kathleen to return.

"You aren't angry with me, are you, Nicholas?"

"How could I be angry, Marcella?" He grinned at her. "I have one question about it, though."

"Go ahead."

"Did you know that Kathleen and I are going to be married before you decided this?"

"Are you and Kathleen going to be married? How wonderful, Nicholas! I am so happy," she said, smiling knowingly. She hurried toward the staircase.

Kathleen returned a moment later and found him standing alone in the hallway. "What are you smiling about?" she asked.

"You," he said, buttoning the front of her coat. "Just you."

Chapter Thirty-four

Within a week of Marcella's announcement, she was planning a short trip to Saratoga. Even with a good deal of coaxing and persuading, Charlotte was undecided whether to accompany her. Marcella, uncertain as to how much she should press Charlotte, turned to Kathleen with her misgivings.

"I don't want to force her to do something she really doesn't wish to do. I have done that too many times—"

"I think it would do her good, Aunt Marcella. She has done nothing but fret and worry ever since Martin came home. It would do both of you good to get away from all of us for a while."

"I thought so, too," Marcella chuckled, shaking her head. "Honestly, Kathleen, what would I do without you? What is it the servants call you? Kat?"

"Miss Kat. It's a pet name Minerva gave me when I was small."

"It fits you. By the way, when am I to meet Minerva? I thought she was coming here."

"She is, but not quite as soon as I had hoped and expected. She stayed behind to help my sister Aggie. She was having her first child, and Minerva wanted to be there. Aggie managed to have twins. Two nephews. Minerva is training a nurse for them now. I expect she'll be coming out in the spring."

"In that case, I guess I'll just have to wait until spring to meet her."

"It is well worth the wait. Minerva is simply marvelous. What a combination the two of you will make!"

"Hmmm. We shall see."

"How long will you be gone, Aunt Marcella?"

"No more than a week, if Charlotte remains behind. If I can persuade her that she needs a change of scene as much as I, then I hope we shall not return for at least two weeks."

Since Charlotte decided to go at very nearly the last minute, there was a great rush to get her packed. Nicholas drove them into the city, where they planned to stay for a few days to shop and go to the theater before they went on to Saratoga.

Nicholas returned to the house the worse for wear. "They argued the entire way to the city." He accepted the drink Kathleen offered him. "Come sit beside me—quietly. Don't utter a single word. I have never heard two women talk as those two can. Lord! I expected it from Marcella, but Charlotte! She is as bad as Marcella, once she is wound up."

"It sounds as though they are going to have a marvelous time!"

"So are we!" He finished his drink in one long swallow and turned to her, taking both of her hands. "What shall we do? Would you freeze to death if I took you to the willow pond this afternoon?"

"Most probably." She smiled and stood up. "Come along. Aren't we going?"

"You just said—"

"That I will freeze and shiver and my teeth will clack unromantically. I still want to go. Can we take skates, too?"

"It should be frozen. Let's take them and see."

Since the day Marcella had made her announcement, no one at Scarborough House had seen much of Martin. Now, with Charlotte's and Marcella's absence, he seemed to be spending more time at home. Curiously, Kathleen thought, Martin was apparently trying to befriend her and Nicholas, though his attempts were pathetic.

One evening after dinner, he turned to Nicholas. "Nick, old man," he said, putting a hand on the taller man's shoulder, "I have a few little business matters I'd appreciate your advice on. If the ladies will excuse us, I'd like to talk with you in the study for a short time."

Kathleen and Rhea nodded to the men and watched as Martin followed Nicholas out the door.

"I don't know why he bothers," Rhea said bitterly. "It is a futile effort. Anyone can see that."

"Probably. All Nicholas can do is advise him about running the business Aunt Marcella gave him. After all, she is still in control of everything. Perhaps they *are* talking about the business. Wouldn't it be marvelous if Martin really began to try?"

"Martin— Oh, what is the point of talking about him? I should never have married him. But I listened to all that talk of his. Such big plans. We were going to have the time of our lives, one big round of parties and fun. The house here for the summer, travel south in the winter. Do you blame me for having my head turned?"

Kathleen remained silent. "Well, maybe that doesn't appeal to you," Rhea continued, "but it does to me. And I wasn't so much of a fool as it might appear. I wasn't the only one taken in by him."

Kathleen tried to be sympathetic. "I am sure what you say is true, Rhea."

"It doesn't matter what you think, anyway—or what anyone thinks. I am married now and can't do a thing about it. That aunt of yours—do you know what she said? Have children. Have children, and that will settle him down."

"She might be right."

"Martin isn't going to settle down to anything. He'll never even give that business a second glance. Do you know he has never said a word about it to me?"

"I don't know what to say to you, Rhea. Perhaps things are not as bad as you think. There are some men who simply do not like discussing business with their wives. Perhaps Martin is one of those, or he may just be dramatizing." Kathleen then wondered why she had said that. She didn't think for one moment that Martin was dramatizing; if anything, his problems were probably more serious than any of them knew.

Martin was every bit as worried as Kathleen supposed. He owed a great deal more money than Marcella realized, and once again he had reached the point where John Munroe, among others, was growing impatient.

Twice he had had a sizable sum of money to pay back a good portion of his debts, and both times, driven by fear and the wild hope that he could free himself from debt entirely, he had taken a chance that he could double what he had. And he had lost.

Now he hadn't any money—not even enough to give him the false hope of one big win—and he had run out of time. When Marcella returned to Scarborough House, he intended to tell her everything. He would make her understand the fix he was in, and how serious it was. After she had given him the money he would ask her for, he would stay clear of John Munroe's world, clear of all the John Munroes.

Marcella and Charlotte were not expected back for at least two weeks, so when a telegram arrived about twelve days after they had left, saying Marcella was ill and they were returning to Scarborough House, everyone was concerned.

"What could be wrong with her?" Kathleen asked.

"I doubt that it is serious. Mother doesn't sound frightened." Martin looked again at the telegram. "It can't be anything too serious, I am sure."

"How can you tell from a telegram if a person is frightened or not?" Kathleen shot back. "It must be serious if they are coming back. Why wouldn't they just stay there and rest? They have doctors there."

"If it were very serious, she would not be able to travel back here," Nicholas observed.

"Perhaps she has begun drinking again and Charlotte can't handle her," Rhea said. "You are the only one who seems able to deal with Marcella when she is in one of her moods, Kathleen."

"But she has no reason to start all of that again."

"What reason did she have the first time?" Martin asked. "Rhea may have something. That is probably what has happened. It isn't Marcella at all who wants to come home. It is Mother."

"I don't believe it. Aunt Marcella is over all that."

"Please," said Nicholas. "There is no point in speculating about this any more. Dr. Agee will examine Marcella on Wednesday when she gets home."

For Kathleen, the next two days were filled with worry, both about Marcella's health and about Martin's state of affairs. She had seldom given Martin two consecutive thoughts, but lately she had noticed how haggard and strained his face looked, how fearful he seemed to be.

However responsible Martin was for his own predicament, she could not help feeling a little sorry for him. For the first time, Kathleen thought her aunt should do something to help him, and she intended to tell her so upon Marcella's return.

When Marcella and Charlotte arrived home on Wednesday afternoon, Marcella was bundled in blankets right up to her eyes. She coughed and barely had a voice left. Immediately Nicholas sent for the doctor.

"I told her before we left the city that we had no business going to Saratoga at this time of year," Charlotte fumed. "Now look at her!" She helped Kathleen put Marcella to bed with hot-water bottles and Minerva's posset.

"I take it all back. I never want to meet the woman who concocted this!" Marcella rasped. "And will you both stop clucking around me?"

"Dr. Agee will be here any time now," Kathleen said and straightened the bed sheets.

Marcella sighed and lay back against the pillows. "It is good to be home. Come sit down, Kathleen, and tell me what you have been up to."

Pulling a small chair up to the side of the bed, Kathleen sat down and told Marcella what had happened while she and Charlotte had been gone. Between Marcella's stories about her trip and Kathleen's stories about herself and Nicholas, the hour until the doctor arrived passed quickly.

After examining her, he emerged from her room, amused and shaking his head.

"She has no more than a bad case of ague and fever, and she seems a bit run-down, but time and rest should cure both of her maladies." He looked at Kathleen. "I was told, young lady, that you have been giving her a posset made from balm. I couldn't have prescribed better myself. She will also be taking fifty to sixty drops of laudanum in tea, with a few drops of peppermint mixed in. When we come to the sweating stage, I will leave you some tartar emetic and dogwood bark, both of which will be a great help. I see no real problems."

Kathleen went back up the stairs to Marcella's room. "He's an utter quack!" Marcella raged. "And a lecher to boot."

"He's no such thing. A bit old-fashioned, perhaps. Nothing worse."

"Bad enough. Why don't you be a dear and fix another of Minerva's concoctions for me? That stuff grows on you." Marcella held her hands to her neck. "It feels as though it is twice its normal size. I'll admit the posset is the most soothing I have ever had. I am still not sure about the taste. It is most vile going down. But then it has a pleasant aftertaste. That is strange, isn't it?"

"I really don't think you should talk so much, Aunt Marcella. Why don't you try to sleep? It would probably do you more good than anything."

For the next two or three days, Marcella was an admirable patient. The others in the house were quiet, and if anything, overly kind to her. Marcella loved the attention, and by that weekend she was considerably better. She still slept a good deal of the time, and although Charlotte and Kathleen both fretted about her using the laudanum again in such quantity, they reassured each other that, after all, the doctor had prescribed it, and Marcella was looking better.

"I suppose we shall always be too cautious with Marcella after that one horrible experience," Charlotte said to Kathleen.

"She does look better than she has in a long time. I do think she took on too much before she was ready. She was inactive for so long, and then once her mind was made up, she was in and out and making all those trips to the city and writing her articles far into the night."

"But you think she has recovered now?" Martin looked from his mother to Kathleen and back again.

"I think she is doing very well, don't you, Kathleen?"

"Well enough for me to talk to her?" Martin asked when Kathleen nodded in agreement.

"I don't see why you shouldn't be able to see her for a short time. It is nothing that will upset her, is it, dear?"

Martin smiled quickly. "I doubt it. It would certainly be unintentional if I upset her," he said, looking toward the doorway. "I think—I think I'll just go up now and say goodnight to her before she goes to sleep. She'll still be awake, don't you think?"

"I think so," replied Kathleen.

"Oh, good. Well, excuse me . . . please." He hurried out the door toward the stairs.

"My, but he is jittery these days," Charlotte clucked, threading her needle. "I don't think he has been taking proper care of himself at all. I suppose he was out every night while we were gone. You would think his wife could manage to keep him in of a night, wouldn't you? How has he been getting along with Nicholas?"

"I don't know exactly, Aunt Charlotte. Nicholas doesn't talk to me about it, but I know that Martin has conferred with Nicholas several times, so I think everything must be going along as it should."

Martin knocked at Marcella's door. She was in bed, reading, and looked up as he came in. Picking up her bookmark from the blanket, she inserted it in her book and laid it to one side. "How are you, Martin? I haven't really gotten to see you since I came home. How are things going for you now?"

"I didn't want to disturb you. I know that seeing me—I have been an awful nuisance."

"Nonsense. I am happy to see you."

"I need to talk to you, Aunt Marcella."

She tried to recall the last time he had called her "Aunt." "Well, sit down. Tell me what you have on your mind—as if I couldn't guess."

"Your guess would be right. I need money again, but it isn't as it seems. It isn't what it has been in the past. I swear to you, it isn't."

"Martin, there is no need for all this breast-beating. Just tell me."

Martin wrung his hands and looked at the floor. "But I want you to understand," he said. "I don't know how to make you believe me, but this is the last time I'll ever go near a gaming table. Please believe me. Just this one time, let me have the money I need, and I'll never ask again."

"Martin, do you realize how much like me you sound? I used to say the same thing. I would look at my vile gin bottle, and I would say, 'When this is gone, I'll never take another sip of it again.' But I did. Every time, until I had someone who helped me become interested in living a new kind of life. Well, I have given you the means by which you can earn the money you need. Have you spoken to Nicholas about what you would like to do?"

He took a deep breath and exhaled it slowly. "Yes. Yes, I did, and that is what—part of what I want you to understand. I want to take advantage of the opportunity, but I need to pay my debts now. I will begin working at the end of this month, and I want to. I have looked over all the possibilities and have found that it is the iron business I like best. Grandpa's old firm. I never paid any attention when Grandpa was alive, although I must have heard him talk a lot about the iron fronts they made for buildings in those days. Nicholas showed me a few that are still there, down on the Wall Street buildings, and I became interested. Can't you see, Aunt Marcella? I am not trying to get out of anything."

"If that is the case, why are you asking me for money now? You will have it soon enough, and it will be yours, of your own earning."

Martin stood up and began to pace back and forth. "It's the *time!* I don't have time. It takes time to earn it. I need it now."

"There is no need to get emotional, Martin. I am listening to you, and I am trying to understand, but I do think you are overestimating the problem. As long as those men know they will be paid, and can count on you as an honorable man, they will wait."

"They'll kill me, Aunt Marcella. It is that bad, or I wouldn't be talking to you about it. You just don't know what they can be like. They don't care about me or honor or anything."

"They are doubtless the worst sort of scum, Martin. They would have to be to prey on another person's weaknesses, but I still feel you are overwrought. Tell them what you have told me and pay them a little at a time from your salary. Set up a regular day and amount. They will listen. You can count on Nicholas as well—he has a level head. Listen to him."

"It isn't that, and I know Nicholas is being fair. More than fair. I have no quarrels with him. But listen to me," he pleaded. "If you can't give me the money, lend it to me. Let me pay you back."

Marcella shook her head. "That was our agreement last time. I haven't seen the first penny. I am sorry, Martin. If this were the first time, I might consider it, but we have been over this ground many times before. I have given you money, I have lent you money. Charlotte told me about the money she gave to you and the promise you gave her. That story was very similar to the one I am hearing tonight. They didn't kill you then, did they, Martin?

"You may have been frightened then," she went on, "but not enough to stop. Well, this time you will have to stop, because I will not give you anything. I cannot do it and feel right about it. Go out and earn it. If you do, perhaps you will be more reluctant to place your own hard-earned money on the red and let the wheel spin."

Martin looked at the ceiling and then at his aunt, his eyes wide and frightened. "I will. From now on, I will. Oh, God, please, Aunt Marcella, listen to me. It isn't a story I'm telling you. It's the truth. If I don't pay them, they'll come after me. You're helping them kill me!"

"I don't like hysterics, particularly if they are men," she said coldly and picked up her book. "I am tired, Martin. We have nothing more to say. My mind is made up. I am not giving you the money, and that is that. Close the door after you when you leave."

"Please. . . ."

"Stop it, Martin! You are humiliating both of us. I can't give you the money!"

"Listen to me!"

Marcella reached up and tugged at the bell to call Gert. "I shall tell Gert I want a cup of tea before retiring, or I shall tell her to get help in removing you from my room."

"Please . . ." he began and looked at her hand on the bellpull as she gave it another urgent tug. He shook his head and began to back out of the room, his hands spread in a pleading gesture.

"Listen to me, please. Believe me," he whispered, his eyes filling with tears. Marcella couldn't bring herself to look at him. She stared hard at the book she had reopened on her lap. As he left the room, she let go of the book and covered her face with her hands.

Had she been right? Was this the best thing for Martin? She had relied on Nicholas's report of the situation, but that had been over a month ago. Things could have changed drastically since then. She promised herself that she would ask Nicholas to try to gather more information about Martin, to find out whether Martin was telling the truth.

Martin staggered down the stairs, trembling with the effort of holding in his temper and his fright. He cursed himself for having gone to her for money so many times before, when he really hadn't had to. And he cursed her for not being able to tell the difference between his lies and the truth. It might have been funny if things had been different. At the moment in his life when he was completely honest and wanted to begin afresh, no one believed him. Each time he had lied and exaggerated and cheated, he had gotten what he wanted. Now he could get no one even to listen to him.

He had known before he saw her that there was very little chance that she would listen, but he had had to try. He had been as calm as he could manage to be, and she had let him talk. Now he had no place left to turn.

Now he cried—out of fear, and anger, and utter despair. Stumbling down the stairs, he sought darkness and a place where, unseen and unashamed, he could pour out his fear.

Kathleen sat alone in the darkened music room. Nicholas would be in the city until the next day; she missed him and their nightly rides along the river. She hadn't felt like sitting with Charlotte any longer, and Rhea had long since gone to her room with a migraine.

Before she turned up the lamp, she went to the window to look out. The first real snow of the winter was coming down, changing the landscape into dunes of white. Another few hours of this, or one more snowfall tomorrow, and they would be able to take their sleigh ride. The hemlocks looked regal in their white coats, and the night seemed to glow with the brilliance of the snow.

She had been there for some time when she heard footsteps. She turned, unalarmed, to see who had entered the room. Martin came in and slumped into one of the huge leather chairs near the piano. He buried his head in his hand on the arm of the chair, muttering and weeping. As she listened, she wanted to comfort him, and knew she dare not—she would only shame him.

Slowly she made her way along the dark wall of the room to the doorway and the safety of the hall.

As soon as she managed to slip out, she went directly to Marcella's room and knocked gently on the door. Gert opened it almost immediately.

"She's asleep, Miss Kat. Is there anything I can do for you?"

"No, Gert. I was just going to say goodnight."

"Well, maybe if you go on in, she'll wake up. She hasn't been asleep more'n a few minutes. If it is important that you see her—"

"No, it's not important," Kathleen said and thought of Martin hunched over in the big chair. "Well, at least not so important that it can't wait until morning. Good night, Gert."

"Good night, Miss Kat. Mr. Nicholas will be comin' home tomorrow. I sure hope all this snow doesn't hold him up."

"So do I."

The following morning Martin appeared at the breakfast table looking tired and haggard. Rhea was not in any better shape. Her hair, usually so carefully done, had been stuffed into a hairnet.

"Didn't you sleep well, dear?" Charlotte asked.

"No, I didn't," Rhea mumbled and began to eat her eggs. After two bites, she pushed the plate aside and glanced over at Martin. "Aren't you going to say anything? Or have you changed your mind again?"

"I am taking Rhea to visit her aunt for a while," he said dully.

"But you have just returned from your wedding trip!"

"That was several months ago."

Charlotte turned to Rhea. "It was just a short time ago. You have hardly been home at all."

"It was at the end of last summer!" Rhea snapped. "And it doesn't matter, anyway, because I am not staying here any longer. It is awful and boring. We never do anything or see anyone. Living up here is like being locked away from the entire world. And now we may well be snowed in. We must get out while we can."

"We shan't be snowed in. And you might do well to think of your husband. After all, Martin is going to be starting his new position this Monday morning. You know how important this is to his future."

"It will be far easier for him to get there from the city than it is from here!"

"I am going to take her, Mother," Martin said, rubbing his finger across his eyebrow wearily.

The rest of the meal was eaten in total silence. When Kathleen finished, she got her wrap and went out into the gardens, now frozen and crackling under her feet as she stepped on the hardened underlayer of snow.

Later that morning she went to see Marcella and told her what she had seen of Martin the night before and then that morning at the breakfast table.

"Is Nicholas back from the city yet?" Marcella asked.

"No, but he should be any time now. Everything is frozen, so I imagine he may be a little later than he planned."

"Well, send him to me as soon as he comes in. Nicholas did some checking for me about Martin. Last time I spoke to him about it, things were not so bad, but that was a good month ago. I don't see how Martin could have made things that much worse in only a month, but perhaps he has."

"Then Nicholas will be finding out about Martin on this trip as well?"

Marcelal threw up her hands. "I don't know. Nicholas is usually so thorough, he may have done it without my telling him. Pray that he has. When does Martin plan to take Rhea to her aunt's?"

"I don't know. I don't believe anyone said anything about when."

"Well, we can take this trip as a good sign, I should think. If things were as dire as he lets on, I doubt that he would be off on a jaunt."

"I didn't get the impression he was going off on a jaunt, Aunt Marcella. It was as though it didn't matter to him one way or another. You know that I do not often take Martin's side, but this time I am really worried about him."

"Send Nicholas up when he gets home," Marcella repeated.

Kathleen left her to go downstairs to wait for Nicholas's arrival. She nearly pounced on him when he came into the house, telling him immediately that he should hurry to Marcella's room.

"No greetings for the wanderer?" He handed her his coat and hat and put his luggage in the hall by the stairs.

"You know I missed you every minute you were gone! But please go and talk to her now. I will tell you later why I am so worried."

"All right, all right," he said and started up the stairs. "The river is freezing. Another few days like this, and it will be solid."

He listened closely to what Marcella told him of Martin's visit to her room and of what Kathleen had related. "What do you think, Nicholas?" she asked when she had finished.

He did not answer but went to the window and looked out at the snow. He turned back to Marcella's inquiring eyes.

"I think you should help him," he said finally. "Lend the money to him. Draw it up like any other legal paper, but help him."

"Then you don't think this is just another of his big splashes?"

"I don't know. I have heard little about him lately. I did ask a few people when I was in town, but no one is saying much. He owes a great deal, but what that means in actual figures, I couldn't find out. The other thing is that this crowd that he owes is—it's a bad one. If Martin thinks they are going to kill him, he may have cause for believing it. It has happened before. If you don't want to help him, I'd like to know, because I will."

"Can you afford to?"

He grinned. "I can't afford not to. Kathleen would never forgive either of us if anything happened to him."

"Thank heavens! For a moment there I thought you had turned noble on me."

"I am practicing it. Anyway, why borrow trouble? I don't feel any real animosity toward Martin, so why should I not help him?"

"But is it helping him? I have given Martin money many times over, and now it seems to me that I do nothing but encourage his weakness."

"Marcella, I have no more answers than you. But this time, he seems to be in real difficulty or has cause to think he is in danger. Either way, the man needs help, and I haven't the courage to take a chance and refuse him."

"All right. I will give him the money he asked for. Can you draw up the proper agreement? I want it written as a business transaction, and give him warning that I will treat it as such. Never mind, I'll tell him that myself. Draw it up and send Martin to me with the paper. You'll have to leave the amount blank, because he never did tell me what he needed."

Nicholas went straight to his study, took from his desk a copy of a similar agreement he had once had with a business partner, and copied the essential parts of it. It took longer than he had expected; he looked up to see Kathleen carrying his dinner in to him on a tray.

"You have had nothing to eat," she said and went about the room lighting the lamps. "I waited for you—and would still be waiting if Carlisle had not seen you come in here and told me. What have you been doing?"

He handed her the paper. "Mind you don't blot the ink, it is still wet in spots. Does that make you feel better?"

"Oh, Martin will be so relieved. May I give it to him? I do hope he has gotten back. This morning he took Rhea to the city for a visit with her aunt."

"Hurry back," he said through a mouthful of food. "If you feel like it, we can go skating. I am certain the pond is frozen. We'll take the torches with us."

Kathleen ran from the room, slowing only when she saw Charlotte walking toward her from the other end of the hall.

"Where is Martin, Aunt Charlotte? Do you know if he has come back yet?"

"Oh, I don't expect him to be back for some time, dear. He went to Rhea's aunt's house. Rhea has been suffering atrocious headaches, and Martin has taken her to town for a bit of a rest and a change of scene. I do hope it isn't too much for him. He does have a good deal on his mind with his new job on Monday and all, but then Rhea never considers him." Charlotte repeated nearly the entire morning conversation, as if she had forgotten Kathleen had been present.

"Oh," Kathleen said, dismayed. "Won't he be coming back? Did they take much luggage?"

"They took everything, dear. There was no purpose in making two trips in weather like this. They left before lunch. There was no point in putting it off. Rhea was very insistent."

"I wish I could get in touch with him."

"Well, he might come back. Maybe he forgot something. You never know."

"If you do see him—I mean, if he stops by the house—would you please ask him to see me before he leaves . . . or Aunt Marcella?"

"Nothing is wrong, is it?"

"Good gracious, no. I just have a message for him, that is all." She smiled reassuringly at Charlotte.

"I'll tell him—if I see him," Charlotte said and bustled off down the hall.

Kathleen hurried back to the study, where Nicholas was waiting for her. On his desk were two packages.

"This one is for you." He handed her the smaller of the two. He opened his as she opened hers. Each of them contained a pair of skates. He held them up and laughed. "I have wanted a pair of skates like this since I was a boy."

"They are beautiful!"

"Let's go find out if they work."

They ran down to the pond, exhaling bursts of steamy air.

"Oh, Nicholas, we are fools. We'll be frozen and exhausted before we even get there," Kathleen panted as they stopped to rest for a moment.

Nicholas built a fire near the edge of the pond and she brought out a container of hot chocolate that Gert had pressed into her mittened hands before they left.

"Did you go to the river to see if it is frozen all the way across yet?" she asked.

"We'll go later tonight. There is going to be a moon tonight, a beautiful bright moon."

"Nicholas, do you ever think of all the years ahead of us?"

"Sometimes. Why?"

"No reason. I just wondered. I do. So many times I have wondered if we would always care about things like the moon and the river. I wonder about us in ten years, or even twenty years. I try to think of you with white hair and a beard, and me with wrinkles and white hair, and I wonder if we will think of the moon and the river then."

"And? What did you decide?"

"I decided we would. I think we always will."

Chapter Thirty-five

Kathleen and Nicholas returned home very late from their visit to the river, singing winter songs, the sounds of their voices mingling with the bells on the horse's harness.

Nicholas brought the horse and sleigh to a stop at the rear of the house and waited until he saw Joe hurrying across the yard to take the reins from him. As they were getting out, Nicholas stopped.

"Stay in the sleigh," he said to Kathleen and put his finger to his lips.

"What is it? What are you looking at?" she whispered loudly.

"Stay where you are! Joe, come with me." Both men hurried around to the front of the house. Kathleen could hear the sound of their feet after she could no longer see them.

As Nicholas and Joe rounded the corner of the house, they saw two men on the front porch. One stood at the front door, peering through the side panels of glass in to the main hall; the other was farther down the porch, looking into the parlor windows.

"You there! What are you doing?" Nicholas shouted, bounding up the steps. "What do you want?"

Both men spun around. The man closest to the front door glanced at his friend and then back at Nicholas. He put both hands up, open-palmed, and grinned broadly.

"Nothin'. No need to get all riled. No one answered the door, but there's lights on in there. We was just lookin' to see if anyone was goin' to come. Didn't know you was out."

"What do you want?" Nicholas asked again.

"We're just visitin'."

"It's past midnight, man! Who are you 'just visiting'?"

"We're friends of Mr. Henderson's. You know, Mr. Martin Hendrson. He told us to come an' visit him whenever we was in the neighborhood. Well, was out. Takin' a nice moonlight ride. Bet you was doin' the same thing now. Afore we knew it, here we was, right in Mr. Henderson's neighborhood. And I says, 'Arnie'—he's Arnie—'let's drop in an' say hello to Mr. Henderson.'" He dropped his hands to his sides and laughed. The other man joined him.

"You wouldn't mind tellin' him we was here, would you, Mr. Dalton?"

"You know who I am?"

"Like I said, Mr. Henderson is our friend. Business associate, more like. Friends know a lot about each other. He's mentioned you a few times. Now you tell him we're here, Mr. Dalton. We won't take up much of his time, but you tell him to come out here and see us."

Nicholas plunged his hands deep into his coat pockets. "You have come a long way for nothing. Mr. Henderson is not here. He has gone away, and none of us has any idea when to expect him back. If you are his business associates, I suggest you get in touch with him through his office."

"Where would that be, Mr. Dalton?"

"I thought you were associated with him. Check with your office. They'll have the addresses of all your customers. Now, *gentlemen*, I suggest you leave. Oh, and I might advise you of one other thing. This is not Mr. Henderson's home. It is mine, and I do not entertain business associates at my home. Good evening, gentlemen." He moved aside to allow them to pass. The man who had done the talking paused in front of him.

"We have no quarrel with you, Mr. Dalton, and we wanna keep it that way, but you tell Mr. Henderson to get in touch. You tell him to do that right away."

"Joe, show the gentlemen to their carriage. You do have a carriage?"

The man gave him a crooked smile. "Down the road aways. Didn't want to disturb nobody. Like you said, it's late for visitin'. Good night to you, Mr. Dalton."

Nicholas watched them walk down the driveway. Joe followed them at a distance as far down as he needed to go to see them get into their carriage and drive off.

After they were out of sight, Nicholas ran back to the sleigh and Kathleen. "Where were you?" she asked. "Why were you gone so long? Who were those men? Nicholas, what is going on?"

He put his arms around her. "Lord, you are cold."

"Who are they? What did they want, Nicholas? Are you all right?"

"I am fine. There is nothing to worry about," he said, smiling reassuringly, and steered her toward the house.

"What did they want?" Kathleen repeated as they walked into the front hall.

He took off his coat and hat and helped Kathleen with hers. "Just two men. They had lost their way . . . Came in here looking for help. It was nothing."

She pulled away from him. "Nicholas! You're lying to me."

He stared at her for a moment and then gestured toward the study. They went in and sat down. "They wanted to see Martin," he said finally.

"Then they are the men he kept talking about!" Kathleen leaned forward in her chair. "The ones he said would come after him. He's in terrible trouble, isn't he?"

"It looks as though he might be."

"Nicholas, Martin said they would kill him."

"We won't let anything happen to Martin. Tomorrow I'll send a message to him. As soon as he knows what is happening, he'll know what to do."

"They are already hunting for him."

"They'll never risk going after him in the daytime, and Martin is smart enough to keep in company at night. Once we can talk to him, he'll have several choices. Until we have the money for him, he can keep himself hidden. Then, as soon as he signs the paper, Marcella will arrange for him to have the money."

"How long will it before Aunt Marcella can get the money to him?"

"I should think he could have it day after tomorrow if he comes here and signs the paper right away."

"What if he doesn't?" She shuddered. "What if Aunt Marcella doesn't give it to him immediately?"

"Martin will get his money, Kat. I promise you that. The main problem is reaching him. I just hope he is staying wtih Rhea at her aunt's house. That is the only address I have for him—that and the plant, but I don't expect to be able to catch him there. Not with this going on."

"But you'll try."

"I'll try both places. Perhaps it would be better if I went to the city myself."

"No! I don't want you mixed up in all of this. Just send him the message."

He laughed and took her hands in his. "Nothing is going to happen to me."

"Nicholas, please don't go. Send a telegram and stay here with me until all of this is over."

"Tomorrow I am going into the city to see if I can find your cousin. I'll be back tomorrow evening. That is all I want you to think about."

Kathleen clung to him. "Please be careful. I love you so," she whispered, stroking the side of his face. "I don't want to lose you, and I am so afraid, Nicholas. I have such a terrible premonition. Don't let anything happen."

"Never," he murmured. "I promise."

Nicholas left for the city before six the next morning.

For Kathleen the waiting began. She knew that if she told Charlotte, it would only terrify her. Twice Kathleen went to Marcella's room to see her, but Marcella was asleep both times. Her cold had gotten slightly worse during the previous night, and her niece decided it was better to let her rest. So she bore her anxiety alone.

Nicholas went first to the telegraph office to send messages to Martin both at Rhea's aunt's house and at the iron works. Then he rode into the city to see Rhea, who told him that Martin had left the day before, almost as soon as they had arrived there, saying he had to make a business trip.

"Did he mention where he was going?" Nicholas asked her. "Did he say anything about seeing anyone in particular?"

"He didn't stay long enough even to exchange pleasantries with my aunt."

Nicholas left her as soon as he could, and not knowing where else to look, went to the iron works. There he was told that Martin had attended a business meeting the previous afternoon. Nicholas also learned that two men had been at the plant on three different occasions in the past week, looking for Martin. From their descriptions, Nicholas was sure they were the same two men who had been at Scarborough House.

Nicholas was at a loss as to where to go from there. He had told both Rhea and the manager of the plant to be certain Martin got the telegrams if they saw him, and had warned them that the matter was urgent. There was little else he could do.

As the afternoon progressed, he began to worry about Kathleen at Scarborough. It was entirely possible that Martin would make his way back there, with Arnie and his friend following. Lord knew what Kathleen or Marcella would try to do.

He proceeded to John Munroe's saloon, where Munroe himself welcomed Nicholas into his office. He offered Nicholas a drink, and in answer to Nicholas's inquiries, claimed to have no information about Martin's whereabouts.

"I am glad to hear he is well," Munroe said, smiling. "With this weather we have been having, I have missed some of my best and most regular customers. But then Marty has just gotten married recently, hasn't he? That may have some bearing on his absence."

Nicholas left knowing little more than he had before, but he was reasonably sure John Munroe had not found Martin, either. He stopped at a few other popular gambling spots, leaving messages everywhere he went, except at Munroe's, that he needed to see Martin urgently.

Before leaving the city to return to Scarborough, he put ads with the same message in the classified sections of all the newspapers. By the time Martin saw them—if he saw them at all—it would be too late, and everyone else would know the message as well. But it seemed worth the slim chance it represented.

Very late in the afternoon, he started for home on horseback, berating himself for having been so slow at his task. Kathleen would be frantic with worry when it grew dark and he was not there. Nicholas had a few fears of his own, not the least of which was that the two men would try to seek Martin at the house again.

The roads were icy, and the snow had begun to fall again. There was no way he could hurry. From time to time a carriage would pass, and he cursed his stupidity for not having taken his own. He had rushed out of the house, riding like an irresponsible young fool across ice, into storms. He had had to be a hero and had failed dismally. He hadn't found Martin, he was cold, his hands were nearly frozen to the reins, and he dared not push the horse beyond sensible limits.

At Scarborough, Kathleen had managed to accomplish nothing all day, although she had tried to sew with Charlotte early in the afternoon. Before long, Charlotte was clucking over her shoulder. "You'll have to redo this whole seam! Look what you have done, Kathleen. You are not at all yourself today. Are you not feeling well?"

"I feel fine," Kathleen replied in a small voice. "It is just an ugly day. It is cold and gloomy."

"I grant you it is a gloomy day, but my dear child, you are being far too sensitive. I do believe you are coming down with something. You haven't caught Marcella's ague, have you?"

Kathleen set the sewing aside and looked ruefully at Charlotte. "Perhaps I will take a short nap."

She went to her room, taking with her a book to read, and lay down on the bed. She read the first paragraph over and over.

Unable to concentrate, she got up and wandered restlessly about the room, looking out the windows, trying to occupy herself by straightening all of her drawers and planning what new clothes to buy before her wedding. But all she could think of was Nicholas.

Near nightfall, she went back downstairs to the front parlor. Kneeling on the sofa, she stared out the front window, but the curve of the drive was barely visible in the falling snow. She left her post at the window dejected and apprehensive.

Nothing felt right.

Kathleen had been jumpy all day, hearing noises in the house where there were none. Somehow, she didn't really believe that her concern for Nicholas was the only cause for the anxiety she felt.

She went back upstairs to talk to Marcella while her aunt ate dinner. I won't say anything, she decided, about what is happening. I'll simply sit with Marcella and talk until she is ready to go to sleep for the night.

Chapter Thirty-six

Arnie and his friend found Martin as he was trying to hire a cab to drive as far as Scarborough House. He was at one of his favorite gaming clubs, just outside the city, where he had been all day long. Not expecting anyone to come looking for him there, he had not been particularly cautious. But when he came out the front door, they were waiting for him. Each of them took one of his arms. As they walked arm in arm down the driveway, they looked like three slightly inebriated friends.

Martin felt as if all the muscles in his legs had turned to jelly. Arnie and the other man half-carried him beyond the row of pines that bordered the club's driveway, out of sight and earshot of the other guests, and began to pummel him systematically.

Through a haze of pain, Martin saw his own blood begin to fall on the snow. This was only the beginning, he knew. By the time they had finsihed with him, he would be dead or begging them to let him die.

He began to struggle, trying to fight off both men; one would have been more than a match for him. They seemed to be playing with him, hurting him, cutting away at whatever strength he had.

Arnie had just begun to beat him in earnest when Martin heard the sound of a horse and carriage. He screamed out, struggling with all his might, choking on the blood that filled his mouth. The two men tried to hold him still until the people had gone on. Martin was close to hysterical laughter when he heard the carriage stop. And then there were men—he couldn't see how many—coming across the drive. Arnie let go of him, muttering under his breath for Martin to stay where he was, behind him and the other man.

Terrified, Martin did as he was told. He remained motionless until the other men had engaged Arnie and his friend in conversation. Then he ran—as fast as his aching body and the snowy ground permitted. He leaped into the carriage the departing men had left unattended and whipped the horses forward.

As he tore down the road toward Scarborough House, the cold night air helped to clear his head. He managed the carriage well for a considerable distance. Then, about two miles from Scarborough House, the carriage took a curve in the narrow road too fast and skidded to the right. The horses screamed, and one of them fell as the rear wheel went off the road into a ditch, tilting the carriage.

Martin, nearly thrown over the side, looked warily over the sloping roof of the carriage. Without better footing for himself and the horses, he would never manage to set the carriage right.

He left the carriage where it was and ran into the woods, abandoning the two animals in the cold, snowy night. Having second thoughts, he returned and turned them loose. Slapping the last horse on the rump, he watched it run from him. Suddenly he realized he could have ridden the horse. He began to run down the road, calling after the animal.

As he ran—and then walked—the hot, sticky pain of the beating gave way to the dull ache of the cold. His eyes stung from the effort of seeing through the driving snow; his face burned, then lost all feeling, as the wind beat against him.

Stumbling alongside the roadway, he staggered from one tree trunk to the next. Quite suddenly—just as he was about to give up—he came upon the driveway to Scarborough House. Not daring to use the road for fear someone would see him, he went along the side and across the lawns to the house.

The kitchen lights drew him to the lattice. His eyes stung with tears when he thought of all the nights he had sat comfortably in that house, safe and warm.

He was tempted to tap at the kitchen window. Gert would hear him and let him in. He would be warm. Just then, he heard the sound of a horse coming up the drive.

Immediately he went into the passageway, seeking the protection of the latticework until he could reach the giant weeping beech tree. On hands and knees he crawled beneath its protective branches. He pressed against its trunk and looked out to see the horse and rider head for the stable area.

It was not Arnie, as he had first thought, but Nicholas.

"I'll get that for you, Mr. Nick," Joe called as he ran from the lighted stables. "Nasty night, this one. You go on inside. They waitin' dinner for you, I think."

Nicholas dismounted, beating his hands together to get the circulation going again. Martin watched as Nicholas walked around to the side entrance and out of sight. He heard Kathleen's cry of joy as Nicholas went in and the door closed again.

Slowly Martin moved from the shelter of the tree. His legs felt like stiff blocks. The wind cut at his wet clothes. He stumbled back to the lattice path along the base of the house, and looked in through the windows. Kathleen came into the kitchen, prepared a tray, then left.

The kitchen was empty again. Martin tried the window first, and then the door. He entered, leaving the door open behind him. Lunging toward the table—and the tray of food on it—he succeeded only in shoving it several feet. It scraped harshly on the floor. Fearful because of the noise, he lurched forward toward the back hall and began to climb the back stairs.

Mrs. Barth, on her way down the stairs to the kitchen, stopped suddenly.

"Who's there? Who's down there?" she called out.

Martin leaned against the wall and tried to be quiet, but the sound of his labored breathing filled the stairwell. Mrs. Barth, trying to see around the turn in the stairs at the landing, took another step. Martin hurried up the stairs to reach her before she stopped asking who was there and began to scream for help.

As soon as she saw him, she screamed. Martin stumbled, grabbing the air to catch his balance. He grasped hold of the hem of her skirt. The tray she was holding clattered down the stairs moments before Mrs. Barth herself pitched

318

forward and fell the few steps to the landing, moaning and crying incoherently. Martin moved past her as quickly as he could, scrambling up the stairs to the second floor.

Gert, meanwhile, had gone back to her kitchen, where she saw the mud and water on the floor and the door standing wide open. The table had obviously been moved; the tray of food teetered on the edge of the table, about to tip over onto the floor. It must have been Joe or one of the stable hands, she decided. She was about to hurry out into the stable yard to give them a bit of what-for, when she heard Mrs. Barth scream and the tray clatter down the stairs.

Hurrying to the back hall, she saw Mrs. Barth. Gert tried unsuccessfully to help her to her feet.

"Mr. Nicholas!" she called as she ran up the stairs and along the hall toward the dining room. "Mr. Nicholas. Mrs. Barth fell. I think she may be hurt. I can't get her up."

Martin ignored the commotion he heard below and concentrated only on what he had to do. As the warmth of the house began to work on his frozen fingers and ears and feet, he ached all over. He touched his face gingerly. One eye was badly swollen, and his mouth had become one large mass of mangled flesh. He choked back a sob.

Nicholas got Mrs. Barth to her feet and into the kitchen. Kathleen rubbed her wrists and patted her face to bring some color back, as Gert tried to force brandy into her.

Charlotte rushed into the room. "What has happened? Such a racket!"

"Mrs. Barth fell, ma'am," Gert said.

"Is she all right?"

"He was awful. A monster!" Mrs. Barth gasped, her great bosom heaving.

"Who was awful, Mrs. Barth?" Kathleen asked.

"The man! The awful man who pushed me down the stairs."

Gert looked at the door and at the floor that she had begun to clean up. "The door *was* open," she said to herself.

"The man did it!"

"Bosh!" Charlotte leaned forward to smell Mrs. Barth's breath. "She's been drinking."

"She hasn't been drinking, ma'am," Gert said. "The door *was* open and—" She looked apprehensively toward the hall door.

"We'll settle this. I'll go see for myself."

"I'll go, Charlotte." Nicholas began to walk to the door.

Charlotte snorted. "It is a storm in a teapot. Get Mrs. Barth to her room where she can do herself no more harm. I'll go see what Mrs. Barth's monster is. She most likely left something on the stairs that frightened her. I want to take some flowers and a magazine to Marcella anyway."

Nicholas nodded. "Come along, Mrs. Barth." He heaved her to her feet. She leaned heavily on his arm as he began to walk her to her room, followed by Kathleen and Gert.

Upstairs, Martin moved slowly down the hall to Marcella's room. He stopped at each door, ready to jump at the slightest movement. Finally he stood at Marcella's doorway.

He stared at it and then turned away and looked back down the darkened corridor. Satisfied he was alone, he turned back to Marcella's door and opened it silently. The empty sitting room was bathed in the soft light of one small lamp. He crossed it to her bedroom door and listened intently for a moment. Hearing nothing—no stirring, no talking, no rattle of a newspaper—he put his hand on the knob and began to turn it slowly.

Marcella lay quietly on the bed. She appeared to be asleep. He walked over to her and stood looking down. Tears began to well up in his swollen eyes. He reached across her and took the pillow from the other side of the bed, holding it in both hands.

"I'm sorry," he whispered softly. "I'm sorry."

Marcella opened her eyes and stared uncomprehendingly at him for a moment. "Hello, Martin," she said softly. "Put the pillow down and talk to me. I—"

Momentarily she closed her eyes, opened them again, and tried to focus on him. "I know you were telling me the truth. . . ." Her voice trailed off, and she closed her eyes again, fighting the effects of the laudanum she had just taken.

"I have something to tell you," she said slowly. "Something . . . something to give you."

"Go to sleep, Aunt Marcella," he whispered. "Please shut your eyes and go to sleep."

She shook her head from side to side. "You mustn't. There is . . . no need . . . Martin." She raised her hand and tried to point to her bureau. Her arm went limp, and she dozed off for a minute.

Martin placed the pillow on her face. Marcella barely struggled.

Martin was still holding the pillow over Marcella's face when he heard Charlotte enter Marcella's sitting room. She had seen nothing of Mrs. Barth's monster, nor any obstacle on the stairs. She was satisfied it had been as she had thought. Mrs. Barth had been drinking and hadn't wanted to admit it. She carried with her a new copy of Demorest's family magazine and the flowers.

"I thought you might like to look at this before you go to sleep," she said from the sitting room, placing the flowers on the table. "Nicholas brought this back for Kathleen, but she doesn't mind if you read it first. Marcella, why must you leave things about? It is so simple to put them away after you use them," she said and picked up a discarded newspaper.

Martin looked frantically from the pillow to the door and the shadow his mother cast as she moved about. He had no idea of how long it would take Marcella to die. Was she dead when she stopped struggling? Or was she merely unconscious? He couldn't release the pillow, not yet. Not until he was sure.

He kept looking at the door to the sitting room, knowing that any second his mother would come through those doors and see him. She couldn't see, he thought frantically; all he needed was enough time to search through Marcella's drawers. She would have money in her room—she always did—and then he could leave. No one would know he had been there, and no one would even realize Marcella had been killed.

If only his mother would think her sister asleep and leave! He pressed down with all his might and then stood up straight, releasing the pillow.

At the same moment, Charlotte walked into the room, looked at him, and screamed. She ran back through the sitting room and out into the hall, yelling for help. "Prowler! Prowler!" she screamed over and over.

Martin ran into the sitting room after her and stood in the doorway, afraid to go out into the hall.

"Mother! Mother, for God's sake . . . please. Please don't call them." He stepped into the hall, reached out for her, and watched the look of horror register on her face as she backed away from him. "Mother, Mother! It's me, Martin!"

She screamed again, and Martin hurried forward, pulling her into the sitting room. He kicked the door shut behind him and put his hand over her mouth, pressing her head against his chest. "Mother, be quiet! Shut up, please. Help me. Don't you see? I need your help. Don't call them."

The door burst open. Nicholas grabbed Martin by the back of the coat and pulled him and Charlotte around.

"No!" Charlotte screamed as she fell heavily.

Nicholas's fist smashed upward, and Martin slumped to the floor.

"It's Martin," Charlotte gasped and began to cry. Nicholas looked down at the man at his feet. Just then Kathleen rushed into the room.

"My God!" she cried. "What happened to him?"

"I don't know. He—I didn't even know him." Charlotte began to blubber incoherently. The only word Kathleen could understand was Marcella's name.

Kathleen hurried to the door of the bedroom and looked in. Marcella appeared to be sleeping peacefully. The pillow was askew, but that wasn't unusual for Marcella, who was a restless sleeper.

Kathleen closed the door. "She is all right. Sound asleep. She hasn't even heard the commotion."

"No, no, no!" Charlotte wailed.

"Take her to her room, Kat. I'll get Martin into his bed. Maybe we can sort all this out later."

Kathleen tried to get Charlotte to her feet as Nicholas picked Martin up, staggering under the weight and awkwardness of his limp body.

"Come with me, Aunt Charlotte. Nicholas will take good care of Martin, and we'll get the doctor to come just as soon as we get you settled. Now come with me. It is the best thing you can do for Martin. He'll be all right. I'm sure he will. Dr. Agee will know what to do."

"Charlotte shuddered. "He killed her," she moaned. "I saw him. My son has killed her. My son. . . ."

"No, Aunt Charlotte. She is just asleep. Come with me, and I'll show you."

Kathleen stood up and pulled Charlotte to her feet. Together they walked to Marcella's bedroom.

"Come along. There is nothing to be frightened of. She is sleeping like a baby." Kathleen opened the door, putting her finger to her lips. Marcella was lying on her side, her face away from them. "See? Sound asleep."

Charlotte removed Kathleen's hand from her arm. "She's dead. Not asleep," she said quietly. "He killed her. I saw him kill her. He took the pillow, and he killed her."

Kathleen walked to the foot of the bed and then along the side until she stood beside her aunt. The light from the bedside lamp was reflected in Marcella's half-open, unseeing eyes.

"Aunt Marcella? Aunt Marcella!" Kathleen shook her aunt by the shoulders. Her head rolled heavily back against the pillow as Kathleen tried to lift her. "Aunt Marcella! Wake up! Aunt Marcella!"

"She's dead," Charlotte said. When Kathleen looked up again, some seconds later, she was gone.

"Nicholas, Nicholas! Come quickly!" She shook Marcella again. There was no reaction. Nicholas came on the run and found Kathleen sitting at the side of the bed with Marcella's hand in hers.

"She's dead," she said tonelessly.

Nicholas stood stock-still. "What do you mean, she's dead? What happened to her?"

"Martin—" Kathleen began.

"*Martin* did this?"

"Aunt Charlotte saw him do it."

"My God," Nicholas breathed. "*Martin!*" Suddenly he looked up at Kathleen. "We'd better get to Charlotte before he does anything to her."

Charlotte had gone back to her own room. In her hand she held Marcella's bottle of laudanum.

"I do hope you left enough for me, Marcella," she murmured.

She wouldn't think of Martin now. She wouldn't think of anything except that she wanted to sleep. She took a drink from the bottle. She didn't like drinking from a bottle. She poured the remaining liquid into a glass and drank it as quickly as she could.

They would hang her son. She wouldn't see that. They would say he was evil. She wouldn't listen to that. He would suffer. She couldn't bear to feel that. He was hers. Her flesh. Her son.

She undressed and put on her best nightshift and robe. As she lay down on the bed, she felt very drowsy and the slightest bit dizzy. For a moment she thought she would be ill, but it passed. She didn't think she could move if her life depended on it. She tried to smile at the thought.

Bits of things she had forgotten long ago formed pictures in her mind—how the wall in her bedroom at Five Points had looked when she had turned her face to the wall to avoid Marcella's chatter . . . the picnic where she had met the man she would marry. That picnic turned into another . . . Martin was a baby, and the three of them had gone on a picnic on a Sunday afternoon . . . There were bees . . . The bees were chasing her, and she couldn't think where she was . . . She worried about those bees coming too near the baby, and so she ran, letting them chase her so he would be safe . . . She ran and ran, her legs getting tired, but it didn't matter as long as she kept them away from the baby. . . .

Kathleen and Nicholas hurried to her room. They rushed to her bedside. Her hands were warm, there was a pulse, and her eyes were closed. When they realized she was breathing, too, they looked up, nearly laughing in relief.

"I think we're both a bit jumpy." Nicholas walked over to Kathleen, took her hand, and led her from the room.

Kathleen stopped long enough to turn down Charlotte's lamp. "She won't need this."

They moved through the sitting room. "While the house is quiet for a moment," Nicholas said, "I'd better get Joe on his way to fetch the sheriff. Meantime, we'd better find Martin."

"I didn't want it to turn out like this," Martin said from the doorway. "I never wanted this to happen. No one believed me. No one believed."

Nicholas pulled Kathleen close to him. Both of them stared at Martin, supporting himself in the door frame. One hand held fast to the jamb, the other held a pistol.

"I don't want to die," he moaned. "I didn't have a choice, but you won't believe that, either, will you? No. You won't."

"Put the gun down, Martin," Nicholas said smoothly. "Let me help you. You're about to collapse, man." He took a step forward, pushing Kathleen behind him.

Martin sniffed and wiped his nose with the back of his hand. "Don't try to take the gun, Dalton. I don't want to shoot you, but I will. I have nothing to lose. You know what I've done already."

"Then why not shoot?"

Martin tried to smile and winced as he opened a cut on his lip again. "Because I have a chance of doing it the way I want. We're all going for a ride. Kathleen, go downstairs and get the coats ready. Stay where you are, Dalton. Don't move until I tell you. And don't you do anything but get the coats, Kathleen. Don't try to warn anyone. I'll shoot him, and I mean it. We'll follow you down."

Kathleen ran to the door, stopped, and looked back at Martin. He hadn't moved, but the gun was still pointed at Nicholas. She ran down the stairs, grabbed both coats from the hall tree, and rushed back to meet the two men at the foot of the stairs.

"You're a smart girl, Kathleen."

"You don't need her to come with us, Martin. A woman will be of no help to you."

"Put your coat on, Kathleen," Martin growled. "Don't you have a scarf?"

"Why won't you let us help you, Martin? Let us send for the doctor and have your face looked at. It should be tended to."

"Let's go," he said, indicating the door with his gun. Nicholas hesitated, wondering if he had any chance of diving for the gun before Martin could pull the trigger. Martin smiled slightly and glanced down at the gun. Nicholas began to walk toward the front of the house.

"Not that way. The rear entrance. To the sleigh."

They walked to the back and out onto the porch. The sleigh was standing there, waiting for Kathleen and Nicholas to take their nightly ride. Joe had brought it around not ten minutes before, and Nicholas cursed the timing.

"Get in, just like you always do."

"It isn't built for three people," Nicholas said reasonably. "Let me tell Joe to hitch the larger one."

"This one will do," Martin said, taking hold of Kathleen's wrist. This time he pointed the gun at her. Nicholas got into the little sleigh and took the reins in his hand. He put out his hand to help her in.

"I'll go next," Martin said and got in. Kathleen squeezed into the cart last. She had to cling to Martin's arm to keep from falling out. The horse halted twice, unaccustomed to the added weight.

"He'll never be able to pull us. It is too much on the ice."

"He'll make it. Drive to the river."

Nicholas obeyed. The horse, one of the smallest in the stable, was breathing hard. "Now what?" Nicholas asked. "What the hell are you doing, anyway? What do you want?"

"Drive down to where they are cutting the ice," Martin said through clenched teeth.

"No one is out tonight. The wind is too high. Can't you see it is dark down there?"

"Drive!" Martin dug the barrel of the gun into Kathleen's ribs, making her cry out. Nicholas drove to the area near one of the largest icehouses. Until the night had turned so raw, he had planned to take Kathleen to that very place to watch the cutting and storing processes.

He turned to Martin. "You see? No activity. It is too windy and dangerous tonight. Now can we go back to the house and get you taken care of?"

"Get out," Martin ordered, nudging Kathleen. He turned to Nicholas. "You next. Go and stand beside Kathleen."

"Run, Kat! Run to those trees."

She began to run, and the gun reported, echoing in the night. She whirled, slipping on the slick surface of the ground. Martin looked from Nicholas to Kathleen and waited until she had come back to Nicholas's side.

"I won't shoot into the ground next time, believe me. It will be you I shoot, Dalton, and don't forget it. Kathleen can run all she likes. She'd freeze before she ever found her way back to the house. Now stand together."

Kathleen's hand sought and found Nicholas's. They stood still as Martin got down from the vehicle. He looked around him. The icehouse was only about twenty feet away from where they stood.

"All right. Both of you, walk toward the icehouse. Stay together! Go on, walk!"

"What are you going to do?" Nicholas asked, not moving.

"Walk right now, or I'll shoot."

"Nicholas, do as he asks, please." Kathleen pulled at his hand.

Nicholas began to move slowly, his eyes on the icehouse in front of them. The icehouse had no windows, no openings, no entrances except those that could be barred from the outside. He squeezed Kathleen's hand until it hurt her and she cried out.

They were but two or three feet from the sluice gate of the icehouse when Nicholas threw his weight against Kathleen, thrusting her from him with all of his strength. She fell and slid across the hard-packed snow. Nicholas dived for the surface of the river, praying that he wouldn't slide into one of the open channels and the rushing water beneath.

The gun cracked again. Nicholas could not stop his slide down the bank onto the blackened surface of the river. He clawed and grasped at the ice and the tools that had been left behind by the ice cutters. His hand closed on one of the great hooks. He swung it as hard as he could, bringing the hook down into the ice. It held fast and he stopped sliding.

"Martin!" he called into the darkness, trying to see through the haze of a new flurry of snow. Kathleen would be far easier to find than he, and he was certain Martin would go after her.

Struggling to regain his footing, he held fast to the ice hook and began to hurry back, looking down every few steps to be certain he wouldn't step off into one of the channels. He heard the gun again and saw a flash of light. Martin was shooting at him, but he was too wide of the mark, and Nicholas realized Martin could see no better than he could.

He crouched down and called out again. The gun went off, closer to him this time. Chunks of splintered ice hit him in the face and shoulder. Again he scrambled to his feet and began to move across the ice. He had no idea how far from the bank he was.

He froze when he heard Kathleen's voice calling out to Martin. The gun went off once, and then he thought it had gone off a second time, but he realized that that had been an echo. Then the echo died away, and there was silence. Had Martin missed her?

"Kathleen!" he shouted and then realized he shouldn't have. "Martin! I'm over here, here!" he yelled and raised his free hand in the air, holding fast to the ice hook with the other.

He heard Kathleen's voice. "Nicholas, I'm all right."

"Martin. Don't touch her. I'll kill you if you hurt her. You can't shoot all night. It's over."

The gun flashed again, and Nicholas felt something hit his side. Strange, it hadn't hurt; just a slight blow. Putting his hand to his side, he felt the warm wetness of blood.

He thought he could see the bank. The last shot hadn't come from a great distance, so Martin couldn't be far from the edge. Suddenly the snow stopped, and the clouds began to clear rapidly. Martin stood fifteen feet from him, pointing the gun directly at him.

"No! No!" Kathleen screamed and came at Martin from the cover of the woods. She ran head down for Martin's back, butting him with all her might. Martin staggered and fell. The gun slithered away on the ice.

Both Kathleen and Martin hit the ice hard and slid at an angle from Nicholas, directly toward the channel. Martin clawed at the slick surface and caught hold of the edge of the sluice, swinging himself around and pushing Kathleen away from him. She spun around, no longer in danger of falling into the channel.

Nicholas lunged at Martin just as Martin managed to gain his footing. The two men squared off, each of them armed with one of the ice cutters' tools. As Martin swung the saw, Nicholas took a step back, slipping and falling. Martin jumped to the bed of the sluice, ready to leap down on his adversary.

Nicholas rolled away from Martin and the saw blade. Martin jumped to the surface of the ice on Nicholas's side, missed his footing, and fell to the surface. Nicholas scrambled to his feet, lunged low, and swung the ice hook at Martin. Martin jumped back, one foot going over the edge of the channel. He fell to the ice, half his body in the freezing water. He clung to the side. The river beneath the surface was a rushing torrent. There was no purchase on the slick ice.

"Help me! Help!"

Nicholas got up on his knees and lunged forward full-length on the ice. He grasped Martin's coat sleeve, but the man was being sucked slowly under by the river below. Nicholas's body moved inch by inch across the ice as Martin clawed at him.

Kathleen screamed. "Nicholas! No! Let him go. You can't help him! Oh, dear God, let him go!" She ran back to the horse, leading him out onto the ice. She had only the reins to use, and had no idea whether she could force the horse to move one way when the rein was being pulled from the opposite direction.

"Nicholas. Take the rein. Take it, Nicholas. Free your hand and take it. The horse will pull Martin out."

She could hear his grunts as he tried with all of his strength to pull Martin from the river, but he neither answered her nor took his hand from Martin's.

Kathleen took the rein and tied it around Nicholas's arm, looped it through, and urged the horse back. The rein grew taut and the horse responded. Nicholas's body had swung around so that it was parallel with the channel. She watched, horrified, as he reached farther into the water to tug on Martin's lifeless arm. Martin slipped under, and Nicholas was forced to release him.

Again Kathleen pulled at the horse, trying to make him back up. If only she had another rope, anything to use but the reins! Nicholas now clung to the rein. If the horse moved one more step, she knew, she would see him disappear into the river as Martin had. She wrapped her arms around the horse's head and pressed down with all her weight.

The horse stepped back, fighting to free his head. She kept pressing with all her might, forcing the head down; the horse took a step back and then another, shaking his head violently and throwing her off-balance several times. Still she clung until she began to get him to turn, slowly, prancing sideways, toward the shore.

Nicholas held fast to the rein with one hand, pressing against the edge of the ice with the other. Once his chest was above the ice level, he released the reins and lay across the ice, coughing and gasping for air. His legs still dangled over the edge of the channel.

Kathleen took hold of Nicholas beneath his arms and dragged him the rest of the way from the channel. She turned him over onto his back. He was still choking. She had to get him back to the house.

Again she went to the confused horse and tugged on his reins, coaxing him as near as she dared to the channel's edge. She had no difficulty dragging Nicholas across the ice to the sleigh.

"Nicholas! Nihcolas, can you hear me? Please, Nicholas, I need your help." A gash on the side of his head was barely bleeding. She couldn't tell if it was serious or not, or if that was why he would not respond.

Struggling with his great weight, she managed to prop him up against the sleigh. But she couldn't lift him into it. She knelt beside him and tried again. She could move him but not lift him.

She began to cry. She *would* lift him. She *would* get him into the sleigh. She climbed into the sleigh, leaned over, took him under the shoulders, and began to tug. He didn't move. She climbed down again. Taking him around the waist, she squatted on the ground and lifted. Suddenly he moved and groaned.

"Nicholas, Nicholas!" she cried. "Get up. Please. Right now. Stand, Nicholas. Stand up. Hold onto me and stand!"

He opened his eyes and looked at her blankly. Pain and fear for her shot through him. He heaved himself to his knees, gasped, and clung to the side of the sleigh.

"Once more! Nicholas, please try one more time. Stand up, Nick, please."

She pushed at him. He pressed down with both arms and fell over the side of the sleigh. She managed to push him all the way in. He sprawled across the seat and the back, his arm swinging down from one side and his legs protruding from the other.

She took her coat off and wrapped it around him. Sitting on the edge of the seat, she urged the horse toward Scarborough House. She didn't take the road but drove straight across the fields, screaming like a banshee. Long before the stable was in sight, she heard Joe shouting back at her. He raced toward her as she pulled in under the portico and jumped down.

"Get him into the house!"

She ran ahead, shouting Gert's name as she went. Gert came out in her nightcap and gown, followed by Mrs. Barth and Carlisle.

"It's Mr. Nicholas! Hurry. He's fallen into the river. Get dry blankets and hot water. Anything you can find."

Joe and the other men brought Nicholas into the kitchen and laid him on the big chopping table. Mrs. Barth began to fill a large copper tub with steamy hot water.

Gert smacked her and shoved her out of the way. "You can't put him in that. Get cool water and plenty of good rough towels. That man's freezing. You want to be the death of him?"

They put him into the cool water, adding warm water little by little. Then they took him from the tub and rubbed him with warm oil and towels, wrapping him in blankets to wait for the doctor. They forced whiskey down his throat, and Gert tried to get him to swallow hot broth and tea. He choked and moaned; each time he responded they looked at each other, thankful that he could respond.

When the doctor arrived, he ascertained that neither the gash on his head nor the wound in this side was serious, aside from the possibility of infection. Pneumonia, they all knew, was the real danger. Kathleen knelt at his side when they took him to his room, as she had once knelt and waited at the bedside of her father. She heard the same tight breathing, felt the dry skin, and sensed the restlessness of his fevered body.

"You go take a little rest, Miss O'Connor," the doctor urged. "This may be a long wait, and we'll all have to take turns. I'll stay right here by his side. You needn't worry. And I'll let you know if anything changes. You have my word."

"I'll wait," she insisted wearily.

"Well, you can at least sleep in here. Is there a cot she can use?" he asked Gert.

"I don't want a cot. I don't want to sleep. I just want to be here."

"I'll go fetch Mrs. Henderson. She'll know what to do with Miss Kat," Gert said.

"Yes, do that. Quickly," the doctor said.

Gert left the room to get Charlotte and to bring down extra blankets for Kathleen. She returned to the room moments later, without the blankets or pillow, her face ashen. She looked for a moment at Kathleen and then at the doctor.

"Can I speak to you for a moment, sir?" she asked and motioned for him to follow her from the room.

"What is it, woman? Are you ill, too? What's wrong?" he asked, following her up the stairs.

"Come along, sir. I don't know—just follow me. Are you there, sir?"

"I'm here, I'm here. What is it?"

They went into Charlotte's room. She was lying just as she had been when Nicholas and Kathleen had seen her, a slight smile on her lifeless face. She wasn't breathing. The doctor closed her eyes and picked up the empty bottle at her bedside. He smelled the glass she had drunk from and put both bottle and glass down again. "What went on here tonight?"

"I don't know, sir. I was wonderin' myself."

"Anyone else in the house?"

"Just us downstairs." Her eyes widened. "And Miss Marcella. I forgot about her. You see, she is ill—I mean, she has a nasty cough and has been stayin' close to her room of late."

"Let's go see her, too," he muttered and walked to the door, waiting there for Gert to lead him to Marcella's room.

Her sitting room was bathed in the eerie half-light from the lamp. They went to the bedroom and looked down at Marcella lying motionless on the bed.

The doctor felt for her pulse and put his hand on her forehead.

"She has a fever," he said, "but she'll be all right until morning. Let's go back down and see to that young man."

In Nicholas's room on the first floor, Kathleen hadn't moved from Nicholas's bedside.

The doctor approached her. "I think, young lady, you had better tell me what has been happening here tonight," he said. "Do you realize there is a dead woman upstairs?"

"Aunt Marcella is dead," she said calmly. "Martin killed her. Aunt Charlotte saw him do it."

"Miss Kat must have it confused, sir, 'cause it's Mrs. Henderson who's dead," Gert whispered.

"Martin is dead," Kathleen said in a low voice that no one heard. She was no longer aware of the others in the room. Her cheek lay against Nicholas's hand, but it was her father's labored breathing she heard with each breath Nicholas drew. She knew it would stop soon. She was waiting.

The doctor turned once more to Kathleen. She was strangely detached, like someone only half awake.

"Can you tell me what happened, Miss O'Connor?" he asked gently.

She looked up at him, made a sign for him to lower his voice. She looked at Nicholas, touched his hand, and rubbed it against her cheek.

"He isn't going to die, is he?" she asked.

"No, he isn't going to die. Not if we have a little good fortune with us."

"Martin almost killed him, didn't he?"

"Martin nearly killed Nicholas?"

"But he didn't," she said, and closed her eyes.

The doctor ran his hand through his hair. "Do you make any sense of what she is saying?" he asked Gert.

Gert shrugged her shoulders and went out to the kitchen to fix a cup of hot tea, laced with brandy, for Kathleen.

When the sheriff got there later, the same questions were asked many times over. Kathleen remained perfectly willing to answer whatever she was asked. But since they didn't know what questions to ask, none of the answers she gave made sense to them.

She was exhausted but wouldn't give up until Nicholas regained consciousness. Only then was she persuaded to take the doctor's nostrums and sleep.

Chapter Thirty-seven

That night was filled with dreams of what had happened. Kathleen awakened in the morning, disoriented and frightened. She lay on the bed, her eyes scanning the room as she tried to sort nightmare from reality. Suddenly she sat up, thinking of Nicholas as she had last seen him the night before. She dressed as hurriedly as she could and rushed down the hall to his room.

The room smelled of ointment and eucalyptus. Nicholas was asleep. Kathleen walked to the side of his bed and sat down. As she watched his chest rise and fall rhythmically, she was filled with a feeling of relief.

"I've been lookin' for you, Miss Kat," Gert said as she bustled in with a tray in her hand. "Why aren't you in your room where you belong? The doctor said you needed a good long rest."

"Hush, Gert. You're going to waken him."

"He's gotta be wakened, anyway. I got medicine to give him, and he's gotta eat, too, just like the rest of you. Now let me get on with my job. You go see Miss Marcella. She's been scaldin' my ears for the last hour askin' for you. Go along."

"Aunt Marcella?" Kathleen said, her face crumpling. "Aunt Marcella is dead, Gert."

"She doesn't sound dead to me. She's healthier than you are right now. Quit your cryin'. I'll take good care of Mr. Nicholas. I wouldn't let a thing harm him."

Kathleen stared at her, open-mouthed. "Aunt Marcella wants to see me?" she asked slowly. "She's really all right? Gert! She's all right?"

Nicholas stirred. Kathleen glanced down at him and then back to Gert. "She's alive?"

She hurried toward the door. "Oh, Gert! Oh, Gert—"

Kathleen ran to Marcella's room and flung the door open. "Aunt Marcella!" she cried, running through the sitting room to the bedroom. She threw her arms around Marcella, crushing against her, and burst into happy tears.

Marcella patted her and comforted her for a moment and then pulled away. "Well, now," she said, ruffled. She handed her niece a handkerchief and continued patting at her distractedly. "Can't you stop crying, Kat? Now, now. That's enough."

"I thought you were dead," Kathleen cried. "Oh, Aunt Marcella, I was never going to see you again. I thought—"

"You can see you were wrong. So stop the crying. What went on here last night? Someone had better tell me soon. I remember seeing Martin come in here, and then everything went blank. What happened?"

Kathleen told Marcella about the previous night. It was a long and confusing story, and it took many times in the telling before Marcella was clear as to what had actually happened.

"Send Charlotte in to me, Kat. She shouldn't be alone now. I want to see her, dear. After all these years Charlotte and I are all that are left. We should be together at a time like this."

Kathleen nodded and left Marcella's room to find Charlotte. Marcella propped herself up in bed, took the medicine the doctor had left for her bronchitis, and thought about Charlotte and herself. Their lives had been strange and stormy from the beginning; now it was Marcella who had to make some sense out of the tragedy that had happened to her sister.

Kathleen went to Charlotte's room. It was much as it had been the night before. The unmade bed still showed the imprint of where Charlotte had lain, but Charlotte was not in the room. Kathleen went downstairs and looked in the morning room and the parlor. No Charlotte. Kathleen went to the kitchen.

"Gert, do you know where Aunt Charlotte is? I can't find her, and Aunt Marcella wants to see her."

Gert looked at her blankly for a moment. "The doctor is with Mr. Nick, Miss Kat. We'd best go see him."

"Is something wrong with Nicholas? I thought he was doing well. What's happened?"

"Nothin's wrong." Gert hurried toward the steps.

The doctor looked up and smiled when they came in. "He'll be fine."

Apprehensively, Kathleen looked from him to Gert.

"She's wanting to see Mrs. Henderson, sir," Gert told the doctor. "Says her Aunt Marcella wants her to come to her room. I thought you'd better—"

The doctor nodded. "Come along with me, Miss O'Connor. It is best we talk somewhere else."

Kathleen followed him from the room and downstairs to the parlor.

"There is going to be no easy way to tell you what I must, Miss O'Connor. Your aunt is dead. We found her last night. Apparently she had taken far too much laudanum, and—"

"But Aunt Charlotte doesn't take laudanum. She—she would never take it. You must be wrong."

The doctor put his hand on Kathleen's arm. "I am not mistaken, Miss O'Connor. Your Aunt Charlotte took the laudanum. I am sorry."

"Then she—"

"She took her own life."

Kathleen looked at him, shaking her head. "Aunt Marcella is waiting for her—upstairs," she whispered.

"Then we had best tell Miss Paxton what has happened. Shall I do it?"

"No. No, thank you, Doctor. I will talk to Aunt Marcella. I should tell her." Kathleen stood up but stayed where she was for a moment, looking at the door.

"Are you certain you are up to it?"

She nodded and left the room. Slowly she went up the stairs to Marcella's room again, and told her aunt what had happened. Marcella was extremely quiet as Kathleen spoke. She asked no questions, nor did she interrupt or comment. When her niece had finished, she sat for some time without saying anything.

"Kathleen, I'd like to be alone for a time."

Kathleen moved to her side immediately. Marcella took her hand in both of hers, smiling quickly. "I am all right, Kathleen. I just need to be alone for a little while."

Kathleen left Marcella sitting quietly in her room and went back to Nicholas's bedside to make her own sense of what had happened.

Chapter Thirty-eight

In the days that followed, both Nicholas and Marcella began to regain their strength. Nicholas would be in bed for some time, recovering from his wounds and his dunking in the river. Marcella, however, was soon well enough to become restless at the restraints put on her activity.

From her bed, and then from her writing desk, she began to make plans to travel to the Centennial Exposition in Philadelphia, where she was to assist Mme. Demorest. Nell Demorest, Marcella explained excitedly to Kathleen, was the only woman who had managed to secure exhibiting space in the main hall of the exposition.

Scarborough House and its inhabitants began once again to move back into the normal patterns of living. The days melted into weeks, and then a month was gone. By the time the new year began, Marcella was making plans to go to Philadelphia.

Kathleen sat at Nicholas's bedside, now able to laugh when he sneezed and complained of having to stay in bed.

"It's January," he sniffled.

She looked at him and smiled. "January—and Aunt Marcella is planning to take her new century by storm."

"I wasn't thinking about Marcella," he grumbled. "And it isn't a century mark, anyway."

"For her it is, and if you would stop complaining and admit to an ounce of patriotism, you would feel the same way."

"Ummm."

"Is that an admission?"

He ignored the question, becoming preoccupied with counting the number of slippery elm drops remaining in the box the doctor had given him.

"Nicholas, let's go to Philadelphia, too," Kathleen said finally. "I'd love to see Madame Demorest's exhibit. It is such an accomplishment for her to be in the main hall. All the others were relegated to the women's pavilion. We could meet Aunt Marcella there. Please. Let's go."

Nicholas looked up. "You're not going to get involved in all that women's business, are you?"

"Aunt Marcella did say she would welcome me in any of her projects. . . ."

Nicholas's eyes widened.

"But if you could devise a way to keep me otherwise occupied, Aunt Marcella agrees that would be my best possible project."

Nicholas sighed in obvious relief. "That is the first sensible thing that woman has said in some time."

At the end of January, Kathleen and Nicholas, newly married, walked into the main hall of the Centennial Exposition Center. Bronze nymphs stood at the four corners of the elegant Demorest pavilion. In the center, Mme. Demorest's gowns were displayed on wax manikins. Cases of polished walnut housed Medallion monograms and the famous patterns.

The most arresting figure in the entire area, however, was a gracious, vividly animated woman talking with a group of spectators. Marcella, as tall and proud and beautiful as she had ever been, had a presence, a self-assurance, that obliterated any flaw of skin or feature.

Kathleen took Nicholas's hand. "Oh, Nicholas! Look!" she breathed, her face shining as she watched her aunt. "I am so happy we came."

Marcella waved when she saw them. Excusing herself from those around her, she hurried over and hugged Kathleen and Nicholas in turn.

"You're radiant," she cried, taking Kathleen by the hand.

Later, after introducing them to her new friends at the exhibit, Marcella took Kathleen aside to talk. She told her niece that she would remain in Philadelphia for a while.

"I want to be active, and to be truthful, I am having the time of my life."

"But we want you at home, with us."

Marcella's smile was mischievous. "You and Nicholas are just beginning. You need to be alone, and I need to be on my own. There will be other times for us to be together."

"But—"

"Oh," Marcella hurried on, "I forgot to tell you. I am going to Ohio. I wrote to Agatha, and she has invited me to visit. I am finally going to meet the rest of my family!"

"Mama would have loved that, Aunt Marcella—and so will Aggie. But you must promise to visit Terry and his family, and Lawrence, and—"

"I am!" Marcella laughed. "I'll see all of them."

Nicholas, standing nearby, was getting more and more restless. He clearly wanted to move on to another exhibit. Kathleen lingered, reluctant to leave her aunt.

"Don't be such a silly goose." Marcella nodded toward Nicholas. "You are going to make him angry—and besides, you are keeping me from my work."

Kathleen touched Marcella's arm. "But I won't see you for so long."

"I'll be back before you know it, and probably too soon, if Nicholas is half the man his father was. You'll not be missing me, Mrs. Dalton." She kissed her niece on the cheek. "Good-bye, Miss Kat," she whispered and walked away.

Kathleen watched her go until Nicholas came to stand at her side. She turned to him and smiled.

"Let's go home."